FIRE IN THE ICE

FIRE IN THE ICE

by

ALAN SCHOLEFIELD

A Congdon & Weed Book

St. Martin's Press
New York

A-1

For Ilsa Yardley

Library of Congress Cataloging in Publication Data

Scholefield, Alan.
  Fire in the ice.
    1. Soviet Union—History—Revolution, 1917-1921—
Fiction. I. Title.
PR9369.3.S3F5 1985   823   85-2143
ISBN 0-312-29101-9

First published in Great Britain by Hamish Hamilton Ltd.

First U.S. Edition

10 9 8 7 6 5 4 3 2 1

CONTENTS

Have pity on us, O our fathers!
Don't forget the unwilling travellers.
Don't forget the long imprisoned.
Feed us, O our fathers – help us!
Feed and help the poor and needy!

Begging Song of Russian Exiles

Prologue

On a dull, close summer's morning in 1921, Sir David Kade flagged down a taxi in the Bayswater Road in London and ordered the driver to take him to the Law Courts. It was barely nine-thirty and his case was not due to be called for an hour, but punctuality was his obsession. The driver opened the sliding window between them and said, 'Oxford Street's jammed, guv'nor, mind if I go another way?'

'Any way you like as long as you get me there by ten-fifteen.'

'Easy.'

The driver left the window open. 'You a barrister, guv'nor?' he asked in a friendly voice.

'No.' It was said shortly to cut off further conversation but the cabbie, a man in his late twenties or early thirties, had half-turned and David had seen the burns on the left side of his face and the pattern of bluish marks where he had been hit, probably by shell splinters as he stood up in a trench. David had been about to close the sliding window to end the conversation; now he found he couldn't.

'I only asked 'cause I had a barrister in the cab yesterday. Changed into his wig and gown on the back seat. Said he was late.' The cabbie swung away from Oxford Street into Grosvenor Square.

David could have driven with his son and daughter-in-law. They had pressed him, but he had refused. His solicitor, too, had offered to call for him. He could even have come in his own Rolls Royce, driven by his own chauffeur, but he wanted to be alone. If he had accompanied his family there would have been emotion. His daughter-in-law would have made him feel even more tense than he already was. So would his

3

solicitor, with his elderly and gloomy face. All would have been warm and loyal, and he did not want that. He did not want to be constantly told he was in the right; he already knew that. But when others said it, he felt they were trying to convince him as well as themselves. He *had* to be right, that was all there was to it.

He had not slept much the previous night and had woken with a headache that had spread from the back of his neck. Now the tension had moved to his stomach and he felt slightly sick.

'You a solicitor, then?' the cabbie asked.

'No. I've got business nearby.'

'Oh.' There was a hint of disappointment. 'I only asked because of the case, see?'

'Which case?'

'The one that's been in the papers. The one where that millionaire's trying to get his child back.'

'Oh, that one.' Again the tone was dismissive.

'. . . owns a diamond mine out in Africa somewhere. Wife left him and took the kid. I don't 'old with blokes like 'im. All that bleedin' money. I mean, what chance does she 'ave?'

David tried to close his ears, but the man went on.

'Not even English. They say he's a Jew. Come from Russia originally. Well, I mean, that's typical, ain't it?' The cab passed through Berkeley Square and into Piccadilly. 'And I read in the papers where it says he done his old partner down in some deal.' He shook his head angrily. 'Now they're fighting over the kid. It's only a baby, poor little sod. What's going to 'appen to it when the parents are finished destroying each other? You tell me that, guv'nor.'

David leant forward and closed the window with a snap.

That was the word Stratos had used. 'You must prepare yourself to destroy her, Sir David,' the solicitor had said. 'That's what she'll be trying to do to you. Custody proceedings are ugly. I beg you to think twice and then thrice.'

Well, he *had* thought. More than thrice. But there was no other way, not if he wanted his child.

The Strand was blocked by omnibuses coming out of Charing Cross Station and the cabbie went down onto the Embankment. It was high tide and the river ran slate-grey under the lowering sky. In his mind he saw another river, wider than the Thames, with black-green trees on either bank. And snow and ice. And the prison barge spinning and lurching and sliding to destruction on the rocks. And the bodies and the screams.

He banged his hand on the glass panel and shouted, 'Let me out here!'

It was five to ten and he was half way between Waterloo and Southwark Bridges. It was only a short walk from the river to the Law Courts. He hunched against a sudden wind and turned up through Temple Gardens.

He stopped on the opposite side of the street from the Courts entrance. Taxis were arriving, then two Rolls Royces came slowly down the Aldwych and stopped. He saw his son, Michael, jump out of one and open the rear door. The former Cossack officer, Maxim Perfiliev, got out, followed by the dark face and plump shape of Annie. And suddenly the flash of Press cameras and the surge of the crowd enveloped them as they struggled to enter the main door.

Then he saw his wife. She must have left her taxi some distance away for she walked down the street, unnoticed. On her far side, in moth-eaten furs, was an old woman with gingerish hair whom David recognised as Princess Gorantchi-koff. Before anyone spotted them they had ducked through the doorway.

Just then a van stopped in front of him and a bundle of papers thudded down at his feet. Before the paper-seller, whose pitch was a few yards away, picked them up. David saw his own photograph on the front page under the heading, DIAMOND MILLIONAIRE IN COURT BATTLE FOR CHILD.

He turned away. Battle. Fight. Destruction. The words were like a knell. Wilde had said you always killed the thing you loved. But did he still love her, and if he did, why was he destroying her? For a moment, a second or two, he thought he could not go on, that he must stop everything, but the moment passed as it so often had in the last days, and he crossed the road.

There was a shout. He heard voices saying. 'There he is! That's him!'

5

Flash-bulbs went off in his face and then he had walked past the policeman on duty at the doorway and had entered the great neo-Gothic building.

BOOK ONE

Russia, 1917

[1]

'Your Royal Highness! My Lords! Ladies and Gentlemen! Pray silence for His Worship, the Lord Mayor of London!'

This was the moment. David Kade touched the cheque in the inside pocket of his evening coat.

The Lord Mayor, Sir Lionel Cowan, was seated four places along the table, past the Duke of Gloucester, the Earl of Kinross and the Secretary of State for War. He rose ponderously to his feet, his face flushed and beaded in the heat of the great room, for the black-out curtains were drawn and the windows shut in case there should be a zeppelin raid.

'It is in the tradition of the City of London,' he began, 'that many of its greatest successes are achieved by men who were not born in this country, indeed, who fled here from their native lands seeking shelter and succour. Such is the case tonight.'

'I speak of a man who came to these shores as a boy, who left again to make his way in the world. In so doing, he made his fortune, then brought that wealth back to the country of his adoption. I speak, of course, of Sir David Kade, in whose honour we are gathered here tonight. . .'

David looked out over the glittering room. In the spring of 1917 such a gathering was rare. He could see the First Sea Lord, a Field Marshall, several Generals, their chests hung with medals, two Admirals, the Bishop of London, the President of the Royal Academy, the owners of two national newspapers, a Lord of Appeal and a dozen other faces familiar to him from newspaper photographs.

Cigar smoke rose lazily. The food had been excellent, if you took into account three years of war. The chandeliers blazed on tiaras and pendants and necklaces, many of which, he thought, contained diamonds which had probably come from his own New Chance mine in South Africa.

At a table to his right were his son, Michael, his daughter-in-law, Jewel. On Michael's other side sat Sarah. David had never seen her look lovelier. She was wearing dark green velvet with a necklace of matched blue-white diamonds at her throat. He knew the necklace well, for he had chosen the stones. She caught his eye and smiled, and inclined her head slightly as though in homage. She had been his mistress now for nearly two years. With her dark hair, grey eyes and her generous curves, she drew attention like a magnet. He would have to make up his mind about her soon, he thought. But not yet. Let the run of the play end, and then he would see.

'. . . breaking no confidences if I tell you that we were not only at school together, but worked in the same banking house,' the Lord Mayor was saying. 'But Sir David was meant for wider horizons. As you know, he went out to South Africa in the early days of the diamond diggings at Kimberley. For several years he and his partner, the late Jack Farson, struggled in heat and cold and dust to win something of value from the ground. The rest is history.

'The great mining house of New Chance is known throughout the world wherever diamonds are spoken of. It has expanded into many other fields: land, property, gold, shipping. But the vital factor from the point of view of the City of London and of Britain as a whole, is that Sir David brought this great company back to the city that gave him his start. It is therefore with very great pleasure that I call on him now. . .'

David rose. He was a man of medium height with broad, powerful shoulders that made him appear somewhat shorter. His dark hair, which gripped his skull like a cap, was touched with grey at the temples. He wore his clothes well and looked younger than his years. He stared down at the representatives of Government, the Establishment, the Arts, all of whom had come to honour him that evening. But would they have come to honour a Jew named Kadeshinsky from Kiev if he did not have a title, and a cheque in his pocket?

He savoured the irony for some seconds, enjoying a moment

of triumph and of power he had never felt before. His knight-hood had been given by a grateful British Government when he had negotiated a land treaty with an African chief – but knighthoods were commonplace in the circles in which he moved. To be honoured with a special dinner by the City of London meant more than that and put him on terms of equality with anyone in the room. There might never, he knew, be another moment like this. Remember it, he told himself.

As he began to speak about his early days in London, another part of his mind worried about the cheque. Was it too much? Was it ostentatious? A figure had been mentioned, but he had added another naught, knowing that, no matter how much it was, there were debts to this country he could never repay.

Only that morning he had walked from his house in Bays-water to the New Chance building in Northumberland Avenue and had passed three crippled ex-soldiers busking in Trafalgar Square. Two had lost legs, one an arm. They were all young and one carried a handwritten sign which read, 'The Golden Warriors.' He had felt a savage anger at what had happened to them and what was happening to others, at his own inability to help. He had turned out his pockets and given them all he had.

'. . . and so when I see the hospital trains and read the casualty figures, I remember that this was the country that took me in, that gave me shelter, a nationality and a name. If I could fight, I would. But even if I can't, at least I can do the next best thing: I can help others fight to keep Britain free so that there will always be a haven for the politically oppressed.' He took out the cheque and handed it to the Lord Mayor.

As he unfolded it, Sir Lionel glanced at him in amazement. He opened his mouth, closed it, then rose to his feet.

'May I just say how grateful we are for this contribution to the City of London's war effort. Ladies and gentlemen, the cheque is for five hundred thousand pounds!'

For a second there was silence, then a roar, a cheer that sent currents of air upwards to disturb the chandeliers.

The hand-shaking and the congratulations were over at last and David found himself with Michael, Jewel and Sarah in the dark windy night, on streets shining with rain. Strangers were still coming up to him and gripping his hand. Then the Rolls drew up to the kerb and Cyril opened the rear door for Sarah.

'Will you come to the flat for a nightcap?' Michael said.

'I don't think so,' David said. 'Speechifying takes it out of one, I find.'

'We're so very proud of you.' Jewel kissed him on the cheek. He had known her since she was a baby and had watched her flower into a great beauty with dark eyes and hair. Now her face was thinner and there were hollows in her cheeks. It gave her added beauty, but David knew the reason and held her close for a moment. 'I wish your father had been here to share it with me,' he said. Their own motor arrived and he stood in the light drizzle to watch them leave. He raised a hand in farewell and as he did so, he felt someone touch his other arm.

He had not heard a footstep, but turned and saw a very tall man in a dark coat and hat, a loosely-furled umbrella hooked over his arm.

'Forgive me. . .'

'Thank you. Thank you very much,' David said automatically.

But he had misconstrued the approach. 'Do you have a minute?' The man's voice was cultivated.

'I'm afraid I must be. . .'

'It is very important.'

David closed the door of the motor and turned. He tried to see to whom he was talking, but the man's hat was pulled well down and a muffler hid his chin. 'My name is Maberly,' he said. 'I thought your speech quite excellent.'

'Thank you.' There was impatience in David's tone.

'It was something you said that prompted me to approach you.'

'It's rather late. . .'

'Does the name Cornelius Amsterdam mean anything to you?'

'Good God, Connie! Of course.'

'I thought it might. I'm meeting him tomorrow. I wondered if you would join us.'

'I thought he was in New York. I don't usually make appointments without. . .'

Maberly bore in gently. 'That was a magnificent gift. Quite magnificent. But if I followed you correctly, you seemed to be making the point that giving money was second best; that you regretted your inability to do something personal towards the war effort. Was I right?'

David felt slightly uncomfortable. 'Well . . . yes.'

'I think I can offer you the opportunity.'

'Who exactly are you?'

'I work for the Government. The Foreign Office, to be precise.'

'Maberly. I don't. . .'

'Of course not. Why should you? Civil servants try to keep out of the limelight, not in it. My office? Sixish tomorrow?' He slipped his card into David's gloved hand and turned on his heel and walked away down Cornhill.

'What was all that about?' Sarah said when David was seated beside her.

'I don't know. He liked my speech. Are you coming back with me?'

He felt rather than saw her hesitate. 'Of course, if you want me to.'

'I always want you to, you know that.' He picked up the speaking tube and said, 'Bayswater please, Cyril.'

The motor went down Ludgate Hill, along Fleet Street and into the Strand. There had been a raid the day before, not by zeppelins, but by the new German long-range bombers based in the French Channel ports. Several buildings had lost their windows.

What could Maberly mean? David wondered. Maberly. The name was not totally unfamiliar and yet he couldn't quite place it. Was he representing the Foreign Office at the Mansion House dinner?

He was aware that Sarah was speaking and he reached for her hand.

'. . . quite ridiculous. I told him at the beginning that if he wanted someone for cheap laughs, he'd better find someone else. After all, the part is meant to show a woman of standing in society, a woman of property. He's trying to turn the character into a giggling ingenue.'

Trafalgar Square and Pall Mall were dark, not a light showing anywhere.

'That's the trouble with working for one of these *finds* from the provinces. They make a name for themselves in Manchester or Edinburgh, but it's not the same thing as London.'

Connie Amsterdam. He hadn't seen him for twenty years or more. Suddenly the name triggered off memories of Kimberley in the early days, so vivid that he could almost taste the dust between his teeth and feel the heat of the sun beating down on his neck.

'What do you think?' Sarah said.

Startled, David said, 'I think you should do whatever . . . you think best. That's the only solution.'

She looked at him for a moment and squeezed his hand and said, 'No one understands me like you do.'

He smiled to himself. On what had been one of the most important nights of his life, Sarah could talk of nothing but herself. But then, that was Sarah.

It was nearly midnight when they reached the house. It had been the fashion among diamond millionaires to make their pile in South Africa and spend it in London. Little Alfred Beit had built himself a Gothic bungalow in Park Lane. J. B. Robinson had built there, too, as had Barney Barnato. David himself, when his wife was still alive and his three children still at home had had a great house overlooking Hampstead Heath, but all that was in the past. His wife was dead, the girls were married and Michael farmed in Sussex. For his London base, David had bought a house in Bayswater overlooking the Park. In normal times he spent about six months in London and six in South Africa, either at the mine in Kimberley or on his grape farm at the Cape of Good Hope. The outbreak of war had trapped him in Britain.

The evening, far from tiring him as he had told Michael, had left him in a state of stimulation and excitement. He took Sarah into the library where a fire burned brightly and then, unwilling to disturb the servants, went to the cellar and brought up a bottle of champagne.

'Here's to the play,' he said.

'And here's to you, my darling. What does it feel like to be able to sign a cheque for half a million?'

'A good feeling, especially in this case.'

'But it's not the first donation you've made.'

He wondered if she was suggesting that he had bought his knighthood and frowned.

She was curled up on the big sofa in front of the fire and her dress had fallen away in front, revealing most of her large, white breasts. He sat on the sofa at her feet and began to rub his hand slowly up and down her thigh.

'David, have you any idea how much you're really worth?' She made no bones about being interested in his money and he did not blame her. Like all actresses, she had had to battle early on and knew the value of a pound note.

'That's a difficult question.'

'You're being evasive.'

'Yes.'

He took her glass and said, 'Let's take the wine upstairs.'

They lay in the big bed, listening to the muffled sounds of London. He was spent, relaxed. Her head was on his chest and when she spoke he felt the vibrations.

'Harry's back in town,' she said.

'Oh?' Viscount Menall was her ex-husband.

'I must say he looks very well in uniform.'

'When did you see him?'

'He came round to my rooms yesterday. He has three weeks' leave.

'Will you be seeing him again?'

'Of course not.' She kissed his neck and then slipped out of bed and began to dress.

'What are you doing?'

'David, I have an early rehearsal.'

'I see. It will mean getting Cyril up.'

'Do you mind, darling?'

'I think I'll take you home myself.'

A shadow seemed to cross her face. 'Don't be silly. That's

15

what Cyril is paid for. I wouldn't have come back if I'd thought you were going to be disturbed.'

He allowed himself to be talked into calling Cyril, but after she had left he lay awake for a long time. Had she gone to bed with Harry yesterday? Was she going back to him now? He felt a sudden spurt of anger. He was not prepared to share her with anyone, and that included ex-husbands.

[2]

Sir William Maberly, Permanent Under-Secretary of State at the Foreign Office, was a tall thin man, round-shouldered from constant stooping to talk to shorter people. He carried his head forward and his silvery-grey hair was thinning. He wore a dusty, dark suit and a high wing collar. He met David in the corridor and ushered him into a large room overlooking Whitehall. Dusk was falling and a gas fire burned. The heavy blackout curtains were already drawn across the long windows.

A vast shape stirred as David entered and began the ponderous process of levering itself out of a deep leather armchair.

'Connie! This is a pleasure.'

'Well, dear boy.' They shook hands. 'I thought you were in Kimberley.'

'I thought you were in New York.'

Amsterdam had always been large, now he was gross, but he still had the mildly buccaneering look that David recognised from his Kimberley days. The sharply-pointed beard, which had once been black, was now grey. David wondered if he still affected the cloak and the large black hat, and then saw them on the hatstand near the door.

No one knew much about him. He had appeared as a diamond-buyer in Kimberley at the height of the rush. There were rumours that he had left Brazil in the nick of time when an emerald deal had gone wrong. People said you had to get up very early in the morning to get the better of Connie Amsterdam. David was confident of his own expertise in diamonds, but Connie knew rubies, sapphires, emeralds, pearls and opals as well. He was more than simply an encyclopaedia. He knew where the gems were, how to get them, where to buy, where to sell. After a great jewel robbery the insurance companies went to Connie to see if he could recover the gems, and often he did. If you were an oil or a railroad or a steel millionaire and you wanted to give your wife or mistress something special, you went to Connie. If you were a faded princess or a marchioness on your uppers and you had the family heirlooms for sale, you went to Connie.

He had always had a certain style, which had made him something of a rare species in the rough masculinity of a mining town. There was a flamboyance about him, almost a femininity, which had attracted disparagement; he had been larger than life in a larger-than-life environment – but in a different way.

His background was a mystery. There was no doubt that he had an accent, but it was difficult to place. He himself claimed that he was half Dutch and half American, and had been expelled from the best schools in England.

From time to time David had seen stories about him in the newspapers, about sale-room coups, about deals running into six figures. It had been said of him that he looked like Diaghilev and it was an image he encouraged.

Maberly gave them each a glass of sherry, took one himself and, once they were seated, said, 'I asked you gentlemen here because we need your help. The subject is Russia.'

David felt himself stiffen.

'As you know, the Tsar has been forced to abdicate and a Provisional Government has been formed under Kerensky. When the Tsar was in power, however unjust and cruel the regime, at least it was consistent. But the abdication has left uncertainty, and the fact that the Tsar is still in Russia adds to that uncertainty.

'Already, there have been mutinies in the Navy and the Army. The whole place is seething with plot and counterplot. Kerensky is said to be a moderate, but moderate by what standards? This is what we don't know. It's as though the country is trying to leap abruptly from the fifteenth to the twentieth century.'

As he talked, David began to get a simplified picture of the confused country in which he had once lived. It seemed that it was split into three parties. There was the Tsar's party, comprising the old aristocracy, the land-owners, the senior Army and Navy officers. They were grouping to put the Tsar back in power. Then there were the Bolsheviks, led by Lenin, whose power-base was among the peasants, the factory workers and the lower ranks of the Army and Navy. They, according to Maberly, were poised for a revolutionary coup. Finally, there was the Provisional Government, under the lawyer Kerensky, which was hanging on precariously to power. It was said to be a party of the centre, and experts in Britain doubted whether it could withstand an attack from the Left.

Sir William went on: 'Russia would like to withdraw from the war. She would like to make a separate peace with Germany. Our information is that the Germans will make such heavy territorial demands that this may not be possible. One hopes this is so, since a great deal depends on Russia holding on. If she ends her part in the war, then Germany can bring men and guns from the Russian front and use them to fight us in France. That could be catastrophic. We have, in turn, been putting pressure on Kerensky to continue fighting.

'But now something odd has turned up. The Provisional Government has been in touch with us. They wish to sell the Russian Crown Regalia.'

David glanced across at Connie and was about to speak when Maberly said, 'I'm sure I don't have to tell you gentlemen the importance of such a collection aesthetically. At this particular time, though, that is of little relevance. His Majesty's Government would sooner have ten more battle-ships than all the diamonds, even in your mine, Sir David. The Provisional Government has indicated that in exchange for the regalia, it wants coal.'

'Coal!' David said. 'Good God, man. . .'

'It's factories are starved of coal. It's munitions works are almost at a standstill because of lack of coal. So that even if they continue the war they won't have the arms and machinery to fight with.'

'How much coal buys a diamond?'

18

Sir William did not reply to the question. 'If it wasn't for reasons I've already outlined, H.M's Government would not be contemplating such a transaction for I have to tell you that Britain is at this very moment in a critical way for coal. What we need is a delegation to go to Russia, make contact, conduct preliminary discussions, find out what the Provisional Government is thinking of in terms of a deal, and see if an agreement can be reached.

'The Foreign Office can field experts in such abstruse subjects as Old Slavonic and Sanskrit, but not, I'm afraid, in precious stones. Now, Sir David, one of the reasons we have invited you to think about this is because if I'm not mistaken you were born and spent the early part of your youth in Russia. Kiev, was it not?'

David nodded. 'I was brought up there by my grandparents.'

'And then, as a young boy, you came to England.'

David thought he had never heard his escape from Russia so beautifully understated. In his mind was the smoke and the fire in Kiev's Jewish quarter when the pogrom began; his race through the burning alleys; the hiding; the running. Then he had been passed through the country like a parcel until he had come finally to his cousin's home in North London.

'Yes,' he said. 'I left Russia when I was a youngster.'

'May I ask if there are any reasons either on the part of the Provisional Government, or your own, that would make it impossible for you to return? If . . .' he added hurriedly, '. . . you should decide to lead such a delegation?'

How do you explain, David wondered, that you would probably always be afraid among a people who had murdered your grandparents and scores of others, and burnt down a whole district of a city?

'No, I don't think so,' he said. 'But how soon would you want to know?'

'As soon as possible.'

'I know some of the Russian stones, of course. Do they want to sell everything?'

'We don't know.'

'The Crown?'

'I have a list,' Connie said.

So he had already known about the proposition, David thought.

'If . . . I'd have to tell my family,' he said. 'I'll let you know in forty-eight hours.'

Connie was staying at the Savoy. In his suite, he poured them each a whisky and soda.

'You knew about this?' David said.

'I was told last week.'

David stared down into his whisky. 'You wonder, "What can I do to help?" You worry about everything, the waste, the young men who are never coming back. A whole generation being wiped out. And doing nothing . . . *nothing* . . . and then they offer you something and your hands begin to sweat. . .'

'I feel the same, dear boy. But remember, it's the greatest collection of jewels in the world. One may never see it all together again. And, of course, there may be other pickings. Who knows what there is? Only the main items are listed.'

David sipped his drink. 'My grandfather, old Moshe Kadeshinsky, would have given an arm and a leg to handle them.'

Connie pulled a list from his pocket. ' "The Orlov",' he said. ' "The Moon of the Mountain", the "Shah." It's fantastic. Who thought we would ever see these or handle them? My dear boy, "The Orlov" is nearly two hundred carats. The "Polar Star" ruby. Two blue sapphires, more than two hundred carats each. And the Crown itself. Listen: "The great Imperial Crown, made by Posier in 1762 in the shape of a mitre. Five diamonds at the summit of a cross, supported by a large, uncut ruby . . . foliated arch containing eleven diamonds . . . thirty-eight perfect pearls in mitre formation . . . twenty-eight diamonds in the band encircling the head." And then there is part of the chain of the Order of St. Andrew and the Imperial Diadem. . .'

'Is there enough coal in the world to pay for them?' David said.

The young man stood in the hall of the Bayswater house and looked about him. He was dressed in Naval uniform and wore the stripes of a Lieutenant-Commander. There was something almost arrogant about the way he took in the furnishings. Kade watched him from the doorway of the study as he completed his circle. They faced each other.

'I'm Guy Jerrold.'

They shook hands and David said, 'Sir William spoke highly of you, Commander.'

Jerrold smiled, but made no comment. Kade heard a sound behind him and turned to see Jewel come from the study pulling on her gloves. She was dressed in cream silk and wore a sable coat. He introduced her to Jerrold. She put out her hand and David saw them respond to each other. He thought that he had rarely seen such a good-looking couple.

'I hope I'm not intruding,' Jerrold said.

'I was just leaving,' Jewel told him.

David directed him into the study and went to the door with her. 'That's a very handsome man,' she said. 'Maybe I shouldn't say it, but being an old married woman gives me some rights.'

David smiled. 'Even I can see that.'

'Is he the one who's going to look after you?'

'You make it sound as though I was in a wheel-chair.' He kissed her. 'Don't forget next Tuesday. He's the Queen's gynaecologist. The best.'

She patted his hand. 'Always the best for the Kades.'

Jerrold was standing in the study, his cap under his arm. 'We were having tea,' David said. 'But perhaps you might like something stronger?'

'Tea would be fine.'

It was a small, cosy, book-lined room with a sofa and two easy chairs covered in a patterned chintz which Jewel had chosen.

'My daughter-in-law asked me if you were the one who was going to look after me,' Kade said.

'I wouldn't use the phrase "look after", sir.' Jerrold smiled. It was an infectious, penetrating smile. He was a lean man with a wedge-shaped face, and David guessed his age at about thirty. His eyes were hazel and his light brown hair had a slight wave and was worn a little longer than Naval

Regulations specified. He was fresh-faced and looked intelligent and decisive.

Sir William had described him as 'capable' and the way he had said it made it sound like high praise indeed.

'Well now, perhaps we should get to know a bit about each other,' David said. 'They've given you my background, of course.'

'A short sketch.'

'We'll get to that later then. You first.'

They talked for more than an hour. Half way through Kade told one of the servants to light the gas, close the curtains and bring in a tray of drinks.

Jerrold spoke with engaging frankness, leaving out information which might have sounded as though he was indulging in self-praise. He came from an old-established Naval family. More than half a century before, his grandfather had joined the Imperial Russian Navy as an instructor at the School of Navigation at the Kronstadt naval base. The family had later moved to St. Petersburg and, on his retirement, had remained in Russia. There had been several children, some of whom had gone into business, importing heavy machinery from Britain. One had become an engineer and had worked on the Moscow-Vladimir section of the Trans-Siberian Railway. Jerrold's father had trained at Dartmouth and had then returned to St. Petersburg as Naval Attaché. He had married the daughter of a landowner near Moscow. Guy had been educated first in St. Petersburg and had then gone to Dartmouth and into the Royal Navy. There had been plans for him to join the Imperial Navy as an instructor at the Naval Gunnery School but, after the mutiny of Russian sailors at Odessa, he had been advised to remain in the Royal Navy. He spoke Russian fluently.

David listened to him without comment, knowing there were two or three things he had learned from Sir William which Guy had not touched on. One was that he had been Chief Cadet Captain at Dartmouth and had won the King's Medal.

As they talked, the two men were judging each other. What would they be like as travelling companions? If they had to share a room? If they had to trust each other?

David sketched in his own background, his childhood in Kiev, his school in London, his struggles at the Kimberley mines. Night closed around them. The fire was lit.

'You met Mr. Amsterdam?'

'Yesterday.'

'I'm sorry I couldn't join you, but I have a good deal of tidying up to do before we leave.' He saw Guy look covertly at his wrist watch. 'Am I keeping you?' he said sharply.

'Oh no, sir, not at all.'

David had not reached his position without an ability to assess people. He needed more time to judge Guy. He decided to test his patience.

He poured them each a glass of sherry and sat back comfortably. 'Sir William spoke highly of what he called your ability to synthesise. Russian politics are in a muddle at the moment, perhaps you could clarify them for me.'

He saw the young man's mouth tighten slightly, but he sketched in the situation much as Maberly had.

'What chance has the Tsar of regaining the throne?' David said.

'I'm not sure, sir. There's certainly a movement in his favour, but not as big as he would like. It's not only the middle and lower classes who have advocated change. There have been a good number of liberal aristocrats who sided against him. He used the Cossacks against them, and that made him even more unpopular.'

'What about the other parties?'

Guy had moved to the edge of his chair. 'There's the Provisional Government, but no one thinks it will last.'

'Even if it gets the peace treaty with Germany?'

'The last news I've heard is that Lenin and the Bolsheviks are planning a counter-revolution. There have been more riots in Petrograd. That's why we're going to meet the Russian delegation in Vladivostok instead of Archangel.'

'Another drink?'

'Really, sir, I think. . .'

'Then we'll go out to dinner. Kettner's still keeps a good table. . .'

'I'd love to, sir, but if you'll forgive me, I'm afraid I have an engagement. I'm taking my fiancée to dinner.'

'Excellent. We'll make it a foursome.'

He waited for a refusal, but the younger man said smoothly, 'Thank you, sir. That's very kind.'

David admired his diplomacy. Guy made his arrangements by telephone, then David telephoned Sarah.

'Tonight?' she said.

'In an hour.'

'But, darling, you should have told me.'

There was a muffled sound in the background as though someone had spoken and she had covered the mouthpiece.

'It's only just arisen. I didn't know myself.'

'David, I'm dead beat. I really would like an early night.'

'It's important.'

'I realise that, darling, or you wouldn't have telephoned me so late.'

'And I'd like you to come.'

There was a pause and then she said, 'It will have to be an early night.'

Elizabeth Lytton, Guy's fiancée, was one of the most beautiful women David had ever seen. She had only been a dark figure in the motor, but once they walked into the restaurant he saw her clearly. The first thing that struck him was her colouring. Her hair was the colour of a copper beech in early summer, her skin pale and her features finely formed, delicate, almost fragile. Her tall figure, though slender, was heavy-breasted and the lines of her thighs were visible as she moved, hinting at unseen delights. For the first time since David had been taking Sarah about, he realised that the heads that turned to stare were looking towards Elizabeth and Guy and not David and Sarah. It was a chastening experience.

He had never seen anyone so completely in love as Elizabeth was with Guy. She hardly took her eyes off him from the time they arrived until they left. He treated her with a kind of brotherly off-handedness, a casualness that bordered sometimes, David thought, on rudeness.

The effect of this on Sarah was predictable. She was used to being the centre of attention and now she reacted badly. She talked about herself with remorseless energy: about her new apartment, her new acting role, her past successes. David watched with fascination. The differences between the two women was striking. Elizabeth had a frankness, an engaging self-deprecation and a sense of humour which he found immensely engaging. She was fresh, untouched while Sarah, by comparison, seemed jaded and temperamental.

They drank champagne and Guy set out to charm Sarah. She was a few years older than he, but David imagined that with his good looks he both reacted to and received a reaction from most women. He complimented her, told her how many of her plays he had seen and, under his flattery, she began to relax.

At the same time, his banter with Elizabeth increased. 'Elizabeth won't understand,' he would say after some reference to the war. Or, 'We'll have to explain that to Elizabeth.'

'Guy doesn't think I've very bright,' she said, smiling.

'I've never said any such thing!'

'No, but you think it. Guy takes all the intellectual magazines. He likes to keep up with international affairs.'

'I find them rather boring,' David said. 'I enjoy books.'

'So do I,' she said.

'Steamy romances,' Guy said.

'Not only steamy romances.'

'What do you like?' David asked. 'Dickens?'

'And Trollope. And Jane Austen. And the Brontës.'

'There's nothing very steamy about *Pride and Prejudice* or *Persuasion*.' He turned to Guy. 'Have you read them?'

'I intend to, when I have time.'

'I shouldn't bother with women novelists,' Sarah said. 'Their characters are talkers, not doers.'

'And I would prefer doers?' Guy said.

'I would say so.'

After they had dropped the younger couple David said, 'Are you coming back?'

She patted him on the arm and said, 'Not tonight, if you don't mind.'

'Tired?'

'Yes.'

'Have you seen Harry again?'

'Why do you ask?'

'I wondered.'

'If you think that's the reason I won't come back with you tonight, you're mistaken.'

'I didn't. Sarah, we won't be seeing each other for some time.'

'Oh? Why, David?'

'I'm going away.'

'Where?'

'I can't tell you.'

'Don't be so silly, of course you can.'

'Please don't make me repeat myself. I don't know how long I'll be away. When I get back, we'll have to work things out.'

'What things?'

'Us.'

'In what way?'

'Either you live with Harry, or you live with me.'

'Is that an ultimatum?' He could feel her anger.

'Just think about it while I'm gone.'

She opened the car door.

'I won't see you up,' he said. 'Good-bye.'

He watched her go into the door of the house in which she had a flat, then glanced up at her windows. There was a chink of light at one side of the black-out curtain. He assumed someone was there, waiting for her.

Three days later he sailed from Portsmouth.

[3]

David stood on the wooden verandah of His Britannic Majesty's Honorary Consulate in Asiatic Russia and stared westward over the country he had fled and had not laid eyes on for more than thirty years. The house was built on a hill above Vladivostok. East and west lay the gulfs of the Ussuri and the Amur rivers, to the south were mountainous islands and rocky headlands separated from the mainland by a strip of water which he now knew to be called the 'Bosphorus of the East'.

Directly below him was the harbour which their ship, the cruiser H.M.S. *Xerxes*, had entered earlier that day. This, too, had been found to resemble the Bosphorus and was named 'Bay of the Golden Horn', its two headlands forming the west and southern shores. It was packed with shipping and he had been surprised at its polyglot nature, but Guy had pointed out, 'We're in a different culture, a different hemisphere. We're farther away from the fighting in France than New York is.'

It was irritating being instructed about a country which was as much his own as Guy's. But here on the edge of Siberia he felt he was on the very edge of the world itself. He had done his reading in the ship and what had emerged was a sense of the hugeness of Russia, which he had never felt as a child in Kiev. In Siberia alone, you could put the whole of North America, the whole of Europe and still have a huge space unoccupied.

Looking down at the harbour now he could make out Chinese junks, ships of the Russian Siberian and Pacific fleets, river steamers that plied up and down the Amur, fishing boats from Korea and Japan.

It was the town itself which brought back memories of his childhood, the golden domes of the churches, the square public buildings, the mass of wooden housing. As he raised his eyes westward he saw the beginnings of the great wilderness of forests and steppes which spread for thousands of miles to the Urals, the natural boundary between Europe and Asia. And in all that enormous mass there was only one road, the great post road, the *Trakt*, and one railway, the Trans-Siberian, which had recently been completed. For the rest, if you wished to travel, you went by river in summer, and when the rivers froze, you walked. There was something daunting about the scale of things that produced in him a sense of unease. He had found America large, larger than southern Africa, which itself was not small, but then he had become used to the scale of London and of England, intimate, almost cosy. He knew that there could be nothing intimate here. It seemed to lack all human scale.

The summer evening was warm, the views magnificent, and he was savouring being alone for the first time in many weeks.

The voyage out had been long, tedious at times and at others full of problems, the most serious of which was the seasickness which had gripped his servant. Cyril Hankey was much more than a chauffeur to David and had come on the journey as his valet and general factotum. They had known each other for a long time. He was a cadaverous man, now about fifty, who had gone out to Africa with the British Army to fight in the Boer war, and had somehow been left behind, a piece of human detritus.

David had come across him one afternoon some miles from Kimberley. His car had broken down and his driver had been unable to fix it. Just then Cyril had come walking along the dusty road, a knapsack on his back. In half an hour he had diagnosed the trouble and had them on the road again.

Later David had seen him in Kimberley and, when his own chauffeur resigned, he had offered the position to Cyril. It was then he had uttered one of the phrases which had now become legendary in the Kade family: 'I don't mind.' This was as near to yes as he ever came. There were other phrases: 'I wouldn't know,' and 'More than likely,' which he used as the occasion demanded. He never said thank you or good-bye, or hello. Nor did he ever respond to David's 'Good morning,' other than by commenting adversely on the weather. Once, on a lovely day, David had said, 'You can't complain about the weather today, Cyril.'

'It'll rain before the week-end, sir,' he had replied.

When David had asked if he wanted to go to Russia he had said, 'I don't mind,' as if they were running down to Sussex to see Michael and Jewel.

At first he had been so ill on the ship they had put him in the sick-bay and then, as he gradually recovered, David had taken him into his own cabin. Cyril had been one of the few men in the experience of the captain ever to be sick in the Suez Canal.

'Don't worry, it's nothing to be ashamed of,' David had said. 'Nelson was always seasick, too.'

'I wouldn't know, sir.'

They had bunkered at Aden, then Colombo, and were a few days out of Singapore when David coaxed him up on deck. It was a glorious, cloudless day with a fresh breeze blowing and H.M.S. *Xerxes* was cutting through the slight swell at fifteen knots. David remarked on the day and Cyril said, 'If it weren't for this breeze we'd catch the 'eat all right, sir.'

It was then that David knew he was on the road to recovery.

He was not David's only worry, for they had hardly cleared the Bay of Biscay when he realised there were other problems: to the ordinary stresses of war and the fear of being attacked by German submarines were added the stresses that grew between men thrown together for long periods.

Although he had known Connie for twenty years he had rarely spent more than a few hours in his company. He hardly knew Guy at all and it rapidly became clear that the three of them were going to have to make allowances for each other and he, as leader, would have to show the way.

Guy and Connie were totally different human beings. Jerrold's background was one of tradition, of a code of behaviour, of roots that went a long way back in the Navy, of a certain style of upbringing, of acceptance that the future held for him an Admiral's gold braid.

Connie was different. Where Guy was straight, he was devious, where Guy lived a Naval life of some austerity, his outlook was sybaritic. He treated the ship's company as he might have treated the crew of a luxury liner crossing the Atlantic. Things had begun to go wrong when he came aboard at Portsmouth.

Because of the confined space in the ship they had been asked to bring as little luggage as possible. Connie had arrived on the Hard at Portsmouth with a Vuitton trunk, three large cases and a hamper from Fortnum's containing, among other items, smoked salmon, paté de foie, tins of lobster bisque and turtle soup, a smoked Parma ham, tins of Palethorpe's sausages and a dark fruit cake rich with molasses. Most of the ship's officers had not seen such foodstuffs since the war began; the crew, never.

'But I *am* travelling light, dear boy,' he had said. 'When I go to New York I take twice as much.'

29

He complained about his berth. He had been allocated a bunk in a cabin with one of the officers and had come to David in a state of high indignation. Had David been alone he might have been firm right then, at the beginning, but Guy was also present and he immediately volunteered to see what could be done. The result was the shifting, not of Connie, who stayed where he was with his luggage, but of the officer. And not only one officer; the move caused a ripple effect as others had to change accommodation. It was felt in some parts of the ship that it was more important to be fighting a war than to be giving up berths to civilians insensitive enough to bring cabin-trunks and luxury food aboard.

When David remonstrated with him, Connie said blankly: 'But you wouldn't expect me to share a cabin with someone who sleeps in his socks?'

As the voyage progressed, it became clear that he was used to luxury and used to getting what he wanted. Every day the ship's company performed one or other of several practise drills and it was often in the midst of fire-drill or gunnery practice that Connie would want hot water for washing or a change of linen or someone to clean out his cabin. Guy put up with these requests and fulfilled them as best he could. David had been tempted to intervene but realised that for Guy's own sake he would have to solve the problem of Connie himself.

Things reached a head on a boiling hot day in the Red Sea. The atmosphere was windless and the air scoops were out at every porthole. In the calm conditions the captain decided to have boat drill. Everyone was called to their boat stations, all were hot and fretful. In the midst of this, Connie demanded ice and fresh limes.

On his way to the deck, David heard the row between Guy and Connie and saw Guy emerge from the cabin, his face a tight knot of anger.

Until then Connie had treated Guy with a kind of avuncular friendliness, 'dear boys' liberally spattering his speech. Now his attitude changed and they rarely addressed each other. To avoid further scenes, Guy left him to his own devices and spent his time with men of his own sort.

Now, standing in the Honorary Consul's garden, David

thanked God that one voyage at least was over and for a while they could be freer of each other.

The house was not large by English standards, but large enough in comparison with those he had seen in the town. It belonged to the Great Northern and Oriental Telegraph Company, whose manager in Eastern Siberia was Harold Wiggins, who doubled as Britain's Honorary Consul. It was built of wood and its charm lay in its position above the town and in the very English garden which spread in front of the verandah.

Much as he was enjoying his solitude, David knew it was self-indulgent and went in to join the others. Mrs. Wiggins, somewhat pink-faced, was being charmed by Guy and left him rather reluctantly for David. 'I hope you'll excuse Mr. Wiggins,' she said, 'but he was called to the office. He should rejoin us within the hour.'

She was a stout plain woman with a trace of Manchester in her voice. As they talked, he discovered that she had lived with her husband in several of the world's lonely places, looking after the company's telegraph repeating stations, and yet she still looked and sounded wholly English. He tried to talk to her about Siberia, but discovered that she knew nothing of it, that she spoke no Russian and read only the English newspapers, which arrived up to two months late. At dinner, she served a meal that might have come from any home in northern England. David wondered how he – and especially Connie – was going to be able to endure her company for the two weeks they were scheduled to be in Vladivostok.

Dinner was over by the time her husband arrived. He was a lanky, freckle-faced man with light red hair and he spoke with the flat vowels of the London suburbs.

'You're very late, Harold,' Mrs. Wiggins said.

'I'm sorry, my dear. But things are hectic just now.'

'Mr. Wiggins is kept at it all the time, with one thing or another,' she said proudly. 'Harold, I've saved you some. . .'

'I have to talk to these gentlemen, so if you wouldn't mind. . .'

'Of course not. I'll leave you to it then.' She smiled at him fondly and, for a moment, David saw into their lives: the two of them alone in an incomprehensible world, possessing only each other.

'I didn't want to speak in front of Mrs. Wiggins, because she becomes easily upset.' David could see he was excited. His freckles stood out starkly against his white skin. He opened a brief-case and pulled out a wad of telegrams, most of which were in code.

'That's only part of the day's traffic,' he said. 'It's been like this since mid-afternoon.'

'You have our attention,' Connie said impatiently.

'There's been a rising in Petrograd. The Machine-Gun Regiment has marched with their weapons through the streets.' He shook the telegrams. 'The sailors in Kronstadt have come out in support.'

'In support of what?' David said.

'They want to destroy the Provisional Government,' Guy said.

Wiggins nodded. 'It's the Bolsheviks, Sir David. They want the power.'

'I realise that. But how does this affect our arrangements? Our people should be arriving tomorrow.'

'That's what I've come to tell you.' He sorted through the telegrams and handed one to David. It was addressed to 'British Coal Delegation,' and read: 'Fraternal greetings. Political events make it impossible for us continue journey. Please convey regrets British Government. Rublyov.'

He passed it on to Guy and Connie, then said to Wiggins, 'I think we must have a talk about this, if you'll excuse us.'

The three of them went out onto the verandah, where it was still broad daylight.

'I don't like the idea of spending six weeks at sea just to return without even a meeting,' he began. 'But apart from any other consideration, our success here might mean the shortening of the war. If Russia collapses militarily, then Britain and France take all the pressure.'

Connie said, 'Is there an alternative?'

David nodded slowly, feeling a movement in his bowels that came from apprehension of what he was contemplating.

Guy put his thought into words: 'The mountain could go to Mohamet.'

'But we don't even know where they are,' Amsterdam said. 'In any case, we have no brief for travelling in Russia.'

David went to the door. Mr. Wiggins was at the table, eating a late dinner. His wife was sitting with him.

'Where was the telegram sent from?' David asked.

'Irkutsk on Lake Baikal.'

'How far is that?'

'By train? Three days. But you couldn't possibly. . .'

'When is the next train?'

'The time-tables are upside down. Half the rolling stock is being used to take materiél to the western front. Sir David, you don't mean. . . ?'

'We've already come half way round the world. Three days more hardly matter.'

'This country is in chaos! They say the *taiga* is full of exiles. Bands of escapees. They're dangerous. Control is breaking down, administration is falling apart. I do beg you. . .'

David turned and went back to the verandah. After briefly outlining what Wiggins had told him, he said, 'Wiggins can send telegrams up and down the line. Even if they've decided to go back to Moscow, they can't have got far.'

'Dear boy, have you thought. . . ?'

David said, 'Guy?'

'My orders were clear: to support you in every way.'

David said, 'I hope you agree, too, Connie. I'm going to need you.' He rose. 'I'll tell Wiggins to get telegrams off to several points along the line and see about accommodation.'

'For God's sake, if we have to do this, tell him to book soft class in the train,' Connie said angrily.

That night David lay in the narrow, uncomfortable bed, finding it difficult to sleep. It had been one thing to conduct talks in Vladivostok under the eyes and the guns of H.M.S. *Xerxes*, it was another to journey back into the centre of the country that had once tried to extinguish him.

Late the following day, they received a telegram saying that the Russian delegation would await them at Symka for a week.

They searched for the town on their maps and finally found a tiny dot on the railway near Irkutsk.

A day later, they left by train.

[4]

The *Rossiya* Express, which it was hoped would complete the 6,000-mile journey from Vladivostok to Moscow, was only five carriages long and was pulled by a locomotive made in Darlington. On the footplate, besides the driver and fireman, rode three armed soldiers. There were more soldiers in each of the carriages. They were there, the conductor told them, to stop bandits.

'Bandits?' Connie said bitterly. 'It sounds as if we're in the Wild West.'

This exchange had taken place at the station in Vladivostok and had provoked another outburst from Mr. Wiggins. 'I wish you'd reconsider, Sir David! If something happens to you, there is nothing I could do.' It was as though he was asking for absolution for events yet to occur.

'We should be all right as long as we stay with the railway,' Guy said.

'I've stated in my report that this was our joint decision and that you had nothing whatsoever to do with it,' David said, and saw a look of relief cross Wiggins' face.

Only one of the coaches was soft class, the rest were hard. A cavalry Major in a dark green uniform with black frogging, long black boots and a large black moustache took the compartment next to David's, followed aboard by a servant carrying his portmanteau and a wicker picnic basket. He stared fiercely at the English party.

The journey started in driving rain and a slatey light. The countryside was grey and sodden and the train chugged slowly through a waste of marshes before crossing the bridge over the Amur, which was more than a mile wide at this point.

34

Their compartments were adjoining and each held two berths. David and Cyril shared one. Amsterdam and Guy Jerrold the other. The soft-class carriage had been designed for comfort on long journeys. The corridor was carpeted and there was a samovar at one end which produced a constant supply of tea. The compartment itself was decorated with etched mirrors, brass fittings; the woodwork was polished mahogany, the bunks were red plush and the curtains tasselled red velvet. There was a thick rug on the floor and an easy chair with an anti-macassar. A small door opened on a lavatory and shower.

'Well, we can't complain about this,' David said after they had looked around. Cyril made no reply, and he let it go. He had pressed Cyril to stay in Vladivostok, but he had refused with a kind of gloomy relish.

At Khabarovsk the train was joined by a slip coach from Nakhoda and then they pressed on into the wilds of eastern Siberia. David had never seen, never even visualized such country. It was of a desolation hard to withstand. Even though it was mid-summer, the rain blew in on an icy wind from the north. Forest alternated with steppe, here and there through the rain he saw a small farm, a field of comfry, and then they were past and the settlement was swallowed up in the mist. He could not imagine what sort of lives such people lived. Once, late in the afternoon, he saw a man walking near the track, carrying a sack on his back. There was no road, no house, no settlement of any sort in that huge plain. There were no fences, no evidence that this was an inhabited landscape. The man walked on as the train rattled past. He looked up once, then he bowed his head and went on walking. David found himself inexpressibly moved by the scene and to break the spell he went next door to see Connie and Guy. Connie had taken to his bed and refused to get up. He and Guy hardly spoke now and Guy spent much of the time standing in the corridor.

David joined him. He started to tell the young man not to let Connie's behaviour worry him, but decided against it, not wishing to risk a snub.

Ever since their evening together in London he had tried to break down Guy's reserve, without success. At first he had put it down to their different backgrounds, but he wondered now if it wasn't the age-gap. He had thought Guy in his uniform one of the handsomest young men he had ever seen. Now Guy was dressed in a soft West of England tweed, and the conclusion still held true.

He said, 'When we get back to Vladivostok there may be mail. They said they'd send it in the Bag. Is Elizabeth a good correspondent?'

Guy's face brightened. 'Very good, sir. She writes well, too. She always has.'

David thought of the tall, full-breasted girl he had taken to dinner. 'Tell me about her,' he said.

'What would you like to know, sir?' The reserve was back, the tone formal.

'I don't mean a curriculum vitae. I just wondered how you had met. Who she was. She's a lovely girl.'

'Yes, she is.' He paused, then said, 'I've known her since I was seventeen. Her brother was at Dartmouth with me. I used to go home with him for the school holidays.'

Having started to talk about her, he seemed suddenly to become another person. The coolness was replaced by a humanity which David found engaging; it was a side to his nature he had not seen before. He spoke of sailing holidays at Cowes and fishing holidays in Scotland with Elizabeth's family with deep nostalgia, as though they formed the most important part of his life. They had gone everywhere together. The Lyttons had treated him like another son and he had treated Elizabeth like a sister. It had been taken for granted that they would marry, not only by Guy and Elizabeth, but by the two families. Everything seemed almost too idyllic, David thought enviously.

In the compartment on the other side of his, the cavalry officer was having an enjoyable journey. He had collected two women with Mongolian features from hard class and they seemed to be having a party. It was well past midnight before the laughter and shouting died down.

There was no dining-car on the train because of wartime restrictions and David was grateful for the hamper Mrs. Wiggins had prepared. The one thing they were never short of was tea and the *provodnik*, a toothless old woman who

36

gossipped with the soldiers by the samovar, was on duty day and night, or so it seemed to David, to supply their needs.

On the second day the weather cleared and the sun came out and they climbed away from the dreariness of the coastal steppe into the *taiga*, that great wilderness of mountain and forest which stretches across Siberia.

This was a different landscape, a trackless, almost impenetrable forest of firs, birches, larches, Siberian cedars and spruce.

In spite of the fact that the sun was out, the forest was dark and gloomy and the air that came into the train was bitingly cold. It reminded David of fairy-tales his grandmother used to tell him, of woodcutters' children, lost or abandoned, of wolves and bears. Occasionally they would pass a small clearing in which men and women in padded clothes were winning timber. What settlements there were comprised small single-storeyed dwellings of silvery weathered wood huddled together as though for comfort. And everywhere he looked, he saw mud and swamp. He thought it must be one of the most terrible places on earth.

They came to stations whose names were blacked out for wartime security, but were not allowed off the train. The platforms were packed with soldiers, most of whom lay on the hard ground, their heads on their packs, rifles by their sides, trying to sleep. David had no idea whether the soldiers were going east or west or whether they were indeed going anywhere. He had lost touch with the war, almost with the world itself, so far away did everything familiar seem. And yet if he journeyed on and then turned south, he would eventually come to Kiev, where Moshe Kadeshinsky had conducted his jewellery business and where as a small boy David had sat in the old man's viewing-room, drinking hot chocolate while his grandfather showed him diamonds and sapphires and emeralds. 'Look closely,' he would say. 'What do you see?'

'Fire and ice, grandfather.'

And then had come the pogrom and he had never seen either of his grandparents again, or their friends, or Kiev, or for that matter Russia – until now.

He was standing in the corridor with Guy, leaning on the

37

brass rail and listening to the low hum of the soldiers and the *provodnik* talking when Guy said, 'Look, there's a road of sorts.'

A wide, muddy road ran parallel to the railway line, cut as straight through the *taiga* as possible, crossing ravines and small rivers on wooden bridges.

'It is *Trakt*,' said a voice beside them, and turning, David saw the cavalry officer. His tunic was undone and his under-vest was showing. He badly needed a shave and he appeared to be very drunk. In his right hand he held a bottle of vodka. 'You know what is *Trakt*? It is only road in *taiga*.' He put his arm around Guy's shoulders. 'You are Englishski. I drink to Englishski.' He drank and held the bottle for Guy, who took it and put it to his lips without drinking.

'Drink, drink,' the officer said. 'You are not girl.'

Guy drank, then David was offered the bottle.

'To Russia,' he said, taking a small mouthful.

'I am Cossack,' the Russian said. 'Maxim Perfiliev, Major.'

Just then the train began to slow down. As it drew into a small station David saw a group of about ten men and women dressed in grey, standing at the trackside guarded by soldiers with rifles. Some had their heads half shaven, others completely. They were all painfully thin, with skeletal hands and skull-like faces. Some were bare-footed, others wore rags tied around their feet. All, including the women, wore leg irons. The train stopped. The soldiers waved their rifles and the group shuffled down the trackside to the rear coach and began to climb painfully aboard.

'Boggerts!' Major Perfiliev shouted at the closed window. 'Dirty boggerts!'

'Who are they?' David said.

He laughed harshly. 'You never hear of General Cuckoo's Army?'

David looked confused, but Guy said, 'They're exiles, aren't they?'

'They run away from prison,' Perfiliev said. 'In winter they work, but in summer they hear cuckoo. They try run away back to homes. Thousands and thousands. And here in *taiga* they die. If they do not die, soldiers find them. I will shoot them.' He drank and passed the bottle to Guy again. 'I drink to Englishski. You like girl? I fetch girl.'

'Not now,' Guy said.

'Later, when it is dark. That is best. You come with me. We find girl. Plenty girls.' He pointed to David. 'We find girl for him.'

The train began to move again and David said, 'Are you going all the way to Moscow?'

'Moscow. St. Petersburg. I go to fight Bolsheviki. I am Cossack. We kill all Bolshevikis.' He laughed uproariously and squeezed Guy's shoulder again. 'Drink! Then we find girls.'

But he was too drunk to find any girls and a little later staggered back to his compartment and fell onto his bunk. David was relieved to be rid of him. He could not get from his mind the picture of the emaciated exiles clambering aboard the train in their chains and wondered if the lonely figure he had seen the day before was such a man. If Perfiliev was right, then all over Siberia there were political and criminal prisoners escaping westward; hearing the call of the cuckoo, unable to endure their terms of exile even though death or recapture lay at the end of their road. After a while the railway and the *Trakt* diverged and there was nothing but the dark forest once more.

The following morning David was to witness another aspect of the chaos which Mr. Wiggins had warned them against before they left. It was a little after six o'clock when the train suddenly jolted, throwing him about in his bunk. He had barely got his feet on the floor when he heard firing.

'What the hell's happening?'

'I wouldn't know, sir,' Cyril said.

He could see nothing but the curtain of black forest from his compartment window, and he went into the corridor. Soldiers were kneeling at the windows, sighting along the barrels of their rifles; the *provodnik* had taken shelter behind her steaming samovar. A locomotive had been derailed and half-a-dozen open trucks lay on their sides, forming a barricade for the men behind them. There might have been ten or a dozen, dressed in uniforms David did not recognise. They

39

had rifles and revolvers and were shouting at the driver of the *Rossiya*.

Major Perfiliev staggered into the corridor.

'What's happening?' David repeated.

'Boggerts!' cried the Cossack.

'Who are they?'

'Dirty Czech boggerts!'

Perfiliev ran back to his bunk and returned with a heavy cavalry revolver in one hand and a sabre in the other. He began to fire through the window.

The train, which had slowed down, now seemed to leap forward in a series of jerks. The firing grew hotter. Major Perfiliev emptied the revolver out of the window and went back to his compartment to find bullets to reload it. By the time he resumed his position the train had passed the ambush and the firing had died down. Guy, Connie and all the other soft class passengers were milling about in the corridor and the Major was waving his revolver, thirsty for blood. When it became apparent that he was not going to be able to shoot anyone he opened his hamper and David saw that it contained nothing but bottles. He opened a new bottle of vodka and they each had a drink. David said, 'Why Czechs?'

The Major said, 'Traitors! I kill Czechs.' He was too excited to make much sense then, but a little later David was able to piece together part of the story. About forty thousand Czech soldiers had deserted the Austro-Hungarian army and come over to the Russian side. Plans had been made to rail them to Vladivostok and from there ship them to France to fight on the side of the Allies. But in the present chaotic state of Russia, arrangements had broken down and they had been stranded. Thousands had mutinied and were camped along the railway, the source of food.

About noon they passed a long goods train travelling east. It was packed with soldiers. They clung to the sides of the locomotive and lay on the tops of the cars, anywhere they could find a handhold or a foothold. These, David learned, were Russian deserters, who were fleeing east as far as they could get from the fighting.

'I kill all deserters,' Major Perfiliev said.

Further down the line they came to a tunnel, on the far

side of which they saw the bodies of several Russian soldiers, some with heads so badly injured as to be unrecognisable as human beings.

'Tunnel low, soldier high.' The Major made a picture with his hands.

All that day they passed groups of Czech soldiers. Some were encamped at the edge of the *taiga*, hunched round fires, others were walking along the track. Occasionally a train passed, going eastward. Sometimes Russian deserters and Czech soldiers were huddled together in cattle trucks. David tried to reassure himself that no-one would harm an official British delegation with diplomatic status.

Late in the afternoon, they reached Symka. He could hardly believe, when he saw it, that this was where they were to have their talks. There was no town, not even a village, only a station.

'Here, here!' Major Perfiliev pressed a bottle of vodka on him. 'In such a place, you must have vodka.'

David, Cyril, Connie and Guy climbed down onto the trackside. The train whistled once and moved forward. David was aware of it leaving with a sinking heart. Guy's face was set, but Connie looked like a frightened and angry child.

Three men stood at the side of the station building. All were dressed in dark suits, wing collars and black homburg hats. With one accord, they moved forward. They stopped five paces from the British delegation. The two groups stood looking at each other in the midst of the Siberian *taiga*, the one almost as far from home as the other.

In those few seconds David inspected the team with which he was to do business. Then the man in the middle stepped forward, bowed and said, 'Rublyov.'

David bowed and said, 'Kade.'

'Allow please. Comrade Letchinsky. Comrade Gudim.'

David introduced Guy and Connie and there was much grave shaking of hands.

In the half light of the forest David had seen the Russians only as shapes, now he was able to differentiate between them. Rublyov was short and squat, a powerful-looking man whose face had been pitted by smallpox. His suit was made of cheap material and fitted him badly. David thought he

41

would have looked more comfortable in a butcher's apron or a peasant's smock and boots. He was clearly one of the new ruling class. Letchinsky was tall and thin and as he removed his hat to greet them, David saw that his silver hair was brushed elegantly back over his head. His clothes were expensive and he wore them well. Gudim was somewhere in between, not of the working-class, not of the elite. Solid and serious. After the hand-shaking Letchinsky said in English, ✳ 'We must aplogise. . .'

But Rublyov held up his hand for silence. Letchinsky turned away, a look of distaste of his thin face. Rublyov took a piece of paper from his pocket and read slowly, 'We welcome fraternal British delegation on behalf of Provisional Government.' He paused, and David realised this might well be the extent of his English. Rublyov turned to Letchinsky and nodded his heavy head.

Letchinsky said, 'We must apologise for asking you to meet us here, but Irkutsk is unsafe at the moment. Allow me to explain who we are. Comrade Rublyov, our leader, is Commissar for Industrial Production in the Provisional Government. Comrade Gudim is secretary of the Committee of the Coal and Iron Federation. I myself am from the Treasury.'

'Would you thank Comrade Rublyov and tell him we're pleased to have been able to make this contact.'

Once again, Rublyov cut Letchinsky short. 'Follow, please!' he said.

There was an arrogance about him that David did not like. It was also apparent that there was tension between him and Letchinsky.

They walked past the station building. It had been carelessly damaged. The windows were broken, the pitch-pine panelling pulled away from the walls and burnt in the waiting-room stove. They followed the Russians along a path that led directly into the *taiga*. The light was dim and gloomy. They seemed to be following a spur-line and after about a mile they came to a clearing. Guy, who had been talking to Letchinsky, told David that the spur-line had been used to bring out timber. In the middle of the clearing stood a single green railway carriage with a gold coat-of-arms on the side, and not far from it, a complex that comprised a saw-mill and a series of five small dwellings, all of which appeared to be deserted. They were led to the largest of them.

'The manager's house,' Letchinsky said.

Rublyov opened the door and stood aside waiting for them to go in. The house was built of split logs and consisted of one large room off which was a cubby-hole, dark and stinking, that had once been a kitchen. Next to it was a room no bigger than a large cupboard with a wash-stand and basin.

The British delegation stood in the middle of the empty room in some bewilderment.

'We apologise, but Irkutsk is full of soldiers,' Letchinsky said.

Connie, a thunderous expression on his face, stalked back and forth, his long cloak flapping. He came to a halt in front of the Russians. 'You expect us to stay here? This is an insult! Not only to us, but to your ally, the British people!'

Letchinsky translated and David saw Rublyov's face darken. He spoke rapidly in Russian. Letchinsky hesitated, and Guy said, 'He wants to know if we are too proud to spend a few hours in a house where a Russian worker lived.'

'Proud!' Connie said. 'If he thinks I'm going to. . .'

'Hold on a minute.' Taking his arm, David led him aside.

In a low, hissing voice Connie said, 'I've been cooped up for weeks in a ship. Then in that train. This is the final straw!'

'Are you thinking about yourself or the British people?' David asked dryly.

'Both. If you let these people treat you like this, how do you think we'll make any headway in the talks? They have a psychological advantage just by putting us in here. Don't you see? That's what it's all about. Why aren't *they* in here? Why haven't they given *us* that carriage?'

'We've come too far to throw everything away because our pride's hurt. In a few days we'll be out of here. You can put up with it until then, can't you?'

'That's not the point!'

'Try and think of an alternative. What are you going to do? We're in their hands.' He turned back to the others and said, 'Where do we sleep?'

Rublyov, who clearly understood more English than he

pretended, walked across the room and indicated the flat top of a huge brick stove. It was warm to the touch.

Letchinsky said, 'You will, of course, dine with us in the carriage.'

David had the impression that he was profoundly embarrassed by the situation.

'Then talk,' Rublyov said.

'Tonight?'

'An engine is coming tomorrow to fetch us,' Letchinsky said.

'But your telegram said you would stay for a week!'

'Circumstances have changed.'

'I think you should tell Comrade Rublyov that we've come half way round the world to have these talks. They can't be rushed.'

'We have come half way across Russia. It is the same thing.'

'It's not the same thing at all,' Connie said angrily.

Rublyov turned away. The other two Russians followed him, closing the door behind them.

'Now, David . . .' Connie began.

David held up his hand. 'For God's sake, Connie, not now. We're all tired. Let's get ourselves cleaned up and see what they have to say.' He turned to Guy, who had witnessed the proceedings in silence. 'What do you think?'

'I think that's a good idea, sir.'

'You would,' Connie said.

Half an hour later, they were called to dinner.

The railway carriage which had been allocated to the Russian delegation was magnificent. According to Letchinsky, it had been one of the Tsar's private carriages on the line between St. Petersburg and his palace at Tsarkoe Selo, and contained a dining-living area, two bedrooms, a bathroom and a small kitchen. Everything was on the most opulent scale. The dining-table and chairs were rosewood, there were tapestries on the walls, the easy chairs were upholstered in green plush. The bathroom was fitted with gold-plated taps and the basin was pink-veined Italian marble.

'What has happened to the Tsar?' David asked. 'We heard he had abdicated.'

Rublyov said, 'He is Colonel in Army now.'

Two servants waited at table. The food was poor: borscht followed by a greasy stew of tasteless, unidentifiable meat, accompanied by vodka and sweet champagne which Rublyov drank thirstily. Connie poked at his food, but ate almost nothing.

When they had finished and the servants had cleared away, the two delegations grouped themselves on either side of the table.

Without much enthusiasm, David opened proceedings with a formal speech about how honoured H.M's Government was to have been approached by the Provisional Government; how they knew that even contemplating the sale of part of the heritage of a great country brought much sadness, but that such sacrifices were sometimes necessary when countries were fighting for freedom.

The word 'freedom' seemed to give Rublyov his cue for a speech that lasted nearly half an hour, with table banging and bluster. He launched into a massive attack on the Allies, and Britain in particular. He accused Britain of being hypocritical, of still trying to deal with the old aristocracy, of denigrating the Provisional Government, of humiliating them, of not fulfilling promises, of denying Russia raw materials such as steel, iron and especially coal. Finally, he accused the Allies of not fighting courageously enough in France, thereby forcing Russia to bear the greater weight of German arms.

The attack had come so unexpectedly and was so violent that for a moment the British were speechless. Then Connie said, 'We've come to talk about jewels. Either we talk about those, or we talk about nothing.'

The Russians sat in stiff silence.

'Ask him if he has the list,' Connie said to Guy. Rublyov took a sheet from a folder and passed it to them. It was printed in English.

After studying it for a few moments Connie said to David: 'I want to talk to you.'

Rublyov indicated that they could move to the sitting-area for private discussions. The Russians remained at the table.

Connie said softly, 'This is rubbish! The Crown isn't there. Nor the Orlov. Nor the Shah.'

45

'Something's happened,' David said. 'I've felt it since we arrived. I'm sure they've had new orders.'

When they returned to the table he said, 'We believe circumstances have changed, that you have let us come here on false pretences.'

Rublyov's pock-marked face reddened with anger and Guy translated his words: 'He says if we feel that way, there is nothing more to be said.'

'This isn't getting us anywhere,' David said. 'Ask him when the engine is coming to fetch them.'

'He thinks tomorrow afternoon.'

'Tell him we're tired, we must rest. After breakfast, we will talk again.'

The British delegation rose and bowed. The Russians inclined their heads, then David led the way across the clearing to their quarters. Connie walked by himself and no sooner had they entered the house than he turned on David. 'I'm giving you formal notice that I'm contemplating withdrawing from the delegation. I'm not used to this sort of treatment, this kind of life.'

David looked at him wearily, seeing, beyond the grossness and the self-consciously struck attitudes, the large black hat, the cloak, the stick, seeing back to the man he had once known in the diamond diggings, the man who had lived in a corrugated-iron hut and who had eaten boiled goat and been thankful for it. The point was that Connie *was* used to worse than this, or at least had been before the good times had come. He heard the man's voice droning on, and at the same time saw that beds had been made up on top of the stove.

He broke away. 'Where on earth did you find those?' he said to Cyril.

'In the carriage, sir. You gentlemen were going it. Each of them Russians had three blankets and two pillows. It didn't 'ardly seem fair, sir.'

'It wasn't. Well done, Cyril.'

He looked at Cyril with new eyes. He had hardly considered him as an ally. But then again, with his experience of war, why shouldn't he be a good forager? He had lived the easy life for the past few years, and there had been no call for such expertise, but before that, he'd had to look out for himself.

46

He turned back to Connie and said, 'At least you won't be quite as uncomfortable now.' He felt his own irritability, but he knew he had to keep the little party together; *his* little party. It had never needed leadership more than it did now.

There was a knock at the door. They froze. It was now nearly dark outside and their earlier experiences had left them tense. Cyril moved towards the door, but Guy was ahead of him. Letchinsky was outside. 'He wants to talk to you, sir,' Guy said.

The tall Russian was nervous. He led David outside, round to the far side of the house, once or twice casting looks back towards the carriage as though expecting to see someone coming after him.

'I have to speak to you on a private matter,' he said.

'I see. But wouldn't it be better if we went inside?'

'Private,' he emphasised. 'It has nothing to do with my delegation.'

David waited. It took the Russian some moments to gather himself, then he said, 'Sir David, can you understand what is happening in this country?'

'Only partly.'

'We are fighting a losing war. Even if the Allies win, *we* will lose. We cannot gain anything. So why should the Russian Army fight? Who will make them fight? One day soon, they will come back. Can you imagine what will happen then? Already there are thousands of Czechs and Russian Army deserters roaming the country. The only power is the Provisional Government. But Lenin is back in Russia, rallying the Soviets to make yet another revolution. And then there are the Army leaders, who are already making common cause with the Tsar. It is well known that they want him back. Soon there will be civil war. People like myself, the moderates, are caught in the middle.'

'Soon?'

'As soon as the war with Germany is over.'

'And when will that be?'

'There are things you should know, but first I want to ask something of you.'

'Ask.'

'When you go, I want you to take me with you.'

47

'Take you where?'

'To Great Britain.'

'Are you serious?'

'Listen, the Russian army is at the point of mutiny. Kerensky is trying to negotiate a separate peace with Germany.'

The importance of this was not lost on David. 'But then why negotiate for coal? Why offer the Crown. . .' He stopped. 'No! It couldn't be! You mean the Provisional Government organised this so that the Allies, or at least the British Government, would not suspect?'

Letchinsky nodded. 'We are negotiating for coal with the French and with the Japanese as well.'

'While the Provisional Government negotiates with Germany.'

'You see how close we are to ruin? If Kerensky achieves his peace we will lose territory and people. You don't think Germany would settle for less. If he doesn't achieve it, the Army will mutiny. Both alternatives will produce civil war. I am no longer young. My family is grown up, my wife dead. My throat is one of the first they will cut.'

'Was there ever any intention of selling the Regalia?'

'To be frank, Sir David, no. It was to give the impression to the British Government that we intended fighting on.'

'Why did you not come on to Vladivostok then, and hold the meeting there? That would have given you the opportunity to. . .' He was about to say, 'defect', but changed the phrasing. '. . . to get to England.'

'After the riots in Petrograd, Comrade Rublyov decided to return to Moscow. It was I who reminded him of the importance of our meeting.'

'For your own reasons.'

'For my own reasons.'

While they were talking, David had come to a decision. If they had been made fools of, then at least he could bring back Letchinsky. As a Treasury official, he would be a source of detailed information to the British Government. It would be better than nothing.

'We'll come into Irkutsk with you tomorrow,' David said.

'I can send telegrams from there. We'll find a way of getting you out.'

Letchinsky held out his hand. 'I lived for a time in England once. In Surrey. It will be nice to see it again.'

[5]

Although it was summer the night was bitterly cold and, in spite of the hardness of the brick stove, they were grateful for its warmth. After first saying that it was impossible for him to sleep in such a place and under such conditions, Connie was the first to start snoring, and even David fell asleep after a short while.

He was awakened by a hand pulling at his arm. 'It's me, sir,' Cyril said. 'There's something going on.' David became aware of a glow at the window.

Guy was stirring. Only Connie was still asleep, like a beached whale. In the distance a shot rang out, crisp and brittle in the stillness. There was a second and a third. They heard a cry.

David crouched at the window. The glow came from the carriage, one end of which was on fire. There were half a dozen figures in the clearing.

'Oh, my God, we're being attacked!' Connie heaved himself off the stove.

'Can you make out who they are?' David asked Guy.

'They look like deserters, but I can't see clearly.' There was an explosion and a tongue of flame shot through the roof of the coach.

There was a second explosion. A rolling ball of fire travelled the length of the coach, racing along behind the windows. David saw a figure jump down and begin to run towards them. Even at that distance the fire was bright enough for them to recognise Letchinsky. The tall Russian had gone only a few paces when a shot rang out and he fell. A soldier walked up to him and used the butt of a rifle on his head, then began to go through his pockets.

49

'We've got to get out!' David said. 'Leave everything.'

'Tell them who we are,' Connie said.

David ignored him. 'If we can hide in the forest for a while they'll finish looting and leave.'

There was a door leading outside from the kitchen. David made for it, the others crowding after him. The small room had an unglazed window. The head and shoulders of a soldier appeared. His face was expressionless. He raised his rifle. David stared into the gaping barrel. But before the soldier could press the trigger a column of blood the thickness of a good cigar erupted from the side of his head and spurted two feet into the air. His expression did not change, but he toppled sideways and disappeared from view.

'Dirty boggert!' they heard a voice say.

Major Perfiliev's face appeared in the window. His uniform was torn and he wore a bandage round his head. He held his big cavalry revolver.

'Englishki! Where is vodka?' he said.

Guy grabbed the bottle he had given them.

'Come!' he said, handing David the soldier's rifle.

They ran from the back of the house into the heavy timber. As they paused and looked back David saw a burning figure fall off the rear of the coach. It could have been Rublyov or Gudim.

'Such fools, those deserters!' Major Perfiliev said. 'They wish food and vodka, but they burn everything.'

'Where did you come from?' David said.

'They break railway, then they kill, just like here. I run. I remember Englishski. Where are Englishski? It is safe where they are. I come back, but it is not safe.'

'Surely they'll move on now,' David said. 'There's nothing more for them here.'

'There are others.'

'An engine is due here from Irkutsk tomorrow.'

'It cannot ride. Railway is break. We must go to *Trakt*. When we find *Trakt*, we walk to Baikal water. We take boat to Irkutsk.'

'How far is it?'

The major shrugged. 'Seventy, eighty versts.'

'How far is that in miles?'

50

'Nearly fifty,' Guy said.

Connie had been catching his breath after the rush to the forest. Now he said, 'You can't expect me to walk fifty miles! We have diplomatic immunity. Tell them who we are and demand protection.'

The last part of the carriage exploded in a rush of flame.

'You saw what they did to Letchinsky,' David said. 'Do you really think they care about diplomatic immunity? We must get to Irkutsk. There must be some authority there.'

'But we have a *laisser passer*. . .'

'That wouldn't mean anything, either to the Russian Army deserters or the Czechs,' Guy said. 'They'd shoot us on sight.'

'So we make for the *Trakt*,' David said. 'We'll follow it westward until we reach Lake Baikal. The steamers still cross. I checked that before we left. In Irkutsk we become the responsibility of the Provisional Government.'

'We haven't an alternative,' Guy said.

Connie said, 'I want to issue a formal protest.'

'Noted,' David said. 'Now let's get going.'

They moved off, Major Perfiliev in the lead. It became instantly apparent that Connie was going to be a problem and David had a quiet word with Guy and Cyril, to take it in turns to walk with him so he would not lose touch with the group.

The terrain was bad. Here in the dense forest the ground was covered in spagnum moss and was treacherously boggy. It gave no hint of change until suddenly someone began to sink in up to his knees. Then they would have to walk laboriously around the area trying to find dry land. The undergrowth itself was often too thick to penetrate. The berry season was at its height and some of the bushes were a tangled mass higher than a man's head, creating thickets hundreds of yards wide and often up to half a mile deep. These also had to be avoided since there was no way through.

Dawn found them exhausted. They had long since left behind any sound of the attack and it was as though they were in a completely different, enclosed world. The dimness and gloom of the *taiga* with its lack of bird-song and its pervading sense of desolation and isolation added a layer of depression to their exhaustion. In the beginning they walked for an hour and rested for ten minutes. But rests gradually lengthened as they struggled through the heavy brush. David and Guy seemed to be the strongest and took it in turns to carry the rifle. Major Perfiliev had lost some blood from his head wound and had relinquished his leadership after a few miles. Cyril did not complain, but it was David who walked at Connie's side, talking to him and trying to keep his mind from his exhaustion and aching muscles. He began to reminisce about the old days in the Kimberley diggings, but Connie showed no interest.

They walked northwards all that day.

'Are you sure we're on the right route?' David said to Major Perfiliev as the afternoon wore on. Too exhausted to speak, he pointed his finger in the direction they must take.

They made slow progress. During one rest the Major said that on the *Trakt* there were way-stations and they might be able to hire a *tarantas* and horses to take them the rest of the way to Lake Baikal.

David passed this on to Connie, hoping to cheer him up, but he was too far gone and did not appear to hear. Each man was now in his own world of physical pain and exhaustion.

Early in the evening, they stopped. The drift of air was from the north and it contained the chill of the tundra. They had no food, but there were plenty of blueberries, bilberries and blackberries and Guy and David went foraging with Cyril. Connie lay stretched out on the ground and the Major sat with his back to a rock, muttering to himself. Neither Connie nor Perfiliev could eat the berries, but both took long pulls at the vodka bottle when it was passed round.

'We'll get as much rest as we can,' David said. 'If we leave again at first light we should reach the *Trakt* sometime in the late morning, if it is where the Major thinks it is.'

'We find,' the Cossack said, but there was little optimism in his voice.

Cold crept up from the ground and down from the air and they lay shivering. The vodka had helped to dull the pain but they found sleep difficult. In the early light, just before dawn, David got up. A man was looking at him from behind a tree about fifteen paces away. David stood very still. The man stepped out and came slowly towards him. He held a billet of wood in his hand as a weapon. David had put the rifle under a bush the night before and was defenceless. Just then there was more movement and he saw other figures step silently out of concealment. Each man was armed with some weapon – a sharpened stick, an old sabre, a piece of rusty iron, a pitch-fork – and all were dressed in grey. Their heads were partly shaven and the bones in their faces stuck out like knuckles. David thought there were about a dozen of them. They closed in on the four men who were still lying on the ground. Guy stirred and looked up. One of the men chopped at him with a heavy stick, hitting him in the small of his back. 'Don't move!' David called to the others. 'Don't do anything. They'll kill us.'

The men were dressed similarly to the group of prisoners they had seen put aboard the train: exiles, convicts on the run, desperate and dangerous.

A tall figure holding a kind of whip stepped forward and said something which David did not understand.

Guy said, 'He wants food.'

'Tell him what's happened to us. Tell him we're escaping, as they are.'

The leader was a gaunt man with heavy bones. His head was half shaven and there was stubble on his cheeks. He was a fearsome sight in the dimness of the forest.

Guy talked rapidly and pointed back along the path they had come. His story, even in these circumstances, was so unlikely that it could not have been a lie, and after a few moments the gaunt man spoke.

'He wants us to take off our clothes,' Guy said.

The Major rose to his feet and spoke harshly. The man drew back the whip and cut him on his left cheek, bringing blood.

'Do as he says,' David said.

They undressed to their underwear, except for Connie, who was almost beyond reach. He lay on the ground and, fearing they might kill him, David called Cyril to help him take off the big man's cloak and outer garments.

'He says he wants everything,' Guy said.

'Tell him we'll die.'

53

'He says if we don't do it quickly they'll kill us anyway. Shoes, too.'

They stood naked in the early cold and watched five of the escaped prisoners pull on their underwear and suits. The discarded grey clothing, the foot-wrappings and two pairs of broken slippers were flung to them. Connie had begun to whimper and Cyril went to help him on with the grey prison clothing.

The two groups finished dressing and looked at each other. Five of the convicts were now dressed in clothes that would have passed in most Russian towns. Their gaunt leader, was wearing Major Perfiliev's uniform. He now walked up to the Major and attacked him with his whip. He lashed him half a dozen times, twice cutting through the thin grey material, drawing blood.

David said in Russian, that suddenly sprang easily to his lips: 'For God's sake, you'll kill him!'

The man turned away and spoke to Guy as he passed. 'He says it is a privilege to kill a Cossack. If we had not been British he would have done so now.'

The gaunt man called his group together and they disappeared into the *taiga*, travelling west. The whole exchange had taken less than half an hour and seemed to David like a dream, except when he looked down at the clothes he was wearing. His shirt was grey flannel, his trousers were also grey. The garments reeked of sweat and filth and he could feel lice move on his body.

'All our papers are gone,' Guy said. 'They're taken everything.'

'We still have the rifle. We'll get to the *Trakt*,' David said. 'It can't be far.'

Connie's clothes were far too small for him, but he did not seem to care. David walked on one side of him and Guy on the other. Each took an arm. Cyril, who had not complained since their troubles began, watched over Major Perfiliev. The Major now seemed to be in terror of his life and this gave him added energy. He talked to himself, muttering in a dialect David could not follow, but the word *brodyagi* emerged three or four times, which David later learned meant 'tramp', but in the present circumstances meant 'escapees'.

54

They came to the *Trakt* at noon. It was more like a ride cut through trees in England than the only major road from west to east. It was not more than thirty feet wide and badly cut-up by iron-shod wheels. In some parts the surface was soft mud, in others it had dried and made walking difficult. Fortunately, the sides were less disturbed and they were able to move along it without too much discomfort.

All that day they walked. The cold wind dropped away and the clouds cleared and the sun beat down. It seemed that within an hour the temperature had risen by thirty degrees. Trapped in this windless space between the trees, the heat was intense. With the warmth came the insects. Mosquitoes buzzed about them all day until they longed for the cold wind to drive them away.

In all that long day they only met one other person, an old man on a horse who, when he saw them, turned and cantered back the way he had come.

It was a deserted, dead world, and David felt that only they were alive in this huge place. But every now and then there were signs of human life, great logs which had been pulled out of the *taiga* and were piled in little clearings on the edge of the *Trakt*.

Towards evening they saw smoke and came to a village consisting of about a dozen small wooden houses.

'There may be a headman,' David said. 'We'll find him and try to get horses.'

'What do we pay him with?' Guy said.

'The rifle.'

But as they entered, it was as though the inhabitants had died of plague. The village was deserted. David and Guy went to several houses, but all were locked and the curtains drawn. Nothing moved.

'Look!' Guy pointed to a rain-water barrel. On top of it was a plate with a loaf of bread; on the ground near another house they saw a small wicker pannier containing cooked potatoes. At a third, they found a plate of stew.

'I think we should take it,' David said.

Guy said, 'Wouldn't that be stealing, sir?'

'For God's sake! Look at Connie. Look at the Major!'

After they had collected the food they sat at the outskirts

of the village and ate their first meal in twenty-four hours. Connie was hardly able to get anything down.

When they had finished Major Perfiliev said, 'It is for *brodyagi*. They afraid. They leave food. They meaning, please eat food and go.'

'They think we're escapees,' Guy said. 'They're bribing us to leave without harming the village.'

They went on into the long gloaming. David had just decided that they must find somewhere to spend the night when they heard voices. They rounded a bend and saw, strolling in the same direction as themselves, half a dozen soldiers, each carrying a rifle. They seemed relaxed. Their uniforms were different and they were altogether smarter than the deserters on the railway line.

Perfiliev started forward. David tried to stop him, but he said, 'They soldiers. I soldier.' He stumbled forward and, when he was about twenty yards behind them, he called out. The reaction was instant. They fanned out, each holding a rifle to his shoulder. The Major went on. One of the soldiers shouted. The Major waved his arms. A soldier fired above him, and he dropped onto the *Trakt* holding his hands to his head. The soldier placed the muzzle of his rifle on his neck, others ran down the *Trakt* towards the British delegation. A soldier shouted an order which David did not understand. The soldier raised his rifle and hit him with the butt.

'He says, put your hands in the air,' Guy called.

The soldiers were excited. It seemed that at any moment one of them would pull the trigger of his rifle. The Englishmen all put up their hands.

'They think we're *brodyagi*,' Guy said.

'Tell them who we are.'

Guy talked for a moment, and one of the soldiers burst out laughing. The others were infected and they shouted to each other in their humour.

'They don't believe us, sir,' Guy said.

The soldiers began to move them along the *Trakt*, pushing them with their gun barrels or jamming the butts of their rifles into their backs.

'At least they must have a senior officer,' David said, and felt another severe blow.

'He says, keep quiet,' Guy said.

Half an hour later they came to a large building with a stockade fence around it.

[6]

In the half-light of the Siberian dusk the building looked like an Army barracks. It was large, single-storeyed and built of logs. It formed one side of a square of which the other three comprised the stockade fence of sharpened stakes. The gate into the stockade was open and two sentries stood on duty. For the rest, the place seemed deserted.

They were herded into the courtyard. The long, low building with its shuttered windows began to look less like a barracks.

Amsterdam was on the point of collapse and David had to help Guy to maintain him upright. 'It can't be long now,' he whispered. 'There must be a senior officer here.'

They were marched to the end of the building. One of their escorts opened a wooden door and indicated that they should enter. They found themselves in a small dark room empty of furniture. The door slammed shut behind them. Chinks of light penetrated the shutters and gaps in the walls themselves, where the logs had not been sufficiently well caulked with moss and mud. They lowered Connie to the dirt floor and David turned to Perfiliev.

'Where are we?' he said. 'What is this place?'

The Major was sitting with his back to the wall, holding his head in his hands. In a low voice he said, 'It is bad place. You Englishski. You talk to them.'

'What sort of a bad place? Is it an Army post?'

But the Major, who seemed to be in a kind of stupor, slowly shook his head.

'It's some kind of prison,' Guy said.

'Then there'll be a governor. Once they establish who we are they might give us an escort to Irkutsk.'

'They don't seem to want to listen to us.'

'Soldiers of that rank never do. It's not their function to listen or take responsibility. You'll see, there'll be someone along in a little while.'

Someone did come to them, but it was not an officer. They heard the wooden bar being taken out of its sockets on the other side of the door and then a lantern shone into their eyes and they heard the jingling of metal chains. A mass of metal was thrown into the room and landed at their feet.

A voice gave a peremptory order. David only caught part of it but Guy said, 'He says, put them on.'

David examined one of the pieces of metal. 'Good God, they're leg irons! Tell him I want to see whoever is in charge here. Tell him we've had enough of this treatment!'

A shadow struck at him out of the lamplight and he felt the butt of a rifle crunch against his cheek-bone, knocking him back against the wall beside Perfiliev, who whispered: 'Do not say I Cossack! Do not say!'

'I think we must do what he says,' Guy said.

They helped each other to put on the leg irons, though it took them some time to work out how to do it. First they put protective leather cuffs round their ankles, then the steel bands, which were locked in place. A voice shouted at them to hurry. They managed to get the fetters onto Connie and brought him onto his feet. They were pushed and prodded into the courtyard. The leg irons weighed about five pounds and the chain allowed each of them only a short step. Cyril fell immediately and David bent quickly to help him before a guard could use his gun.

It was not yet fully dark and they could see that they were being herded along the shuttered side of the building. They came to a door which swung open as they approached and they heard a kind of low hum. Beyond the door was a corridor which ran the length of the building. Other doors led off from it. They stepped into a corridor and were assailed by a smell so rank that David choked and covered his mouth and nose with his hands. A guard who had a bunch of keys at his waist, opened one of the doors. There was a sudden rustling, then silence. They were pushed through the door. They heard it slam behind them, heard the key turn in the lock.

The room was about forty feet long and twenty wide, and,

packed into it were nearly a hundred men. The air in the confined space was mephitic. The hum they had heard had been the murmur of voices which had ceased when the guards had opened the door.

Around the walls small wicks burned in grease, giving a low light.

The two groups stared at each other in silence. David was almost too bewildered to take in their precise situation, but slowly his senses cleared. Each man in the room was dressed similarly to the way they were dressed themselves, except that these people all wore a kind of visorless Glengarry hat.

Suddenly the prisoners – for this, it soon became apparent, was what they were – resumed the positions they had been occupying before they were disturbed. Against the facing wall were two sloping wooden platforms running the length of the side. They were about two feet above the dirt floor and there was a scramble for places. Some men were forced off them and had to make do with the floor. In the dark corners there were bundles of rags with pale thin faces above them; these had not moved. A large wooden tub stood in the middle of the room. It was from this that the worst of the smell arose. David did not need to be told what its function was.

At that moment, Connie fell. He collapsed like a balloon from which the gas had suddenly been expelled. He dragged Guy down with him. The floor was earth and was damp and partly churned up. They pulled him to a section of the wall near the door where there was a little space. He was breathing rapidly and his body was shaking.

'I'm going to die,' he said.

'No,' David said. 'We'll get you out of this, we're in some sort of prison. It's because we're wearing these clothes. In the morning I'll speak to an official. You'll see, we'll be away from here by lunchtime.'

But Connie was hardly listening. He floated in and out of consciousness, and in both states was lost to them.

The prison room was almost entirely airless. The windows were shuttered and the door was closed. As in the other small room, the only air to reach them came through cracks in the shutters and the walls where the logs did not meet.

The smell was horrendous. David found himself trying not

to breathe, yet in that oxygen-starved air being forced to breathe more rapidly than normal.

'We've got to get through the night,' he said to Guy. 'That's the first objective. And Amsterdam is the immediate problem. I'll deal with him. You keep an eye on Cyril and see if you can keep the Major going.'

Connie's mind was wandering. David took his head onto his lap and wiped the rivulets of sweat from his face.

'Remember how we used to sweat in the desert?' he said. 'Remember those tents and corrugated-iron shacks?' He talked on about the early days, trying to rouse Connie, who occasionally groaned and drifted in and out of sleep. David's own mind went back to the diamond diggings. He had never experienced heat like that. But it had been a clean, dry heat. This was filthy, miasmic.

Then the door opened. He looked around, expecting to see soldiers, expecting someone to have discovered that a mistake had been made. Instead, a group of women entered. They were dressed in blouses, shirts and shawls. The men had clearly been waiting for them. They called eagerly to each other and David realised that some of the women must be their wives. They squeezed onto the platforms beside their menfolk, some on the floor. Each had brought a little food tied up in a scarf or napkin, and shared it. But other women had come for other reasons and later, among the dying in their bundles of rags, David was aware of the heaving bodies of couples rutting like animals on the dirt floor.

One woman in particular caught his attention. She was dark and had a gypsy cast to her face. She was below medium height and thin. Even though she wore the grey clothing of a prisoner, she had managed to invest it with a kind of elegance. She wore a headscarf tied in such a way that it reminded David of women in England. In her arms she carried a small white Pekingese. She bent her head and kissed it. Then she turned to one of the men on the floor and spoke. He shook his head. She threaded her way through the prisoners. Once or twice he saw a man pass over a small piece of bread and she fed it to the dog. Once a prisoner tried to grab her arm and almost succeeded in pulling her off her feet. The dog barked and snapped at him and she managed to jerk her arm free. The expression on her face did not change, but she moved away to the far side of the room to continue her begging.

A man left the platform and went towards the prisoner who had grabbed her. He slapped him several times in the face until he put his hands up in supplication. The man who had dealt out the punishment then stopped in front of David.

He had enormous shoulders and powerful arms, square hands and a square face. His head was shaven and there was a white scar running across the top of his skull from above his right eye to the base of his left ear. He looked at David and the others without welcome, without even humanity, and then began to speak rapidly. At first neither David nor Guy could make out what he was saying, for his accent was thick, but then it emerged that he was giving them an order. They were to do as he said, and only as he said. Did they understand? His word was law. They must ignore the prison authorities. They must behave and, above all, not try to escape or else he would cut their throats.

Guy tried to convey to him who they really were, but he waved the speech away. 'Do you understand?' he said.

Without waiting for an answer, he pushed his way back to the platform, where his place had remained unoccupied.

'You're not going to take any notice of that!' Guy said angrily to David. 'You must see the officer-in-charge. It's our only chance.'

'Forgive me,' a voice said in English.

The speaker was lying against the wall and all David could see was a thin, pale face and sunken eyes.

'You are English?' he said. 'Truly English?'

'Truly English,' David said.

He moved along towards them on his elbows. 'How have you come to such a place?'

David told him. The man pulled himself upright, with his back to the wall. A thin hand emerged from the rags. 'Belkonski,' he said. 'Dmitri Belkonski. I am teacher of English, or I was. Now I am traveller.'

David said, 'Do you know that man?'

'He is Zagarin, leader of *artel*.'

'*Artel*?'

61

'I will explain you. It is commune of prisoners. Zagarin is leader. Called *starosta*. He make arrangements with guards for food, for transport for people like me who are sick, for vodka, for women. That is why women here now. It is arrangement made between *starosta* and guards. It is also bargain. We do not give trouble to guards. We do not try to escape, we do not try to kill them. That is bargain. He is sick?' He pointed to Connie.

'Yes.'

Belkonski shrugged. 'We are all dying.'

David said, 'I must get him out of here. All of us.' He repeated what he had tried to tell the *starosta*.

The Russian said, 'They think you are Poles or Finns. They think all foreigners are Poles or Finns. Maybe Czechs. Everyone is confused.'

'Yes.' David remembered the words of Mr. Wiggins in Vladivostok. How far away that seemed now, both in time and space.

'When I first saw you I thought you were Ivan Neponootchis.'

'Who is that?'

'Ivan Dontremembers, John Knownothings.'

Confused, David shook his head.

'Do you not know where you are?'

'In some kind of prison, I assume.'

'This is called an *etape*. Do you know of it?'

'No.'

'A prison on the *Trakt*. You English call it a way-station. We are all prisoners here. Exiles. We go to Siberia, to gold mines at Kara. We have been travelling for months. We started from St. Petersburg by train and then by boat and then by train and boat again. Then there are no more trains because they must go to war, so now we do what exiles did twenty years ago. We walk. We have been walking for four months, here on *Trakt*. We must walk for four more. Men become desperate. They run away into *taiga*. Later sometimes they are caught far away. They say they do not remember their names. They are sentenced for vagrancy. These sentences are always lighter than those they had. Those they

62

don't remember. You understand? Johnny Dontremember. It is what they are called.'

David was silent. For the first time, he was really afraid. He realised he had moved into a world which he could not control, where wealth and position meant nothing. He turned to Connie, but he was asleep, as were Cyril and Major Perfiliev. Guy was awake, leaning back against the wall, his eyes half closed.

'Difficult to understand how someone like that gets to a place like this,' he said.

David followed his gaze and realised he was looking at the woman with the dog.

'She's different from the others,' Guy said.

'She is Countess,' Belkonski said.

'What is she here for?' David asked.

He shrugged. 'Such questions we do not ask.'

'It's just that she looks . . . it's difficult to explain. She doesn't seem to belong here. She's beautiful,' Guy said.

For some reason, David felt a touch of irritation. 'Beautiful women commit crimes, too.'

'I suppose so.' Guy followed her with his eyes as she went from group to group, begging for the dog. No one else tried to molest her. She was not wearing leg-irons and her movements were smooth and supple.

'We have been here twenty-four hours,' Belkonski was saying. 'Tomorrow we walk again. Twenty English miles. The next day twenty. Then we rest for a day. Then two days walking, then rest for a day. So it goes. It has been like this since the Forwarding Prison in Tiumen. Do you have any food? Fresh food? Oranges?'

'We have nothing.'

'It is a pity for you. For nothing, you get nothing.'

They were silent for a time, then David said, 'I must speak with the officer-in-charge in the morning.'

'It is Captain Lychenko. Do you have proof . . . papers that say who you are?'

'No. They were stolen from us.'

'Do not hope too much. Let me show you something.' He lifted one of the small candles and played the light over

63

the walls. Thousands of names were scored into the wood. 'Travellers like us,' he said.

The word 'us' chilled David. 'May I ask why you are here?' he said.

'I am thief. I teach English, but I am thief. Soon I will die.' He touched his mouth. 'Scurvy.' He slid down the wall until he was lying against it. 'Do you have vodka?'

'No. We have no vodka.'

The women began to leave. David was overwhelmed by exhaustion and depression. The Countess was the last to leave. As she reached the door she paused and turned. Her eyes strayed around the room. They paused briefly on Guy, and then she was gone.

Half lying, half sitting, with Connie's head on his lap, and supported by the pressure of other bodies around him, David allowed himself to fall into the kind of stupor which had earlier gripped Perfiliev. In the morning, he told himself, things would be different.

Morning came at last, but it was not as he had imagined. The prisoners were herded out of the rooms a little after seven. Connie could scarcely walk and had to be half carried out into the courtyard. Soldiers were everywhere, David spoke to one of them, but the man shouted at him and pushed him back into the crowd. There were about four hundred men and women and they assembled in lines. The sky was overcast and there was a light drizzle. Already the yard was covered in mud.

At this moment a group of old women carrying baskets made their way through the door in the stockade. Each was made to show what the baskets contained and each, with much broad humour, was searched. They formed a line on the far side of the courtyard, placing their baskets in front of them.

'Food sellers,' Belkonski said. He had joined them and now for the first time David could see him clearly. He was painfully thin and wore the regulation grey clothing, dirty rags swathing his feet. His face, like those of most of the men, was bony and gaunt. His head was shaved and his gums, when David could see them, were purple.

A prison blacksmith came into the yard bringing a small portable forge, a lap anvil, several hammers and an armful of chains and leg fetters. A group of soldiers formed a semicircle around him and slowly the prisoners began to shuffle past. The blacksmith inspected each one's chains to see if they needed repair. Beyond him was an under-officer holding a heavy leather bag. As each convict passed him, he gave him a few copper coins.

'Be careful of them,' Belkonski said as they shuffled forward. 'The money must last two days.' David helped Connie towards the blacksmith and as they reached him an officer appeared at one of the windows and shouted to a guard. The British party and Major Perfiliev were rounded up.

They were taken back into the building, along the corridor to an office at the rear. An officer was sitting at a long table. He was dressed in dark green and David assumed he was Captain Lychenko. A clerk, also in uniform, sat at a smaller table. Shelves round the walls held piles of paper bound with ribbons. Some of it was yellow with age and a coating of dust lay over everything. The captain was writing with a scratchy nib and looked up as they entered. David examined him carefully, for he was, as Guy had said, their only hope. He was of medium height with the flat face and high cheekbones of the Mongolians they had seen on the train. When he looked up, David thought he had never seen such cold eyes. They were not so much hostile as indifferent.

David and Guy had discussed what they were going to say. At first they had thought of taking a strong line, of making a protest, then they had decided that this might be unwise. David was glad, for the man did not look as though he would stand for anything like that.

As Guy began to speak, he held up his hand. 'Name?' he said.

David said, 'We wish to –'

The captain said softly, 'Silence.' He turned to the clerk and pointed his forefinger.

The clerk said, 'Name?'

When it came to his turn, Connie was unable to speak,

65

and they told the clerk his name. Perfiliev said, 'Neponoot-schi, your nobility.'

The captain nodded and pointed to the far side of the room. Perfiliev moved away from the group.

The clerk stood in front of Guy with his pad and pen. 'Crime? Sentence?'

'Look, this is nonsense!' David said.

The captain picked up a large, flat ruler and slammed it into the palm of his hand.

'Sir,' Guy began. 'We –'

But the captain nodded to the clerk, who stood before Cyril. 'Crime? Sentence?'

When Cyril did not answer he made a note and moved on. He asked the same question to each man in turn.

The captain spoke, and Guy turned to David. 'He's going to have us flogged for not answering.'

David stepped forward. He was afraid, but he was also angry. 'I protest most strongly!' he said in English. 'We are members of a British delegation – '

The captain rose. For a moment David saw death in his eyes, but he was committed.

'Translate,' he told Guy. 'Tell him who we are. Tell him what happened.'

It might have been that the captain had never been treated like this by any of his charges, for he paused and listened as Guy spoke. David found that his own grasp of his first language was becoming firmer in the crisis.

Lychenko resumed his seat as Guy continued. Finally, when Guy stopped, he said, 'You are lying. You are Czechs. I will have you shot.'

'That is untrue!' David said.

'You stole a rifle. It is a Berdan. Our soldiers only have Berdan rifles. To steal it, you must have killed one of them.'

'For God's sake,' David shouted. 'We've told you. If you don't believe us, send one of your men to the railway. You'll find the burnt-out carriage. Send a telegram to Petrograd. Or to Vladivostok. We met a delegation from Moscow. They are dead. Comrade Rublyov, Commissar for Industrial Production, Comrade Gudim of the Iron and Coal Federation, Comrade Letchinsky of the Treasury.'

66

For the first time, an expression of uncertainty crossed Lychenko's face.

'Send a telegram to the Provisional Government. May I remind you that if you harm us, you harm your ally, Great Britain.'

The clerk was standing stiffly to attention, fear on his face. It was apparent that the captain had never been addressed in such a way before.

Lychenko said, 'I cannot send a telegram. The wires are cut.'

'Release us, then.'

He shook his head and tapped the ruler on his palm. After a moment he said, 'I will write to Petrograd.'

David seized his initiative. 'We cannot wait here while you write letters. Our business is important. It has to do with the war.'

But the captain had had enough. He put the end of the ruler against David's chest. 'No more! I will write. You will go with the others. I don't believe you. When the reply comes I will personally shoot you. Go now.'

'But – '

'If you speak, I will have one of your people shot. Not you. You must have a reply to your letter.' He tapped Guy on the chest. 'But you, and you,' He tapped Connie 'And you.' He tapped Cyril. 'You will get no reply. For stealing the rifle it is the death penalty. If you are who you say you are, Petrograd will know of you. Then you can go home if you are still alive.'

He opened the door and stood to one side.

David hesitated. From what he had understood from Belkonski, they would walk twenty miles today to a smaller wayside prison called a *polu-etape*. The following day they would walk another twenty miles to a regular *etape*. There would be another officer in charge there who might be more amenable. But Connie could not walk one mile, much less forty.

'What about my colleague, Mr. Amsterdam?' David said, indicating him. 'He is ill. He can't walk.'

'Then you must leave him. There is a lazarette.'

67

Connie, hearing his name, had guessed what they were saying. 'For God's sake, don't leave me, David!'

'He'll walk,' David said.

The captain shrugged.

They were escorted back into the courtyard. The prisoners were filing past the food sellers, buying bread and pieces of dry sausage and small yellow turnips.

At that moment a number of small carts came through the main gate. These, they were later to discover, were called *telegas*. A single small horse drew what appeared to be a huge barrel cut in half lengthwise and mounted on four unsprung wheels. In the front was a single seat for the driver and the guard. In the bottom of each, a layer of dirty straw had been placed. One of the under-officers shouted: 'All prisoners who have certificates from the doctor, step out!' About forty convicts separated themselves from the main body and shuffled across to the *telegas*. Belkonski was one of them. Painfully, they climbed over the sides and lay in the straw. As quickly as his chains allowed, David hobbled over to Belkonski and said, 'My friend is sick. How can he get a seat in one of these?'

'You must have a certificate.'

'Is there a doctor here?'

'No. He was at the Forwarding Prison.'

'I spoke to Captain Lychenko. He said there was a lazarette. Is there no doctor there?'

The pale, skull-like face broke into a smile and David looked away from the rancid gums.

'If he goes there, say good-bye to him. No one comes out from the lazarette.'

David spoke to a guard. For a moment, he did not understand, then as David's Russian grew more fluent with desperation, he shook his head and said, 'Certificate! Certificate!' and pushed him back towards the crowd of prisoners.

'Look for Zagarin,' Belkonski called from the *telega*. 'Maybe he help.'

David hobbled up and down the lines until he saw the leader of the *artel*. He was sitting with his back to the stockade fence eating a kind of porridge from a small basin. He broke off pieces of black bread and stuffed them into his mouth.

68

The Countess stood near him, holding the dog in her arms, scratching it behind the ears. In the daylight he could see that she was older than he had thought, perhaps in her late thirties. Her thin face was very pale and her eyes such a light brown as to be almost golden. She looked worn and ill.

David crouched in front of Zagarin and explained what he wanted.

'Who are you? A Pole? A Finn?' Zagarin said, with his mouth full.

David told him, 'English,' but it seemed to mean nothing. Poles, Finns, English, political exiles, murderers, thieves: all were the same to Zagarin. Finally he wiped the basin with a piece of bread and finished his meal.

'Half his money,' he said.

David looked round for the officer with the bag of coins, but he was nowhere to be seen. 'We were with Captain Lychenko. We have no money,' he said.

Zagarin shrugged. 'You waste my time.'

'If he's left here, he'll die.'

'Better for him.'

'That's not the point! We're a British delegation!'

'If you have money, he rides. If not, he walks.'

Two copper coins dropped into the mud in front of Zagarin and David looked up at the Countess. 'Take them,' she said in English. Her voice was low and throaty, but the expression on her face was cold, almost dead.

Zagarin pocketed the coins. 'Today he can ride. But from tomorrow, half of all your money, otherwise he walks.'

Tomorrow was in the future, it was the moment that counted.

'Thank you,' David said. Then to the woman: 'Thank you. We'll repay you.' She turned away and said a few words to her dog.

Zagarin spoke to a guard, orders were given and Connie was helped into one of the *telegas*.

'Ready!' a guard shouted.

An under-officer with a muster roll checked off the prisoners. Every prisoner had a grey linen bag, in which was stored his scanty personal effects. Many had copper kettles which dangled from the leather belts that supported their leg chains. David wondered how, with nothing, he was going to keep his party alive.

'Party – to the right! Party – march!' With a clinking of chains, the grey throng shuffled slowly out of the main gate of the *etape* into the thin, cold drizzle. For the first time David noticed that some of the women had babies in their arms, or small children at their skirts.

The main body of convicts was closely followed by the *telegas* with the sick and infirm. Next came four carts loaded with grey linen bags, and finally a *tarantas*, a two-wheeled cart with a canvas hood, drawn by three horses harnessed abreast. This was a sprung vehicle, and on the seat sat Captain Lychenko. There was a rear-guard of soldiers, some on horse-back, some marching. Others walked on either flank of the column.

The rate at which this mass of people moved was slightly over two miles an hour. Soon they had left the *etape* behind. Their world was the muddy *Trakt* in front of them and the *taiga* on either side.

[7]

David's memory of that first day remained in his mind as long as he lived, like a black and white photograph grainy with rain, its chiaroscuro moving from the light grey of the rain-sodden sky through the grey of the shaven heads and the clothing of the prisoners, to the darker grey of the mud and the blackness of the trees.

The column stretched for nearly a mile, moving with the sound of some great animal in chains, a sound that was flung back by the trees so that talking, if they had felt like talking, would have been a strain. But even above this noise came the occasional cry of a child, a wail of terror and pain, snatched away like that of a gull at sea, and the creaking and crashing of the unsprung carts.

David, Guy and Cyril walked near the rear of the column. Perfiliev was behind them. His head had already been shaved and he looked a different person from the ebullient, vodka-swigging Cossack of the train. As a child, David had feared the Cossacks. Like the wolves of the forest, it was a word to instil dread; 'If you don't eat your cabbage, the Cossacks will take you.' It was no wonder that Perfiliev sought anonymity. David could imagine how little interest would be paid by the guards to a prisoner with his throat cut: one less to worry about.

The members of the British party still retained their hair. David saw this as a hopeful sign. Perhaps they had managed to sow a seed of doubt in Captain Lychenko's mind.

Their main difficulty for the first few miles was the length of the chains which confined them to a shorter stride than they would normally have taken. A walk became a shuffle. David's boots were worn. Soon the mud had seeped into them and each time he put down a foot he could feel the cold slime squeeze between his toes.

They passed again through the village where food had been set out for them the previous day. It was closed up tight, the curtains of rain causing it to seem even more desolate. Word must have reached the inhabitants early for no smoke showed in the chimneys, the doors were barred and shutters closed. The long column moved slowly up the single street. Men and women, too exhausted to avoid the puddles of grey water, splashed through them, adding to their misery.

A few ranks ahead of them walked the Countess with her dog. She stroked and fondled it constantly, letting it lick her face. Occasionally she would turn and look down the lines. Once David thought she was looking at him, and smiled. There was no answering smile, and it occurred to him that she had been looking at Guy.

Ever since they had reached the *etape* he had been aware that Guy had been a centre of interest. He looked different from anyone else: the handsome, wedge-shaped face, the luxuriant hair, the aristocratic structure of his chin and mouth. Among these starved, shaven, miserable ghosts, he must have appeared like some Apollo. Eyes had followed him. Words had been exchanged between men.

Soon after they had begun the march a guard, walking some few paces to the rear, had lengthened his stride and caught up with them. David had been unaware of it at first then, turning, he had seen the man speak to Guy out of the side of his mouth. Guy had kept his eyes on the ground in front of him. The guard had come closer, said something more, laughed softly, then gone on up the line. Guy's face had darkened with anger.

David had never fathomed the young man. He had always believed that if you lived in close confinement with someone, you must come to know him well: his worst and his best characteristics. He had achieved this with Connie in the ship, but not with Guy. Guy seemed to have areas of his psyche into which he could withdraw. It was as though all the years of training as a cadet and then as an officer, living among other men, sharing cramped quarters, had caused him to learn to live within himself; to guard his tongue and his emotions.

David recalled their dinner in London with Elizabeth Lytton. That was the only time, he believed, he had seen Guy acting naturally, though perhaps even then his own presence might have made Guy's behaviour less than relaxed.

Since they left England Guy had done his duty superbly, and it was a difficult one, for the three other men were his flock to succour and protect, yet he could not give orders, could not pretend to lead them. Under the present circumstances, how long could his restraint last? There was not only cool English blood in Guy, but Russian blood, with all its unpredictability, excess, wildness. David wondered how and when this blood would show itself and thought that if Guy was bothered by the guards it might well burst out sooner than later; and then God help them.

He wondered how he could tell a man who was already controlling himself that the need for even greater control was just around the corner.

Cyril was walking between Guy and David. Of the three, he had taken longest to get used to the leg chains. He had stumbled more than once and they had managed to catch him before he fell. Now he did so again, tripping on a root which had become exposed on the surface of the *Trakt*.

'Thank you, sir,' he said, as David caught him by the arm. 'Don't 'ardly seem like a road at all. Wouldn't like to bring

72

the motor 'ere, sir.' His face was pinched and he had every right to despair, yet ever since the real troubles had begun he seemed to have lost the faint whine in his tone, the sense of impending doom. Soon after they had set off this morning, David had said, 'I can't tell you how sorry I am that this has happened, Cyril. Especially to you. I'd give a lot to get you out of here and back to London.'

'And what about you, sir?' Cyril had said mildly. 'And Mr. Amsterdam? And the Commander? Don't worry about me, sir. I got used to this in the war. Them Boers had us marching all over the place. The 'eat was terrible and when it wasn't 'ot, the cold was perishing.'

'But no chains.'

'No, sir, no chains.'

'We'll get out of it, Cyril, don't worry. It's just a matter of when.'

'I'm not worried, sir. Especially not about you, sir. You got determination, sir. Well, I mean, stands to reason, being who you are. You could walk right through Siberia.'

These were the two longest consecutive speeches David had ever heard him make. It seemed that adversity had cheered Cyril up.

They walked for five hours, and then halted at the entrance to a village. They were not allowed in, but on a piece of open grassland nearby a small market had been set up. A dozen women in shapeless garments, with scarves tied under their chins, were there with baskets of provisions, bottles of milk, jugs of kvas, fish pies, hard-boiled eggs and black bread. By then David, Cyril and Guy were walking in a kind of closed world of numb exhaustion. They heard shouting from the front of the column and then the word came down the line: '*Prival! Prival!*' announcing the noonday halt.

Like many of the other prisoners, the three of them collapsed on the wet grass, too exhausted and weak through lack of food to move. Others, the strongest, were already lining up in front of the market. The women who sold the kvas – fermented mares' milk – had the longest lines in front of them, and David saw the Countess drinking from a large pewter mug.

73

After a while Guy said, 'I'll go back and see how Mr. Amsterdam is.'

'No.' David pushed himself up. 'That's my job. I should never have let him come.'

The carts were drawn up at the edge of the grassed area. Connie was in Belkonski's cart and it was clear that he was worse than he had been the night before. The carts themselves were only marginally better than walking. The unsprung wheels crashed on every rock and every root and every pothole. The sick were almost as exhausted as the marchers from trying to cushion the sudden shocks.

'How are you, Connie?' David said, wiping the rain from his face.

'He will get used to it, or he will die,' Belkonski said.

Connie's lips were blue and the veins in his cheeks, usually an unhealthy red, were mauve. His breathing was hoarse. He opened his eyes and said, 'I'm hungry, David.'

'I know. We'll get food tonight. Can you hold out till then?' He turned to Belkonski. 'What rations do we get? Is there soup?'

'Rations? There are no rations. We buy food as we go.'

'You mean they supply nothing?'

'They give us money.'

'That's all?'

'Every two days. It must last two days.'

David stayed with Connie for a short while, trying to comfort him, then he shuffled back to the other men.

The Countess was standing a yard or two away from them, stroking her dog. Guy was examining the contents of a grey linen bag.

'She's brought us food,' he said. David saw three hard-boiled eggs, a bunch of small onions and part of a loaf of rye bread. He thanked her, but her face remained expressionless. She leaned forward, nuzzling the dog, and looked down at Guy.

'I must take something to Connie,' David said.

Just then there was a commotion and Zagarin pushed his way through the crowd. He shouted at the Countess. She ignored him. He caught her by the shoulder and pulled her away. The dog was barking and snarling, but she made no protest. Guy began to struggle to his feet, but David held him back. 'It's not our business!'

'She brought us the food!'

'We don't know what the situation is. Let's find out before we do anything that will endanger Connie.'

All through that long afternoon the column shuffled along the *Trakt*. Once they passed a roadside shrine consisting of an open pavilion in which hung an effigy of Christ on the Cross. Most prisoners removed their caps and crossed themselves as they drew abreast of it.

In the early evening, after another five-hour march, they came to the *polu-etape* where they were to spend the night. It was much like the previous prison. The prisoners were stopped outside the stockade, drawn into line and counted. Then the order was given for them to go in.

With a great cry and a rush of stumbling, clanking feet, the male prisoners pushed and jostled each other to get through the gateway. They ran across the courtyard as best they could, some falling, some being shoved out of the way, some being held back by their clothing.

David was to learn that this happened every night. The race was to secure places on the wooden platforms so that they would not have to sleep on the muddy floor near the excrement barrel. Some had found a way of making money out of it. They would sell their places for a few kopecks and have more money to spend on kvas the following day. By the time David, Guy and Cyril had brought Connie and Belkonski from the cart, all they could find was a patch of mud in one of the corners.

It took nearly half an hour for the tumult to subside, then the convicts began their preparations for supper. They bought soup from the soldiers, who had stolen it from their own kitchen. Some had saved their fish pies and black bread and ate them now. David shared out the onions and Belkonski added a loaf of black bread.

'It's not much,' David said.

'But you eat,' Belkonski said. 'Remember, the market women do not have to bring food for sale. Sometimes they have none and they bring none, then we starve and die.'

'It's almost as though they want us to die.' David registered

75

with dismay the word 'us' and how naturally it had fallen from his lips. They must *not* identify with the prisoners. It was part of his plan for their release that they would not identify, that they would maintain themselves as a separate group.

'The more that die, the better for the *chinovniks*,' Belkonski said. 'When we leave Forwarding Prison there is register of all prisoners. Some die, some escape. Thirty per cent of all prisoners in Siberia are loose in summer. But registers remain full. No names are taken off. So in prison food is supplied for convicts who are not there. So food is sold and money put into pockets.'

The onions and the bread were soon finished. 'Listen,' Belkonski said. 'You like joke? There was town once called Zashiversk in north. A hundred and fifty years ago it was centre of fur trade. Fifty years ago no more fur trade, no more town. Buildings fall down, forest grows. But on maps still is Zashiversk. So in city of Irkutsk civil servants are asking government every year for money to look after buildings, streets, water, everything, just like proper town. They putting money in pockets.' He laughed softly. 'I tell you, *chinovniks* can do anything.'

Major Perfiliev came to sit near them. He seemed undecided how to treat them. He could not afford to allow his true identity to become known and yet the English, whom he had once seen as allies to whom he might attach himself for safety, now appeared as helpless as anyone else.

A short while later the women were let in. It was a repetition of the night before. They watched the Countess move slowly among the men, bending and talking and occasionally being handed something. On one of the wooden platforms, Zagarin was eating, surrounded by three or four of the *artel* members. His eyes followed the woman. She was wearing her scarf lower on her face and as she came nearer, David could see the swelling on her cheek-bone. She leaned against the wall nearby and Guy began to pull himself up. They looked at each other. David felt himself gripped by bitterness over and above the despair from which he was already suffering. Even in their present circumstances he could not help but envy Guy his youth and his physical attraction.

She bent and spoke into the dog's fur. Her voice came clearly to them in English. 'Don't let anyone know you are talking to me.'

Turning away from her, Guy said, 'Did he hit you?'

'It's not important.'

'Was it because you brought us the food?'

'Don't worry about it. Who are you?'

He told her, briefly, what had happened to them.

'They think you are spies.'

'Who?'

'Captain Lychenko.'

'How do you know?'

'Zagarin knows everything and I know Zagarin.'

'Lychenko's a fool,' David said. 'There must be other officers. There'll be one at the *etape* tomorrow night.'

'They are all the same. They will never let you go. You will die on the march like your friend.' She glanced over at Connie.

She drifted slowly away, stepping carefully between the bodies, accepting a crust here, a few crumbs there. She fed everything to the dog.

[8]

David had fought against adapting to his surroudnings because of his feeling that it would lead to identification with the other prisoners and remove the Britons from any special category in which they might have been placed. But within days he had realised that unless they adapted, they would die.

Death was no rarity in the *etapes*. It was not an uncommon sight when they were being released from the over-crowded rooms in the morning to see a bundle of grey rags against a wall with no life left in it. There was always the lazarette, but the prisoners would do anything rather than be left behind. David often saw them pleading with Zagarin or

77

another member of the artel, but unless they had certificates or could pay, they did not ride.

The days began to merge into weeks. At each *etape* David made his protest to the captain in charge of the new guard, but it was as the Countess had said: no one was going to take the responsibility of believing them. 'Wait until Kara,' they said. Others threatened them with beatings. After several such interviews, David realised they were not going to be released on the march, therefore they had to survive; to survive, they had to adapt. He had no hope of anyone coming to their aid. Power was in the hands of the guards and the *artel*. No one would even know where they were. It was as though they had entered a fourth dimension.

Their world was the long trail of marching prisoners and the inside of the stinking *etapes*. They began to lose all sense of time and place. Soon they did not know where they were, except that it was somewhere in Trans-Baikalia. They walked in mud and choking dust. Once they were herded into cattle trucks, but how long they travelled by train or how far they did not know, for the trucks had no windows. Then they were off-loaded and the march began again.

They were aided in their adaptation by the fact that they were a unit of three in a mass of individuals, and could use this to help themselves.

They had not been marching for more than a week when they realised that handing over half their money so that Connie could be transported in the *telega* meant that they could never buy enough food on which to live. So in the evening rush to gain places on the platforms David, Guy and Cyril formed a team. Guy was one of the strongest men in the column and David was also fit. They had only suffered a few days of hardship by comparison with the months and years of sickness and confinement of the other men. It was comparatively easy, therefore, to use their strength to gain places. They would always keep one for Connie, whom they would fetch later, and one spare for sale. The money brought in this way checked their slow starvation.

Even so, Connie was shrinking and sinking before their eyes. As the weeks passed, his skin hung on him in folds. David looked after him with great solicitude. At night when

78

he lay next to him on the platform he would talk about the old days, trying to interest him in something other than his own misery. Occasionally it worked and they would talk of the wide-open town of Kimberley in its early days; the deals in diamonds; the larger-than-life characters.

Over the weeks they had learned a little about the Countess. Her name was Alexa. What her crime was, they did not know, but she was being sent to the mines at Kara, so they assumed it must have been something serious, perhaps political.

It became even clearer that she was interested in Guy and that he was interested in her. One night, to test him, David recalled their evening in London with Elizabeth. 'You'll see her again, I promise you that,' he said.

But Guy had turned over, unwilling to discuss it, and David felt bitterness sweep over him. All his adult life Guy had probably only had to crook his finger for women to come to him. David hoped that for all their sakes that he would not become involved with Alexa, for Zagarin was already restive about her contact with the British group.

It was at the noon-day halt that she would seek them out, after she had had her mug filled to the brim with *kvas*. She made no bones about her needs. 'I would stay drunk all day if I could,' she said once. At the end of the first month David himself would have given half his fortune for a bottle of vodka and the oblivion that would follow.

Like many of her class in Russia, she spoke fluent English with only a slight accent. This she owed to an English nanny and to a partial education in England. Her father had been in the Russian Foreign Service and had been chargé d'affaires in London and Washington. Later she had married Count Leonid Kropotkin, but what had happened to him they did not know, for she never spoke of him or her immediate family.

She was a mystery, which made her even more interesting. David found her beautiful in a dark, gypsylike way. She was too thin for his taste, but he could see past this to a time when ease and food would have put flesh on her bones. He could imagine the effect she would have had on men. Even as she was, he was drawn to her. There was something undefeated and undefeatable about her. She was the sort of woman for whom he had been searching subconsciously. The irony was that he had found her here and that she was interested, not in him, but in a man years younger than herself.

They never saw her without the dog. Occasionally, when she thought it safe, she would let it trot at her side, but most of the time she held it in her arms. 'You know what they would do to Chen if they could?' she said. David thought of the soups made in the *etapes* at night. Chen's little body would be no great enrichment.

It was about five weeks after they had been captured that they began to talk about escaping. Until then, they had kept telling themselves they would soon be released. Guy mentioned it first, though it had been in all their minds. They no longer believed that letters would come for their deliverance. They were part of a system, of another world. They talked about it academically at first because, in reality, it was Connie's death warrant since there would be no one left to help him. Belkonski was the only friend they had made and he was so weak the task would be beyond him. Perfiliev was still only on the fringe of their group, keeping his options open, waiting to see what would happen.

'I suppose there's the Countess, sir,' Cyril said as they marched along one day. 'She could look after 'im. Then once things got sorted out, we'd come back for 'im.' They were brave words, David thought, for Cyril's chest had begun to bother him, and the likelihood of him getting away was becoming less certain.

'You heard what they said about the telegraph,' Guy said. 'The line's been cut. The whole place is in uproar. We'd never get in contact again.' He paused, then said, 'Anyway, she wants to come with us.'

'You've discussed it with her?' David said sharply.

'Only in the most general terms.'

'You mean, out of the country?' A disturbing new picture was emerging.

'Yes.'

After that it became more and more a topic for their conversation, until David had to remind himself each time that they could *not* leave Connie.

Other prisoners did not have the same constraint and there

were several escapes. It was not too difficult. The essential prerequisite was to be sure one could remove the leg-irons. This was achieved by hammering the metal anklets into an oval shape so they could be slipped over the heel. To do this, a prisoner first had to find a stone heavy enough to use as a hammer, and then find the time to use it. It had to be done in the hubbub of the noon-day halt as everyone crowded around the food sellers, or during the din at night as people scrambled for places on the platform, and so blanketed the noise.

It was part of the bargain struck between the *artel* and the guards that there would be no escape attempts, but this did not stop men who were desperate enough.

The escapes took a standard form. A man who had worked on his leg-irons would release himself opposite a particularly dense part of the *taiga* and then wait until the guards' attention was elsewhere before bursting from the column and trying to reach the covering scrub. If he could get a lead of fifty or a hundred yards before being brought down by rifle fire, his chances of evading capture were excellent, for the forest made pursuit almost impossible.

This occurred with a Finnish prisoner, a murderer, who managed to evade capture for three days. But he had the ill luck to become trapped in a bog and was pulled free by villagers who took him back to the column. He was placed in what were called 'travelling irons'. These consisted of heavier irons joined to his throat by thick steel chains. If he tried to run, he would strangle himself. As it turned out, there was no need for such security, for he was found dead the following morning, with his throat cut. No one had the slightest doubt, including the guards, that Zagarin had killed him, but nothing was said. It was a lesson for the others and there were no further attempts made to escape for a week. But finally they began again, for death, in these circumstances, was no great deterrent.

It became increasingly obvious to David, and to those who lived closest to them, including Belkonski, that the feelings between Guy and Alexa were deepening.

Belkonski said, 'It is problem for you.'

'Why?' David wondered if Belkonski had divined his own feelings.

'She is Zagarin's woman.'

He decided to speak to Guy, but each time an opportunity arose, he found himself unable to. What if Guy told him to mind his own business? Perhaps he might even guess that there was a secondary reason for David's concern. So he kept his own counsel but watched closely what was happening.

The two met whenever it was possible, but that was only twice a day. Instead of joining the others at the noon halt, she would wait for Guy and they would take their food apart from anyone else. In the evenings when she came round to beg for the dog she would stand close to Guy and talk to him with her head buried in Chen's white hair.

She was not the only one to show an interest in Guy. Several of the guards had made overt friendly gestures but he had managed to avoid them. About this time a prisoner called Muravieff began to pay attention to him. He was a huge man, the biggest in the *etape*, but slow-moving and slow-thinking, more of an animal than a human; he was said to have killed his mother and father over a few kopecks. He began to pay court to Guy, trying to walk with him on the march, or join him in the *etapes*. In the evenings he would come to wherever the group was sitting and squat down in front of Guy and talk to him in a low voice.

The other prisoners watched with amusement, especially Zagarin and other members of the *artel*. Zagarin had named Guy 'pretty boy' and now people watched to see what would happen. It added a certain interest to their terrible lives.

It was obvious that Guy was acutely embarrassed, especially as Muravieff would approach him when Alexa was near, and David began to wonder if the whole thing had not been organised by Zagarin to make Guy look like a fool in her eyes.

They did what they could for him. On the march he walked between David and Cyril and in the evenings they would form a group around him, making it difficult for Muravieff to get near.

But whatever they did seemed inadequate, for the big, simple-minded, shambling man continued to seek Guy out.

He began to bring scraps of food, a hard-boiled egg, a piece of black bread.

'I don't want it!' Guy pushed it back into his hands. 'Don't you understand? I don't want it!'

'Hey, pretty boy,' Zagarin called. 'He's fattening you up like a goose. They say he likes 'em plump.' This brought laughter from the other prisoners.

The next time Muravieff brought food, Guy gave it to Connie.

Muravieff said, 'It is for you, not for him.'

Guy ignored him. He broke up a piece of black bread and fed it to Connie.

Muravieff said, '*You* eat!'

Again, Guy ignored him. Muravieff gripped his wrist and held it. Guy opened his hand and dropped the bread into the mud, then slowly ground it in with his foot. Muravieff stared in disbelief, then with a roar, he pulled Guy towards him. Guy's free hand held the chain of his leg-iron. He swung it. There was a sickening crunch as it met the bone of Muravieff's skull, and the big man fell away, blood spurting from his head.

From that time, the other prisoners were wary of Guy. If he could do that to Muravieff, it was apparent that he was much stronger than any of them, and no-one cared to test his strength again, not even Zagarin. But there was a look in the Russian's eyes as they rested on the British group that told them what would happen to Guy if he got the chance. It was then that Belkonski gave Guy a weapon: a heavy canvas needle sunk into a handle of wood. 'I will never need it now,' Belkonski said.

Guy thanked him and kept it in the lining of his coat. The word went about that he was armed. No-one molested him after that..

They marched on. Days became difficult to separate. Each one was much the same as the one before. Sickness was taking its toll. The main danger was typhus, but many had scurvy and syphilis. It was the beginning of autumn and days of rain alternated with days of still, golden sunshine. But the prisoners were too far gone to appreciate that. The nights were either wet or frosty and when the exiles reached the *etapes* their body heat in the cold rooms would cause steam to rise from their damp clothing and they would begin to shake and sweat. These were known as 'gypsy sweats'.

With the cold weather, the death rate increased. The weak were carried off by pneumonia and at night the *etapes* were filled with coughing and raucous breathing as those with chest trouble gasped for air in the foetid, freezing rooms. The children began to die. Rainy weather set in and the *Trakt* became worse. Many people now had no shoes and walked bare-footed through the freezing mud.

David had never conceived that such misery could exist, nor such desolate country. For much of the time, the column seemed to be the only living unit in the endless *taiga*. True, they passed through villages, but these were so sad themselves that they heightened the air of desolation.

It was during this period, when David had reached the very bottom of his own emotional and physical resources, that he experienced something that was to leave a permanent mark on him. Late on a day of freezing drizzle, they came to a large village. The weather had been so bad that the food sellers had not been seen at noon and now the prisoners faced a night of hunger.

On the outskirts of the village Zagarin went to speak to the captain, who was sitting in his *tarantas*, and the column was stopped. About a hundred prisoners, including Alexa, formed a group and, with clashing chains, walked slowly up the village street. Then they began to sing. No attempt was made at harmony, or even to keep in time with each other. The sound was low-pitched and quavering. The singers seemed constantly to be breaking in on one another as though in a round. David had never heard anything so sad.

Have pity on us, O our fathers!
Don't forget the unwilling travellers.
Don't forget the long imprisoned.
Feed us, O our fathers – help us!
Feed and help the poor and needy!

The mournful threnody was broken constantly by the counterpoint of the chains and it seemed to David that this moment expressed all the grief and despair that had been felt by the hundreds of thousands of prisoners over the generations who had walked from the Forwarding Prisons to imprisonment in Siberia.

> Have compassion, O our fathers!
> Have compassion, O our mothers!
> For the sake of Christ, have mercy
> On the prisoners – the shut-up ones!

He realised that for the first time in these terrible weeks he was on the edge of tears. Part was self-pity, but part was a genuine feeling for the misery of Russia, a misery he had experienced himself, in a different way, as a child.

> Behind walls of stone and gratings,
> Behind oaken doors and padlocks,
> Behind bars and locks of iron,
> We are held in close confinement.

Doors in the grey log houses which had been firmly shut when the singing began, slowly began to open. Peasant women and even children appeared with their hands filled with bread, meat and hard-boiled eggs. Behind the singers came another group of convicts holding out their hats and linen bags to collect the food.

The singers walked along the cross streets. The dirge continued

> We have parted from our fathers,
> From our mothers;
> We from all our kin have parted.
> We are prisoners;
> Pity us, O our fathers!

The wailing voices grew fainter, orders were given to start the march again. In the courtyard of the *etape* that night the food was shared out and soup was made with the meat, but not all benefited equally. The *artel*, which had organised the begging song, took most.

A few days later Zagarin sent for David at the noon halt. The leader of the *artel* was hunched over a small fire watching soup bubble in a pot. He added more sticks to the fire.

'What do you want?' David said.

Zagarin poked at the fire, then said, 'Where is the other one?'

'Which other one?'

'The young man.'

David knew where Guy was. He and Alexa were sitting under a cart eating their food. 'I don't know.'

He had been waiting for such a summons. He had also been waiting for Zagarin to use the power everyone knew he possessed. But something seemed to be holding him in check. Perhaps it was because the British party was still an enigma and to harm one of them overtly might bring retaliation. They still kept their hair, they still received half-promises that, once they reached Kara, their case would be investigated. Perhaps Zagarin was restrained by the same influence. The Britons may have come from Mars as far as the prisoners were concerned. What no one knew was what power was wielded by Mars. Now, as though to underline what David had already surmised, Zagarin approached his object obliquely.

'You cannot keep places on the platforms.'

'Others do it.'

'They are prisoners. It is allowed for prisoners.'

'We are prisoners.'

'But you say you are not.' He looked up over the soup spoon and David saw the peasant cunning in his eyes.

When he returned, Guy said, 'You know what that means: we'll starve if we can't sell the places.'

'What about our own, sir?' Cyril said. 'Couldn't we sell them? I'd sooner eat than sleep on the platforms.'

'We don't have places even for ourselves any longer,' David said. 'The platforms are reserved for Russian prisoners from now on.'

They marched in silence that afternoon, each knowing the real reason for the new restrictions, but unwilling to mention it.

It was at this point, for the first time, that David thought he might die. His weariness was like a sickness so great that death seemed welcome. But there was some reserve inside him, some hard core that had been created in the early days of struggle, some power of will to survive that kept him on his feet and in movement. The hours of the march were torture and to take his mind off his misery he would plan areas of his past to revisit. For the five hours of the morning march he might, for instance, decide to try and remember his

86

childhood in Kiev, the house in the *podol*, the Jewish ghetto, where his grandfather, Moshe Kadeshinsky, carried on his jewellery business. He would remember them walking by the Dnieper, the old man's hair blowing in the icy wind, he would remember sitting in the room in which the business was conducted, holding a diamond in his hand, hearing the old man saying, 'What do you see, David?'

'Fire and ice, grandfather.'

'Good boy. Drink your chocolate while it's hot.'

He remembered his English tutor, Mr. Hemlow, and he remembered the golden light of Kiev when it burned with autumnal fire. And then the pogrom and the running and the fires and looting. He would spend a whole morning thinking about this period, trying to remember the minutest details. One thing would lead to another and he would save areas to think about later. In this way he lived in another world, a mental world, while his tired body shuffled on and on.

He thought of Michael and Jewel and their house in Sussex. He tried to visualize the interior exactly and move from room to room. It was there that his grandson, John, had died of diphtheria. He thought of Michael as a child and of Jewel and her recent miscarriage, which finally meant the end of any chance that she could have another child. He thought of the New Chance building on Trafalgar Square and of his house in Bayswater; of books he had read; lines of poetry; bars of music.

He found he thought of Sarah very seldom, and when he did so, it was as a man might recall a possession, a beautiful painting, perhaps, with pleasure, but without the zest of one human-being for another. He hypnotised himself with the memories, prying and prising and digging more deeply into the past than ever before. He came to believe that they kept him alive.

At night now they slept in the freezing mud of the floor. Alexa began to smuggle them part of the food she begged for the dog. It was not much, but it was something. What made everything worse was that Connie complained constantly. The *telega*'s crashing had bruised his flesh and made his bones ache. He had shrunk to the size of a normal man and his gums were purple with scurvy. He complained about the *telega* and the cold and the lack of food. It took all David's patience to comfort him. At night, he would moan and beg for food and blankets. All David could do was lie by his side and try to take his mind off his misery by talking of the old days.

They had lost so much weight that they were now indistinguishable from the other prisoners. 'If we don't leave soon, we won't have the strength,' Guy said. 'I think one of us, at least, should go before it's too late.'

'Who?' David said.

'We'd have to decide that. Whoever it was must try to reach the authorities, then obtain the release of the others.'

It was obvious that Guy was the youngest and the strongest. 'Would you take Alexa?' David said, not mincing matters.

'She knows how to organise an escape.'

One morning when they were released from the *etape* they entered a different world. The courtyard was covered with snow and the wind was in the north. Autumn had suddenly gone.

'We *must* do something,' Guy said that day. 'Otherwise we're never going to make it. We'll starve before we reach Kara.'

'He can't last much longer,' David said.

'That's what you always say.'

The distinction between leader and subordinate had disappeared long ago. They were simply two men struggling to survive.

That night, lying next to David, Connie said, 'I know what you're planning. You're going to leave me.'

'I won't leave you,' David said. 'I think it's time for Guy to go, though. It may be the only way out for us all.'

'You promise?'

'Yes.'

There was silence for a while and then Connie said in a low voice, using the phrasing of childhood, 'Say, "I promise." '

'I promise,' David said.

But the fear of being left ate into Connie, and the following day he was more lively than he had been for weeks, and stopped complaining.

[9]

Guy talked constantly about escaping. It possessed him completely, and Connie seemed to sense that there was a streak of ruthlessness in him that was dangerous. He kept close to David whenever he could so that David and Guy would have no opportunity for private discussions. Zagarin was also suspicious and kept the Countess with him. She did not appear at either the noon halt or to beg in the *etape* at night. She marched with Zagarin. She ate with him.

The effect on Guy was dramatic. His face, already drawn, became sharp with anger, and there was disagreement between him and David.

'If we're caught and she's with us, we lose any credibility,' David said.

'What difference would it make?'

'We're supposed to be a diplomatic mission. She's a convicted prisoner, a Russian.'

'She's not a criminal.'

'How do we know that?'

'Because she says so.'

'She would, wouldn't she? But even if she was telling the truth, she'd slow us down.'

Guy said: 'I've done talking. I'm going. She's coming with me. You must make up your own mind.' He had never gone this far before and, as though aware of it, he said, less aggressively: 'You think everything will be put right when we reach Kara. But that's only a guess. You don't know. No one knows.'

David realised he was right. It was true that Alexa might cause problems, but basically he knew that his reasons for not wanting her to accompany them were more complex than that. The problem reduced itself to one simple equation: if they took her, she might or might not hinder them; if they did not go, they would die. And if they left Connie, he would die.

Slightly warmer air had come up from the south in the past twenty-four hours and melted the snow. It was an ideal time to leave, since they could not be tracked. Guy planned to make his break two days later after the noon halt, so that they could save as much food as possible.

Through Belkonski they managed to get a message to Alexa and heard in return that she would put aside food.

David found himself full of conflicting emotions: anger at Guy's callousness, yet aware that it was their only hope; envy at Guy's freedom to escape with Alexa; irritation at Connie for holding him back.

His emotions were a waste of energy. For the following day, twenty-four hours before the planned escape, the prisoners were all put aboard a prison barge.

The transfer came without warning. One day they were trudging through the *taiga*, the next they were in a barge being towed upstream.

Shortly after leaving an *etape* they had reached a river. It was wider than those they had already crossed by ferries. At first they thought the barge was another, larger ferry, but their leg-irons were removed and once they were aboard they were towed upstream by a paddle-steamer. Where are we going? What river is this? The questions received five or ten different answers. Most of the prisoners did not care. Like Belkonski, they were simply grateful to be resting. 'Thank God for a river, not a road,' he said. To be moving without bumps or crashes, without the leg-wearying weight of the irons, without freezing mud between their toes, was like a holiday.

The barge was a large floating hull about two hundred and fifty feet long and thirty feet in the beam. It had been built expressly for the transport of convicts. Below were sleeping holds with wooden platforms like those in the *etapes*. At either end of the barge were deck houses about eight feet high. One contained the lazarette, the other was where the guards slept. The space between was roofed over and the sides closed by bars and wires, creating a cage. The vessel had neither masts nor engines and looked, David thought, like a child's drawing of Noah's Ark.

Guy tried to find out from the guards where they were going, indeed, where they were, and how long they would be in the barge, but either they had been given orders to say nothing or they were uncertain themselves. Because of the leaden grey sky they could not even be sure in which direction they were travelling.

The barge had been built many years before. The decks were rotten, the paintwork had flaked and there was rust everywhere. In the holds it was like a fine powder that caused them to sneeze and choke. From what they had seen, the paddle steamer did not look much better. It had obviously suffered from years of neglect and hard usage.

The grey river was almost half a mile wide and the current ran strongly in the mid-channel. On either bank black-green trees acted like curtains, cutting off all views.

They kept going through a day and night. The following morning, after the prisoners had come up to huddle in the cold of the cage, away from the excrement barrels and the powdery rust, the tow-rope parted. One moment they were being towed serenely up the great river, the next there was a sound like a rifle shot and they were slowing down, then moving backwards. As it did so, the barge turned broadside on to the river and started to spin slowly.

Some of the women and children in the cage began to scream. David's own view at the centre of this huge, spinning hulk was of trees, then water, then trees and water as the vessel moved through 360 degrees. At first the gyrations were slow, but as the current caught her she began to skid downstream in a series of swings and jerks, throwing them off balance.

Away behind them, the paddle-steamer was turning. There were shouts from the guards for calm, but it was impossible to control the prisoners. To be locked up in a cage when his life was threatened was the most terrifying thing that had yet happened to David and he found himself beating on the bars with the others and screaming at the guards to open the door. By his side, Connie, too, beat at the bars, terror lending strength to his muscles.

The guards were equally terrified, of the river and of the prisoners. Some locked themselves into the deck-house, others stood by the cage, rifles pointed, ready to shoot. All was pandemonium. Some of the prisoners were kneeling in prayer. Children were weeping.

David saw Guy force his way across to Alexa. Zagarin had climbed up the cage and was yelling for the Captain. Guy pulled Alexa through the mob of hysterical prisoners. She was clutching her dog, but looked neither panicky nor afraid.

'If we're lucky, we'll have a chance when she strikes,' Guy said. 'Depending on *what* she strikes.'

'You all right, Cyril?' David said.

'I'm fine, sir.'

'We must keep close together.'

'There's a bend coming up,' Guy said. 'She won't take it.'

There was a scream and a shot. Someone had caught a guard, pulled his head through the bars and cut his throat. Another shot sounded. David saw the door of the cage fly open. Prisoners poured out onto the narrow deck. A guard raised his rifle, but he was charged down by three or four men and thrown into the water. Others began to jump.

'We'll be safer at the stern,' Guy said. They followed him aft.

Zagarin had grabbed the barrel of a rifle. He was shouting at the guard. The man was terrified. Suddenly he pulled the trigger. Zagarin fell sideways, bouncing first against the cage and then sliding across the deck into the river.

They reached the stern. There were few people here. Most had climbed on top of the cage. The hulk was moving faster and faster, spinning and sliding. It reached the bend and its own momentum carried it out of the current and sent it skidding towards the bank. A line of black rocks like decaying teeth stood in its path.

'Hang on!' Guy put his arms around Alexa and she turned to him, cradling the dog in her arms. The impact threw them all on the deck. 'Come on. Quickly!' Guy shouted.

The rocks had ripped the bottom out of the barge and she was sinking.

They lowered themselves into the water. Connie started thrashing his arms and choking. Cyril went to his aid.

The water was bitterly cold. All around them, people were trying to swim, some screaming for help, some already drowning. Too far away to reach him, David saw Belkonski's gaunt face rise above the water, once, then disappear. They grabbed for the rocks. The current was less swift and they were able to pull themselves along until they reached the bank. David looked back. The hulk was fast, but only the stern was showing. Hundreds of prisoners and guards were struggling in the water. Bodies were drifting downstream. Others were splashing up onto the mud and into the trees.

They reached the bank together.

'Which way?' Guy said.

'Let's just get away from here.' David led them into the thick and overgrown forest.

They walked for about half an hour, hearing all about them the sounds of other escaping prisoners. David saw this as potential disaster. He stopped and said, 'It's like Piccadilly Circus. If we're not careful, we'll be rounded up with the rest of them. In a few hours every soldier in the district will be combing the forest. Half of these prisoners don't know what they're doing. They're simply running. That's the quickest way of getting caught. We have to make a plan.'

'What about going south, making for the railway?' Guy said. 'Dressed like this, we'd have no trouble from the deserters or the Czechs.'

'If I were a Russian soldier, that's the first direction I'd look. South, and then west. So we'll go north.'

'North?'

'They'd assume that no-one would go north at this time of year.'

Alexa stared at David over her dog's white head. 'Can you say which way is north?'

It was Cyril who spoke then. 'You look at the moss, sir.' He pointed to the trees. 'You can always tell, sir. Grows on the north side.'

They were standing in a small clearing in the midst of a dense thicket. As they studied the moss, they heard a movement nearby. They turned towards it. Guy bent and picked up a heavy stone. There was a crackling of branches and a voice said softly, 'Englishski? Englishski!'

'It's that damned Cossack,' Guy said.

'Englishski!' It was louder this time.

'For God's sake, he'll wake the forest!'

Perfiliev pushed his way into the thicket. He was smiling. 'Maxim Perfiliev,' he said, bowing to Alexa. There was an unctuousness in his manner which David did not like. He preferred the raucous drunkard of the train.

'I look for Englishski,' he said. 'We march together. Old friends.'

Alexa said, 'I don't want him.'

'Have you any food?' David said.

Perfiliev unhooked a good-sized pot from his belt. Then he dug into his pocket and showed them a knife and a box of matches.

'For cook food,' he said.

'I don't want him with us,' Alexa repeated.

'He may be useful if we find food and need to cook it,' Guy said.

'Tell him to go! I don't want him!' Her voice was imperious, a reminder of a past when she had given orders that were automatically obeyed.

'I'll look after 'im,' Cyril said. 'I'll see he don't give no trouble.'

Guy said, 'If we leave him and he's picked up, he'll tell them exactly where he saw us.'

'Kill him, then,' she said.

They stared at her. Perfiliev smiled again. 'It is joke.'

'All right, you can come,' David said, and saw a look of intense anger cross Alexa's face.

They pressed on, walking as fast as they dared in their weakened states. David found he had been wrong about Alexa; she did not hold them back. Even Connie, in the beginning, seemed to find a new source of strength.

They kept to the bank of a river, thinking it more likely that they would come across a settlement there. People represented danger, but they also represented the only opportunity of obtaining food. In the early afternoon they hid in the undergrowth as a steamer came downstream past them. The decks were lined with soldiers.

They fought the *taiga* all that day and saw no other living

94

soul. The weather was cold, but dry. Guy and Alexa walked together. Sometimes she carried the dog, sometimes he did, and once or twice when they came to an open space, they allowed it to run free.

They risked a fire that night, to dry their clothing, and slept in dense undergrowth. They built primitive shelters of branches to keep off the wind, and slept on mattresses of greenery. They were drier and more comfortable than they had been in the *etapes*. Guy and Alexa slept apart and David watched them prepare their bedding with the same envy that had ebbed and flowed in him since he had first laid eyes on her.

They continued to march north for four days. In that time they came across two settlements. Remembering what had happened at the village they had reached before they had been captured, David and Guy worked out a strategy. They allowed themselves to be seen, not distinctly, but as grey shadows at a distance, so that the villagers never knew how many they were. On both occasions, food was left for them on the outskirts of the villages: bribes to leave the inhabitants in peace.

After the fourth day, they turned eastwards. David knew that somehow they had to get further east, somehow they had to find other clothing, somehow they had to reach a telegraph or some form of responsible government. And somehow they had to keep alive.

The countryside gradually changed. The dense *taiga* gave way to more open grassland with stands of silver birch. Here they saw herds of elk, but they were far away. Occasionally they would come across a track and follow it for a while, only to find that it had been made by deer and led nowhere.

They were looking for villages, but the area seemed to be uninhabited. In the distance there were mountains with caps of snow and they knew these would be a formidable barrier, impossible to climb. They would have to find a way through and hoped there might be rivers along the banks of which they could walk.

They went one whole day without food. That night as they lit a fire and huddled round it, Perfiliev said, 'It is dying time for *brodyagi*. I tell you story.'

He told of an old man who had been exiled for most of his adult life. Each summer he would escape and wander in the *taiga*, only to be recaptured. One year in spring he had gone to the governor of the mines and asked to be confined so that he would not escape. 'He knew he die in snow,' Perfiliev said. 'Like we.'

All the following day they marched, looking always for smudges of smoke in the sky or any signs that would show them they were near human habitation. But there was nothing. They began to string out.

Guy and Alexa walked in front. They formed a separate unit and David had no doubt that if something went wrong with any of the others Guy would not hesitate to leave them and go on into the wilderness with her alone. Then came Perfiliev and Cyril. They seemed to have formed a kind of companionship of mutual assistance and would help each other out of bogs and up screes. Connie fell further and further behind. David had realised that a great deal of his collapse in the *etapes* had been self-indulgent, which had cost the others dear in terms of reduced food. But now it was not possible to be angry with him. He looked like a ghost. David stayed with him as much as possible, at other times rounding him up like a sheep-dog and bringing him into the main group. He thought they must look like a detail from a Breughel: dark figures against the empty landscape and the grey sky.

About noon the wind, which had been blowing from the south, dropped suddenly, and for a time everything was still. But it was an uneasy calm. They felt a sense of portent, of something gathering in the stillness. Then a new wind came, bringing with it a new sensation. It blew on David's back and it was as though someone had opened the door of an ice-house as he walked past. It was so marked that they stopped as one and turned, staring at the north-west as though the wind might be visible.

It came first as a slight breeze, gradually increasing in strength during the afternoon. At one of their rest periods Alexa said, 'I think a *purga* is coming.'

'We must find some shelter,' David said, looking for a thick stand of timber.

They entered the forest again, but the trees were sparser

than in the *taiga* farther west. There were drifts of snow in the hollows.

They were very weak. It was nearly forty-eight hours since they had eaten. Connie collapsed, his back to a tree.

David saw Alexa speak to Perfiliev. This was unusual, for she had not addressed a word to him on the journey. She took something from him and walked into the forest. 'Let's gather some branches,' David said to Guy.

The four of them began to rip branches from birch trees and build up a windbreak. They worked as fast as they could, fearing what was coming. They laced the branches in and out to try to give the windbreak strength and they were almost finished when Alexa returned. She was carrying something red and dripping in her hands. Perfiliev untied his pot and gave it to her. She moved into the shelter of the windbreak and started a fire. To the contents of the pot she added handfuls of snow, a bunch of wild garlic and several sprigs of wild herbs.

They watched her across the fire. Her dark, thin face was set and her golden eyes were cold. The inner light seemed to have gone out. They began to smell the soup and, like a magnet, it drew them nearer. It smelled so wonderful they could hardly bear to wait. They watched the liquid bubble and saw tiny globules of fat rise to the surface. She cooked it for an hour as the afternoon wore on. She divided the meat. There was not much to share between five people, but there was enough. They ate, and they drank the soup. David felt the warmth spread through his body until it reached the very tips of his fingers.

No one spoke, no one mentioned the dog's name. David saw Guy put an arm around her shoulders, but she twisted away and sat by herself, staring at the fire.

Half an hour later the *purga* struck them.

David had heard about these storms. He was not sure when, it may have been in his reading on the journey to Russia, but he thought it was an older knowledge, part of his inherited tribal memory.

The sky went suddenly dark and in the distance they heard a booming noise. He could feel its vibrations inside his chest. The air was filled with driving snow. The latticed windbreak was lifted as though it was a toy and went spinning out of sight. One moment they were crouching behind it, the next it was gone. The booming turned into a roaring and it was all around them. It was so cold that the exposed parts of their bodies burned as though heated by irons. David knew they must die, just as Perfiliev had forecast, unless they got out of the wind.

'Dig!' he shouted. 'Dig down into the snow.'

They burrowed down, using the holes as windbreaks. But the snow was so heavy it soon began to bury them.

Guy said, 'This is how sheep die. They're frozen in.'

The snow wall offered them some protection, but it took all their strength to keep themselves from being covered, and David knew they had only a limited amount of energy left from the meat and the soup.

'We must find a better place.' He forced them to their feet, all except Connie, who said, 'I'm done, finished.'

'Get up!'

'It's no use.'

'We can't carry you, if that's what you want. If you don't get up, we'll leave you.'

'You promised!'

David grabbed him by the shoulder and, with Cyril's help, got him to his feet.

Guy was already moving off with Alexa and Connie whispered: 'You would have left me!'

They could only travel in one direction, and that was with the wind behind them. Where the trees were thinnest they were blown off their feet. David was looking for some rocky defile or dense stand of timber which would offer shelter. But in the snow, visibility was down to a matter of yards.

They staggered on, holding each other like blind persons following a sighted leader. The wind gradually increased and with it the snow. The roaring was all about them. They could see nothing. David knew that if they stopped, they were finished. 'Keep walking,' he told himself. 'Keep going.'

They kept moving in this way for the better part of two hours. David and Guy took it in turns to lead; David and Cyril shared responsibility for keeping Connie on his feet. David was already bruised from crashing into trees when he walked into another. He hit it with his shoulder, then tried to feel his way round it. But the trunk was not vertical, it was horizontal. He loosened his grip on Connie and, using both hands, began to feel above and below. There were several trunks. They seemed to be stacked to a height above his head. He realised he must have walked into a log pile. Two facts registered in his mind: first, a log pile would make a windbreak; secondly, where logs were piled, there must be human hands.

He felt his way to the end of the logs, but there was another stack at right angles to them. He followed the stack. His face hit something hard and after a second he realised it was the horns of a deer. His hands were so cold they were almost numb, but there was no mistaking the antlers. But who would put antlers on a wood pile?

With a surge of hope, he began to grope below the antlers. There was an indentation, smaller logs. He brushed the snow away. His hands touched something marvellously familiar: a door-handle.

He called Guy and the others. They cleared the snow and managed to open the door. They pulled Connie into the dark interior of the building and slammed the door behind them. In the sudden silence it was as though their ear-drums had burst and they had gone deaf. Perfiliev struck a match.

'There's a lantern!' Guy reached for it and Perfiliev lit it. They looked around their sanctuary. The hut was about twelve feet square. On one side was a narrow bunk under which were piled billets of wood. There were other piles against two of the walls. Opposite the bunk was an iron stove on which stood a pot containing ice. Half a dozen split, dried fish were hanging on a piece of rope in one corner. It seemed that the hut had been equipped and left ready for occupancy.

Perfiliev had begun to cut shavings from a billet of wood and soon he had the stove alight. Slowly the ice in the pot melted and Alexa put several of the fish into the water. They looked at each other as though surprised to find themselves alive.

David turned to her and spoke for them all: 'If it hadn't been for you, we would be lying out there. . .'

As he spoke, the door burst open and a huge figure looked

in on them. He might have been a bear, except that he held a rifle in his hands.

He stared at them without speaking, then closed the door behind him and squatted in front of it. Even squatting, his size dominated the room. The skins he wore were powdered with snow, his eyebrows were rimed, and so were his moustache and beard.

David was convinced that he had been tracking them, that there were others outside. There seemed no point in greetings or talk. David was so weary that he was almost glad they had been found and, as he looked around at the other faces, he saw a reflection of his own feelings. Guy turned away and lay on the bunk, and Alexa sat with him. Her cheeks were hollow with exhaustion and yet, with a scarf around her head, she still managed to maintain an air of distinction. She took a piece of rag and wiped the melted snow from Guy's face. It seemed that by some subconscious mutual consent they had decided to treat the new arrival as though he did not exist, that they were saying, 'Take us if you want to, but don't talk to us.' Connie had collapsed onto the floor.

David finally broke the silence. He pointed to the fish broth which was bubbling on the stove. 'Do you want soup?'

The man nodded and pulled an enamel mug from a small hide bag hanging at his side. He took off his fur hat and sipped the soup, watching them through the steam. His head was bald and bullet-shaped, his moustache and beard, now dripping with water as the rime melted, were grey. His eyes, set wide apart, were slanted and his features were Mongolian.

At last he spoke: 'I am Tungus Munku. I am sixty years old.' His Russian had a guttural accent; it was clearly not his first language. 'Where do you go?'

'Vladivostok.'

He looked down at the floor and laughed.

Outside the storm raged, but inside the stove had heated the small room to a point where Munku was steaming. He rose and took off his outer clothing, which comprised trousers of white reindeer skin, a fur jacket made from the pelts of Arctic fox, white deerskin mittens and long boots above hare-skin socks. Underneath he was dressed in a loose Buryat gown of coarse grey material, not unlike the prison-weave the others wore, caught at the waist with a sash. The wrists were turned back and faced with black silk. From the bag at his waist he pulled out a small felt hat shaped like a deep pie-dish and placed it on his head. He had put the rifle behind him and now picked it up again.

'Do you have vodka?' he said.

'No.'

'Do you have tobacco?'

'We have nothing but soup.'

'Where are we?' Guy's voice was flat and listless.

'Yakutsk Territory.'

'How far are we from Vladivostok?' David asked.

Again he laughed.

'Why does he laugh?' Alexa said in English.

David shrugged.

Munku said, 'You are *brodyagi*. I am hunter of *brodyagi*. For each I get ten roubles.' He held up the fingers of both hands.

'We are not *brodyagi*,' David said. He told the story of their hold-up in the *taiga* and how they had been forced to give up their clothes. He did not disclose what had happened afterwards.

Suddenly, Munku moved. It was as though a snow-leopard had sprung forward. His hand closed on Perfiliev's leg and he pulled him along the floor. As he did so, he jerked up the cuffs of his trousers and held up his ankle. The marks of the fetters were plainly visible.

David said wearily, 'Guy, you'd better tell him. You can make him understand better.'

But Guy did not reply and Alexa said, 'He's asleep.' She wiped his face again.

David turned back to the man: 'I will tell you the truth,' he said.

'The truth has many faces,' Munku said.

What difference would the truth make now, David thought. Outside was the *purga*, inside they faced a man with a rifle. In any case, he was too tired to think of lies. As simply as he could, he told their story. Even as he spoke, he could hardly imagine a more unlikely setting for a more unlikely tale. Munku listened impassively.

At last he came to a halt. His despair was deep. He could

not imagine the man understanding, or even taking in half of what he had said, or indeed, believing what he had understood.

Munku was silent for a while, then he say, 'Why are you not shaved?' He pointed to his head. 'Are you politicals?'

David realised that he had not comprehended anything. He said, 'What are you going to do with us?'

But Munku was feeling in his hide bag. After some moments his hands, covered with scars and ingrained with dirt, came up with a small tin. David looked at it in astonishment. It was an English cigarette tin, square and flat, with the words 'Churchman's No. 1' still visible on a dark green background.

'You know diamonds?'

'I told you. I'll give you anything. . .'

'I, too, know diamonds. Here in Yakutsk Territory, I look for diamonds and gold. I trap, I hunt, but always I look.'

He opened the tin. It was lined with moss on which half a dozen small stones lay. The thick, spatulate fingers lifted one and let it roll into the palm of his hand.

As far as David could make out, it was a diamond. Munku took each out in turn until he had all six in the palm of his left hand. He moved them gently with the index finger of the other hand, and pushed one stone towards David, watching him. At length he said, 'You know diamonds. Look.'

David was puzzled. The man seemed to be asking him to admire the stones, but what could he want with their admiration? Then, suddenly, he wondered, was it possible that this was some sort of test? He had told Munku that he owned a mine, had even told him its name. In any other part of the world the name New Chance would have meant something to anyone who was interested in diamonds. Here in Yakutsk Territory, it meant nothing. So Munku was testing him: if his story was true, he would be able to judge the stones. If he could not judge them, Munku would turn them in, at a profit of ten roubles each.

But what if he judged wrongly? What if Munku was also an expert, having spent a lifetime collecting these small stones and selling them, learning to read their interiors and appraise them?

Again he remembered his grandfather handing him one cut gem-stone after another and asking, 'What do you see, David?'

'Fire and ice, grandfather.'

Fire and ice. It would not be enough for Munku.

Like all diamonds in their rough state, these looked like chips of dirty bottle glass smoothed by water action. Munku's index finger constantly moved them into new positions on the horny palm of his hand.

'What does he want?' Alexa said.

'I think he wants me to value them.'

'Can you?'

'I don't know.'

The irony of the situation was not lost on him. Now that Rhodes was dead he was probably the most notable diamond figure surviving from the great days of Kimberley. That was where he had learned his trade the hard way. But it had been years ago. He no longer looked into the cold-hot hearts of gem stones. He had other experts to do that. He had rooms with tables where they sorted them by colour into yellows and browns and whites and by shape into macles and cleavages and flats and half a dozen other categories.

Only he and Alexa were awake. Guy slept on the bunk, Connie on the floor. Cyril and Perfiliev lay against the wood piles along the walls. It was as though some runic game was being played out with an audience of one.

The thick fingers stirred the stones. 'Look!' Munku said.

David reached forward and took one. It was opaque and dirty. It *might* be diamond. It might also be ilmenite or zircon or corundum or a common quartz. He could not see in the poor light. He thought of the loupes and the enlarged windows that were concomitants of diamond-sorting. Here he would have to guess, and if the guess was wrong, it would be hard luck on everyone.

Since Tungus Munku had come into the hut he had dominated it by his size, his personality and by the rifle he carried. Now David gathered what remained of his energy and said, raising his voice: 'How can I look without a glass?'

Munku delved into his hide bag and came out with a small, battered magnifying glass.

David took his time. He looked at each stone in turn, then replaced it in Munku's palm and picked up another. By the end of nearly fifteen minutes he had examined them all. He arranged them in three groups, one of four stones, two of single stones. The slanted eyes and impassive face watched him.

'What are they?' Alexa asked. He was glad she was there, awake beside him. He seemed to draw strength from her presence.

He pointed to the four. 'Those are diamonds. And so is that one.' He indicated the best stone of all, a white diamond of about one carat. 'In fact, it's not a bad stone.' Then he touched a greenish stone to the left of the central group. 'I'm not sure of this one . . . and that's the trouble. He's been more interested in it than the others. He knows what it is, and if I'm an expert, I should know as well.'

He picked it up again and looked at it against the light. There was something familiar about it, but what it was escaped him. It was as though he knew a tune, only to be confused by hearing it played on the wrong instrument: a violin concerto on a piano.

He looked into Munku's face, but the eyes told him nothing.

'I don't want to make a guess,' he said to Alexa.

He bent down and shook Connie's shoulder, calling his name. Connie did not move. His face was blue and his breathing rapid.

Cyril had coughed himself awake and said, 'He's bad, sir.'

'Connie! Wake up!'

Connie blinked. 'David . . . you promised. . .'

'Yes, yes. I want you to look at this stone.'

'My left leg . . . I can't feel it.'

'It's gone stiff, that's all. Connie, tell me what this stone is.'

'I can't feel anything! David, I. . .'

'Pull yourself together! Here. . .' He made Connie take the magnifying glass. 'What stone is this?'

Connie held the glass and looked at the stone. 'It's a garnet.'

'But they're usually red!'

'Occasionally you find a green one, especially in Russia. David . . . you've got to help me!'

'Of course. Go back to sleep now.' He turned to Alexa. 'What's the Russian word for garnet?'

She told him, and he saw a slight reaction on Munku's face. For a moment, he felt triumphant. But Munku did not speak. He put the diamonds away one by one, snapped the tin shut and placed it in his hide bag. He picked up the rifle and sat against the door where he would watch them.

David realised that he had not been convinced. He wondered if the man, hearing Alexa speak the word for garnet, might have thought it was she and not David who had recognised it. Who could tell what went on in his mind?

He remembered the treaty negotiations he had carried out with a tribal chief north of the Limpopo River in Africa many years before, a land agreement that had eventually given the British Government a corridor to the sea and David his knighthood. That chief had the same simple-cunning mind as Munku. To deal with him, David had had to think on his level, to dismiss the civilised subtleties and replace them by an understanding of a different set of needs.

Munku was a hunter and in his spare time a prospector. In his role of hunter he sometimes hunted men, for which he was rewarded. David was certain that the 'civilised' attitude of social revenge would have no place in his thoughts. He would hunt them for the ten roubles. He would feel neither sorry for them nor guilty nor glad nor justified. He would hunt them because he was a hunter and he needed money for certain staples he could not make or catch or grow. His life in this desperate place depended on his skills and his skills were sometimes employed in hunting escaped prisoners.

Skills. That was the factor that dominated life here. Munku knew how to live in a climate that would kill the five of them within hours; he knew how to feed himself and to keep himself.

But David also had skills. In one area, his skills at least matched those of Munku. Diamonds. If not, his life was a fake. It would mean he had built everything on a supposition that did not exist. It would also mean that the first time he had been really tested – by a simple man in a wild place – he had failed; that is, if he did fail.

He decided to gamble.

'How long have you been collecting stones?' he said.

'From a boy.'

'Do you sell them?'

'Always.'

'What do they pay you?'

'Money.'

'They will laugh at you this time.'

'Laugh?'

'You say you know diamonds?'

'I know diamonds from a boy.'

'In that tin you have only four diamonds.'

'Five. A garnet and five diamonds.'

'Four.'

'Five.'

'Show me.'

Munku looked at him for some moments, but did not move. His face remained impassive, but the eyes held a mixture of puzzlement and anger.

David continued to bait him. 'Are you afraid to show me? You say the truth has many faces. A diamond, too, has many faces, but they all look like diamond.'

Tungus Munku dipped into his bag and brought out the stones. Once more he arranged them on his palm. This time it was David's forefinger that pushed and sorted the stones into the same three groups.

'Which are the diamonds?' he said.

Munku indicated the four smaller stones and then he touched the one-carat white.

Alexa said, 'Why are you doing this?'

David said, 'He was playing a game with me, now I play one with him.'

'And what about us?'

'If I win, I think we have a chance. If not, at least I've tried.'

'You don't play games with a man like that.'

'It's the sort of game he might understand.' He turned back to Munku and indicated the stone. 'Are you sure?'

Munku nodded. David put the glass to his eye again and moved nearer the light. It was a diamond all right. He could make out the structure. This one was an octahedron. He placed it on the stone hearth of the stove and then took up a piece of steel about a foot long which was used for raising the lid of the stove when it was hot. He brought it down sharply on the diamond. There was a crunching noise and the diamond disappeared. In its place was a small blob of coarse powder.

Tungus Munku stared at the powder in disbelief. David knew that the next few seconds would determine whether or not he would shoot them.

'You see,' he said, smiling. 'It was not a diamond.'

Then Munku did a curious thing: he leant forward, placed the tip of his finger in the powder and, like a child, brought it to his mouth, tasting it.

'No diamond will crush,' David said. 'You should know that. It is the hardest thing on earth.'

Munku stared at him, tiny particles of powder clinging to his lips.

'The others are diamonds,' David said. 'Be sure of that. And I will buy them from you.'

Munku picked up his remaining stones, one by one, and placed them back in the moss. Then he closed the tin and put it, with the magnifying glass, in his bag. He reached for his rifle. Everything was suddenly still, even the storm seemed to stop for a few seconds. David felt Alexa's fingers on his arm, biting into the flesh.

'How much will you pay?' Munku said.

Alexa said quietly in English, 'Don't offer too much. He won't believe you.'

David estimated that the four stones and the garnet might be worth between a hundred and two hundred roubles. He offered a hundred. Munku shook his head. David raised it by twenty. Again Munku refused.

'What do you want?' David said.

Munku opened the breech of his rifle and took out the bullet. The rifle was an old Winchester repeater, but the stock was damaged and the barrel scarred. He held it out.

'Done,' David said. 'I'll buy you any rifle you choose, but only in Vladivostok, only if you take us there.'

Munku held up the bullet and said, 'One thousand.'

'Only in Vladivostok,' David repeated.

Munku bent his head, listened to the wind, and finally nodded. Then he smiled. It was like a ray of sunshine.

'He thinks he has got the better bargain,' Alexa said.

Still smiling, Tungus Munku stretched out in front of the door, his rifle by his side. David felt numb, and sick with exhaustion.

'Why did you break the diamond?' Alexa said.

But he sat with his head on his arms, too tired to answer.

[10]

David came awake slowly. He was slumped against the bottom of the bunk and so stiff he could hardly move. Cyril was pulling at his trouser leg.

'Sir!'

'What is it?'

'It's Mr. Amsterdam, sir.'

Connie was lying against the opposite wall, his legs curled up in a foetal position. It was bitterly cold. The stove had gone out during the night and the fish broth had frozen. David moved across the room, pain shooting up his stiff muscles. The blue he had noticed in Connie's cheeks the night before had gone, they were now greyish-white. He touched him, and it was like pressing his fingers onto concrete.

'He's dead, sir.'

Alexa lay on the bunk with Guy. Both were asleep. She had her arm about his shoulders, his head lay on her breast. His skin was shiny in the lamplight and he groaned and ground his teeth. Tungus Munku lay across the doorway. He had pulled his heavy coat over his body. He must have woken when Cyril spoke, for his eyes watched every movement.

'My friend is dead,' David said. It had been expected for so long that he found he could speak of it without emotion. In any other place and time he would have felt sadness for the passing of this companion from the old days. But here death was a commonplace and treated matter-of-factly. Belkonski had once described it as like going to see an old friend.

Munku rose and bent over the body. 'Better for him. He die in snows.'

They cleared the snow from the doorway and carried Connie outside. The world was white. The noon sun was just above the horizon. There was no wind and everything was crackling with cold. The hut was almost drifted in on the windward side, but on the lee there was less snow. David saw a large mound and several smaller ones. The smaller ones suddenly erupted in a chorus of barking as his dog-team greeted Munku. The larger mound was a sled and when it was uncovered Munku took off several skin rugs and distributed them among the party. Then he threw pieces of frozen fish to the dogs.

In the hut Alexa said, 'Guy is sick.'

David looked at him in the light of the lantern. The shine on his skin was sweat.

'What is it?' he said.

'Gaol fever.' Her face was haggard.

'How bad is he?'

'Bad.'

'Do you know what to do?'

'There is nothing to do but wait. I've seen it often. Some lived, some died.' Her voice was flat, controlled.

David had seen men with fever in the crowded tent camps of Kimberley. There too some had died, some lived.

Munku loomed over him. 'It is time. Wind stops but comes again. Voosh!'

They left half an hour later after eating what was left of the soup, Alexa feeding Guy with a spoon like a child. Munku cleaned the cabin stove and tidied up and David learned that they had been in a *povarnia*, a travellers' hut, built specially in the remoter parts of Yakutsk Territory to perform the function it had for them the night before.

They could not bury Connie for the ground was frozen. Instead they dug a shallow grave in the snow and David recited the Lord's Prayer in English. They knew that within a few hours the body would be dug up by bears or wolves.

109

Guy was laid on the sled and covered in skins, the dogs were harnessed. 'Poz-za!' Munku shouted. 'Poz-za!' The dogs leapt forward and the birch runners began to hiss.

They staggered forward. In parts the snow was almost up to their knees but as they moved away from the shelter of the trees they found the going better because it had begun to freeze. The sun remained low on the horizon and was only visible for a few hours before the sky turned grey. They travelled through a white twilight. Soon a three-quarter moon lit the snow-field, causing their bodies to throw long black shadows. It was a strange, eerie landscape.

Everything was still except for the breathing of the dogs and an occasional call by Munku of 'Norakh-Norakh!' – To the left! – and 'Takh-Takh!' – To the right!

Around them now were wild mountains. They were travelling along the bottom of a valley and in the distance David could see the glint of a river.

Eight hours after they had left the *povarnia* Munku built a fire and made another fish broth. They drank it standing up, too afraid to sit in case they could not rise again.

Alexa took a mug of soup to Guy.

'How is he?' David said.

'Sleeping.'

Again the soup worked its miracle. It kept them alive.

'Poz-za! Poz-za!' Munku cried and the dogs leant into the harness.

They travelled for nearly five more hours. Munku drove them as he drove the dogs. Occasionally he looked over his shoulder at the sky to the north. The gesture lent renewed energy to their muscles. They knew that if they were caught by the returning storm it would be the end.

The mountains closed around them and they travelled on the bank of the river. Cloud obscured the moon, but in the brilliance of the snowlight David could see ice-floes, some of them as big as a tennis-court, slide silently by.

The wind found them again, not with an initial hesitation as it had the first time, but in a squall that came racing up behind in a cloud of ice dust. They drew the skin robes more tightly around themselves.

'Keep together!' David shouted.

Cyril was very weak. Sometimes the wind brought him to his knees and each time he took slightly longer to struggle to his feet. His coughing was worse. He would be the next to die, David thought. Either Cyril or Guy. Perfiliev seemed to endure. He was the sort of man who was outgoing when things were good but kept to himself in adversity, watching and waiting for opportunities to improve his condition.

There was nothing David could do at the moment for Cyril or Guy. It had become purely a matter of personal survival. If he took his hands from the robe he would get frost-bite. Already his toes were numb.

Ahead of them always was the towering figure of Tungus Munku. David had had his eyes fixed on the man's back for the past thirteen hours. At times he hated him, at times admired him. Ultimately, Munku offered him a challenge. He was sixty years old; if he could survive, David could, too.

Just as they were reaching the end of all their resources, Munku's voice rose above the wind: 'Norakh-Norakh!' The dogs yelped in anticipation, picked up speed and the sled veered away from the river and entered the trees.

Soon they came upon a clearing. In it stood a building with fire and sparks spurting from the centre of its roof.

It was built of big logs placed at an angle so that it looked like a huge conical tent. The spaces between the logs were filled with brushwood which, in turn, had been covered with mud and earth and, more recently, with snow mixed with water, which gave it a windproof sheath of ice. Piles of wood surrounded what David was later to learn was called a *yurta*.

Munku picked up Guy as though he were a child and led them inside. The *yurta* was warm and David felt his fingers begin to burn as though dipped in acid.

His first impressions were confused because of the state of his body and mind, but he gradually became aware of his surroundings. He might have been standing in a Red Indian teepee, except that this one was so much bigger. Its windows were plates of thick ice and it had only one entrance. All along the walls were bunks covered in deer-skins which served both as benches and beds. The walls were lined with skins: caribou, Siberian tiger, snow leopard, lynx, bear and wolf.

The floor was covered in hare-skin rugs and softly-worked reindeer hides. In the centre of the room was a raised fireplace on which were burning logs nearly six feet long which sent tongues of flame and sparks up through the wide opening at the apex of the roof. This had been plastered with mud on the inside to stop the wood catching. The fire was the only light source.

A steaming copper samovar stood on a stone hearth next to the fire and beside it was a young woman dressed in a loose gown of dark blue cotton with red silk facings. Her face was round and pretty, like a Russian doll's, and her eyes were bright with curiosity. She was Tungus Munku's new wife – his fourth – and her name was Bou-Ta.

She gave them a stew of some kind of venison and cups of brick tea laced with mutton fat which would normally have made David feel ill. Now he gulped the hot liquid gratefully. They crawled onto the bunks and covered themselves with skins. Guy was shivering and sweating by turns and Alexa lay under the skins with him, wiping his face and talking softly to him. David fell asleep almost instantly, but kept on waking during the night. He heard her low voice as she talked to Guy and he thought of how he had talked to Connie to keep him alive when they lay on the floors of the *etapes.*

The fire was allowed to die down and freezing air entered the *yurta* from a hole in the roof; by the time morning came everything was covered in a layer of snow and the liquid in the samovar was frozen solid.

Bou-Ta re-lit the fire and soon flames and sparks were shooting up into the sky and the air in the *yurta* grew less cold. They were given a breakfast of curds and *salamat*, flour boiled in sour cream, and brick tea to which mutton fat had again been added, this time with salt. Munku had been outside seeing to the dogs, and he called David. He gave him a coat made of deerskin, heavy hide trousers, long boots and a hat of fur which covered his ears and nose like a balaclava.

He led the way down to the river. The wind was still blowing, but not as strongly, and in the grey morning light the river presented a bleak and dismal picture. It was about a quarter of a mile wide at this point and the ice-floes looked larger and more menacing than they had the night before.

Sometimes they bumped into each other with a grinding noise, occasionally they were caught at a bend and became stuck. It was obvious that the river was beginning to freeze.

'Are we going by river?' David asked.

Munku began to talk rapidly and David had difficulty following him. As far as he could make out, there was an annual goose hunt at the mouth of the river to which 'foreigners' came – David assumed him to mean either Japanese or Koreans – and it would be in their boats that they would reach Vladivostok.

But the hunt was imminent and they must leave immediately. David thought of Guy shivering and sweating under the skins in the *yurta*. There would be no question of his travelling down a freezing river. It would finish him. Yet if they tried to over-winter here, the police would find them. Indeed, Munku himself might give them up. Ten roubles per head now might be worth more than the promise of a new rifle some time in the future.

Munku walked to a mound in the snow and began to clear it. A rowing boat about fourteen feet long became visible.

'How long will it take to reach the sea?' David said.

Munku shrugged, indicating it would depend on the ice, then he said, 'Eight days.'

David explained the situation to the others. Guy was unconscious but Alexa said, 'It would kill him.'

'I know, but what can we do?'

'How long will the river take to freeze?'

'A week, maybe more, maybe less.'

'He's at the crisis now,' she said.

'The only alternative would be to stay here until spring.'

'Impossible! You think we are alone here with this man? All through the forest people live like this. There are villages. People travel. Even if Munku said nothing about us, others would know. Here they can look at a footmark in the snow and tell you who came this way.'

All that day and the following one they waited for Guy to recover, but either Alexa had misread the signs or the crisis was taking longer than normal. He was desperately ill, and David took turns with Alexa to sit with him.

The wind died completely and the cold became intense.

David had never known anything like it, had never even imagined such cold. Sometimes when he went down to the river to look at the ice, the cold pierced the fur garments and he even felt the moisture on his eyeballs begin to freeze. The river was taking on a new look. Where only a few days before there had been separate ice-floes, now they were joining to make islands. Tongues of ice crept out from the shallow water at the banks and gripped them, grinding and groaning and slowing them down until all motion ceased and the floe became part of the ice canopy of the land itself. Channels of dark water flowed between the ice islands, but these seemed to grow narrower even as David looked at them.

They all made several trips each day to the river bank, sometimes together, sometimes individually to stare at the ice. Munku had managed to clear the boat. David, Cyril and Perfiliev helped him run it out onto the ice from where they could launch it. Everything now depended on Guy.

By the fourth day it was apparent that the river was freezing more quickly than Tungus Munku had anticipated. The boat was loaded with dried fish and smoked deer meat. Each of them had been given heavy fur clothing. The weather remained calm and the cold remained intense. David took Alexa aside. He had been putting this off as long as he could, and the irony was that he was now planning what he had scorned when Guy had suggested it.

'I'm afraid we will have to leave him,' he said. 'He'll have no chance on the river. I've spoken to Munku. I've told him that if they look after him, I'll give him anything he wants. But if we all stay, we're finished. I don't think Cyril will survive a winter here and I'm not sure that Munku has supplies, or could get enough to keep us all alive.'

She watched him, stony-faced. He went on, 'Anyway, as you said yourself, with all of us here the news would get around.'

He knew that what he was saying was basically true, yet it sounded specious. He tried to tell himself that conditions were not the same as leaving Connie behind in one of the *etapes*.

'Once we reach Vladivostok we can contact the Russian

114

Government, tell them about Guy. All the circumstances will change.'

'What do you want from me?' she said.

'I want to know what you plan to do. Are you coming or are you staying with Guy?'

She turned away without answering, crossed the room to Guy's bunk. Her action was more eloquent than anything she might have said.

When David told Munku, he said, 'We go now.'

It was early afternoon. The three men followed Munku down to the river. The boat's keel had frozen to the ice and they had to cut it out with an axe. The sun had gone and the snowscape, with the grey-green water of the river, the ice and the black trees, looked like a steel engraving. They climbed into the boat. Munku gave them each a heavy pole about eight feet long and then he sat in the thwarts and took up the oars.

They were about to push off when they heard a cry and saw Alexa standing at the edge of the trees about four hundred yards away. She called again, and waved, and began to run clumsily towards them. She came onto the ice and stood by the boat, her face hidden by a cowl of fur.

'He's dead,' she said.

'I'll come,' David said.

Munku pointed to the narrow channel of water and said, 'We must go.'

'We have to bury him.'

But Alexa climbed into the boat. 'She said her brother would bury him.' She repeated it in Russian and Munku nodded. David hesitated.

Perfiliev said impatiently: 'How can bury him? Everything ice.'

Cyril tried to speak, but began coughing. Finally he managed to say, 'You could say a prayer, sir.'

For the second time, David spoke the Lord's Prayer, in English. When he had finished, Munku pushed the boat out into the stream. As they were caught by the current, David saw a figure at the tree-line. Bou-Ta was calling a faint farewell and waving to them. David waved back, then his whole concentration was focussed on the river.

To him, the journey down the frozen river had all the qualities of a nightmare, a dream in which some parts remained clear and others were telescoped or lost in blurred memory. In a curious way, they owed their survival to Guy. Had they left Munku's house sooner, the river would have killed them. Those four days of waiting for him to break through the crisis of his fever had allowed them to build up strength by rest and food to a level just sufficient to cope with what they had to do.

At first David had not known what function the wooden poles had, but almost immediately they were in action, used to fend off the ice floes that threatened to crush them. They did this hour after hour, day after day, while Alexa sat enveloped in furs in the stern. Munku, that iron man, kept the oars. Occasionally David would offer to take his place and then a small smile would come over his face as though to say, 'What good would you be?'

They took six instead of eight days to reach the sea. They were driven on by Munku, who slept only three times. Otherwise they were in constant movement. When they did stop he built a huge fire and made soup with the fish or the meat. Then they all slept and it was Munku who woke them and drove them on as the black channels of water grew narrower and narrower.

The river began to widen out as they left the mountains behind and as it did so the flow grew slower and the ice thicker.

Sometimes they would stick fast and Munku or David would chop a way through to another open channel. It was like travelling through a maze. A channel that looked promising would grow narrower and narrower and finally they would grind against the ice and stop and the axe would have to be used to break through to another channel which might close up in a few hundred yards.

At last, on the morning of the sixth day, the ice seemed to grow thinner. Mud flats appeared and the river was so wide it stretched from horizon to horizon. David thought they must be at its estuary. In summer these would be marshes, now most of the area was frozen. Munku took off one of his hare-skin mittens, put his finger in the water, then in his mouth. 'Salt,' he said.

All that day he rowed them through the marshes. It was a place ineffably bleak, with yellow reeds bending in a wind from the Sea of Okhotsk. Above their heads was the constant honking of geese. In the afternoon they heard the booming of guns as though a naval battle was taking place and soon they saw, on rising ground, a group of wooden huts, some built on the mud, some built above the water on stilts. In the distance, eight large fishing-boats rode at anchor.

The marshes at this point were dotted with hides and in each hide was a punt gun with a barrel like a cannon. As the geese came in and formed groups on the water the nearest gun would fire and twenty or thirty birds would die in a single shot.

Munku stopped at the first hut and there they waited until the hunters returned. It smelled strongly of dead birds and fish and it was surrounded by heaps of bloody bodies.

The returning hunters were short sturdy men dressed in quilted jackets and trousers and covered in blood and mud and feathers. One of the skippers could speak a little Russian and, with Alexa's help, David reached an agreement with him. They would be taken off when the goose hunt was over. In the meantime, they could wait at the hut.

They spent the following two days sleeping and regaining their strength, and then the waiting began. From the moment it was light enough to see until it was too dark to distinguish the incoming birds, the Koreans were in the marshes. David had never imagined so many geese to exist. There were white geese and brown geese and multi-coloured geese, the names of which he did not know. He assumed the marshes were a rest area on a migration route to the south. Every day the air was thick with geese coming in from the north and those that did not die in the marshes took off again, circling and then heading south in V-shaped skeins.

They were left alone in their hut for the hours of daylight, and even Munku went off to join in the sport. Alexa had kept herself apart since their arrival. David had wondered if this might be because she feared the Koreans, but they offered no harm. Most returned to their vessels at night, only a few

117

sleeping in the huts, and these men were so tired and cold at the end of the day that they fell asleep around the fire immediately after their evening rice bowl.

During the day she went out by herself, walking on the frozen mud. She often spent hours in the biting wind, staring across the marches. David found her there one day as darkness was falling. He realised she had been crying for the tears had frozen on her face. He wanted to say something to comfort her and yet had nothing to say. He assumed she was crying for Guy. He could say that he mourned him, too, but how would that help? It might only make it worse for her. She turned and began to walk slowly towards the hut. He caught her arm and stopped her.

'Do you want to talk about him?' he said.

She shook her head.

He wanted to break through the barrier of silence. He thought to ask about her background, but hesitated, thinking she might be just as unwilling to talk about that. In any case, her past was something he did not wish to investigate. He was not sure why, but he felt a resistance in himself. They were here on the very edge of the world and her past and, to a certain extent his own, lay behind them in Russia. He had already begun to project himself back into his life in England, to look forward rather than back. But what about her?

'What will you do in Vladivostok?' he said.

'I don't know.'

'Do you know anyone there?'

'No one. But if I did, it wouldn't help.'

For a moment he had forgotten that her status was not the same as his own. He was not a convict. He thought of Mr. Wiggins and Mrs. Wiggins in their English garden overlooking the Golden Horn. It was unfair to involve them in what was in effect a criminal conspiracy, but there was no other way. He would tell them as little as possible.

'Would you allow me to help you?' he said.

She had walked on a few paces. When she turned he was again struck by the thin beauty of her face.

'Are you really a man who owns a mine?' she said. 'Was Guy really a naval officer? Or is it just a dream and will I wake in another *etape*?'

'If I am who I say I am, will you let me help you?'

She stared at him for a moment as though still wondering whether this was a dream. Then she nodded. 'Of course.'

Three days later the sky was empty, the geese had gone. The following day they sailed for Vladivostok.

BOOK TWO

Cape of Good Hope, 1920

David stood waist deep in the river. The water was freezing and ice-floes were slipping silently past. He had lost Alexa. She had been with him a moment before, but she was not there now. Instead, a different figure came floating up from the icy depths. David lowered his hand and caught the body, pulling it slowly to the surface. It turned. Where the face should have been was a blank. Yet the body was dressed as Connie's had been dressed. He knew he must warn Alexa. He shouted. But there was no reply. The body's arms floated like seaweed and gently encircled him. It began to drag him under water. 'Alexa. . . !'

He woke. A black face was above him, the eyes wide with apprehension. A hand was shaking him gently by the shoulder. He was in a bath of sweat and terribly afraid.

'Tea, masteh!'

Gradually the river faded, as did the blank face and the twining arms. He knew he was at his home at the Cape of Good Hope and the face he was staring at belonged to his house-boy, Jackson, who brought him his tea every morning.

Jackson said, 'Is masteh all right?'

'Yes.'

'Miss Jewel says masteh must remember he going riding.'

He had forgotten, but said, 'You can tell her I'll be down in a little while.'

When Jackson left, David slumped back on the pillows, feeling drained and weak. He had not had the dream for some time and he had begun to think he had finally escaped from it and that he was over the physical and mental reactions to the Russian experience.

He had given up trying to isolate the stimuli which

triggered off the dreams. They seemed to come from nowhere, suddenly bursting in on him, either waking or asleep. The dream of this faceless figure which he knew to be Connie's was particularly vivid. It was also the most frightening, leaving pale images in his mind that often took hours to fade completely. It was the dream that had haunted him most and had frightened him most.

He got out of bed and stood at the window, sipping his tea. It was one of the views he loved best in the world. The house was built on a slope of the great massif that comprised Table Mountain and Devil's Peak. It stood above the Constantia Valley and he could look across the acres of vines to the sea in the distance. He had chosen the spot carefully. The house was surrounded by trees: huge old oaks, silver trees, pines, aspens and eucalyptus. It was large, but not as big as those built by his fellow diamond-magnates. Round the shoulder of the mountain Rhodes had built *Groote Schuur*, a great Dutch-gabled mansion, and less than four miles away Sir J. B. Robinson had his Victorian manor, *Hawthorndene*. David had built his own house because, as Chairman of New Chance Mining, he had to spend part of each year in South Africa and did not wish to live in the hot desert town of Kimberley itself.

He had told his architect that he wanted all the bedrooms and public rooms of Constantia House to have a view over the valley. The result was a three-storeyed building with a wide front. The deep verandahs of the public rooms on the ground floor had sliding glass windows so that even in winter or windy summer weather he and his family could look out over the valley.

Now, even as he looked, it seemed to change. Snow covered the vines, the trees became stark and the sky turned navy-blue. He was behind the sledge of Tungus Munku. He could see Guy, wrapped in furs, and Alexa hurrying next to him. And Cyril and Perfiliev behind him. It was as though he stood outside his own body and watched this tiny caravan move across the vast snowscape of the Yakutsk steppe. Then, as in a kaleidoscope, two images overlapped and blurred and, abruptly, he was looking again at the Constantia Valley on a summer's morning.

By association, the memories brought back a picture of Elizabeth Lytton. He had cabled her from Vladivostok and also written, giving details of Guy's death. When he returned to London he had telephoned her and she had come to see him in Bayswater. Again he had been struck by her loveliness, the magnificent copper hair, the tall, full-breasted body. But this time he viewed her from the security of his own love for Alexa and their recent marriage.

They had sat in his study and talked about Guy.

'It seems impossible that he's dead,' she had said. 'Guy wasn't the kind to die.'

He had remembered the golden young man who had sat in this same room. He said, 'I know what you mean.'

Then she said in a puzzled voice, 'I don't understand why *he* died and not . . . well, he was much. . .' He knew she was about to say 'younger' but caught herself. 'He was always so fit.'

'Fevers don't discriminate between people. They strike anyone. And by that time we were all weak, all vulnerable.' He paused and saw that she was waiting for him to continue. 'He just . . . slipped away. Nothing could have been more peaceful. I'd have given anything to have saved him.'

'I'm glad he didn't die alone in that awful place. I'm glad he had you with him. He respected you.'

'We were all with him. We all loved him.' He knew it was what she had wanted to hear.

'It's odd. He wasn't obviously lovable, if you know what I mean, and yet one *loved* him. I've never loved anyone else.' It was then she had begun to cry.

David finished his tea and went through his bathroom into Alexa's bedroom. Mosquito netting at the windows diffused the light, making it cool and soft. She was still asleep. She had thrown back the blankets and sheet, and lay on her side. Her nightgown had fallen open, exposing one of her breasts, and in the grey light he could see the pink nipple. He felt himself gripped by desire. He sat on the edge of the bed and she opened her eyes. His hand went out to cup her breast. She turned so that she was on her back and brushed back her hair. He bent and kissed her.

Her lips were cool and there was a slight resistance. He

would have drawn back, but he wanted her. He lay down beside her and took her in his arms. She responded in the way she always did, the way he had become used to. He stroked her body and kissed her face and she lay there, not quite passive, but giving nothing in return. When he penetrated her, he heard her breath in his ear, but as usual did not know if her response was real or just pretence. And as he raced to his climax he felt her body jerk and twitch as though in mutual passion, and all the while a voice inside his head was telling him that it was not real, that she was being a wife, doing her duty. As he lay, spent, beside her, he felt, as he often did, anger at betrayal, at the knowledge that whatever was within her he had failed to arouse, and he wondered what it had been like for her with Zagarin or with Guy. Had they managed to make that body move with real passion? Had they managed to bring the breath from her in gusts, a cry to her lips, perhaps? He had her body, but the central core of her being eluded him.

He had thought that once she had a child things might be different, that the physical barriers might come down, opening a way to her psyche. Well, the child had arrived. Sophie was in her nursery along the corridor. But her coming had opened no door.

'When do we go back to England?' Alexa said.

'April or early May. I haven't decided yet. Why? You're not bored, are you?'

'Of course not.'

'I'd hoped we would have had more of a holiday, but there are things that have to be sorted out with Nash at the mine. It never occurred to me I'd be this busy.'

'I told you I'm not bored.'

'No, but we're not seeing enough of each other.' She was silent where he had hoped she might agree. 'Is there anything you want?'

'Want? I have cars, servants, a beautiful house, I have everything, even diamonds. What else could there be to want?'

'I hope you're not disparaging diamonds,' he said, trying to make a joke of it. 'We owe our lives to them in more ways than one.'

126

He thought of Tungus Munku's diamonds which lay, still in their battered little cigarette tin, in a vault of his London bank. To his mind, they were the most important stones he owned.

Her remark stayed with him while he was dressing. There was an arrogance in it that irritated him. She had contrived to make diamonds sound faintly ludicrous. Sometimes it was difficult for him to understand her remarks, perhaps because it was difficult to understand Alexa herself. If she had been one person it would have been easier, but there seemed to be at least three Alexas.

There was the woman of the march, of the stinking *etapes*, a remote figure, drifting among the men, begging for her little white dog. What he had so much admired about that Alexa was her preservation, in the midst of such squalor, of some elegance: the way she wore her scarf, the belt that drew in her shapeless prison clothing. She'd had to make an effort to remain a woman. It would have been so easy to give up, as others had done, yet some spark in her kept her going. No one who had not gone through the Russian exile system could ever know what an effort that had cost.

Then there was her bravery on the march. He remembered how she had taken Perfiliev's knife and gone into the *taiga* to kill the dog. Without that food, they would have died, they would never have had the strength to reach the *povarnia*. And her loyalty to Guy during those endless days when they had waited for him to recover, as the river began to freeze. She could, at his expense have made certain of saving her own skin.

He had come to know, or perhaps not to know but to observe, another Alexa after they had reached Vladivostok.

Suddenly, when the Korean boat had landed them in the city, it was as though the major role in her life had been removed, the role she had been forced to find in the *etapes* and the Forwarding Prisons which had allowed her to survive.

He had told the Wigginses the story they had agreed on, which was that Alexa was not a prisoner, but had been accompanying her husband into exile when he died and she had chosen of her own free will to come with them. He wasn't sure if they believed him, but the word 'Countess' had impressed Mrs. Wiggins. Alexa needed to keep to the house for safety, but this was no hardship as they were all exhausted or ill.

One day Mrs. Wiggins had come to David and asked if there was anything lacking in their hospitality towards Alexa. When he asked her what she meant, she had taken him to Alexa's room and pointed to the bed. 'She hasn't slept in it. Not once. The maid says she sleeps on the floor. And look here. . .' She had opened the bedside cupboard and David saw an assortment of foods: an apple, a piece of bread and cheese, a half-eaten slice of cake, a small piece of bacon, a hard-boiled egg.

'Where did these come from?' he asked.

'From the dining-room. She smuggles them out. I don't understand it, Sir David. Does she not like the food? Is there something wrong with it?'

'There's nothing wrong with it, Mrs. Wiggins. You must remember that for months she has never had enough, never even known where the next meal was coming from. She's not used to plenty.'

He had realised then that the habits formed by years of imprisonment would take some breaking. Alexa had learned how to control her world in the prisons, now she was confused. He, by the same token, had never been in control of his life in Russia; now he had assumed control again.

That was how he had seen it then, not foreseeing the nightmares, the insomnia and illness that would invade his life. At that point, she had taken on an entirely different role. She looked after him in the same way as she had cared for Guy. He remembered waking up some nights in her arms, struggling and shouting, and how she had soothed him back to sleep.

The irony, he came to believe, was that, after the prison years, she knew how to act in adversity but not in normal life. This had been borne out to a certain extent in London and at the Cape, where it was as though her behaviour was based on some blurred memory of her early life in an aristocratic Russian household. He noticed her arrogance, the way she spoke to servants. There was no malice in it, it was simply the part she was now playing. Then there had been New

York. That was when he had seen beyond the role-playing and it had devastated him.

Jewel was waiting for him at the stables. His spirits rose again when he saw his daughter-in-law. From her childhood she had been a favourite of his and nothing had pleased him more than her marriage to Michael. She was in her mid-thirties, a few years younger than Alexa. She still had her looks, the dark eyes and black hair, and still retained the gentle facade which caused many people to misjudge her. Underneath it was a toughness which had always surprised him.

She was looking a great deal better than she had when she had arrived in Cape Town. Her miscarriage, the war years, the worry about himself and finally a bout of shingles had all taken their toll. He had invited her out for a holiday and postponed Sophie's christening so that she could be present.

They hacked towards Tokai Mountain, then turned back through the vineyards. David dismounted to look at the maturng grapes. 'Muscat d'Alexandre,' he said, indicating the luscious green bunches. 'What they call *Hanepoot* out here. And over there I've got Waltham Cross. Don't like them so much, they draw the mouth. The wine grapes are down there.'

'You've done wonders since I last saw it,' Jewel said as they walked the horses down into the valley. 'Alexa must love it.' When he did not reply, she said, 'I thought she liked riding.'

'She hasn't been out for months. Before Sophie was born she rode every day, sometimes twice. She galloped all over the valley. We used to have races. I was often afraid for her – and the baby.'

'I hope her stopping is nothing to do with my being here.'

'No, no. It's probably the heat.'

'Have you settled when you're going back to London?'

He told her and she said, 'I'll come back with you if you can stand me until then.'

'You know we love having you. I just wish Michael could have come out too. It would have made everything perfect.'

She smiled. 'It seems to me things are perfect as they are.'

He nodded. 'I never thought that I'd get a second chance. Sometimes I have to pinch myself to prove I'm not dreaming.'

'You deserve it. And so does Alexa after what you both went through.'

'Mine was nothing to hers. She won't speak of it, but I can guess.' For a second he saw Alexa's face on that steely afternoon at the goose hunt, the tears frozen on her cheeks. It was the only time he had ever seen her break down.

'She'll get over it, especially now she has Sophie.'

'I hope so. Sometimes I. . .'

'What?'

'Nothing.'

They reached the stables and dismounted. 'What would you like to do today?' he said.

'Anything. Nothing. I'm so pleased to be out of the English winter that just to sit in the sun all day would suit me fine. That's after I've said good-morning to Sophie.'

They went up to the nursery. Sophie was being fed by Annie, who had been at Constantia House for years and had a grown-up family of her own. She was a Cape Coloured, one of the race that owed its existence to miscegenation between Whites and non-Whites over the centuries. She was a plump, motherly person who doted on Sophie.

Jewel said, 'May I please, Annie?' and took over the feeding. Sophie had her mother's golden eyes and brown hair. When she had finished eating, Jewel picked her up and said to her, 'What shall we do today? Would you like to go to the sea?' She turned to David. 'What about Alexa? Will she come?'

'I don't think so.'

'What about you?'

'Work, I'm afraid.'

'Then I'll have Sophie all to myself. Do you think Alexa will mind?'

Annie answered for him. 'Madam won't mind. Madam don't see Miss Sophie in the mornings.' Her thick lips pressed together, forming a thin, disapproving line.

The New Chance Mining group was far too great a company now for one man to run, but David still kept much of it under his control. He had an office in the city and sometimes he would work there, in constant touch with Kimberley and London by telephone, cable and letter; or else a secretary would come out to Constantia House and they would put in a morning in his study.

At the back of his mind, though, was the idea of a slow withdrawal from the fiscal life. He wanted to see as much of his new family as he could, wanted to watch and be part of Sophie's growing up, and spending weeks and weeks in a Union Castle liner travelling between Southampton and Cape Town, and more time on the train from Cape Town to Kimberley and back, was not his idea of how this was to be achieved.

In spite of unexpected pressures, he found time to organise picnics and drives and take Sophie to the beach as often as he could, for he loved to sit with her and watch her play in the sand. Usually he was accompanied by Jewel and Annie; sometimes by Alexa.

Alexa seemed content to let Jewel entertain the baby and spent large portions of the day by herself, reading or walking in the vineyards. Sometimes David would go with her, pointing out how the bunches of grapes would be trimmed into shape once they had matured, showing her the soft, powdery bloom on the skin, explaining the different forms of trellising and a host of other things he thought might interest her. Although she nodded and listened, he began to feel that she would rather be alone, and again he was reminded of her lonely figure standing on the edge of the Sea of Okhotsk. It was this quality of separateness she had, of remoteness, that had first caught his imagination. Now it had begun to torture him.

It was as though she lived in her own world and by her own values, and many men before him, he thought, must have wanted to break into it and share those values. He wondered if Guy had managed it in the short time they had known each other, and he wondered if he ever would. Perhaps it would come eventually through shared experiences, and certainly he and Alexa were rich in those.

They had arrived in Vladivostok to find Russia in greater chaos than before. While they had been escaping through the frozen snows of Yakutsk Territory, the Bolsheviks had won the counter-revolution, and civil war had broken out, Reds against Whites, with half a dozen war lords fighting for easy pickings on the side. To Mr. and Mrs. Wiggins, themselves caught up in events far beyond their imagining. They had been like people returning from the dead. Mrs. Wiggins had been terrified of Tungus Munku, who slept outside David's room on the passage floor, unwilling to let him out of his sight until he had completed the bargain they had struck.

It had taken David several days to establish links between himself and the Foreign Office in London and, through Maberly, with New Chance. Within a fortnight he was solvent and Tungus Munku had the finest sporting rifle and shot-gun money could buy. There had been no sentimental parting, no thanks expressed. He had looked at David for a moment as though to memorise his features, then he had gone, a huge, bearlike man wrapped in skins against the cold, clutching his two new guns and his boxes of ammunition – much to Mrs. Wiggins' relief.

There were no British ships in harbour at the time, but they managed to get berths in a Japanese vessel sailing for Yokohama. Perfiliev had become a permanent member of their party. Being a Cossack, he was in danger in Russia, for now in the civil war old scores were being settled. To have left him would have possibly meant his death. In any case, David felt that after everything they had endured together, there was a bond. Perfiliev had, in fact, saved them just as surely as Alexa had in her turn and Tungus Munku in his: without his matches and pot, they would not have been able to cook any food.

From Japan, they had managed to get freighter passages to America. It was on that slow voyage across the Pacific that something in David seemed to buckle. Until then he had been in constant movement and in a position of responsibility, and he had been living on nervous energy. Now, with nothing to do, with the immediate goal achieved, reaction set in. The voyage was a blur of recurring dreams and nightmares; he was racked by insomnia and lost his appetite. He grew thinner and finally fell ill with Spanish influenza which drained him of energy and left him weak and depressed.

Cyril's chest trouble was worse and when his sea-sickness started again he had to be taken to the small sick-bay, leaving David alone in his cabin. Alexa spent much of each day with him. She would read to him if he wished or sit quietly, allowing her presence to calm him so that sometimes he would doze off. Often he would wake trembling and shouting. It was during this period that he realised how strong she really was.

New York changed everything. It was spring and the city was a world away from anything they had been experiencing. It had a fairytale quality built on luxury and plenty. Even by comparison with London there were no bombed buildings, no glass in the streets, no burst water or gas mains. True, the town was filled with khaki uniforms and there were cripples to be seen – as in London – selling matches. They hardly noticed these things. New York was so majestic, so filled with splendour that even David found it difficult to adjust to it after the horrors of the *taiga* and the *etapes*.

He moved back into his familiar world. New Chance had a building on Fifth Avenue and for the first time Alexa saw him against his true background. There were chauffeur-driven cars, luxurious hotel suites, newspaper interviews. He went to Washington for meetings with the British Ambassador and there were conferences with members of his staff as he caught up with what had been happening to the company in his absence.

This sudden flurry of activity helped him recover and the frozen wastes of Russia were gradually pushed to the back of his mind. He took up again responsibility for others. Cyril had developed a spot on his lung and David sent him to a TB sanatorium in the Rockies near Colorado Springs. Perfiliev was no problem: he took to New York as though born there. Its hustle appealed to him and he responded by allowing his own bragadoccio full rein. David found him a job in the New Chance organisation and he moved to Staten Island, where there was a growing community of White Russians.

But the major change was in Alexa. At first she hardly left the hotel: she disliked and was frightened by the speed with which life moved in New York.

133

He tried to persuade her to go out. 'You have a car and a chauffeur. Surely there must be something you would like to do?'

'I'm all right. Stop worrying about me.'

But he did worry. Sometimes she would not leave her suite all day. She would have her meals sent up and often he would find fruit or bread put away in her drawers against a time of need. He told himself he would have reacted the same way if he had been imprisoned as long as she.

One day he said gently, as he dropped a mouldy orange into the waste-basket: 'You don't have to do this. There are more where these came from. You only have to ask and you can have everything you want. Everything and anything. Nothing is going to be taken away from you.'

She gave no indication of believing him, but the following day, before he left for Fifth Avenue, she said, 'David there is one thing I'd like.'

He smiled. 'Only one?' Then he realised she'd had to steel herself to ask. 'Tell me. Anything.'

She had been wearing a scarf over her hair as she had in the *etapes*. It was almost the first thing he had noticed about her, that small effort at elegance. Now she took it off and her hair, lank and unkempt from the years of privation, fell to her shoulders. 'I would like to go to a hair-dresser,' she said.

He frowned. 'But there's one in the lobby. You only have. . .' He stopped and, understanding, picked up the telephone and was put through to the hair-dresser. 'They can take you now,' he said and saw a look of part excitement, part apprehension on her face. 'I'll come down with you.'

At the door of the salon she clung to his hand, reluctant to leave him. 'Countess Kropotkin,' he told the receptionist, and she looked impressed. Alexa was led away. She looked over her shoulder as he stood at the door. He had waited until she had been seated and saw her slowly relax in the chair. He had waved reassuringly and she waved back.

Later, when he had returned to the hotel, he hardly recognised her. Her hair was drawn back into a shining knot at the nape of her neck and she looked five years younger. Her skin was glowing and he realised that she was wearing *maquillage*. She had on a new dress of turquoise silk that brought out the gold flecks in her eyes.

'Do you like it?' she said.

'It's magic! I think you look wonderful.'

He had placed money at her disposal when they arrived, but as far as he knew she had never used any.

'I saw the dress in a shop in the lobby when I was leaving the hair-dresser's.'

'Will you wear it out to dinner?'

She had hesitated, then said, 'If you want me to.'

From that moment, his life seemed to take on a new dimension. If he wasn't quite creating a personality, it was at least as though he was treating a palimpsest, bringing out what was there already. Now that she had taken her first tentative step into the new world, she grew in confidence. She began to go out by herself, not very far nor for very long at first, but increasingly. He felt that she enjoyed going out with him, too. He could hardly believe the change in her. It was both radical and eccentric. Sometimes she seemed to be a young girl, so great was her delight in a new blouse or pair of shoes; sometimes he saw in her the woman he would recognise a few years later, already gaining the confidence she would have when she married. Then abruptly, she would become uncertain; both images would disappear and she would shoot back into her shell and become the remote Alexa of the *etapes*. He realised how fragile her grip on her new life was and he trod carefully.

He wanted to lavish money and presents on her, but realised that excess might alienate her and so, as she gradually blossomed, he kept his excitement and his pleasure in her to himself. He accompanied her everywhere, even shopping for a completely new wardrobe. She, who had not seen such creations for years, agonised over styles, colours, materials. He might have bought whole shops for her, but instead he discussed the options, helped her to make her choice. Again this increased her confidence.

Once they had left Russia she had retreated from making decisions, now the decision-making machinery began to work again. In all the time they had been in Siberia, he could not remember her smiling. Now she smiled often, and each time

135

he felt it as a sudden flash of excitement, like an electrical impulse.

At this time, too, she began to put on weight. 'I eat like a camel,' she said one day in a restaurant.

'Like a horse,' he said.

'Do you say like a horse?' She laughed. 'This dress is new. Soon I may not be able to get into it.'

As she put on weight, her beauty increased. Her face became less gaunt, her thighs and buttocks were outlined under the skirts of her new dresses.

He wanted people to see him with her. One evening he took her to a recital at Carnegie Hall. The tickets were a hundred dollars apiece in aid of war funds. It seemed that every elegant woman and smartly dressed man in Manhattan was there. Yet he was aware that when Alexa entered heads turned towards them and eyes filled with speculation and, in some cases, envy. He was reminded of the night Guy had walked into Kettner's in London with Elizabeth Lytton, but this time he was the focus of attention. It was a heady feeling.

The pace of their lives accelerated and he found himself caught up in an emotion beyond anything he had anticipated. He was obsessed and infatuated with her. Her fascination for him was overwhelming. She reminded him of a diamond called the Southern Cross. He remembered that when he had bought it as a lump of opaque glass, dirty and uncut, it had only hinted at beauty, but once cut and polished it had taken everyone's breath away. He had recognised a unique quality in the Alexa of the *etapes*, in her grey prison clothes, now he knew that his judgement had not been wrong. He had once owned the Southern Cross. Would he ever own Alexa?

Time was not on his side. He was more than ten years older than she and there was an urgency in him he found difficult to control. He wanted her physically, but he also wanted more. There was deep in him the old Jewish need for family, line, survival. He wanted a child by her and wanted to see it grow up before it was too late. So far he had not tried to touch her, always telling himself not to rush things in case she turned against him. He knew there was a ruthlessness in her, otherwise she could never have survived her past in Siberia. He could not have born her rejection, for he felt it would have been total and humiliating.

At that period of the war it was difficult to get berths in a ship bound for Britain and the weeks in New York lengthened into one month, then two. They went to the opera and to symphony concerts, to theatres and restaurants, and Alexa absorbed it all as though she were a traveller from some far distant place where civilised values had not penetrated – which, in fact, was true. In those days of spring they drove out onto Long Island or across into New Jersey to Atlantic City. They seemed to enjoy themselves so much that he found it difficult to exclude the possibility that a mutual feeling had begun to grow between them. Increasingly, he wanted her to himself, away from his office and staff and acquaintances. He felt that if they were alone, their relationship might ripen quickly. He suggested that she might like to see Florida or take a train to the West Coast. He was prepared for a refusal, but instead she said, 'Take me north.'

'It will be colder.'

'I know.'

They had gone to New England and spent a few days in Provincetown on Cape God. It was much colder than New York and winter seemed to linger. The village was charming in a European manner, the food good, their rooms comfortable, the scenery beautiful.

On the second afternoon, they walked along the beach in the direction of Race Point. There was an icy wind off the sea and the immense sky was a flat, uninterrupted grey. She stopped and turned towards the water and let the wind blow in her hair and she seemed unconscious of his presence.

After a while he said, 'What are you thinking of?'

She shook her head.

'You look as though you've come to the edge of the world without finding what you're looking for.'

'Does one ever?' It was as though a shutter had closed behind her eyes.

'It depends how much you want it.'

'Do you think you can say, "I want that, so I will have it?" '

'Up to a point, yes.'

'What point?'

'Whether it's available.'

The beach was littered with flat stones and he picked one up and skimmed it across the surface of the water, something he had not done since he had walked along the Dnieper as a child with his grandfather.

'You're lucky if that's your experience,' she said. 'With me, it has been the opposite.' He waited for her to continue, but she turned and began to walk again.

He caught up with her and held her by the arm. 'Alexa, I want to talk to you.'

He felt her muscles stiffen under his fingers and regretted his impulse. 'You must have known these past weeks that things between us – at least, I mean, on my part, that things had. . .' He found, under her penetrating stare, that his thoughts did not translate easily into words.

'You want to make love to me?'

'Of course. . .'

'But why not?'

The way she spoke made it sound like an acceptable quid pro quo, a payment for services rendered.

'Not just that. I want more.'

'Perhaps there is no more.'

'I don't believe that.'

She walked on and he stayed by her side. 'You're not helping, Alexa.'

'I've tried to.'

'No, I don't think you have. You know what I'm trying to say, but you're putting me in the wrong, somehow.'

'Perhaps that's what should happen once in a while to people who always get what they want.'

That night after dinner she said, 'Do you wish to come to my room?'

'No.'

They motored back to Boston. The weather was brilliant, but cold. They lunched in an oak-beamed restaurant overlooking the sea near Plymouth, and had the place almost to themselves. They had spoken little on the drive. The sunlight on the sea, a martini before lunch, the blazing log-fire, the general atmosphere of cosiness, seemed to relax her, for she said, 'You are very serious today.'

It was unlike her to make statements that might lead on to personal subjects.

'I was thinking about yesterday,' he said. 'I put things badly.'

'How would you put them today?'

He said, rashly: 'I could say I want to look after you, but that would be the wrong way round. Ever since coming back from Russia I've known that my life lacked purpose and direction. I work, but for whom? I've built up New Chance, but for whom?'

She said, 'I'd be no good to you, David.'

'Let me judge that.'

'There's only half of me left, if that.'

'He's not coming back, Alexa. You've got to believe that.'

She shook her head. He wanted to say something more, but the waiter brought their fried clams and the moment was gone. Other people entered the booths on either side of them. There was no chance to talk without being overheard.

They finished their lunch and walked through the cold sunshine to the motor. He helped her in, tucked the rug around her legs, then sat beside her. After a few seconds silence he said urgently: 'The most important thing is that I love you. I didn't dare allow myself to think of such a thing until we were clear of Russia, but it started a long time ago.'

She put out a gloved hand and he held it.

'You have all your life to live,' he said. 'You can't let the past engulf you. At the moment, you're not living, you're drifting. For God's sake, don't you understand? I love you and want you and need you!'

When she did not respond, he started the car and drove off. They had not gone far when he felt her hand come to rest on his thigh. He put his own over it. 'Give me a little more time,' she said.

'As much as you want.'

A month later they were married and spent their honeymoon in the S.S. *Richmond Bay*, in a convoy bound for Liverpool. Maxim Perfiliev had elected to remain in the city that appealed to him so much, and Cyril remained in the Colorado sanatorium, where his progress was slow but sure.

[2]

The Constantia Valley, near Cape Town, filled with expatriate English, was as snobbish as the shires of England. Consequently, a Russian Countess and her husband, a wealthy knight, were in great demand. There were visits from neighbours and visits to neighbours and there were acquaintances from London wintering at the Cape whom David felt obliged to entertain. Alexa played her part in all his arrangements and when he looked down the long dining-table at Constantia House – a room glowing with stink-wood and yellow-wood and old Cape silver – towards her at the far end, he knew he had fulfilled a dream.

Sometimes the mixture of people in their drawing-room would suggest a European *salon*, but the impression was superficial. The conversation concerned grapes and wine and servants and local politics, none of which interested Alexa in the slightest. Sometimes she allowed her feelings to show and eventually she acquired a reputation for arrogance.

As the summer wore on, there were other visitors. These formed the umbilical cords which bound David to the New Chance mine in Kimberley, six hundred miles to the north. There was, for instance, Crossley Nash, his personal assistant. He was in his early thirties, a quiet, sharp-faced man, who sat at the dinner-table without saying much, but who never missed a point in the conversation. David had not met anyone who worked so hard, and even at Constantia House his light would burn far into the night. But as a visitor, he did not add much of a festive note to proceedings. This was left to J.J. 'Jimmy' Cairns, who came down to Cape Town to fetch his ailing wife, Molly, from the mailship which had brought her from England. Jimmy turned Constantia House upside down.

He was a big, bluff, genial man who wore loud tweeds in

140

winter and baggy cotton drill in summer. He seemed always to be laughing or on the point of laughter and when he did burst out, he completely closed his eyes, so intense was his enjoyment. He was almost bald and the last of his thin grey hair was brushed over his sunburnt skull. He smoked constantly – dark brown Trinchinopoly cheroots – and drank prodigious amounts of whisky, most of which seemed to burst out in perspiration. His face was highly coloured and his eyes, embedded in wrinkles, were deep blue. His energy was boundless and he found it difficult to be idle. He seemed to be constantly in motion, stirring up others, carrying them off with him or leaving them gasping.

He had known David since the early days of the Kimberley diggings and was now the general manager of the New Chance Mine. He liked nothing better than to sit down with a bottle of whisky and reminisce about the old days, telling stories to Alexa and Jewel of some of the characters he had known and some of the times he'd had.

He stayed a week at Constantia House and in that time he organised more entertainment than they'd had all summer. On his arrival he instantly suggested that, it being Saturday, they went out to lunch and then on to the races. Alexa at first demurred, but it was like trying to say no to a grizzly bear. He swept the four of them up and drove them to a beach restaurant, then to the race-course.

David had at first worried about what Alexa's reaction might be, but he was delighted to see that she was enjoying herself as she discussed weights and form with Jimmy.

'You have a real gambler here,' he told David. 'You'd better watch your cash.'

She smiled and said, 'I used to go to the races in St. Petersburg before. . .' She stopped. There was a moment's silence, then Jimmy said, 'Come on, Alexa, we can't stand here. We must get our bets down.' And he drew her away.

'I'd forgotten how energetic he was,' Jewel said. 'I hope Alexa can keep up with him.'

'She'll keep up. He'll do her the world of good.'

The pace set that first day was never allowed to slacken. There were visits to nightclubs, the opera, restaurants. He even organised a sheep roast. Soon they were all complaining of exhaustion, but David thought he had never seen Alexa looking better.

Then they went down to the docks to meet Molly Cairns, and suddenly it was all over. David, who had known her for years, was shaken at the sight of her. She had been a woman whose appetite for enjoyment matched her husband's. Now she was old and frail and Jimmy looked after her like the child they had never had. It was clear that she was desperately ill. He had sent her first to Zurich and then to London. She had been in a sanàtorium in Switzerland for several months, then gone into hospital in London for an operation. Now the prognosis was only fair.

They left on the noon train for Kimberley and the Kades trooped back to Constantia House tired, exhilarated and sad all at once.

Sophie was christened in February and they had a large party to wet her head. Before it Alexa said, 'I wish it were only the three of us. A child is being christened, that's all. It's a personal thing.'

'It's not often someone my age gets to attend the christening of his own child. It's a time for celebration.'

Alexa's appearance at the christening was brief. She attended the service, carrying Sophie, but later at the party excused herself and it was Jewel who held the child at the centre of an admiring crowd. David had been looking forward to the occasion for weeks and Alexa's absence spoilt it for him. For the first time since they had been married he let his irritation at her behaviour show. After the guests had left he found her reading in her sitting-room. He stood by the window, staring out over the valley.

'Are you angry?' she said.

'What did you expect?'

'I'm sorry, David, it's just that sometimes your friends. . .'

'They're not *my* friends, they're *our* friends.'

'However you like to describe them. They make such a big fuss over small things. This isn't the first baby to be born and won't be the last. But for weeks everyone has been talking about the christening, what presents to give, what to wear, what lovely names for the baby. . .'

'Don't you bother to christen babies in St. Petersburg?' he said acidly.

She did not reply and he said, 'What did you do there, anyway? You never speak about it. You never touch on the past at all. At first I thought I understood, but now I think it's unhealthy.'

'Unhealthy?' There was a flash of anger in her eyes.

'It's as though you push it away. Bury it. As though you're afraid of it.'

She closed the book with a snap and stood up. 'I don't want to discuss it.'

'That's the trouble. You never want to discuss anything. We circle each other like strangers. We make no real contact. I feel that after all this time I hardly know you. We sleep together, we have a child. We *made* the child together. And yet. . .' He tried to check himself. He knew he was suddenly launched into deep water and that the usual control was missing. He floundered on. 'I can't seem to get through to you. I have your body, but not *you*, somehow.'

'I told you in America there was only half of me.'

'It's not enough! Can't you understand? I want what's inside the body!'

He was holding her by the shoulders and now the anger coalesced into something different and he bent and kissed her, crushing her body against his, forcing open her lips, tasting her saliva.

She tried to twist away, but he gripped her. He heard fabric rip as he fumbled at the front of her blouse. She fought him. He felt the soft warmth of her naked breast. Then, abruptly, she stopped fighting. Her arms dropped to her sides and she stood passively, obedient, a receptacle for his flesh.

He turned away and went into his own room, slamming the door behind him. For the rest of that day, which should have been one of the happiest of his life, he kept to his study, filled with self-disgust, but also with a feeling of surprise that his own coolness had been breached by feelings so powerful that they thrilled and at the same time alarmed him by their very unfamiliarity.

The atmosphere between them remained strained for several days then, one evening, there was a telephone call from Kimberley. They were sitting on the big verandah in the dusk having an aperitif before dinner, and David was called to his study. He came back looking troubled and said, 'I have to go to Kimberley sooner than I planned.'

'Why?' Jewel said.

'That was Crossley. There's been a problem with smuggling. We've been working on it for weeks. It's on the increase and now it's beginning to affect the price of stones. It's got to be stopped.'

'Smuggling what?' Alexa said.

'Diamonds. What else?'

'I thought perhaps brandy or. . .'

'You're thinking of smugglers who operate on ships. These are a different breed. They smuggle diamonds out of the mine to sell. It's been going on since the industry started and there seems no way we can stop it completely.'

'How do they get the stones out?' she asked.

'They used to swallow them and recover them afterwards.'

'After. . . ? Oh, yes, I see.'

'That's why we keep our mine-workers, or the black ones anyway, in compounds. They stay there until their contracts end.'

'And the white ones?'

'We search them. Keep an eye on them. The system isn't perfect, of course. You can't anticipate everything. People have gone to the most extreme lengths. We've had cases of men cutting themselves, placing diamonds in the cuts, then sewing up the flesh. They stick them up their noses, into their ears. They'll do anything to try and hide a good stone.'

He turned to Jewel and said. 'Would you like to come back with me and see the old place?'

Jewel looked swiftly at Alexa, then said, 'If you want me to.'

Later, when Jewel had gone to bed, Alexa said, 'You didn't ask me if I would like to come with you to Kimberley.'

'It never occurred to me that you'd want to. It'll be as hot as hell and, anyway, I thought that sort of business trip would bore you.' But they both knew that the real reason dated from the day of the christening.

'I don't get bored.'

He was about to remind her of her attitude to their friends, but decided against it. 'I'd like nothing better,' he said. 'I'd love to show you Kimberley. But don't expect too much. It's only a small town in the desert.'

The following day, when his secretary was making their arrangements, Jewel said, 'On second thoughts, I don't think I will come, if you don't mind.'

'Oh?'

'It's so beautiful here now that the south-easter has dropped, and Kimberley will be so dusty and hot.'

'That's not the real reason, is it?'

She smiled. 'When will I have a baby to myself again?'

[3]

The town of Kimberley had come a long way in the fifty years or so since the world's largest pipe of diamonds had been discovered under the surface of the semi-desert. In place of the old tent town there were rows of Victorian bungalows with painted corrugated-iron roofs and deep verandahs, with flowers in the yards and small lawns in front which had to be watered every day.

The Kades reached Kimberley in the early evening of a late summer's day when the sting had gone out of the heat. It was covered by a haze of grey-blue smoke as evening meals were cooked on a thousand coal stoves. There was no wind and the air felt warm as it brushed across the skin. As he often did when he came to Kimberley, David thought of the first time he had seen it. He had walked into it then and the haze over the diggings had been dust.

They were met at the station by Crossley Nash, who took them to the North-Western Hotel in the centre of the town, where a suite was kept for David when he was in the country. They bathed and changed and David said, 'Crossley's been busy and we have a pretty full diary. There's dinner tonight at the Victoria Hotel and then. . .' He glanced at his small pocket diary. '. . . lunch tomorrow in the board-room and. . .'

He saw Alexa's face fall and said, 'Most of it is in your honour. They want to do well by the chairman's wife.'

'Does it have to be like that? David, couldn't we be together? Just the two of us, for a little while? It's the week-end. Do they all work at week-ends? Don't they have wives and families?'

'Of course they have.'

'Don't *they* want to be together? Why should we ruin their free days? Then on Monday we go to the luncheons and the dinners and you do what business you have come to do and you are Sir David and I am Lady Kade.'

He felt a moment of pleasure that she would want to be with him and that she, normally so reserved, had suggested it.

He had sensed a difference in her when they were in the train. The journey had been hot and dry and boring. Most of it lay across the huge semi-desert called the Karoo. She had been content to read or talk, to watch him as he worked at his papers, or simply to stare at the brown landscape that passed slowly by.

He had glanced up once and caught her looking at him, and she had smiled. It was a rare moment of shared intimacy.

Now he said, 'I can tell Crossley to cancel everything until Monday.'

He kept a change of clothing in Kimberley and the following day he put on an old cotton drill suit and a Panama hat and showed her what there was of the town and the Big Hole on the outskirts, nearly half a mile in diameter, in which he and thousands of others had dug and sweated and tried to make their fortunes.

They had worked in burning heat and bitter winter cold until the skin on their hands had cracked and their lips had cracked and each day had been a kind of torture.

From the Big Hole, he took her to the old cemetery. It was a derelict-looking place. Most of the graves were covered by dead weeds. It lay on the slope of a slight hill with the sun winking on the occasional jam-jar filled with everlastings that decorated a few of the graves. Sand had covered the paths. Few of the gravestones were upright and most graves were unmarked mounds of earth. He walked up and down in the heat until he found what he was looking for. This grave was neatly kept and outlined with granite blocks. The chiselled letters in the stone were legible. The inscription read:

JAMES MCIVER SANDIESON
Born Moy, Inverness-shire
Died Kimberley, Cape Colony
'He was a Digger'

Underneath that, in fresher lettering, was the sentence:

'Original owner of New Chance Mine'

'That's where it all started,' David said. 'He was dying when we got here. We bought his claim. He hadn't taken much out of it.'

'You had the luck,' she said.

'Yes, we had the luck. He died and we didn't.'

The night was hot and they lay in the big double bed with the windows open, listening to the sounds of the town.

'In the old days you'd be lucky if you got to sleep before midnight on a Saturday. Lucky if you didn't hear a gun go off, someone getting shot, glass breaking, police whistles. Now listen.'

All they could hear was an occasional motor or the footsteps of home-going pedestrians.

'It's become very sedate,' he said. And he thought: like me.

He woke early. The air entering the room on the grey morning light was the cool air of the desert. Alexa was lying with her back to him. He knew he had only to stretch out an arm and she would come to him, for she had never refused him. Even as he looked down at her, she twitched slightly in a dream.

Lying there, thinking of her, looking at her, wanting her, he felt a surge of affection and love, and with it a superstitious gratitude. To have someone like Alexa in his life, not only Alexa, but Sophie as well, was something he had hardly dared hope for. He told himself that these were things that outweighed the sexual problems.

He remembered the first night of their honeymoon in the Bradford House Hotel in Boston. She had been as stiff as a stone statue and afterwards she had apologised.

He had said, 'Don't ever say you're sorry. It's almost never good the first time. People have to get used to each other.'

147

Now his hand went out to pull her towards him, but he checked himself. At that moment, he did not want mere acquiescence. Instead he slipped quietly out of bed and went into the next room and rang for tea.

After breakfast he ordered a picnic hamper and they drove out into the desert and soon left the town behind. 'I can remember this road when it was just a track,' he said as the car bounced over the gravel corrugations.

After a while they came to a gate in the barbed-wire fence and turned onto a farm track that wound in and out of low hills. A line of trees indicated the course of a river.

They went through several gates. As the car approached each one, black children came racing across the veld to open it. They stood, staring at the motor, their skins dusty, their clothes ripped and patched and ripped again. David threw them a few coppers. There was a swift scrabbling in the dust, raised voices from those who had lost, and then the motor lurched forward. Finally they came to a large brick bungalow surrounded by gum-trees and acacias and what had once been a lawn. It was shuttered and locked and David wandered along the side, looking in at the windows. 'This used to belong to Michael and Jewel. They sold it to the mine when they moved to England. We use the farm to raise sheep to feed the black workers.'

He drove a short distance and pointed to another house. This was a ruin. Trees and bushes had grown through the mud walls and a grape vine had crawled over what had once been a verandah. 'This was the first homestead in the valley,' he said, opening the car door for Alexa. 'It was called Portuguese Place. Jewel's father married the daughter, a woman called Marie Delport. I used to come out here quite often.' He took off his Panama and began to fan his face. 'It always was hot here in summer.'

They walked down to the river, David carrying the hamper and a rug. They found a stretch of soft green grass in the shade of a weeping willow next to a long clear pool with a sandy bottom.

'They used to call this the Breakfast Pool,' he said.

As she unpacked the hamper he looked at the hard-boiled eggs and dry beef sandwiches. 'It's not much of a feast, but the wine should be cool.' Two bottles of Tattinger had been packed in ice in a wooden cooler. The ice had melted but the wine was still cold. They drank thirstily. He remembered how she used to drink *kvas* in Russia, how she was often the first in line for it. There had been a kind of frenzy then, a need to blot out not only the past, but the present. With Zagarin's death and the escape from Russia, all this had changed.

They nibbled sandwiches and tried the eggs, but the food was unappetising in the heat. He opened the second bottle of wine and lay back on the rug, trying to settle his head comfortably on the hard ground.

'I wish I'd been here in the early days,' she said. 'I'd like to have known you then.'

Startled at her unusual directness, he pushed himself up on his elbows and looked at her.

'You're different here,' she said.

'In what way?'

'In Russia you seemed so strange. You spoke with the assurance that only men who have wealth and power can. Yet they treated you worse than they treated anyone else. Then you said that you would get us out, and you did. And in the middle of a war you said you would get us to New York and London, and you did. It was like a fairy-tale. When we got there, you were like an emperor. You actually did have money, houses, power, a family. You had told me about all these things in Russia, but I had not believed them. It was too difficult to believe in someone like you.'

'I don't understand. . .'

'I couldn't find *you*. Real people have weaknesses.'

'I have lots of those.'

She shook her head. 'Once we came here I began to see you as you might have been. When you were poor. When you were struggling. Look at this hat. It's old and stained. You would never wear such a hat in London, or even at the Cape.'

He inspected the old Panama. 'I've never thought about that. Well. . .' He raised his glass. 'Here's to the real me. I'm not sure you'd have liked the David Kade of the early days, though.' He lay back again and put the hat over his face.

It was the hottest part of the day. In the trees around them, doves were calling softly. He was drowsy with the wine. He closed his eyes and for a few moments drifted between wakefulness and sleep. The doves began to sound a long way away. Then he felt her hands on his trousers. Her fingers fretted with the buttons until she undid them. She pushed up his shirt then drew down his underpants. He raised his buttocks from the ground and she slipped the pants down around his knees. Then he felt her mouth.

His heart was racing, but he lay still. She had never done this before, the impetus had always come from him. He was savagely tumescent and elated at the same time. He stroked her hair. He felt her move up his body. She eased herself onto him and her mouth found his. He could not wait. He rolled over so that she was beneath him and he took her, there on the hard ground, experiencing a brutal joy he had not felt with her before.

When it was over he looked down at her and saw the perspiration on her face and the slackness of her muscles, the half-closed eyes, and knew that perhaps for the first time since their marriage he had reached the inner core and she had responded.

'I love you,' he said. 'Always remember that.'

She reached up and pulled his head down onto her shoulder and they lay like that until the sun found them through the branches and they had to move.

'Could we swim?' she said.

'Of course. I used to swim here often.'

They took their clothes off and swam in the cool water and later let the air dry their bodies and it was evening before they drove back to Kimberley.

That night as they put out the light she held him longer than usual and said, 'Thank you. I've been happier this week-end than I have for a long time.'

During the next few days they saw little of each other. David spent his time at the mine or in the office building in the Old Cape Road with Crossley Nash. A police captain called Diekes, of the local diamond squad, came to see him. The week-end became a memory only. He was irritable with the hotel staff.

One evening they went to dine with the Cairns, who lived in a large new house in a suburb. It was surrounded by well-watered lawns and jacaranda trees.

'There'll only be the four of us,' Jimmy Cairns said as he welcomed them. 'Molly doesn't feel up to large gatherings.' Some of his bluffness had gone and he seemed to have lost weight. His face was flushed and his speech was slightly slurred and David frowned as he saw the size of the whisky he poured for himself.

Molly was brought down to dinner by a uniformed nurse and David, who had been silent before dinner, did his best to take her mind off her illness by talking of shared experiences. But it was not a success. It was apparent that she was in pain, and she hardly touched her food. At the other end of the table Jimmy watched her with stricken eyes, drinking whisky throughout the meal. It was something of a relief to them all when the nurse took her back to her bedroom.

The three of them went into the drawing-room for coffee. It was a large room with French doors opening onto a wide, red-flagged verandah. Alexa refused a liqueur and Jimmy brought out a bottle of malt whisky and two glasses. While he was removing the foil he said, 'What did you think of her?'

David said, 'I thought she was looking a bit better.'

'That's a bloody lie and you know it. She's dying. Christ Almighty, anyone can see that. Sometimes I feel like taking a gun and putting her out of her misery. It'd be kinder. Still . . . it's not your *indaba*. There we are. Glenfiddich. That's a good drop of Scotch, not like the rotgut brandy we used to drink in the early days.'

'Not for me, thanks.'

'Don't be bloody silly, of course you'll have one. Here's to us. Survivors.'

David held up his glass and took a small sip. Cairns said, 'It won't hurt you.' Then to Alexa, 'David was always a careful chap. That's how he got where he has. Being careful. And taking his opportunity when it came. One day I'll tell you about opportunities.'

They left as soon as they could and neither said much on the way to the hotel. Crossley Nash was waiting for them. In spite of the heat he was dressed in a dark suit with waistcoat and a high collar. His sharp face was drawn and his eyes worried. 'I'm sorry to intrude at this time of night, but something's come up.'

'Don't make him work too hard,' Alexa said.

While she went up to the suite David and Nash sat in Nash's motor.

'Well?'

'We know who the smuggler is. The police trapped an illicit diamond buyer last night and he talked.'

'Who?'

'Jimmy Cairns.'

'What!'

'It's true.'

'It can't be.'

'I'm afraid it is. The police came to me this afternoon and I went to see his bank manager. I've done him a couple of favours in the past. He let me look at Jimmy's statements.'

'And?'

Nash passed him a set of pages. 'It's all down here. Stock market speculations that went bust, horses that finished last. It's being going on for more than a year.'

'What a bloody mess.'

'Recently he's been getting greedier.'

'What's the total loss from the mine?'

'Sixty thousand. At least, that's what's gone into his account during the period.'

David sat quite still for a long time and Nash did not disturb his thoughts. Then he said, 'Thank you, Crossley. You've done well. I wish you hadn't, but there it is. Tell Jimmy I want to see him here at the hotel tomorrow. Then get some sleep. I might need you later.'

Alexa was in bed when he reached the suite. He poured himself a whisky and sat sipping it by the window. She came into the sitting-room. 'Bad news?'

'The worst.'

'Was it about the smuggling?'

'It's Jimmy Cairns.'

'Oh, David! Are you sure?'

'Pretty sure. He's been at it for more than a year.'

'What are you going to do?'

He rose. 'I don't know.' He turned and stared out of the window, but saw nothing. 'I'll have to put a stop to it.'

'Do the police know?'

'So far it's not their business. There's no law against carrying diamonds out of a mine, especially if you're the general manager. Selling them is illegal, but he hasn't been caught selling them. I'm going to deal with this myself.'

'It's a bad time for them.'

'I realise that.'

She put an arm around his shoulders. 'Poor David.'

He shook his head slowly. 'A bloody thief. You know he went bust once? Absolutely flat. And I took him on and gave him every opportunity. Damn it all, he was sitting in my house at the Cape, drinking my wine, and stealing from me!'

'Don't think about it that way. Remember he's your friend. You've known each other half a lifetime. Don't let it end in bitterness.'

'I suppose you're right. What usually happens in cases like this is that the person is moved sideways. Maybe I can find something for him. Somewhere he won't be tempted.' She kissed him on the cheek. 'It must be like kissing a hedgehog,' he said, smiling wearily.

Jimmy Cairns came to the hotel at three o'clock on a dry, hot day. He ambled around the suite in his crumpled cotton drill, taking in the decorations and the furniture.

'They do things pretty well,' he said. 'I've always liked this place. Food all right?'

'About the same as always,' David said. 'The hotter the day, the hotter the meal. How's Molly today?'

'As well as can be expected. I think that's the phrase.' The bitterness was back in his voice.

'Is there nothing at all that. . . ?'

'Do you think I haven't tried everything?' he paused, then in a quieter voice, said, 'How's Alexa liking it? Kimberley, I mean.'

'Surprisingly well. I took her to see the sights, such as they are, and we picnicked out at Portuguese Place. She's gone to have her hair done today. What about some tea?'

'I'll have a whisky.'

'Help yourself.'

Cairns poured himself a measure and added water from the terra-cotta 'monkey'. 'Not drinking?'

'It's a bit early for me.'

'Still being careful.' He smiled. The hostility of the night before had not quite dissipated. David ignored him and Cairns said, 'Is this a social meeting?'

'Not really. I want to talk about the mine. Before the war, when diamonds boomed, we put on a lot of fat. Now that things have swung the other way, we have to slim down.'

'We're modernising as fast as we can. We've got new drills and crushers on order. They'll cut the work force.'

'Yes, I know. But we need to look at other areas.'

'Meaning?'

'The management.'

'I wouldn't have said we were overmanned there.'

'I think we are, Jimmy.'

'Now hang on . . . wait a minute. . .' He pushed himself out of the chair and poured another drink. 'I don't think I like what I'm hearing. If you want to take an axe to my staff I'll fight you all the way.'

David did not reply and Cairns stared at him for some moments. His brick-red face became blotchy, some areas turning a dirty white. 'Me?' he said softly.

'No one's going to be dismissed. We thought. . .'

'We?'

'I, then. I thought that natural wastage would suffice. In your case, with Molly so ill. . .'

'Leave Molly out of it.'

'. . . you might think of early retirement.'

'Retirement?' He looked at David blankly. 'Retire? Are you saying I'm not up to the job?'

'Of course I'm not, but we all have to retire some time.'

'Because even if I was, you wouldn't know. You're like an absentee landlord. You live with your snobbish friends in London, or in your house at the Cape surrounded by your vines. You get out of Kimberley as quickly as you can. It's we who get our hands dirty, not you.'

David had been holding himself in, but found it becoming

increasingly difficult. 'What I do isn't in question,' he said. 'It's what you do.'

'What's that supposed to mean?'

'For Christ's sake, Jimmy, I'm giving you a chance to get out with a decent pension, a chance to look after Molly. Take her away from this place. Go somewhere by the sea.'

'You're giving *me* a chance?'

'Do you think we're all blind and deaf and dumb? Do you think that because I'm not here I don't know what's going on?'

Cairns shook his big head from side to side. 'You'll have to explain that. I don't know what the hell you're talking about.'

'Don't say I didn't give you your chance. I'm talking about sixty thousand pounds deposited in your bank account in just over a year, over and above your salary and bonuses. And don't tell me you won it on the horses or the stock-market, because I know you didn't.'

Cairns leant back in the chair. His eyes slid away from David and fixed themselves on the far wall. After a moment he said, 'So that's what it's all about.'

'Yes.'

'How did you find out?'

'I don't think that matters.'

'It was Nash, wasn't it, the young prick? Pawing over my statements. That's illegal, you know.'

'I know.'

'Well, there it is. . .' He smiled confidingly.

'You seem to think it's a trifling matter.'

'Listen, David, you're a man of the world. You know what it's like here. Everybody does a bit of smuggling now and then. I mean, when we started off here the niggers used to steal from us. They used to swallow the stones or stick them up their arses. Everyone was in the smuggling business and the illicit diamond-buying business. It's part and parcel of this place, of the whole country, for that matter. It's ridiculous making laws saying that private persons can't buy or sell diamonds. There are places on the west coast where you can bend down and pick the damn things up – then they slap you in gaol if you try to sell them. They're asking for it.'

155

'Not *they*,' David said. 'It's not illicit diamond-buying I'm talking about, it's smuggling stones from the mine you work for.'

'Don't tell me you're going to miss a few stones.'

'You seem to be taking it very calmly.'

'You're making a great fuss about nothing.'

'I'm talking about the general manager of one of the biggest mines in Kimberley, smuggling stones like a poor white or a black.'

'That's a bloody awful thing to say.'

David felt his anger begin to get the better of him. If Cairns had showed the slightest sign of remorse he might have felt differently. 'You're worse than a poor worker. You're stealing from yourself. And you're stealing from me.'

'That's it, isn't it? It's not so much the stealing, it's the fact that they're *yours*. Everything is *yours*, haven't you any idea why I did it? Don't you have any understanding?'

'That's what I'm waiting to hear.'

'Can't you even imagine how much the bills have been for Molly, or are you so bloody wealthy that you've forgotten what real money is like when you have to earn it?'

'I knew you'd say that. I knew you'd use her as your excuse. Well, it won't do, Jimmy. You've been losing heavily on both the horses and the stock-exchange. No one knows yet except Crossley and me. You've got a chance to. . .'

'I won't retire!'

'I'll make you, then.'

Cairns rose. 'Do you think I'm going to take this sort of shit from you?'

David looked at him for a moment and then said, 'Goodbye, Jimmy.'

He sat for a long time by the open window after Cairns had left, then he poured himself a strong whisky. He felt drained and weak. His anger had always been cold, but none the less savage for that.

He telephoned Nash and discussed with him the gist of the interview. He did not want to be alone, yet he did not want to be with people, either. He put on his Panama and went into the hot afternoon streets, and walked. He walked for more than two hours, criss-crossing the town, north to south, east to west. Occasionally he was greeted by an acquaintance, but did not reply. Once, thirsty, he stopped in a rough bar and ordered lemonade. There were half-a-dozen men drinking beer who smiled with derision, but he did not notice them. It was evening before he returned to the hotel. The anger had passed and he was exhausted and depressed. He refused food and took a drink into the bedroom. Alexa followed and, sensing he did not wish to discuss the meeting with Cairns, said, 'Turn over and I'll rub your neck.'

She gently massaged the muscles and after a while said, 'Why don't you take off your clothes.'

'I'm afraid I wouldn't be much good tonight.'

'I didn't mean that. You don't have to prove yourself every time.' They lay in each other's arms and he was asleep in a matter of moments.

The following morning he closeted himself in his office with Nash. 'If it wasn't for Molly I'd sack him,' he said.

'That would cause a stink. The town's too small.'

'The hell with that. I started here when the place was a tent town, when the few buildings there were didn't have wooden floors. I'm as much part of this town as anyone — more in fact. If it wasn't for New Chance hundreds would be on the bread line. No, I'm not going to worry too much about the town. But it would kill Molly off.'

'Why not send him to Durban on compassionate leave? The company owns a couple of houses there. Let him stay on in one until his wife dies, *then* if he won't resign, sack him. By that time he'll realise there's no way back.'

'I want him out now,' David said. 'I won't have him in the building. Where is he, by the way?'

'I haven't seen him.'

'Get his things together. Have a letter typed . . . no, you'd better type it yourself. A letter of resignation. Leave the date off, but get him to sign it. If he won't, then tell him he's out without a pension. Tell him I don't owe him a damn thing.'

'What about his wife? I mean, he'll need money for medical bills and day-to-day living.'

'Let him sell his house. You know, Crossley, the word "smuggling" doesn't really describe what he's been doing. It softens it. Smugglers have a sort of romantic aura about them. This was stealing. Jimmy's a thief. He was stealing my property just as if he'd come into my house and taken things from my drawers. It makes me feel sick to think of it.'

Alexa had left a message at the desk that she was in the garden at the back of the hotel. It was not a garden in the true sense, but an area of gravel paths edged with bricks and dotted with pepper trees. She was sitting on a bench under one of the trees and her face was like stone. She looked up and smiled briefly as he joined her.

'You look as though you'd seen a ghost,' he said.

'Jimmy was here.'

'I don't want to see him.'

'He came to see *me*.'

David frowned. 'Why you?'

'To beg for his job.'

'But what's that got to do with you?'

'He said you'd listen to me. David, you should have seen him. I think he'd been drinking all night. His face looked like dirty water. His hands were shaking. He even cried. It was terrible.' She was silent for a moment, then said, 'I saw a man beg once. At Kara. His child was sick and he asked the prison governor if he could visit him. A boy. Seven years old. His face was also grey. And his hands shook. He went down on his knees and begged. But he was refused. I've never forgotten that.'

It was one of the few times he had heard her recall the past, but now the circumstances made him less interested in it than he might have been, less sympathetic.

'What did you tell him?'

'I told him I'd talk to you.'

'You shouldn't have said that! You've given him hope.'

'Why not? That's all he has.'

'He stole from me.'

'People do such things. No one is perfect.'

'Alexa. . .'

'It's true. Anyway, he said he wants to keep his job, not so much for himself, but for Molly. He said what she has to face is bad enough.'

'When I offered him the chance to resign yesterday because

158

of Molly's health he said, "Leave Molly out of it." I think perhaps he was right.'

'But you can't leave her out. The town is small, you've said so yourself. She'll hear about it eventually. People talk. Why has Jimmy Cairns resigned? They'll ask. And someone will say there are rumours about smuggling. It will get about.'

'He's hiding behind Molly now. He's making her the excuse for what he did. But she isn't. I paid him well. He could have taken care of everything on his salary and bonuses. But he gambled on the horses and on the stock-exchange. You can't have it both ways.'

She was silent for a moment, then said, 'Haven't you ever done anything you were ashamed of?'

He thought he saw contempt on her face and said angrily, 'You don't understand how things work in Kimberley. Everything depends on your reputation. When I first came here diggers said, "Watch out for Kade, he's a Jew." But I became a digger like them and then I began to deal in stones. I never did anything dishonest and there were plenty of times I could have got away with it. I knew I had to build a reputation. That was everything. In this business there are no contracts. People shake hands, give their word, and if their word is no good, then nothing is good.'

Two days later Alexa left for the Cape alone. David stayed on to help Crossley clear up the mess Cairns had created.

[4]

'You must be pleased to be home,' Jewel said to David. They were in the nursery at Constantia House and David was holding Sophie while Jewel brushed biscuit crumbs from the cot and picked up a rattle from the floor. Alexa had gone into town soon after lunch and it was time for Sophie's afternoon sleep. The curtains were closed and the room was in soft gloom.

'Never more so,' David said. 'Have you felt her grip?' He

159

offered Sophie his finger again. The small hand curled around it like a sea anemone.

'She's been wonderful,' Jewel said. 'It's been like having. . .' She broke off, then said, 'Did you miss her?'

'We both missed her, at least until the Cairns business.'

'Jimmy, of all people!'

'I couldn't seem to make Alexa understand that I couldn't let it go. If she'd had your upbringing and your experience of Kimberley, she would have realised. Even so, I blame myself for part of the trouble. I should never have lost my temper. She was fond of Jimmy. I should have remembered that.'

'So Jimmy has gone?' Jewel took Sophie from him and put her into the cot.

'We finally made him see sense. He's taken Molly to Durban. Crossley is acting general manager and when the board meets we'll confirm the appointment.'

When Sophie had settled they walked out into the vineyards. The early April day was still. The oaks were turning and the vine leaves were shades of tan and yellow. In the shade, the air had a crisp quality and the orange sunshine had lost its heat. Jewel was right, he was very pleased to be home, not only because it signalled the end of the Cairns affair, but because he had missed his family.

'How has Alexa been since she came back?' he said. He had arrived late the previous evening.

'She's been . . . restless,' Jewel said cautiously.

Later that day David found that, while they had been separated, Alexa's life had developed into a different pattern. She would spend a brief part of each morning with Sophie and then either lunch at the house or go into town. He gathered that she had her hair done, went to beauty salons, shopped, lunched with friends, some of whom were their neighbours. When he looked surprised at this she said, 'But you told me to make friends with them.' Which was true.

She was, at least on the surface, the Alexa he had known before Kimberley: polite, friendly, but without the warmth that he now knew lay inside her. There were moments when he could see how troubled she was. Her face was thinner, the smudges under the eyes larger. He knew there was something deeply wrong and assumed that she was still upset about Jimmy and Molly Cairns. One morning, as he took his tea into her bedroom, he began to talk about Cairns and saw a shadow cross her face. What could he say? He could not go on apologising, he could not repeat over and over again that what he had done was justified.

His own days were busy. He, Alexa, Jewel and Sophie were booked to sail from Cape Town on the *Sutherland Castle* in mid-May and he had many things to attend to first. But he put aside a part of each day for Sophie, his delight in the child growing stronger and stronger.

One warm autumn day he and Jewel took her to the promenade at Sea Point and pushed her pram along the front. David saw a newspaper-seller and crossed the road to buy a paper.

At that moment, a man and a woman came down the steps of one of the many boarding-houses that faced the sea and walked slowly away from him. They had not seen him. He stood for a moment like someone in catatonic shock. Then he began to tremble. He felt as though he might vomit, and moved to stand by the gutter. When he recovered, the couple had vanished.

He found himself back with Jewel.

Seeing his white face, she said, 'Are you all right? You look as though you've seen a ghost.'

'I think I have,' he said. 'I think I've just seen Guy Jerrold!'

'You couldn't have!'

'Alexa was with him.'

'It was someone who looked like him. Perhaps it wasn't Alexa, either.'

But the picture of the couple was firmly in his mind. The two of them, coming down the steps, their faces grim, then turning along the pavement, Guy talking and gesticulating as though trying to convince her of something. They were gestures and facial expressions he knew well. Guy had used them when he had argued the case for escaping even at the risk of Connie's life.

They hardly spoke on the way home. Jewel watched him with worried eyes. His face remained drawn and white and there was a sheen of perspiration over it. When they reached

Constantia House he said, 'When Alexa comes back I'll be in my study.'

He locked himself in and began to pace. The study windows commanded the loveliest of all views over the valley, down to the sea, but he was unaware of it. His mind was thousands of miles away from the Cape of Good Hope. Instead of vineyards and oaks he was seeing a dark green river, snow-covered banks, black trees; his ears, instead of hearing the soft catlike sounds of his shoes in the deep carpet, were full of the growling and grinding of the ice floes in the river, the shouts of his companions in the boat, the crack of the ice poles as they crashed against the floes; he was experiencing again that desperate journey to the sea. He could see the faces: Tungus Munku, with the straggling grey hair on his face, Cyril Hankey, Maxim Perfiliev, and beside him in the stern, the wrapped figure of Alexa, her face expressionless. And all the time they were fighting the ice, Guy Jerrold had been fighting his sickness. Connie . . . Zagarin . . . Belkonski . . . names he had thought were fading were suddenly there in the forefront of his mind.

He was a mass of conflicting thoughts and emotions: jealousy, astonishment, confusion, anger. But all were overshadowed by an appalling despair, a feeling of guilt for what he had done to Guy.

His mind picked over the details. The sweating face of Guy among the furs in which he had been wrapped; the decision to leave . . . they *had* to leave! Guy was not his only responsibility. What about Cyril? And Perfiliev? Were their lives not important? If they'd stayed, they might all have been dead now. And then he saw the picture of Alexa coming through the trees towards the boat. He had known then what she was going to say, felt it in his bones. He had almost willed her to say it, and she had.

But Guy had not died.

There were other pictures: Guy and Alexa together in the *taiga*, building a sleeping shelter for themselves; Guy and Alexa in the storm-bound hut; Guy and Alexa together in the *yurta* of Tungus Munku. Always Guy and Alexa.

He saw Alexa on the banks of the Green River near Kimberley, for the first time in their married life entering

162

totally his sexual world; Alexa rubbing the back of his neck on the bed in the North-Western Hotel. And, earlier, Alexa by herself on the frozen mud of the eastern sea, Alexa in New York. . . The pictures were like photographs on two facing pages of an album with Alexa as the common factor. He found himself wishing that Guy had died when he was supposed to have died, because he knew that neither his power nor his wealth were a match for the one thing that Guy possessed: his youth.

He stopped pacing and sat in his office chair and allowed his head to drop into his hands. It was always said that the worst enemy was the memory of a martyr or a dead lover. But how did you fight a lover who had returned from premature burial to claim what was rightfully his?

There was a knock at the door and he let Alexa in. 'Jewel said. . . Are you ill?'

He shook his head. 'I was at Sea Point this afternoon. We took Sophie for a walk in the sun. I saw you and Guy.'

She took out her hatpin, tossed her hat on his desk and sat down by the windows. 'Thank God you know. I've been wanting to tell you and at the same time wanting not to hurt you, and trying to find a way and trying to see what was best for everyone. Sometimes I've hardly known where I was. There never seemed to be an opportunity, a right time. But now you know, and I'm glad.'

'All those hair appointments and lunches with friends.'

'The lying was worst of all.'

'Tell me about him.'

She leaned back and chose her words carefully. It had happened, she said, three or four days after she had returned alone from Kimberley. She had been in the garden and seen a figure near the gate at the end of the long drive. She had not given the person a second thought, but he had not gone away and after a while she had walked down to see what he wanted.

'You've seen him,' she said. 'You know how changed he is. Thinner and older.'

'Yes.'

'Do I have to tell you what it was like to see him?'

'No.'

163

'I asked him to come in, but he wouldn't. He had come out by tram as far as Claremont, and then he had walked. His shoes were all dusty. We talked in the road and then we went to a tea-room and we talked again. I went with him back to the boarding-house and we went on talking.'

'We left him to die,' he said. 'Is he bitter?'

'Yes.'

'Of course he must be. Anyone would. I never thought . . . it just never. . .'

She looked down at her hands for a moment and then said, so softly that he could barely hear, 'We were all to blame.'

'No. At that stage Guy was my responsibility. I should have made certain. . . What happened to him?'

'He regained consciousness and the fever left him. Bou-Ta nursed him back to health. He says Tungus Munku went back on his agreement when he got back from Vladivostok and handed him over to the soldiers, but by then word had come about you all from St. Petersburg and his credentials had been established. Instead of arresting him, they gave him an escort to Vladivostok.'

He had stayed there at the Wiggins' house, but as the weeks passed and no Royal Naval vessel put into harbour, he had taken a passage to Singapore. By the time he reached England the war was over. His privations had left him weak and ill, and he had spent some time in a Naval hospital. But he had never really recovered and eventually, instead of being invalided out, had been allowed to resign with a small disability pension.

'What is his disability?' David asked.

'He suffers from severe depressions.'

'I can understand that!'

'After his resignation, all he wanted to do was find out what had happened to us.'

'To us?'

'Yes, us.'

'That couldn't have been too difficult.'

'No. He traced us, then he followed us here.'

'What about Elizabeth? Has he never mentioned Elizabeth Lytton to you?'

'He told me about her in Russia.'

She had recounted it as unemotionally as possible, but the pictures in his mind were vivid. 'What happens now?' he said.

'He wants me to leave you. To go back to London with him.'

'And you?'

'David, for God's sake, I don't know. I just don't know!'

'That's it? We both have to wait for you to make up your mind?'

'You make it sound easy. But that's your world: black and white, yes and no; come, go; do, don't. Can't you understand what has happened to him? We left him to die.'

'I understand that perfectly well. Perhaps as well as you. But life has moved on. We're no longer in Russia, we're no longer in a dwelling in the middle of the *taiga* with a man who has typhus. Decisions were made at the time. They were wrong, but the one thing I've learned in my life is that any decision is better than no decision. We thought he was dead. I'll never forgive myself for having left him, but that is what happened. And now we have different circumstances. You are my wife, we have a child. Suddenly, out of nowhere, Guy comes back into our lives to start a chain reaction. Other lives will be dislocated and other people will suffer.'

'He suffered.'

'The past is the past. Isn't that your philosophy? I'm your husband, yet I know almost nothing of your past because you've never chosen to tell me about it. I've respected the fact that you want it closed, finished. I understand there are terrible things in it that make you ache every time you recall them. But what difference is there between the past and the recent past, unless you yourself want to go with Guy?'

She was silent.

'Do you?' She shook her head from side to side, but it was not a negative. It was a movement that indicated uncertainty, unwillingness to say 'Yes,' or 'no,' or even, 'I don't know.'

'Do you?'

'You have every right to be angry, but you must give me time.'

'Do you love Guy?'

'It's more complicated than that. You were talking about

the past. No one can bury the past completely, but I was beginning to forget Guy. I was making a new life, which was something I never thought I could do. Guy was someone I never thought I could have. For me, in Russia, life was over. I was going to the mines at Kara and that's where I would have died. You once said you never thought you would be given a second chance. You were, and it was good fortune. Mine was a miracle. Guy was part of the miracle. Not all of it. You were part of it, too. I didn't ask Guy to love me. I'm older than he is. He already had a woman of his own. But it was me he wanted. Do you realise how long it had been since a man wanted me as Guy wanted me? To live with, to be with always. The guards in the fortress of Petropavlovsk in St. Petersburg . . . they didn't want to live with me. The men in the Forwarding Prison at Tyumen, or in the *etapes*, men like Zagarin . . . then suddenly from Mars, there was Guy.'

He went to stand by the window. 'It isn't possible to conduct life in a series of greys like this,' he said. 'You decided to be *my* wife, to have *my* child. In my world, we have to stick by those decisions.'

'That's all you talk about. *My* wife. *My* child. *My* diamonds. Decisions! Like the one you made about Jimmy Cairns!'

'It had to be made. It was the right one.'

She leaned back wearily.

'I want you to bring Guy out here,' he said.

'He won't come. He doesn't want to see you.'

'He's embarrassed?'

'You still don't understand. Let me explain in your terms: I was his woman before I was your woman.'

The words had the force of a blow.

She went on: 'He does not feel *embarrassed* about you. He doesn't feel he owes you anything. He hates you, David.'

'I'm damned if I'm going to sit back and watch a ghost from the past come and break up my family!'

'But it isn't like that. Or at least. . .'

'At least you don't know. That's putting it at its best, isn't it?'

'Yes.'

'If he won't come here, I'll go to him.'

'Please don't. Give me time. Let me try to work things out.'

'I think that the longer you take, the more difficult it will become. One has to act quickly and finally.'

'As you did with Jimmy.'

She pushed herself out of her chair and picked up her hat.

He heard her cross the hall and go upstairs to her suite. While they talked the room had gradually become dark. The nervous perspiration had dried on him and he felt chilled. It was as though he were hollow inside.

He bathed and changed and at about 8.30 he stood outside Alexa's room. The light was on and he heard movement inside. He went to the garage and got out one of the motors. He drove down the muddy streets until he came to the main road linking the southern suburbs with the city. It was almost deserted except for an occasional tram that clanked mournfully along the tracks. A north-wester was blowing and the squalls lashed down as he drove through the industrial suburbs and the centre of the city.

At Sea Point he could smell the brine and hear the roar of the waves as the wind drove them against the sea wall. He drove slowly along the deserted promenade looking for the boarding-house, but the surroundings appeared different at night. He continued all the way along the front, turned and came back the way he had been walking that afternoon. The houses reminded him of terraces he had seen in English Channel ports like Dover and Newhaven, solid brick houses, some double-fronted, of two and three storeys. He reached an area that was familiar and was able to visualise the ice-cream vendor's stand. On this side of the Peninsula the night was dry, although the promenade itself was being drenched with sea spray. There were lights on in the house and he went to the front door and rapped on the knocker.

A middle-aged woman with a fringed Spanish shawl round her shoulders answered the door and he asked for Guy Jerrold.

'That's the English gentleman,' she said. 'Is he expecting you?'

'Yes.'

'Room number four on the first landing.'

The door was wrenched open at his knock, and Guy stood there, looking at him. His face had been alight with expectation, but it went dead as he saw David. They regarded each other for some seconds before David said, 'May I come in?' Guy stood aside, and he entered the room.

It was large, with windows facing the stormy sea front, but it was poorly lit by gas and there was a dingy quality about it. The furniture was cheap. There was a double bed, a table with two upright chairs, a grate in which a coal fire burned smokily, two Morris chairs with wooden arms and stained cushions; in one corner a small screen partially hid a wash-stand bearing a bowl, jug and chamber pot. On the table was a bottle of whisky and a glass, next to it a plate containing half a pork pie and a couple of tomatoes.

Guy was dressed in the trousers and waistcoat of a tweed suit. He had taken off his collar and tie and his shirt was open at the neck. His hair was still worn long but it had not been trimmed for some time and was ragged at the back. He was still a handsome man, but he had lost that look of golden youth that David had seen in London. There were lines on his face now, his mouth was thin and his eyes were hard.

'How did you know where to find me?' he said. 'Did Alexa tell you?'

'I saw you together this afternoon. Pure chance.'

'Does Alexa know you've come.'

'No, but I've spoken to her. She asked me not to. Did you tell her to say that?'

'Why should I?'

'I thought you might perhaps feel some guilt.'

'Why would I feel guilty?'

'About what you're trying to do.'

Guy lit a cigarette from a packet of Officers' Mess on the chimney-piece, then leaned against the table. 'I think we should get one thing straight. I don't feel any guilt about what's happening. After what you did to me the best thing I can say is that I don't feel anything about you at all. As far as I'm concerned, you're a non-person.'

'I can understand that. In your circumstances I might feel the same way.'

'I'm not sure you do understand. Let me put it as simply

as I can. Alexa and I were very much in love. You left me to die and then you thought you would have her for yourself. But you were wrong on all counts.'

It was much what Alexa had said when she spoke about being Guy's woman first, and he wondered if that was her reasoning or Guy's.

'Circumstances change,' he said. 'Alexa is now my wife and we have a child. Our actions, or I should say your actions, will affect us all. You cannot simply say that earlier conditions prevail and make it right.'

'I've told you how I feel. I plan to marry Alexa.'

'Have you asked her?'

'Not yet. She isn't free.'

'And she won't be. Because, don't make any mistake, I won't give her a divorce.'

'I had hoped you would do the honourable thing.'

'Is it honourable to come between a husband and his wife? Is it honourable to cause that wife to commit adultery? Come, man, don't be a sophist.'

Guy shrugged.

David said, 'And Elizabeth Lytton? She's another whose life must be affected.'

'She's none of your business.'

It was like speaking to a wall, David thought. Guy's voice was a monotone, hardly rising or falling, as though he lacked any interest in what was being said and was simply waiting for him to go. All his gestures were brittle and nervous.

'Listen to me, Guy,' he said urgently, his eyes straying around the room. 'I don't know what your circumstances are, but I know you've resigned from the Navy. Do you think you could keep Alexa?'

Guy's face changed from its mixture of aloofness and arrogance, to anger. 'That's what it comes down to in your mind, doesn't it? Money! Let me tell you something: I could never understand why the British Government sent a man like you on a mission like ours, but I understand perfectly why Alexa married you. It was money, and only money. She had nothing, no love, no family. She married you for money, for security. She doesn't care about you or your child. Don't you understand that?' His voice had risen. 'That's all you've ever had to offer, and all you'll ever have. Now I ask you to leave me alone.'

David drove aimlessly through the dark streets for hours and it was well after midnight when he reached home. It seemed he had hardly gone to sleep before his house-boy, Jackson, was shaking him by the shoulder.

'Tea already?' he said.

'No, Masteh. Telephone.'

The morning was stormy. He went downstairs to his study and took the call. It was Crossley Nash, telling him that Molly Cairns had died late the previous day in Durban. They had received the news in the night.

Jimmy was already on his way back to Kimberley with her body, according to Nash, and David knew he would be expected to attend the funeral.

'I'll leave as soon as I can,' he said.

It was mid-morning by the time he had made his arrangements. He told Jewel he was catching the afternoon train and sent for Jackson to do his packing.

'Where is Miss Alexa?' he said.

'In her sitting-room, Masteh.'

To reach her sitting-room, he had to pass the nursery. The door was open a few inches and he heard the low murmur of a voice and the gurgle of a baby. He paused and looked in. Alexa was standing at the window, holding Sophie. They were alone. The baby was trying to feel Alexa's face with her fingers and Alexa was pretending to bite them. They were totally absorbed in each other and there was an expression in Alexa's face he had never seen before. He watched for a few moments, profoundly moved by the sight, then tip-toed to her sitting-room. He felt suddenly optimistic about their future. He heard Annie's voice and soon Alexa came into the room. Her face still retained some of the tenderness he had observed in the nursery, but as she saw him, it vanished and her features took on the grim, taut look of the previous afternoon. He felt as though he had been let down in some way.

He told her briefly why he was leaving immediately.

'Tell Jimmy how sorry I am,' she said.

'I saw Guy yesterday.'

'I asked you not to. I asked you to give me time, to let me do things in my own way.'

'You'll have time while I'm away. This will give you a chance to think it over without pressure. When I get back, we'll talk.'

He had a first-class compartment to Kimberley to himself. He had made the journey so many times that he seemed to know every hill and fold in the ground. In the late afternoon the train steamed through vineyards and orchards and then wound up through the Hex River Mountains onto the great arid plateau which stretches over the greater part of southern Africa. He sat at the window, staring at the semi-desert without seeing it.

The xylophone sounded for dinner and by the time he returned to the compartment the bed-boy had made up one of the lower bunks with blue blankets bearing the red railway crest.

He worked at papers for a while but he was exhausted and found it difficult to concentrate. Finally, he gave up and went to bed. Usually the rocking of the train acted as a soporific, but not now. Eventually he pulled a blanket round his shoulders, switched out the light and sat by the window, staring at the night. Occasionally he saw a pinpoint of light in the vast darkness, the only evidence of some lonely farm. The iron-stone hills were lit by lightning as storms accompanied the train up-country.

Suddenly he felt more lonely than he ever had in his life before. He seemed to be the only living thing in a black desert. He was speeding away from the only people in the world he loved. What he was doing was totally unnecessary. They could bury Molly Cairns without him.

He thought of the conversations he'd had with Alexa and heard again the harshness and self-righteousness in his tone. It seemed now that everything he had said might have been calculated to leave her more vulnerable to Guy's pressure.

The train was due to stop at Touws River, a small railway town in the desert, about midnight. He decided he would telephone her, say a few words of kindness and comfort. At that time the lines would not be busy and he might get straight through.

He dressed, and waited. The train came to a halt in heavy rain. He jumped down onto the platform and ran to the station master's office. 'I'm Sir David Kade,' he said. 'I need to use your telephone.'

The station master was a small, wiry man with a deeply pitted, bulbous nose. He glanced up from his desk. 'Who?'

'Kade. Sir David Kade. I must make an urgent call.'

The man had never heard of him. The office was brightly lit and a fire burned in the grate. There was a telephone stand on the desk.

'This is railway property.'

'I'll pay.'

'Only railway personnel can use this telephone.'

David took out his wallet and put a pound note down on the desk. The station master looked at it for a moment, and covered it with his hand. 'I suppose it'll be all right,' he said.

David turned the handle of the telephone and finally heard the sleepy voice of the exchange. 'Can you put me through to a Cape Town number?'

'There is a fault on the line because of the storm,' the woman said. 'It won't be fixed for a few hours.'

He replaced the receiver and went to the door. The engine was taking on water, but that was the only movement. His need to talk to Alexa became more urgent now that he had been frustrated. If he could only get back and make her understand how much she meant to him.

His mind, filled with these racing thoughts, began to be overtaken by something resembling panic.

'When's the next train to Cape Town?' he said.'

'Seven o'clock. But it's running two hours late because of the storm.'

'When will it get there?'

'Maybe four, maybe five o'clock.'

He tried to visualise her in her room. Was she lying there, awake, remembering what they had said to each other? Or was she lying with Guy?

'Where can I hire a motor?'

'A motor? Man, we don't hire out cars in this town.'

'I want to get to Cape Town quickly. Where's the nearest garage?'

'Behind the hotel.' He pointed across the tracks and David could see a building with a painted sign advertising Chandler's Beer. 'He's my brother-in-law.'

'Ring him and tell him I want a car.'

'You're mad, mister. He won't hire you a car.'

'Tell him I'll pay him fifty pounds if he drives me to Cape Town. If he says yes, there's a fiver more for you.'

Fifty pounds was a staggering sum. Even a fiver was a quarter of the station master's monthly wages. He picked up the phone, gave the exchange a number and spoke rapidly in a low voice. After a moment he hooked the receiver on the stand and said, 'He'll be here in fifteen minutes.'

'Ring this number when the lines are working. Tell Lady Kade I'm on my way back.'

It took fifteen hours to drive the hundred odd miles to Cape Town; and in all that time, David hardly spoke. During the night, the noise of the wind battering at the canvas hood of the Buick and rattling the celluloid side panels made speech impossible and, later, David was too tired to talk.

He and the garage owner took it in turns to drive, an hour on, an hour off. The surface was like a quagmire. Three times they skidded off the road and had to push the car back. It took them almost four hours to get over the high pass called Bains Kloof, threading their way between rocks brought down by landslides. But the farther south they drove, the better the weather became, and once out of the mountains they were met by bright sunshine. They reached Constantia House at three o'clock in the afternoon.

He was not sure what he had expected, but had prepared himself for the worst. In the event, everything seemed just as he had left it. The house dozed in the late autumn sunshine and only the mass of leaves and branches on the ground were evidence of last night's storm. He paid off the driver and went into the house. No one was about, and suddenly he was afraid.

'Annie!' he called. 'Annie!'

'Yes, Master.' She came from the kitchen.

'Where's Sophie?'

'Miss Alexa took her out for a drive, Master.'

'And Miss Jewel?'

'She gone to town, Master.'

He went up to his room, showered and changed and lay down on his bed to wait for Alexa's return. He tried to doze for a short while, but his mind was too active and his body, after the tremendous activity of the last hours, still seemed filled with nervous energy. At about five he went in search of Annie again.

'Did Miss Alexa say when she would be back?'

'No, Master.'

'When did she go?'

'I think, after Miss Jewel went out.'

'Didn't you see her?'

'No, Master. She tell me to go and buy things at the shop in Wynberg.'

'When was this?' He could feel his heart racing.

'This morning, Master.'

'This morning!'

He turned away and ran upstairs. He looked into Alexa's bathroom. Her toilet things were missing, most of her clothes were gone. He ran downstairs, calling for a car. The traffic was heavy in the evening rush-hour, and it was past six o'clock before he reached the boarding-house in Sea Point. He hammered on the door and the same woman in the same Spanish shawl opened it.

'My name's Kade. I want to see Mr. Jerrold.'

'You're the gentleman who came before.' He tried to push past her. 'Mr. Jerrold isn't in, sir. He paid me. He's gone. He said he was going to stay the whole month, but this morning. . .'

'Where did he go? Was there a lady with him, and a baby?'

'Yes, sir.' She reached for an envelope which was lying on the hall-stand. 'This is for you, sir. The lady asked me to put a stamp on it and post it. But that would be a waste now, wouldn't it?'

The urgency suddenly drained out of him. He held the blue envelope in his hands as though it were some alien object he had never seen before.

He wandered out onto the pavement, crossed the road and sat on one of the benches facing the sea. He knew what was inside the envelope.

'Dear David,' he read. 'The station master at Touws River telephoned me this morning to say you were returning by car. I don't know why, but I can guess. I asked you for time, but you've given me none. I cannot live this way. . .'

The words were jumbled together, unlike her usual handwriting, and the sentences, short and breathless, were written as though she had been on the edge of hysteria.

He read on: 'There are other reasons why I must go with Guy; reasons I have never been able to discuss with you. I have had to live with myself all this time and it has been painful. I am taking Sophie. I know this will hurt you, but she needs me, and that is everything. When you read this, I will be in the mailship. God bless you. Alexa.'

He sat for a long while, looking out at the darkening sea. Two or three hours earlier he would have seen the mailship. Now the ocean was empty to the horizon.

He walked stiffly to the car. 'Take me home,' he told the chauffeur.

BOOK THREE

London, 1920

1

The Rolls Royce crossed Lambeth Bridge and turned left along the Embankment. A fog lay over the Thames, the October night was cold and the air was filled with the acrid smell of coal fires.

'We must turn down somewhere along here. Take the next street to the right,' David said.

The motor nosed slowly into that mass of criss-crossed streets that lie between the Thames and the Buckingham Palace Road. At nine o'clock on a Sunday evening, the area was dead. Occasionally the lights of another motor bored through the fog as it came towards them, and once or twice David saw a hurrying figure, hunched against the chill.

'Warwick Square should be on our left,' he said.

Merrow had not been his chauffeur long. David supposed he was adequate, but he missed Cyril. He had come back from Colorado eventually with what they said were healed lungs, but it was clear that he was never going to be able to work again, so David had bought him a cottage on Michael's estate in Sussex, and given him a pension.

'That looks like a church, sir,' Merrow said.

They had come in on the east side of a square and as they drove along it, with the gas lamps picking up the dripping plane trees, he saw through the fog a church spire. Merrow pulled up outside the building and a figure detached itself from the shadowy doorway and came towards them.

'Sir David? It's me, Currie, sir.'

'Sorry I'm late. There's been fog all the way up from Sussex.' David turned to Merrow. 'You wait here.'

He stepped out onto the pavement and Currie said, 'It's not more than two minutes away, sir.'

He was a large man in a creased navy-blue suit, a white celluloid collar, dark tie, and black bowler on his head. The bottom buttons of his waistcoat were unfastened to give his belly room to bulge, and his fleshy face was made even larger by a soft double-chin. At one time he had been a detective-sergeant in the Metropolitan police, now he was the Currie of Currie and Linton, Private Inquiry Agents, of Number Nineteen, Soho Square.

'It's been a long time,' David said.

They crossed the road and were enveloped by the fog. Soon David had no idea where he was.

'How did you find them?'

'We watched the White Russian groups, sir, as per our discussions. There's one in Maida Vale, one south of the river and one not far from here, sir, just off the Pimlico Road. That's where we spotted the lady.'

'But you've been watching them for months.'

'That's the way of it, sir. Happens when you're thinking it's time to give up. Maybe she felt lonely, her being a foreigner and all. Wanted to see a bit of her own people. They're like that, sir.'

They came into Gloucester Street. There was a small group of shops on the right and opposite them a public house called The White Hart, its illuminated windows like beacons in the fog. The houses, like most of the others in this part of London, were three or four storeyed, with pillars supporting pediments over the doors. Each had a basement area cut off from the pavement by iron railings.

'If you'll follow me, sir.' Currie opened one of the basement gates near the pub and walked down a few steps. David joined him. They were hidden from the road and from the surrounding houses. Currie pointed to a house on the opposite side. 'Number thirty-two. First floor.'

It was part of a terrace of houses, the ground floors of which were shops. There was a dairy, a greengrocer's, a coal merchant, a stationer and Number Thirty-two, which was a dress shop with the sign 'Princess Fashions' lettered on the window. The first floor apartment occupied the front of the house.

The curtains were not drawn, but Holland blinds were down and one of the rooms was lit.

Since he had received Currie's telephone call at Downlands late that afternoon, David's stomach had twisted into a tight hard knot. He had been searching for so long that he had reached a point where he had told himself they must have gone to live in France or Italy and he would never find them. All that summer he had searched, and Currie had searched and now, suddenly, there was a sighting. Or so Currie said.

'That'll be the lady, sir.'

Shadows moved behind the blinds. Someone had walked across the windows and turned up the gas and now it seemed that there were two shadows, the one a woman, the second a child she was holding in her arms. Was it Alexa, with Sophie? He had only Currie's word for it, and twice before Currie had thought he had spotted her, and been mistaken.

Then he thought he heard Sophie cry out and his heart seemed to turn over. What should he do? He couldn't force his way in and demand the child. He stepped up onto the pavement.

The door next to the shop opened and light streamed out briefly, illuminating the figure of a man before it was cut off. It was Guy, and he was carrying something. He came towards them, then turned into the public house. David moved along the pavement and looked through the heavily-patterned window.

Except for a group at a table playing cribbage, the room was empty. Guy stood at the bar. He had brought back an empty bottle and was pocketing the deposit. He looked thinner than he had in Cape Town and was wearing a tweed jacket and waistcoat and a pair of grey flannel bags. He ordered what appeared to be a large whisky and drank it quickly. The barman brought him a bottle of whisky and he paid for it. David moved back into the shadows as he crossed the road again. There was another flash of light from the opening door and, a moment later, they saw his shadow on the blinds.

'Well, sir?' Currie said.

'You've done it. I'll make it worth your while. I don't need you any longer tonight, but tomorrow I want you to follow the man. Find out what he does. Find out all you can about them both.'

'Right you are, sir.'

Currie pointed out his way back to the motor, then disappeared into the fog.

David stood on the steps for more than an hour, watching the house. The lights behind one set of windows went out, then came on behind another. That will be their bedroom, he thought. The anger which had been lying beneath the surface of his mind gripped him, so that he began to shake. But he knew that there was nothing he could do just then, not if he wanted to make sure of Sophie.

He reached his house in Bayswater a little after eleven. He had promised to telephone Jewel. The lateness of the hour meant that the lines were not busy and he got through to Downlands in less than five minutes. She answered so quickly that he had the impression she had been sitting by the instrument.

'Did you see her?' she said.

He explained how he had watched the house. 'I'm almost sure it was her. She was walking up and down behind a blind.'

'Walking? No, no, I don't mean *her*. I mean Sophie. Did you see Sophie?' There was a shrillness in her voice that he had last heard at Constantia House, the day Sophie had been taken away.

'I thought I heard her cry once. All I saw was her shadow, being carried.'

'How do you know it was them?'

'Because I saw Guy come out.'

'I'll come up to town at once. I should be there in a couple of hours.'

'What for?'

'We must talk! We must think what we're going to do.'

'I've asked Currie to make further inquiries.'

'You're wasting time! They could move.'

'You can't imagine we could force our way in and grab the child! Kidnap her?'

'Alexa did.'

'Yes, and that could help us to get her back.'

There was a pause, and the line crackled. 'What are you going to do?' she said.

'I haven't decided. I want to get all the facts, and then I'll make up my mind. But I'm not going to do anything illegal. That way I could lose Sophie for ever.'

'Don't you want me to come up?'

'Not at the moment. I've told Currie to find out what he can about both of them, then we'll think about it calmly.' He knew he had to control his own anger.

That night he couldn't sleep. What he had seen and heard, and the conversation with Jewel, went round and round in his mind, finally distilling out in pictures and memories of that day in Cape Town when he had sat on the bench at Sea Point staring out over the sea on which Sophie had been carried away.

He did not remember getting home. It must have been dark, for he recalled the house with every light on and every door open. Coming up the drive he had thought it looked like a great liner itself.

All the servants were in the kitchen, their faces solemn, their eyes wide. Annie was crying. Jewel was white-faced and bitterly angry.

'We must cable the ship,' she said. 'Tell the captain what's happened. He'll put them under guard. I'm sure it can be done. Then they can be arrested in Southampton.'

'Arrested? What for?'

'She's kidnapped Sophie.'

'You can't kidnap your own child. She's Sophie's mother.'

'There must be something that can be done! We'll get private detectives to meet the ship. See where they go. Watch them.'

He had considered it for a moment, then said, 'I'd have to involve people in London. What if the story got out? There'd be a scandal. And any scandal. . .'

'You're not putting New Chance before Sophie!'

'Of course not. But can you imagine what our lives would be like if the newspapers got hold of it? Reporters at the house in Bayswater. Reporters at Downlands. We'd none of us have a peaceful moment. No one would be immune. Whatever we do, it must be discreet.'

She saw the sense of his argument, but even as he was talking, he had known it was only a half truth. His own pride was at stake. He could imagine the bar-talk at his club:

'Heard about Kade?'

'Seems his wife ran off with a young Naval officer.'

'Took her baby with her.'

'He's much older than she is, of course.'

'Middle age in pursuit of youth.'

He cringed. He must involve as few people as possible. When he returned to London he would hire an inquiry firm himself. It shouldn't prove too difficult to find her.

His office in New Chance House overlooked Trafalgar Square. He stood at the window watching the autumn dusk begin to creep over the city and the starlings come back in their thousands to roost on the National Gallery. There had been a letter from Crossley Nash that day with a postscript about Jimmy Cairns. It seemed he was drinking heavily and there were rumours that he had been mixed up in some unsavoury deal. As long as it was simply talk, it probably wouldn't harm the company. David looked at his watch and saw that it was nearly four-fifteen. He had an appointment with Currie at half-past. He told his secretary he was leaving for the day.

The Tropicana Club, Currie's choice of a meeting-place, was in Shepherd's Market. From the outside it wasn't much more than a doorway; inside there were two glass cases of tropical fish lit from behind, bad murals of palm trees and white beaches and a small bar of bamboo behind which a black bartender was reading the racing edition of *The Star*. The lighting was dim and the place was deserted except for Currie, who sat at a round table under a beach umbrella. Dressed in his dark suit and black bowler, he looked distinctly out of place. He rose and said, 'I didn't think you'd be recognised here, sir.'

'You're probably right.'

'I wouldn't have any of the cocktails, but the whisky seems genuine.'

When they each had a drink David said, 'Are they still in Pimlico?'

Currie looked surprised. 'Oh, yes, sir.'

'How long have they been there?'

'They moved in about six weeks ago.'

'Do you know where they were before that?'

'Not yet. I didn't want to appear too nosey. You said not to make anyone suspicious, sir.'

'Tell me what you have.'

'Seems the house belongs to another Russian person, sir. A princess.' He pulled out a notebook and consulted it. 'Princess Gor-an-tchi-koff. I've got it spelled here, sir, but it doesn't come easily to the tongue.'

David remembered 'Princess Fashions' on the shop window.

'It seems that your ... that Lady ... that the Countess works for her ... this princess, sir. Her being one of them White Russians.'

'Works for her?'

'In the shop. I've been watching the house for nearly a fortnight, since we went there, sir, and she comes down every morning at the same time. Half past eight. Opens up the shop. Takes in the milk. Lets in the seamstresses who work in the basement.'

'What about her child?'

'She brings it down, sir. She's got a cot and a playpen down in the basement. That's where the child goes. The girls love it. I was in the day before yesterday. Said I was from the gas board. Baby was having the time of its life.'

'What else?'

'During the day she does her own domestic shopping. That's when Princess Gor-an ... when the owner comes in. She's usually there for an hour or two and that gives your lady a chance. Just local shopping. Food.'

'Does she ever go out to the West End, or anywhere else?'

'Not that I've seen, and I've had two men on the house round the clock. Lives a very quiet kind of life.'

'What about Commander Jerrold?'

Currie turned another page of his note-book and pushed it under an elastic band with the other used pages.

'Gentleman leaves Number Thirty-two about eight o'clock every morning to go to his place of employment.'

'What sort of employment?'

'He works at the Anglo-Russian Society in Emperor's Gate. Librarian there, sir. Been working about a month.'

'Do you know what he earns?'

'Couldn't say, sir, but it can't be much. Rather a rundown sort of place, if you ask me.'

'And I suppose he lives a quiet life, too.'

'Takes sandwiches for lunch. Sometimes walks to the park. Nothing exciting there.' He flipped over one or two pages. 'Except. . .'

'What?'

'He's been visiting a house in Walpole Street, Chelsea. Twice last week. Three times this week.'

'During the day?'

'After work. Takes the bus to Sloane Square and walks along the King's Road.' He glanced at the book again. 'Tuesday last week was the first time we spotted him. Stayed there forty-two minues. Then again on Friday. Stayed an hour and five. Monday, Wednesday and Thursday this week. All more than an hour. Once nearer two. Then walks back to Pimlico or catches a bus to Victoria and walks home from there.'

'Who does he see?'

'Don't know, sir. Let's himself out. No name on the door. Just the number. Didn't want to make myself conspicuous, as per your instructions.'

David thought about this information for a few moments, then said, 'Fine, Currie, you've done well. You watch the Pimlico flat. Don't worry about Walpole Street.'

'Right you are, sir. Can I get you another whisky?'

'No thanks, I have an appointment.' He laid a five-pound note on the table. 'But have one on me.'

'Very kind of you, sir. Thank you.' A large, soft hand closed on the note as David rose.

2

It was Saturday morning and David had risen early. He had
driven to Chelsea and now sat in the motor at the end of
Walpole Street. He was wearing a macintosh and a trilby and
felt more as Currie must feel, he thought, than the chairman of
a mining group. The house was on a corner, part of a Geor-
gian terrace. Its plaster was painted pale pink, the window
sills white and the front door black. The surrounding area
was raffish but Walpole Street had a kind of neat, bourgeois
quality.

At nine o'clock the street, which had been quiet, came to
life. A coal merchant's dray drawn by a Clydesdale came
slowly along and several deliveries were made through the
coal-holes in the pavement. Then a dairyman came by. Doors
began to open, people began to emerge from the houses.

David saw the door of the house he was watching open,
but it was only a maid who collected the morning's milk. A
light drizzle began to fall. He waited. About half past ten his
patience was rewarded. The door opened again. This time a
woman dressed in a long coat, a head scarf and carrying a
basket on her arm, came out. She put up a black umbrella
and walked towards the King's Road. David followed and
saw her go into a butcher's shop on the far side of Royal
Avenue. He crossed the King's Road and waited. She took
her time. From the butcher she went into a grocer's and a
greengrocer's, then a newsagent's. He turned into a side street
and stood behind an apple barrow. When she came out of
the shop she would have to pass him. He had been there for
a matter of seconds when he saw her coat, and then she
stepped off the pavement and he saw her face: it was Elizabeth
Lytton.

He followed her back to her house and as she was putting her key in the lock he said: 'Miss Lytton, may I talk to you?'

She turned, startled, and looked at him without recognition. He removed his hat and her eyes cleared. 'Sir David!'

'I won't keep you long.'

He thought she was as beautiful as ever, but that quality of innocence that had so beguiled him was no longer there.

Her eyes surveyed him coldly. 'I have a luncheon appointment.'

'I'll see that you keep it.'

They went up to her drawing-room on the first floor and she ordered coffee.

'I know what you've come about,' she said.

'I'm sure you do.'

'Guy said you'd probably track them down.'

'It took longer than I thought it would.'

'You wouldn't have found them if he hadn't wanted you to.'

'Then it would have saved a lot of time if he had sent me a note.'

She watched him in silence.

'You're hostile, and that's a pity because we have mutual interests,' he said. 'I assume you want Guy back.'

'Of course.'

'And I want you to have him back. I never wanted it any other way.'

'You knew what was happening in Russia.'

'Yes.'

'And did you want her too? Guy says you did.'

'I don't think anything is served by this kind of talk.'

'Is that why you left him to die?'

Coffee was brought in and she poured him a cup. After the maid had gone she said, 'Do you remember when I came to your house in Bayswater you told me how you were with him at the end; how much you all loved him. Those were lies.'

'Not in the way you've put it. We thought he was dead. He had been desperately ill.'

'But he wasn't, and you left him.'

'I won't argue. Do you think I haven't thought about it?'

'Guy hates you.'

188

'I know.'

She looked at him over the top of her coffee cup and he knew that she hated him too, though perhaps hate was too strong a word, perhaps she only despised him, and he felt a sadness that such a beautiful woman should judge him that way.

'And now he's damaged me,' he said.

'It's hardly the same. You could have stopped him! You knew about Guy and me.'

'How could I? I didn't know what they were going to do.'

She rose and walked restlessly to the window. The grey morning light glinted on her copper-coloured hair.

'She must be very beautiful,' she said.

'You've not seen her?'

'No. From what I've heard, in a way I don't blame Guy. Every emotion must have been heightened, dramatic. And there's his Russian blood. It's been impossible for him: all that drama, then he's suddenly had to learn how to be ordinary again. With Guy and me, that's how it's always been. We like the same things. We grew up together.'

'What has happened to them?'

'What do you think? He's been living in rooms, with a crying baby, damp nappies – and the baby not his own. And with a woman who was different from the one he knew in Russia.'

'Has he told you what they did when they arrived in England?'

'He didn't want to come to London. First they stayed in Winchester.'

'Why there?'

'Because no one knew them there. They had one floor of a small brick villa on the outskirts of the town. Not quite the thing for a Countess.' There was a bitter note in her voice. 'So she came up to London and made contact with other Russians and she was offered a position in that Pimlico shop, with the rooms above it. They had to take it, they had no money. Can you think what that means to a man like Guy? Being kept by a woman! Then he found a job in the library of that Russian society, but even then he's had to live partly off her earnings.'

189

Alexa had left behind most of the jewels he had given her, except a pendant of matched Brazilian emeralds. It was as though she had spurned the diamonds. He wondered why she had not sold the emeralds, if they had been so hard up.

'So he began looking for you?'

She said, almost to herself: 'I knew he'd come back to me.' She forced a smile. 'It's not the first time it's happened. Guy can't help it, really. Women throw themselves at him.' David remembered Sarah's reaction and how he, himself, had guessed precisely what Elizabeth was confirming. 'It's been happening since he was in his teens. But I understand. I don't make a fuss. Sooner or later, I know he'll come back. I'm the only one he really loves, you see.'

'And now what?' he said. 'He saw you twice last week and three times this. Is it over between them?' She did not answer. 'It *is* my business, you know, and we *are* on the same side. I want you to have Guy as much as you want him.'

Still she hesitated, then she said: 'Guy said it's finished. He's going to leave her. I believe him.'

'Does Alexa know?' It was the first time her name had been spoken.

'He's going to tell her this week-end. He might be telling her now, for all I know.'

He should have felt a surge of pleasure, but his feelings for Alexa were too complex now; his focus was, as it had been for months, on Sophie.

'And then?'

'He's been offered a position with the Transatlantic Line, first officer in the *Olympia*.'

'I know her. She's a fine ship.'

'I shouldn't have told you all this.'

'I promise I won't do anything to complicate matters. But I'd like you to do something for me.'

'What?'

'Telephone me when he comes back to you.'

She thought about it, then nodded.

'Thank you,' he said.

The coldness had not left her eyes.

He rose. 'I'll let myself out.'

He spent most week-ends with Michael and Jewel at Downlands, which lay in West Sussex near the Hampshire border.
The house dated from the 1850s and was built of knapped
flint and yellow Cotswold stone. It was tucked into a fold of
the Downs with its back to the north-east wind which, on
this Sunday, was blowing a bitter gale. He had his own
apartment and had spent most of the day, except for a brisk
walk before lunch, working on business papers and keeping
half an ear open for the telephone. By five o'clock he was
bored and restless, and decided to go for a swim despite the
chilly weather. The pool was a new addition, built since the
war and heated by an anthracite boiler. It looked more like
a Victorian plant house at Kew than a private swimming
pool, for there were exotic plants in pots around the sides
which were supposed to give a bather the feeling of being in
a tropical river. David swam up and down a few times but
by himself it was a cheerless pastime and he thought of all
the days he had taken Sophie to the beach and held her in
his arms as the wavelets surged around his ankles. If only
she had been with him now. . .

After supper he sat with Jewel in the library in front of the
fire while Michael poured a glass of port. He was similar in
build to his father, of medium height, with powerful shoulders, but his face was narrower, and whereas David looked
younger than his years, with his cap of dark hair sitting
closely to his skull, only touched with grey at the temples,
Michael was now bald and looked older. They could have
been taken for brothers.

David had not enjoyed this week-end. He had come down
after talking to Elizabeth and since then he had gone over
and over the conversation and had concluded that there were
many gaps in his knowledge, the most important of which
was that he had no idea how Alexa felt. Was she also weary
of the liaison? He was impatient for a call from Elizabeth.
The telephone had rung several times, but each time it had
been for Jewel or Michael. He knew the situation was on
their minds, too, and that there were unspoken thoughts lying
just below the surface of all their conversations.

Now, because there was a dangerous lacuna which might
be filled either by unwelcome questions or opinions from

Jewel, he said, 'Jimmy Cairns is in a bad way. I had a note from Crossley the other day. He's drinking heavily.'

'He always drank a lot,' Jewel said.

Michael was stretched out in front of the fire. 'I don't think I saw him drunk in all the years I knew him, though. He was just Uncle Jimmy to me when I was a kid. I loved being with him. He was always full of fun.'

'Alexa thought so, too,' Jewel said.

'He did her a power of good. I've never seen such a change.' David told Michael briefly about Cairns' visit to Cape Town.

'She stuck up for him over the smuggling business,' Jewel said.

David was remembering the scene in the garden of their hotel in Kimberley, the scene he wished now had never taken place, for he dated all the subsequent events from that time.

'She didn't understand,' Jewel said. 'That was always her trouble. She never did understand.'

'Perhaps we didn't make enough effort to understand her,' David said.

'Anyway, that's not the point now,' Jewel said. 'Sophie's the important one. Are you going to see your lawyers this week?'

'I don't know. If Guy does leave her, I'm going to ask her to come back.'

'After what she did to you!'

'The child needs both parents.'

'We can give Sophie everything she needs, can't we, Michael?'

'Not everything.'

'But enough! We can give her more than she's getting in a couple of rooms over a shop!'

David rose. He had not wanted this conversation. 'I have work to do,' he said. 'Would you switch the telephone through to me?'

He kissed Jewel on the forehead, sensing her resentment, and waved a hand at Michael. 'I'll be up early. Don't worry about breakfast. I'll have it when I get to London.'

He worked for an hour, but the telephone did not ring and at last he went to bed. This was the time he feared. Often when he closed his eyes the picture on the inside of his lids would be of Russia, of the prison barge careering downstream, the gunfire, the rocks, then the screams and the groans and the bodies floating by.

Since Alexa had left, there had been another dream. Now he seemed to stand outside himself watching a figure on a bench looking out over the darkening sea, reading the letter that told him his second chance had come to nothing. Now the vision would fade into Alexa with Sophie in her arms, moving behind drawn blinds.

There was a knock on his door and Michael came in. He sat down on the bed and said, 'I'm sorry about that.'

'It was nothing.'

'Even if you don't want another child it's hard to be told you can't have one. And Jewel did want one.'

'I know.'

He rose early the following morning and was putting his papers into his brief-case when she came in. She was still in her dressing-gown and her eyes were tired.

'Would you like coffee?' she said.

'I've made myself a cup, thanks.'

'Sophie and Alexa have been on my mind all night. I've been thinking. If you go to her immediately Guy leaves her, she'll be angry and confused and. . .'

He did not want to discuss the matter, but could not ignore her. 'I should have thought it would be just the opposite. That's when she'll need someone.'

'Then you don't know Alexa. She's far too proud for that. She'd think you were patronising her. Wait a fortnight or three weeks. Let her come to her senses, let her see what it's like living by herself, looking after a tiny baby. If you go to her too soon, she'll refuse you, and then you'll have to fight for Sophie.'

She went to the door with him and as he left she said: 'You know that I only want what's best for Sophie, don't you?'

'I know.'

There were no messages from Elizabeth in Bayswater, nor at New Chance House.

Monday passed, then Tuesday, without any word. On

Wednesday he lunched alone at his club and when he returned to his office his secretary gave him several messages, one of which was unsigned and read: 'Guy returned to Chelsea for good last night.'

Every instinct urged him to rush to Pimlico, but the more he had thought about Jewel's warning, the more he had come to see the psychological sense in it. He set himself to endure two weeks of waiting. And waiting did not come easily to him.

During the second week he had an unexpected visitor in Bayswater. The servants had already gone to bed and he answered the door himself. In the half light, all he could make out was a figure in a heavy fur coat, and a dead white face.

'I wish Sir David Kade,' the woman said.

'I'm David Kade.'

'I am Princess Gorantchikoff. I have informations.'

He took her into his study, where he inspected her more closely. She was elderly, extremely thin, with a bird-like face which was caked with white powder. Two bright areas of rouge burned on her cheek-bones and her lips were a slash of red. Her hair had been dyed a gingerish tint but grey roots were showing. She wore a great number of bangles on her bony wrists and several rings on skeletal fingers. She made a jangling noise when she moved and she reminded David of a marabou stork.

He offered her a drink, but she said, 'By me alcohol is poison.'

'What can I do for you?'

'It is for you what I can do. That is question. I have informations about your wife.'

For a moment he thought wildly that she had come to tell him that Alexa had fled, but Currie had reported by telephone less than an hour before that everything was normal.

She took out a black Russian cigarette and placed the cardboard mouthpiece in the side of her mouth. The room was suddenly filled with the smell of latakia.

'What information?'

'I am business woman. Here in London I am by myself. I have no one. You understand?'

'You have information to sell, is that it?'

'Just so.'

'I don't buy information.'

'But for divorce.'

'What divorce?'

She inhaled deeply and let the smoke drift from her nose. 'You have wife and baby. She is living with second man. Is no divorce? Please, I am not child.'

'How did you come by this information?'

'I have dress shop. She is working for me.'

'I have that information already.'

'I don't believe. . .'

'Your shop is in Pimlico. And I have a lot more information. I know how she got the job and when, and that she lives above the shop.' He felt an angry satisfaction in confounding her.

'So,' she said. Then her expression changed. She smiled, showing her dirty teeth. 'Maybe newspapers wish such informations.'

He said: 'You can do what you like with your information, but I'd advise you to think very carefully first.' There was no mistaking the threat in his tone.

She rose and stubbed out her cigarette. 'It is joke. I am Princess. You understand joke?'

'Yes,' he said. 'I understand joke.'

[3]

Alexa stood in the doorway with the light from the hall behind her, but the street light threw a soft glow on her face.

'Aren't you going to invite me in?' he said.

She hesitated, then stepped aside so he could pass her. She closed the door and led the way along a passage. It was lit by a single gas-jet and looked dingy. The lower half of the walls was painted an institutional brown, the upper half a dirty cream. On the floor, a patterned linoleum had worn in places, showing the fibres. She was wearing a shapeless grey smock and as he followed her all he could see of her body were her legs. They were shapely, but thin; she had lost weight again.

He had timed his arrival for the early evening when the shop would be closed. He had been tense all day. As he mounted a rickety staircase he could feel the tension move to his stomach.

She opened the door on the landing and he followed her into her apartment. The inner doors were all open and as he took off his coat he could see it in its entirety. Two rooms faced the street, with a third at the back. There was a small kitchen which also contained the bath. The sitting-room, which doubled as a dining-room, was a fair size, with long windows. Under them were a square table and four chairs and at the other end of the room a gas-fire made a low, gurgling sound. Two Morris chairs and a sofa covered in grey-green corduroy were grouped around it. A clothes horse on which nappies were drying was in front of the sofa.

It would have been a dismal place indeed, but for the fact that Alexa had imposed her own sense of style and colour on it. On the dining-table was a large orange begonia in a pot. Its twin made a splash of colour against the far wall from the top of a pine chest of drawers. A *ficus* broke the outline of the windows and its small green leaves threw patterns of shadow on the walls. She had put some cheap Kashmir rugs on the floor and spread a shawl along the back of the sofa. The chairs were hidden under brightly-coloured throw-rugs. The walls had been covered in a strange collection of posters, many of which advertised Christian missions in China. Others were emblazoned with copies of ikons. All this David absorbed in a matter of seconds. Then Alexa said, 'I was putting Sophie down. I'm sure you want to see her.'

Sophie's bedroom was at the back. It was small and cramped and there was barely enough room for her cot and a small cupboard. She was sitting in the cot after her bath. Whereas the living-room smelled of food and drying nappies, this one smelled of talcum powder. She was holding the bars of the cot, shaking it. David stopped in the doorway and stared at her. He had forgotten exactly how she looked, but now he realised she had changed. She was bigger and had more brown hair. His pleasure in seeing her was momentarily blighted by the thought that he had missed more than six months of her life.

Here, too, the porridge-coloured walls had been covered by posters to give them warmth and brightness. He went towards the cot and was about to say, 'May I pick her up?' when he thought: She's mine. I don't have to ask permission.

He lifted her and held her in his arms. At first she put her hands out and began to pull his nose, but after a few moments, started to wrestle away from him. Her face went red and her mouth puckered. 'It's all right, you know who I am,' David said. But she began to cry and Alexa, watching from the doorway, said, 'She's always shy with. . .'

She checked herself, but the implication was clear, and he said, 'Did she always cry when Guy picked her up? Or didn't he pick her up?'

He put her back in her cot and opened a box with a Harrod's label. It contained a doll about the same size as his daughter. He put it into the cot. It was a crying doll and as the body bent, so the eyes turned and it gave a low, wavering cry.

Sophie screamed in fright and Alexa hastily removed the doll. That seemed to reassure the child, for soon she lay on her back and put a thumb in her mouth.

'She's tired,' Alexa said. 'We went for a long walk just before you came.' She turned the gas down so that there was only a faint glow and then, as David walked back into the living-room, she half closed the door.

'I'm sorry,' he said. 'I shouldn't have said what I did. Let's start again. How are you?'

'Better than I've any right to be. I'd offer you a drink, except I don't have anything. I could give you a cup of tea.'

'No thanks.' He stood in the middle of the room, looking at her, then he said, 'I really could do with a drink. I'll go over to the pub. What do you fancy? Whisky?'

'That would be fine.'

He walked across the road. The public house was full and it was some minutes before he could be served. He bought a bottle of whisky and one of brandy and had a quick double whisky as he waited. He thought of Guy doing much the same when he had seen him a few weeks ago. He realised he had not been into a public house in England for years.

She had changed out of the smock and was wearing a tweed skirt and a camel-hair jersey with a yellow scarf tied at her throat. She had put a comb through her hair and touched up her lips and cheeks. The clothes-horse was gone from the room.

'Presents for the house,' he said, putting the bottles down. He gave them each a drink and they sat in the Morris chairs on either side of the gas-fire.

He felt tongue-tied and even the drink did not do much to help. He wondered if she felt the same way. She seemed so calm and collected.

It was she who cut through the genteel preliminaries. 'You know Guy's left, don't you?'

'Yes.'

'I'm told you know a great deal about me.'

'Oh?'

'The Princess told me she'd visited you.'

'Did she tell you why?'

'She said she wanted us to get together again. I don't believe her. I suppose she wanted money.'

'If I were you, I'd be careful of her.'

'You can't blame her. She's on her own. She's old and she's frightened. She's in terror of dying a pauper and not having a decent funeral. But she's been good to me.' He glanced around the room and she guessed what he was thinking. 'It isn't much, but it's better than nothing. And she doesn't pay me a fortune, but it's better than nothing. Sophie and I can live on it.'

'But Guy couldn't?' he said dryly.

'Do we have to discuss Guy? It's finished. Done with.'

'I saw Elizabeth Lytton.'

'Ah, so you knew about that.'

'It was nearly three weeks ago.'

'If you knew where we were, why did you wait this long? Didn't you want to see Sophie?'

'Very much. I wanted to see both of you. But after Guy left, I didn't want to rush in and, maybe, make things worse for you. I wanted you to find your feet.'

She gave him a searching look and said, 'That was very sensitive of you.'

He covered his discomfort by saying, 'Have things been bad?'

'Before or after Guy left?'

'It can't have been much fun for either of you these last few months. Elizabeth told me you'd lived in Winchester.'

'That was Guy's idea. He was embarrassed that his friends might discover us in London. He's very conventional in some ways.' She held up her glass and he refilled it. 'No, it wasn't much fun. And that should please you, because you were right. It was day-to-day living that killed it. The great drama ended in cheap rooms and drying nappies and Sophie always on top of him.'

'He knew what to expect when he came to Cape Town.'

'I don't think he did. I think that mentally he was still in Russia. I believe he thought I would leave Sophie, but I'd rather have died.'

He frowned, remembering her apparent indifference to the baby, but also remembering the moment when he had surprised the two of them in the nursery.

She was sitting forward, staring into the gas-fire. 'And of course, when I took Sophie's part, he resented it. Aren't you pleased you were proved right?'

'I am pleased that he's gone. I'm pleased to be able to see you. Both of you. That's why I've come. I want to ask you to come back to me.'

She shook her head slowly. 'You don't want me. You want Sophie. I think she's all you ever did want. New life. People say that when you get older young things have more importance.'

He flinched. 'Of course I want Sophie back, but. . .'

'And there's Jewel.'

'What has she to do with it?'

'At the Cape it almost seemed that you were Sophie's father and she was the mother.'

'That's nonsense. You knew she'd lost her boy John. Then she had two miscarriages. It was only natural that she felt drawn to the baby.'

'She took her over.'

'You let her! You didn't care.'

'Did you ever ask me if I cared?'

'Why didn't you say anything?'

'I was in your house, your world. Sophie was part of *your* family as Jewel is, in a way I could never be. I was trying to fit in with your attitudes and your way of life. You were happy to let Jewel spoil Sophie – smother her with her own frustrated love.'

'It wasn't like that. . .'

But she went on. 'You know, David, at one point I did think of leaving Sophie. Not because I don't love her. I do, more than you could ever begin to imagine. If I didn't seem sufficiently affectionate there were . . . reasons. I thought it might be in her interests to leave her with you, that her life might be more secure. But I wasn't going to leave her with Jewel. She needed a real mother, not someone who treated her like a doll!'

'That's exactly why I want you to come back. She needs her real mother and her father.'

It was only once he caught her look that he realised what he had said.

'I want you both,' he added hastily. 'I want to take you away from this.' He waved his hand around the room, and the gesture encompassed the street and the area as well. 'I want to give you both everything you should have.'

'You want Sophie,' she said.

'Of course I do!'

'And I'm to come along as nurse-maid.'

'It's not that at all. I don't want my daughter brought up here under these conditions.'

'No, David.'

'What does that mean?'

'It means we're not coming back to you. During the past two weeks, something has happened to me. If you'd come on the day Guy left, it's possible things might have been different, I don't know, but two weeks is a long time. For the first time in my life, or for as long as I can remember, anyway, I'm under no pressure. All I have is Sophie, and she's all I need. We have each other. And I have some security. I don't have to tell you, of all people, after what happened in Russia, how important that is. To know where your next meal comes from, to know that you have shelter, to know that you have a child to love and who loves you; to know that no one is going to brutalise you or force you to do this or that or take your child from you. Above all, to know that you can exist independently of everyone else. It's a kind of paradise.'

He opened his mouth to reply, but she went on talking, almost to herself. 'I'll be able to watch Sophie grow up. I'll be able to care for her as I was never able to care. . .' She stopped abruptly.

'Don't I have any say in my own daughter's future?'

'It depends what you want to say, how you want her to grow up. If you want to pay for her schooling and her clothes, then we'll both be grateful. But I know now that we can manage without you, and no amount of money is going to make me change my mind.'

'Wait a minute! Sophie's only a baby and you're already talking about her education. You're taking too much on yourself and I won't have it. You're not going to dictate to me the future of my child. As far as I'm concerned, she'd be better off at the Cape.'

'You see . . . it isn't really me you want. And now I've got something to ask you. I want you to give me a divorce. In the circumstances it would be best. Then we can . . . or the lawyers can . . . reach agreements about money and about Sophie's future.'

He suddenly felt bitterly angry. It seemed that in all this emotional upheaval he had been the party most injured, yet she had said no word of apology, had shown no gratitude for his concern. His anger stemmed mainly from humiliation. Guy had left her and she had no one. David had overcome his own pride and agreed to take her back. She had rejected him. In other words, rather than have him, she would be happier with no-one. The unjustness was so manifest that he rose to his feet, gathered up his coat and said, 'I'll never divorce you! Never! And I tell you now that I'm going to have Sophie.'

She stared at him with her large golden eyes. 'You'll have to fight me.'

'Yes, I'll fight you.'

David first met Edward Maxwell, Q.C. in the barrister's chambers in New Square, just north of the Law Courts in Lincoln's Inn. He had been taken there by his solicitor, Sir Gregory Stratos, for the first of what became a series of conferences between the three men. Maxwell's rooms were like the man himself, perhaps a trifle too elegant. There was a subtle aggressiveness about them that was reflected in their owner. There were Persian rugs, antique tables and desks and large animal paintings by Landseer and Stubbs. In the midst of this stood the Q.C. himself, a large, florid man in his early forties who must once have been good-looking, but who was now running to portliness. He had been elegantly suited by Huntsman in a dark blue pin-stripe. He wore a shirt of blue Bengal stripes and a stiff white collar and his black shoes came from Lobb. Across his plump belly he wore a gold watch and chain. A white silk handkerchief drooped from his coat pocket. He could as easily have been a famous theatrical impresario as a barrister.

'Specialises in this kind of case,' Stratos had said earlier. 'One of the most destructive cross-examiners in the civil courts. He could get enough criminal work to fill his diary ten times over, but there's not the money in it for him.'

Maxwell had ordered tea for the three of them.

'I think I should explain the law as far as this . . .' he had begun.

'I don't think we need to go over that again,' Stratos said, but Maxwell turned to look at the wall. He reminded David of a politician who, when interrupted, retains his thoughts in the original order, waiting only for a chance to continue where he had left off.

He took up a piece of buttered toast and laid on it a thin smear of Patum Peperium. 'Before the eighteen-eighties there would have been little doubt of the outcome of this case,' he said. 'The custody of an infant then belonged, against all other persons, to the father, who was said to be the guardian by nature and nurture, and it was his responsibility to do with his children almost as he wished until they had achieved the age of twenty-one.'

He finished his toast, drank his tea, wiped his hands and lips with a napkin and went to stand at the window. 'In 1886, Parliament passed the Guardianship of Infants Act, which placed the mother almost on the same footing as the father. The relevant section states – and I hope I quote correctly – "The court will, in a proper case, give a mother custody of the father's infant children notwithstanding that the mother may have been guilty of matrimonial misconduct." So you see, Sir David, this is not as open and shut a case as it might appear.'

'Just because Lady Kade has committed misconduct doesn't mean that the court will automatically side with you. And if she is, as you say, now living on her own, is looking after her daughter with care, has created a life for herself which is at once moral and industrious, the court might well take the view that she has put her mistakes behind her – they like that sort of thing – and is the best person to look after the child. *Might*. But when we're finished, *won't*. I am quite certain of that.'

The assurance was what David needed. Stratos had not been encouraging. He was a man who favoured settlement if at all possible and his vaguely pessimistic demeanour had been annoying. Maxwell did not seem like a man who lost.

'The court would want to know who would look after the child were you granted custody,' the barrister said.

'My daughter-in-law. She knows and loves Sophie already. She has offered.'

'I see. Certainly the child's future would be guaranteed.'

'I could give her everything,' David said fiercely.

'Yes, well, we won't press too much on that point. Judges have been known to take a violent antipathy to men who exhibit their wealth.' He moved away from the window and went on, 'Court cases are like buildings, some are small and nasty and others are large and nasty, but each has a style of architecture. In a case such as the one we are discussing, the foundations are particularly important.'

He was standing with his back to the window, one hand behind him, the other constantly feeling for his gown, which was not there. David felt for a moment that he was being addressed as an officer of the court. Maxwell's voice was deep and velvety and he spoke in orotund prose.

'In short, it is rather like a divorce suit: one wants to know what ammunition the enemy has so that one can defend oneself. In your letter to Sir Gregory you say you know little about your wife's early life. Does the contrary also hold true? Does she know as little of your life as you know of hers?'

'She knows everything, at least, as much as one can know from being told. I certainly didn't consciously keep anything back.'

'Everything? No one tells *everything* about oneself.'

'No, perhaps not,' he said, thinking of Sarah and one or two other women, 'but I can't think of anything that could be used against me.'

'It's difficult to make judgements about oneself. What I would like you to do is to think carefully about all aspects of your life since you met your wife and write down for me anything, however trivial, that may occur to you. I must stress at the outset that what seem everyday occurrences sound very different in a court of law. You have only to hear someone on a motoring offence plead in mitigation that he had scarcely two or three glasses of gin before going out in his car to know that such a phrase sounds his knell in court. Even the word "gin" begins to sound like treason or murder. So think carefully, Sir David, I beg you. What we do not want at any cost is to be taken unawares.'

'I'll do my best.'

Maxwell walked to his desk and lifted a page of notes. 'You see, I can already point to an area where awkward questions might be asked. For instance, when you were taken prisoner in Russia, you did not protest to each of the officers who were in charge of the prisoners, but only to the first few. Why was that?'

'It became hopeless. They all said the same thing.'

'But your wife's counsel may ask you how you could foretell such a thing. He might put it to you that you had been, if not derelict in your duty as leader of the delegation, at least feeble. Feebleness does not necessarily make for a good custodian for an infant.'

David looked up angrily. 'You weren't there! You don't know the circumstances! Anyway, there was a possibility that they might have made things harder for us. For instance, had I continued to pester them, they might have made Mr. Amsterdam walk, instead of allowing him to ride in the carts. They might even have shot us.'

'Don't ever say in court: "You weren't there," or "You don't understand." Nothing antagonises a judge more. You are there to *make* us understand.'

David was about to retort, but Maxwell held up his hand. 'You didn't go on protesting because you feared reprisals. You feared they might take it out on Mr. Amsterdam. Excellent! Quite right! A leader acting in the best interests of one of his men. Be positive, Sir David.'

David nodded. 'I understand.'

'Good. Now that you have seen the kind of trap, let me return to what we know – or don't know – of Lady Kade. As you say, it is not very much. We have no *foundation* for our structure. We have to know everything about her. Or as much as possible. And here I find a difficulty. Who is to tell us? Were this a case where her early life had been spent in Scotland, or even Ireland, I know a reputable firm whom we could engage to dig and dig. But Russia! St. Petersburg. Moscow. Who can dig there? Why, I doubt there is a firm of private inquiry agents anywhere in the world which would send a man to Russia. Do you see the difficulty?'

'I know someone I could send.'

'Who is that?'

'My general manager. He's due in London on business in a week or so.'

'Loyal?'

David recalled the Cairns affair. Nash had shown complete loyalty there. The fact that he had gained by it would only make it more significant. David had no objection to that.

Perhaps Nash had it in his mind that one day he would step into David's shoes, and he had no objection to that, either. He said to Maxwell, 'Totally.'

He spent a sad Christmas with Jewel and Michael in the country, missing Sophie so much that he almost decided to withdraw his petition and try some other way of winning them back. But on his return to London he received a call from Stratos telling him that Alexa had applied for an injunction restraining him from removing Sophie from her custody while the case was pending.

'My God, as if I would!' he had shouted into the telephone.

'You implied as much when you said the child would be better off at the Cape. She was protecting both of them, it is not unnatural.'

'I wasn't implying anything!'

'You sowed doubt. That's why, if you've any idea of seeing her or talking to her, I must ask you to forget it. Don't get in touch with her under any circumstances.'

It was the injunction which had put the iron into David's soul. Before that he had wavered; after it, he was determined.

'By the way,' Stratos said, 'it's unlikely the hearing will take place before the summer. When does your Mr. Nash arrive?'

'Day after tomorrow.'

'That should give us plenty of time.

David met the mailship and drove Crossley Nash to London. They had lunch in Winchester on the way and used the time to talk of matters concerning the company.

'How's Jimmy?' David asked. 'Still drinking as much?'

'He's dropped out of touch,' Nash said. 'The last I heard he was going to live with a widowed sister in Port Elizabeth.'

As they drove out again to the London road, David looked at the little brick terrace houses they passed, remembering that his wife and daughter had lived with Guy Jerrold for a time in one of them. He could think of no background less likely for Alexa.

Nash said little, as usual, at either of the two conferences they

206

had with Maxwell and Stratos. He looked, in his neat, dark suit, like a bank clerk, someone who would get lost in a crowd. Only David knew his nervous energy and tensile strength, and his capacity to act incisively on his own.

Sunday morning was cold, but sunny, and David drove him up to Hampstead Heath for a walk before lunch. Again, he was assailed by memory, for the big house he had occupied with his first family lay just over the brow of the hill and he and his children had walked many times on the Heath.

On this day, hundreds of others had had the same idea and had brought out their children and dogs. There was an air of relaxed urban pleasure about the scene, except for the two men in dark blue overcoats and black homburgs who strode along the paths, deep in conversation.

'I know it's asking a lot of you, Crossley,' David was saying. 'But you're the only one I can trust.'

'I just wish it hadn't arisen. I've always wanted to go to Russia, but I'd rather have gone for other reasons. I liked her very much.'

'I know. I hate the situation myself. But as Maxwell says, in a case like this there are no holds barred. We've tried to get an agreement, but she's holding to the injunction. We've given her every chance, but it boils down to this: I want to see my daughter grow up in the best circumstances possible. I think that those lie with me and not with Alexa. She feels the opposite. Unfortunately, to prove our points we have no other means at our disposal but to attack each other.'

They lunched at David's club and later in the smoking-room Nash took an envelope from his pocket and handed it to David. 'I almost forgot these. They came out just before I left. I thought it would be quicker if I brought them rather than put them in the post.'

The envelope contained cuttings from South-African news-papers. One said: DIAMOND MILLIONAIRE TO SUE FOR CUSTODY OF CHILD. Another was headed: COURT BATTLE LOOMS OVER MILLIONAIRE'S DAUGHTER. A third described Alexa's injunction.

'Where did they get all this stuff?' David said.

'From their London offices. They've probably been inter-viewing Lady Kade.'

David shook his head angrily. 'One or two reporters have been on to me. I've said, no comment.'

'Once the case starts the papers will be full of it.'

'Stratos says it'll be held in camera because of the age of the child.'

'I still think you'll be lucky to escape. From what I know of the press they'll find a way of publishing something. It's too good a story to miss. A millionaire and a Russian Countess. People love to see titles and money ground into the dirt.'

'I hope you're wrong!'

But Nash wasn't wrong. A fortnight later on a Sunday evening the *Morning Post* telephoned David at his house asking him to comment on a story that had appeared that day in the *Sunday Examiner*.

He said: 'I don't know of any story. I don't read papers of that sort. And I have no comment to make.' He put the telephone down, went back into his study for a few moments, then picked up his coat and scarf and walked to the Edgware Road, where he found a paper-seller huddled in a shop doorway. He bought an *Examiner* and stood under a street light, turning over the pages. The story led page five.

The heading read: 'CHEAP' DIAMOND IS BASIS OF MILLIONAIRE'S FORTUNE. He felt a momentary clenching of his stomach, then he was flooded by anger. He went home and read the story through.

'Sir David Kade, the well-known diamond magnate who is suing his wife for the custody of their infant daughter, founded his huge empire on a single stone which he bought, at much less than its true value, from his partner.

'The stone, called the "Southern Cross," was lost after a shell exploded in Kimberley during the Boer War, but it was the largest diamond ever found in the Kimberley diamond diggings.

'Few people know that it was not discovered by Sir David, as is generally thought, but by his partner, Mr. Jack Farson, who died in the desert nearly twenty years ago. . .'

David read the jumble of half-truths, some facts and some

outright lies, and wondered what he should do about the story.

In the early evening of the following day he and Stratos went to see Maxwell.

'I don't like it,' Maxwell said. 'This is just the sort of surprise I was talking about. Where do you think they got hold of the story? It's unsigned.'

'I have no idea.'

'Is it true?'

'Parts of it are.'

'What about this diamond? It says you paid your partner a thousand pounds for it, but really it was worth thirty thousand.'

'Well, first of all, he wasn't my partner at the time, and he was down on his luck. He needed money badly. I had to borrow it to pay him. Anyway, it was a private deal.'

'But you knew what you were getting?'

'If you mean that I was getting a beautiful stone, that's true, but it happened to be worthless at the time. The market was depressed and even if I'd wanted to, I couldn't have sold it.'

Maxwell went into his ritual of looking out of the window and pacing up and down restlessly.

'Did you really found your company on it?'

'Not at all. The company was founded because I had information about a different soil structure which people thought did not hold diamonds, and which I knew did. So I bought up as many claims as I could.'

'So this stone had nothing to do with it?'

'Only in the sense that I used it as collateral for a loan in order to buy the claims.'

'I still don't like it,' Maxwell said. 'But I don't see how they can use it. There is nothing about it in their petition so it can't be introduced by them and *I'm* certainly not going to introduce it. Is there anyone who is trying to attack you?'

'Not that I know of.'

'Does your wife know about the stone?'

'I've never discussed it with her.'

'We'll just have to ignore it. The press loves a case like

this, so I suppose there's no point in getting upset about publicity.'

'There'll probably be more,' Stratos said gloomily.

As they were leaving Maxwell said, 'By the way, have you heard anything from Nash?'

'Not yet. I told him to take his time and find out as much as he could.'

'Time has a habit of slipping away, you know.'

Nash's first communication was a short note from Moscow before he took the Trans-Siberian railway for Vladivostok. It simply stated that his inquiries were 'progressing'.

It was not until March that David received the first report in what became known both to him and to his legal advisers as the Nash Letters, which eventually formed the foundation for which Maxwell had been looking, on which to build their case.

[5]

An important part of the relationship between David and Crossley Nash had depended on letters between them, but these up to now had been business communications. Nash's letters from Russia were entirely different. Before he left, David had told him that he wanted to know every detail of his investigations, and Nash took him at his word. Instead of the dry impersonality of their business letters, these revealed that Nash possessed the observing eye of a good journalist.

The first letter was written over a series of days and formed a journal.

'I arrived in Vladivostok from Moscow a week ago,' he wrote. 'You have made part of the journey by train, so you know what it is like. But there has been almost constant fighting along the railway line since you were here and it is only recently that the Reds have been able to destroy the White armies operating in Siberia. Much of the line has been destroyed and temporarily repaired, and some of the bridges are so badly damaged that we had to leave the train and walk across them.

'My time in Petrograd was frustrating. There are – or I should say, were – several aristocratic families named Kropotkin, even a prince, but he died a long time ago. The difficulty in trying to discover anything about the nobility is that no one will admit to knowing them. They have ceased to exist, or at least have effaced themselves so well that it is difficult to discover them. The joke here is that there are more Russian nobles driving taxis in Paris than hiding under their beds in Petrograd.

'On the other hand, the new ruling class is extremely difficult to approach. After their experiences in the Civil War they are suspicious of everyone, including the British, whom they dislike for siding with the White Russians.

'My only hope was the old middle class. They have suffered almost as badly as the nobility. Most seem to live in genteel poverty. After one or two false starts I met a music teacher who spoke good English and who agreed to act as my interpreter. He is very poor and does not have sufficient fuel to heat his rooms. We have come to a financial arrangement and the result was that he took me to the fortress of St. Peter and St. Paul, where, many prisoners are held before making the journey to the east.

'At first it was difficult to find anyone to help. It seems that the administration has denied that prisoners are still being exiled, but my information is that numbers have actually increased since the Revolution of 1917.

'My friend, the music teacher, made contact with one of the clerks in the Fortress. He was difficult to persuade, but again a financial agreement was reached. He has provided documentary evidence, of which I have a copy, that a Countess Kropotkin was held in one of the casemates – these are apparently dark, solitary, bomb-proof cells – for nearly a year. She had arrived from the gold mines at Kara and was sentenced in St. Petersburg to return there and serve life imprisonment. If this is the same person, and there is no reason to doubt it, she must have been returning to Kara when you met her. But I cannot discover the charge. The files have all been removed by the new secret police, who are feared here above everyone.

'I tried again in Moscow, but since none of the records are there, I found myself always being referred to Petrograd. It seems to me that Kara is the most likely place to discover exactly what happened and I have managed through the Ministry of Mines here – I had discussions on the possibility of marketing gold and diamonds for the new administration in London – to obtain permission to go there. I can travel by river steamer, but I shall have to wait until the Amur River unfreezes.

'In the meantime, I have been at work in Vladivostok. You described to me the house of Mr. and Mrs. Wiggins, but it is all changed. They are no longer in residence and it is occupied by a local official and his family. The garden, which you remember as being very English, is at the moment under snow. The weather has been bitter and I will never complain again about Kimberley's heat.

'The Wigginses have suffered a reversal of fortune. He is no longer honorary consul, nor indeed is he anything at all. The Great Northern and Oriental Telegraph Company has been taken over by the new administration and Mr. Wiggins has been replaced by a Russian manager.

'It took me two days to track them down. They are living in reduced circumstances in rented rooms near the docks where they wait first for money owed to them and then a ship to take them back to England.

'I took them out for a meal and this was all they talked about. Apparently the Soviets have not compensated the telegraph company yet for taking over its business – there is some doubt that they will – and until they do Mr. Wiggins will not receive his last three months' salary nor the payments he made towards a pension.

'I am doing what I can for them in the way of meals, etc., and in return I have received information concerning Commander Jerrold which Sir Gregory and Mr. Maxwell might find useful.

'As you already know, he had recovered from his illness by the time a detachment of soldiers arrived at Tungus Munku's home to escort him to Vladivostok. It is ironic that, had the barge not foundered and had you not escaped as you did, you, too, would eventually have been brought there under escort.

'Commander Jerrold spent some months with the Wigginses. They say he was in a very emotional state, whatever that means. Tense, I expect. And who wouldn't be after his experiences? Apparently he suffered deep depressions.

'Some weeks after his arrival (Mr. Wiggins cannot recall how many) a woman came to the house looking for him. Neither of the Wigginses know much about the various peoples of Siberia, but they said she was dark and pretty, very young, and wore a long gown faced with silk. They described her as "Mongolian", but I suppose that description would fit any of the Golds, or the Buryats.

'Mr. Wiggins told me that neither he nor his wife could understand her – they cannot speak Russian – but that Commander Jerrold had known her and had spoken to her. He had not asked her into the house. Mrs. Wiggins said she thought the woman was pleading with him for something. She says he seemed to speak harshly to her and finally she left.

'She returned every day for a week and sat in the lane outside the house, waiting for Commander Jerrold to come out. Every day he ordered her to leave.

'The Wigginses have no explanation for all this except that Mrs. Wiggins felt sorry for the girl, for she seemed so wretched.

'Perhaps I am less innocent. It seems clear what had happened. You told me yourself that Munku's new wife was young and attractive. She was left alone in the wilderness with Commander Jerrold while her husband brought you and your party to Vladivostok. During that time, he recovered. It is not, I think far-fetched to suggest that he may have taken advantage of her during the weeks they were together and while her husband was away. She probably fell in love with him.

'If I am right, then she left her husband, made her way to Vladivostok, searched for Commander Jerrold, found him, but was instantly rejected.

'Mrs. Wiggins tells me she has seen her several times here

in Vladivostok in recent weeks. I imagine she could hardly have gone back to her log-cabin in the snows after leaving her husband as she did.

'If my hypothesis is right, it throws an interesting light on Commander Jerrold, don't you think?'

Here the letter ended.

As winter turned to spring and the case loomed ever nearer, David felt an increase of tension. Sometimes, when he found himself wishing that he had never started it, he thought of Alexa's injunction and the article which had appeared in the *Sunday Examiner* and they corrected the balance. The *Examiner* story was not isolated. There had been other references to David's early years. Although some expressed admiration for his achievements, others seized on past incidents and distorted them. There was, for instance, the knighthood he had been given for negotiating a treaty with a tribal chief which had given Britain a corridor from Central Africa to the sea.

The corridor had never been used and public feeling, which had once supported Rhodes and the Empire builders, was beginning to change. Deals, which offered illiterate blacks insignificant sums of money for territorial rights in perpetuity, now seemed rather shameful. As the stories were written, it appeared that David had instituted the idea of the corridor in the way that Rhodes had taken over territory, whereas in fact the British Government had approached him for help. The country had been grateful then; now the very ethos of Empire was decaying.

Then there was the question of his donations to the war effort. The sum had finally reached nearly a million pounds. Yet one or two reports managed, by subtle phrasing, to leave the reader wondering what his underlying motive had been.

He had other worries. Michael was knocked down by a young heifer and broke three ribs. He took a long time to recover and Jewel no longer came up to London so often. In a way, David was glad to have a break from her. She seemed to think he needed constant encouragement and would inveigh against Alexa whenever she saw him. If anything, that turned him towards, rather than against, his wife.

Then, one Saturday afternoon, Sarah arrived at the Bayswater house. He had not seen her since before leaving for Russia.

He brought her into his study, where there was a fire, and took her coat.

'Surprised?' she said.

'Very.'

'You looked as though you'd seen a ghost.'

'You took me unawares. You're looking well, Sarah.'

'Well? Ooh, I don't like that!'

'If I said, as lovely as ever?'

'That's better.'

She had put on a little weight, but she was still an attractive woman.

'I was passing,' she said. 'I thought I'd drop in and give you some moral support.'

'That was kind of you. Tea or a drink?'

'I think a drink would be nice. Scotch?'

He handed her a glass.

'Well, what a fuss!' she said.

'Isn't it? How's Harry?' He knew she had remarried her first husband, Viscount Menall, while he had been in Russia.

'We've split up again.'

He remembered the light behind the curtain when he had taken her home after that first dinner with Guy and Elizabeth. Harry Menall had been there then, waiting for her. It was because of him that they'd had their final row before David left for Russia, when he had gone to her rooms and she had refused to open the door. He had realised Menall had been with her.

'That's rather why I'm here,' she said. 'You know Harry came into the family fortune, such as it was? Not nearly what he hoped for. Anyway, he's gone out to Australia, poor lamb.'

David understood why she had come. 'And he doesn't send you anything?'

'That's it, darling.'

He decided that he was not going to play her game, and said: 'How's the acting? I saw your name recently. You were in a farce, weren't you?'

'That was a year ago. Since then things haven't been all

that bright. I've been offered parts in Birmingham and Manchester, but you know what I think of the provinces.'

She finished her drink and he gave her a second.

'Is there anything I can do?' he said. 'I don't know any theatre managements, but I might be able to get you a position somewhere else. I know someone on the board of Whiteleys.'

'Selling knickers and gloves? You're not serious!'

'Well, what then?'

She drank again. 'You see, I've had this proposition. The *Sunday Examiner* want a story about you. The real Sir David Kade. What it's like being the . . . let's not mince our words . . . the mistress of a millionaire. They'd get one of their staff people to write it, but they'd use my name.'

'I see.'

'You know I wouldn't dream of doing anything of the sort, except that circumstances –'

'May I ask how much they've offered you?'

'Rather a lot, as a matter of fact. A thousand guineas.'

He leant back in his chair and nodded. 'That is a lot.'

He knew she was lying. Probably doubling the figure. And lying again when she said they had come to her. Almost certainly she had gone to them.

She lit another cigarette and looked at him through the smoke. 'Being rather hard-pressed, darling, makes it just a teeny bit difficult to turn them down.'

'Let's see if I can guess what you're suggesting. If I give you the thousand guineas, the *Sunday Examiner* doesn't get the story. Is that right?'

'That's it, exactly.'

'You know, Sarah, I have a peculiar aversion to blackmail. I always have had. There was a time once when I might have cared what you wrote, now I don't.'

'Do you realise what you're saying?'

'I'm saying, give the *Sunday Examiner* the story. Get the money from them.'

'Do you know the sort of things they'll write?'

'Dirt.'

'They'll ask me about our love life.'

'You've heard of the laws of libel and defamation?'

'So have they. They have lawyers too. They know just how far to go.' Spots of colour had appeared on her cheeks. 'What sort of lover you were. That sort of thing.'

He rose and handed her her coat. 'Goodbye, Sarah.'

'Lover!' She laughed harshly. 'My God, if I really told them! You don't think you were my only lover, do you? I had *real* lovers. Men half your age. I could have had anyone I wanted! You thought it was Harry all the time. It wasn't. Remember that night when I wouldn't open the door? It wasn't Harry who was with me, it was Guy Jerrold. He must have laughed!'

The second letter arrived from Nash.

'The first thing to tell you,' he wrote, 'is that I have had a bit of luck in finding an interpreter. Vladivostok is not the same as Petrograd or Moscow and interpreters are difficult to find, at least one who would accompany me to Kara.

'I now have all the permissions I need, even a letter to the Governor himself, but there would have been no point in going alone.

'This is where the Wigginses have been of great help. They have introduced me to a former Post Master of Vladivostok with whom Mr. Wiggins was in close contact in his telegraph work, and he in turn has introduced me to his brother-in-law, a Mr. Vladimir Kononovitch, who was himself an exile in a remote Siberian village for five years. At the end of his sentence he came here, eventually marrying the Post Master's youngest sister.

'Kononovitch plays the saxophone. Another musician! He was exiled from Moscow because of his political writings. Now that his side has won, it might be supposed that he would be supporting the present regime, but he seems to believe that they are not much better than the last lot, and hankers after America.

'He speaks English fluently, having spent some years in the United States as a journalist. He is keen to go to Kara, which is quite famous in these parts, as you must know, for he says he will be able to write about it and sell the articles in America, which will in turn pay his passage there if he can obtain permission to emigrate. He is a large, friendly man

217

who laughs loudly. He is bald, with a tonsure, and makes me think of a wrestler turned monk or vice versa.

'We shall make part of the journey by train then take a river steamer up the Shilka River. The weather has been warm this last week and they say the season is early and the ice on the rivers is breaking up.

'I have been searching for the woman I think is Tungus Munku's wife. Mrs. Wiggins said she last saw her talking to a man near the docks. I have spent some time near the spot without any success.

'There is no news yet about the money owing to Mr. Wiggins and I have made them a small payment for helping me in the matter of the interpreter. Mrs. Wiggins has undertaken to try to find the woman while I am away at Kara.'

The letter broke off, then started in much smaller writing on different paper.

Kara Goldfields. Chita Oblast.

'We reached the goldfields early this afternoon. I have not seen the Governor yet, nor anyone, in fact, other than an officer who is giving us accommodation in his house, but I thought I would let you know that I have arrived.

'Our journey was a strange one. We came the major part by train, but could not travel up the river because the warm weather has gone and winter has returned. Ice is everywhere and some snow has been falling almost every day.

'When we left the train we had to make a long journey to Kara and we did so in what I think is called here a *narta*, a very odd kind of sled, which we had to hire.

'The exterior was made of thick canvas like a tent. The floor was covered in a deerskin and Kononovitch and I were able to lie on it under a fur rug. In a way it resembled a hut, for it had a small iron stove in it, with a smoke pipe going out of the roof. The driver kept checking the stove as we went along. It was quite warm and Kononovitch, who had travelled in such a conveyance before, made us tea on the stove.

'We were drawn by three small but sturdy Siberian ponies and reached Kara at midday, having travelled all night. The weather was so cold that Kononovitch's thermometer registered minus 30° Centigrade and the ponies and driver were covered by frost.

'The final part of the journey we did on foot because of the mountainous road. The ponies were unharnessed and used as pack animals.

'Until he was forced to abdicate, the goldfields at Kara were the private property of the Tsar and, according to Kononovitch, were worked entirely for his benefit by convict labour.

'They are not really mines in our sense, but a series of open gold placers situated at intervals along a small river called the Kara. The diggings are roughly divided into lower, middle and upper, and cover a stretch of twenty miles or more. The Governor has his headquarters at the lower diggings, and we made for that.

'It is a truly terrible place. If I go on at some length about it, please remember that you asked for details and it will give you some idea of where Lady Kade was forced to exist.

'We reached the lower diggings through a small valley bounded by low hills covered in scrub and snow. The floor of the valley comprised mound after mound of washed gravel and reminded me of the worst of our slag heaps. But in Africa at least there is sun. Here everything is bathed in a grey half-light. The snow on the valley floor is dirty from prisoners walking backwards and forwards over it and everything is in the grip of frost and ice.

'The lower diggings consist of a straggling Siberian village of low white cabins, long, unpainted log barracks, officers' houses with corrugated iron roofs, and a large, black, gloomy log building which houses the prisoners.

'On the outskirts of the village, hidden among trees and gravel heaps, are dozens of unpainted shanties and dilapidated cabins. I found out that these were inhabited by ticket-of-leave prisoners, some of whom had brought their wives and children to live in this ghastly place. Whole families crouch in these shacks while the men work out the last of their sentences.

'Everywhere there are convicts in long grey coats with yellow diamonds on their backs, being herded by Cossack soldiers in heavy sheepskin coats, felt boots and muff-shaped caps.

'Several fires burn out in the open and the Cossacks stand

by them, warming themselves. No prisoner is allowed anywhere near them.

'We went at once to the house of the prison Governor, Colonel Nikolin, but he has had to go to Chita on business and is not due back for several days. We have been given accommodation in the house of an under-officer called Koriak. The room, which Kononovitch and I must share, has two beds and not much else. There is no heating and the water in the jug on the wash-stand is frozen.

'Kononovitch knows a great deal about Kara and has been able to supply me with certain facts. Apparently the penal term of a Russian convict here, either criminal or political, is divided into two periods. During the first he is held in the prison building under strict guard. If he behaves himself, he is allowed out of prison for the last part of his sentence and can live either by himself or with his wife and children in one of the shanties in what is euphemistically called the "Free Command".

'If he is a criminal, he will have to work during the day but can go back to his hut at night. He cannot put his toe out of the limits of the penal settlement. Nevertheless dozens, if not hundreds, of convicts escape every spring and summer simply by vanishing into the *taiga*. Most are eventually recaptured; some die.

'When the prisoner has served the whole of his sentence he is sent as a "forced colonist" to some part of eastern Siberia for the remainder of his life, never being allowed to return to European Russia.

'There are also women prisoners, both political and criminal, and the women, too, have a "Free Command" and live in the little shanties of the lower diggings.

'The under-officer has promised to take us over the prison buildings in exchange for a fountain pen. We will go tomorrow before the Governor returns.

'Our guide who brought us here in the *narta* is to leave tomorrow and I will send this letter with him so that he can post it at the railway station.'

The second letter ended at this point.

'It's all very interesting,' Maxwell said, tapping the letters, 'but it's not helping us very much. We don't know why Lady Kade was kept in prison. If she *was* kept in prison. There's no proof one way or another. And Nash says that wives and children could live in this "Free Command" at Kara. It seems to me that if she had accompanied her husband into exile a judge would be profoundly moved by her devotion.' He paused. 'We go to court in less than a month.'

'I've cabled Nash at Vladivostok, but there's been no answer,' David said.

Maxwell changed the subject. 'I suppose you've seen this week's *Examiner?*'

'It's required reading,' David said lightly.

'I imagine this "Viscountess Menall" is a pseudonym, for the same person who wrote the first story.'

'No, she's real enough. She's someone I used to know, someone I thought of marrying, as a matter of fact.'

'Perhaps you were well out of it. She doesn't seem to like you much.'

David told him briefly what had happened, then Maxwell said, 'Odd things happen when a case like this gets publicity. I've seen it before. People you've forgotten or thought were friends suddenly come crawling out of the woodwork to settle old scores. Anyway, there's nothing about this that you . . . we . . . should worry about. Not as far as the case is concerned.'

David wished he would stop talking about it. When he had first read the story he had been filled with angry embarrassment and this time it was combined with a feeling of squalor.

'The trouble is, everything is innuendo, not enough to get one's teeth into as libel or defamation. Anyway, I wouldn't advise it.'

'I had no plans about that at all. One case is enough.'

'I don't suppose there's much left, is there?'

'Left?'

'Of your private life. I mean, to come out in the press.'

'Not that I can think of. I'd always thought I'd led rather a dull life.'

The days dragged on into a week and then a fortnight. David sent further cables to Nash, but received no reply. Then one morning he found a large brown envelope covered in foreign stamps on his breakfast table. It was post-marked

'Chita.' Above the letter proper Nash had scribbled in pencil, 'A merchant who supplies Kara with food returns to Chita tomorrow and has agreed to post this for me. It may be quicker than if I were to take it out myself. Our departure is problematical, for a thaw has set in and the countryside is running with water. Will write again as soon as I have anything definite.'

The letter began where the last one had left off: 'It is snowing again. We have been here three days and the Governor has yet to arrive. We are told that the bad weather has held him up.

'In the meantime, the under-officer, Koriak, has seen in us a situation he can exploit. He is an unctuous individual of peasant stock, but there is cunning in his eyes. He now has two of my pens. He also has one of my ties and, from Kononovitch, who must see everything he can for his articles, a cigarette case and socks. In exchange, I have seen more of this dreadful place than I had bargained for.

'He took us first to Ust Kara, which is probably the worst of all the prisons here, for it is built on low, marshy ground. It looks like a block of stables. The logs are unpainted, but black with age, and are now decaying. Koriak seems to have an agreement with the guards, for there was no trouble about taking us in.

'The floor of the building was spongy with damp and slimy under our feet. Kononovitch felt faint at the smell, a mixture of decaying wood, human excrement, carbolic acid and ammonia. Koriak took us through seven huge cells filled with convicts. They all rose and stood to attention as we passed, which made me feel ashamed, since some of them could hardly stand. Koriak told us that most of them had scurvy. I said I wanted to see the women's prison and he winked at me as though we shared lubricious thoughts.

'Their building was smaller and contained large cells opening into each other. The rooms were well lit and warm but the sanitary conditions were little better than the men's. The floors were uneven and decayed and in places the rotten planks had broken, leaving dark holes. The women used these holes to throw their rubbish so that the smell was almost as bad as in the men's prison.

'There was no furniture but the sleeping platforms. I never saw a blanket or a pillow. The two large cells contained forty-eight girls and women and at least half-a-dozen were carrying sickly babies in their arms.

'Next our guide took us to the shanties in the "Free Command". They were made of planks and pieces of corrugated iron. It seemed incredible that human beings could live in them through the Siberian winter. I saw women and children huddling around small fires. Their expressions were hopeless and, in some cases, vacant.

'He then asked if we would like to see the "secret cells". Needless to say, it cost me another part of my clothing. He went to fetch a lamp and we went to a building which was separated from the others. Here he showed us small cells which had no windows, no furniture, not even a sleeping platform. There was only an excrement barrel, four walls and a concrete floor. Prisoners confined in these cells lived in what he said were "dungeon conditions". He told us that most men died or went mad in these cells. Women are also sometimes confined in them.'

When David reached this point in the letter he found that the memories of the *etapes*, the smells, the despair, came back so vividly that he began to feel afraid again. He told himself he had nothing to fear, he was safe in London, but he became prey to an all-pervasive anxiety, as though his present life was the dream; the mud floor and the excrement barrel the reality.

The letter broke off at that point, and restarted some days later: 'Colonel Nikolin, the Governor of Kara, arrived back from Chita four days ago. He is a very big man, bigger than Kononovitch. He fought against the Germans, but he has the ramrod back and straight neck of a Prussian officer.

'At first we thought he was a cold man. Although I sent in my letter and permissions the moment he came back, he kept us waiting for forty-eight hours, and then in the middle of the afternoon, he sent for us.

'He wears a large moustache and he has shaved his head so that it is covered in bristles. The under-officers and staff-officers seem much afraid of him.

'He told me that it was not in the best interests of Kara to have strangers here. He knew that in years past visitors had sometimes been allowed by the Tsar's prison service, but had he known that we were coming, he would have tried to stop us.

'When I told him as near the truth about my reason for being there as I saw fit, his manner changed. Here I must confess to bending the facts slightly. In Moscow an official misunderstood me. He thought I was part of a prosecuting team and that Lady Kade had committed some crime for which I was gathering evidence. This greatly eased my way. I let Colonel Nikolin believe much the same.

'He seemed to recognise the name Kropotkin, but no more than that. When I told him that Lady Kade had escaped to Britain he was incensed.

'That evening he sent for us and we went to his house. It was larger and better equipped than Koriak's. There were carpets on the floor and wall-hangings from Bokhara and Samarkand. The furniture was painted. There was a large porcelain stove and on the other side of the room a player piano.

'He lives alone with a body servant. He had been drinking and there was an open bottle of vodka, and several small glasses, on the table. His tunic was loose and in the heat of the stove he was sweating profusely.

'He poured us drinks and sprinkled cayenne pepper on the raw spirit. It is a lot more powerful even than Cape brandy. He told us about his war experiences and how his wife and children had disappeared into the area of Russia taken by Germany under the treaty of Brest-Litovsk; how he had searched for them without finding them.

'He drank a great deal and then he played us the piano, pumping with his feet and conducting with his hands. I think he wished to see new faces. That's the only reason I can give for his invitation.

'He became very drunk and as we were leaving about midnight he told us he had found someone in the men's prison who knew of the Kropotkin affair. We should be in his office at nine o'clock the following morning.

'We were there with time to spare, but he kept us waiting in the outer room for nearly two hours. We saw him once or twice as he came out to talk to his clerks, but he ignored us. The camaraderie of the night before had gone and he was the straight-backed officer we had first met.

'There were times when Jimmy Cairns did the same thing. You got drunk with him one night and he let his hair down. The next day he regretted it. It is a difficult situation.

'Around noon, a prisoner was brought to the building. He was dressed in the regulation long grey coat with the yellow diamond sewn onto the back. His hair was shaved and his feet were wrapped in layers of rags. He appeared to be a very old man, but Kononovitch had told me that all prisoners look older than they are because of their suffering. He was extremely thin, of medium height, and his eyes had sunk deeply into his bony face. He had a thin hooked nose and looked Jewish.

'He stood in the doorway of the outer office. He was so afraid of this unexpected call and what might happen to him, that he was belching and breaking wind. He closed the door behind him but the clerk made him go outside and wait in the cold. As he returned to his desk the clerk said, according to Kononovitch's translation, "He smells."

'A few minutes later we were taken into Colonel Nikolin's office and the prisoner was brought in. His name was Lazaref. We sat on a bench at one side of the room, the Colonel sat behind his desk, Lazaref stood against the wall.

'Colonel Nikolin put several questions to him which, of course, I could not understand. Lazaref opened his mouth to speak, but instead began to cough. His lungs sounded like jelly.

'He brought himself under control. He spoke hesitantly and gave the impression that it had to be dragged out of him. I had the feeling that he thought that after all these years some event was coming back to haunt him. Kononovitch translated.

'He told us that Count Kropotkin had been serving the first part of a sentence at Kara. His wife was living in one of the shanties in the Free Command. He was to live with her when he had completed the custodial part of his sentence.

'In those days, according to Lazaref, the political prisoners had a reasonably comfortable prison house with windows which gave a view of the *taiga*. One day the Governor of

Chita Oblast came to inspect the prison, saw the view and forced the prison authorities to build a stockade fence a few feet from the windows because he said the men had come to serve a sentence in a prison, not to live in an hotel.

'They could now see nothing but the wooden fence. After several months some of them grew melancholic and six decided to escape before they went mad. Count Kropotkin was implicated in the plan.

'He did not attempt to escape himself, but helped the others. No one would have known about his part had not one of the escapees been recaptured and blamed him in order to lighten his own sentence.

'Lazaref cannot remember exactly how long Count Kropotkin was serving. He thinks it was five years, two and a half of which would have been served in the Free Command with his wife. He was now sentenced to an extra three years in the prison building, but first he had to serve a period of four months in one of the secret cells. Two months later, he died.

'I tried to question him about the events in more detail, but this appeared to be all he knew. Finally, I had to give up, for Colonel Nikolin was becoming impatient. I asked permission to make a deposition of Lazaref's statement and this was witnessed by the Governor and Kononovitch. I enclose it with this letter.

'I am afraid it is not as detailed as I would wish, but it seems to me a vital piece of evidence.

'There has been a great change in the weather. The clouds have gone and the sun is shining, but not even sunshine can change the bleakness and despair of this place.'

That was the last letter from Nash. He seemed to disappear completely into the vastness of Siberia and there was no way David could get in touch with him. Cables, letters, even the help of Sir William Maberly, all came to nothing. They could only wait.

The Royal Courts of Justice lie at the top of the Strand where it merges with Fleet Street. When the building was put up in the 1870s it looked like a great abbey, white and startling among the grimy buildings around it. Someone viewing it then, with its towers and turrets, its flying buttresses, its pointed arches and stained glass windows, might have been forgiven for thinking it more ecclesiastical than judicial. Now, nearly fifty years later, its grandeur remained but its walls had become like its neighbours, blackened by smoke and soot.

David had left his cab on the Embankment, had walked up through Temple Gardens and stood on the opposite side of the Strand, watching a milling crowd of newspaper reporters and photographers. His solicitor, Sir Gregory Stratos, had assured him weeks before that because the case concerned an infant they would make application for it to be held in private; there would be no reporters present.

He had seen taxis arrive with Maxim Perfiliev and the nanny from Cape Town, Annie Bester; he had seen his wife and Princess Gorantchikoff enter unobserved. Now it was time for him. He crossed the road and immediately the press spotted him. 'There he is!' 'Look this way, Sir David!' 'Here! Over here!' He was blinded by flashes from the cameras. Then Stratos fought his way through the crowd and together they pushed the reporters aside and finally managed to reach the huge hall, which looked like the nave of a cathedral.

'Are you all right?' Stratos asked.

They stood by the glass cases which housed the Daily Cause Lists while David straightened his tie. 'I'm fine.'

Stratos led him across the black and white marble floor,

up a stone staircase and into corridors that were like the galleries of a castle, off which were the court-rooms.

The room in which his case was to be heard was much smaller than David had imagined, a sombre place of dark wood and dark blue leather, with a high ceiling in which there was a large window so covered in grime that it let in almost no light. His first impression was that everything was crowded together: benches, tables, chairs, people. He took his seat next to Stratos, directly in front of the judge's bench. Stratos was dressed in a dark suit with a white wing-collar and tie, and his face wore its perpetual look of gloom.

'You cut things rather fine,' he said.

'I didn't want to be here too early.'

'Let me take you over the ground again: Maxwell will outline our petition and present a general view of the case and the law. He'll also give the facts which are not in dispute and which we've agreed. You'll remember that in our petition we said that. . .'

They had been over and over this ground and David allowed himself to look about the court while he half listened. There were two tables in front of the judge's bench. He and Stratos were at one and, to their left, Alexa was sitting at the other with her solicitor, Lawrence Mathers. David had not known the name, but Stratos had described his firm as 'very sound'.

David was caught again by her beauty. She had regained some of the lost weight and looked well. He felt her appearance was the barometer of her happiness and was irritated that she should be happy without him. She seemed unaware of his arrival, occasionally leaning towards Mathers as he spoke. Otherwise she sat, composed and silent, giving David only a view of her profile; she seemed almost too calm, too relaxed. He wished he could find it in himself to hate her.

As Stratos stopped talking, he felt a touch on his arm. It was his counsel, Edward Maxwell. 'How are you feeling?' he said. 'Nervous? Don't worry about it, everyone does.'

'I'm not,' David said, but Maxwell did not seem to hear.

'Just answer clearly and slowly. Remember, the judge will be writing much of it down. Nothing makes judges more irritated than witnesses who speak too fast or mumble.'

'I'll remember.'

Maxwell leant back, one arm lying negligently along the back of his bench, the other hand flipping through his notes. He looked formidable in his wig and gown, totally at ease. He was like a predator in his own territory, David thought, afraid of nothing.

A door opened and the clerk of the court came in and took his seat directly beneath the judge's bench. Alexa's counsel, Russell Ashton, Q.C., was talking to his junior, who was sitting behind him. Ashton was a small, thin man with a quiet manner and a habit of placing his hand on the back of his wig as he spoke. At first David had wondered how Alexa had managed to finance such a defence. He had considered the Princess as a source of funds, but then had remembered the emerald pendant which was the only piece of jewellery Alexa had taken from Constantia House. There was always a good market for emeralds.

He turned to smile at Jewel and Michael. There was Annie. There were Perfiliev and Cyril. He could not see Guy anywhere.

He felt a hand on his arm and saw that the judge was coming in. Everyone rose. Sat. Were silent. Mr. Justice Cole made himself comfortable. He was a tall man with a sharp, intelligent face marked by an incised line running down each cheek. They gave him the cruel look of an inquisitor, someone to whom the law might mean more than justice. When he had adjusted his papers and his cushion to his liking, he glanced towards David, looked past him and said, in a voice so soft it could hardly be heard, 'Mr. Maxwell?'

Maxwell rose, holding his gown in one hand and his notes in the other. 'May it please you, my Lord, I appear on behalf of the petitioner, whose application this is, and my learned friend, Mr. Russell Ashton, Q.C., on behalf of the respondent.' He then went on to outline the case of Kade versus Kade.

David had attended trials both in the criminal and civil courts, but he had forgotten how slow the pace was. The whole of that first morning was taken up with details of the petitions and discussion of the law involved. Although there was a short-hand writer, it seemed that Mr. Justice Cole wrote almost continuously on a yellow legal pad. Everything was low-key. The voices of the counsel became almost monotonous in their seeming lack of interest. Occasionally the judge interrupted to ask a question or put a point but, for all that it mattered, it appeared that there were only three people in the courtroom, the two counsel and the judge, and that they were discussing among themselves something that did not involve anyone else.

David became aware that the court had grown silent. Stratos was looking at him expectantly and, as he stood up, whispered, 'Good luck.'

'My Lord,' Maxwell began once David had been sworn. 'It is not in dispute that Sir David Kade was asked by His Majesty's Government to lead a delegation to Russia in 1917 at the instigation of the Russians themselves to negotiate for the Royal Regalia. Nor is it in dispute who accompanied him, how he got there, nor what occurred, until such time as he met his future wife. Your Lordship will have read the facts of their capture and the unwillingness on the part of the Russian authorities to accept who they really were. But our petition depends greatly upon the understanding of the course of events occurring directly on their capture. I will ask Sir David to go into greater detail of what happened when they were sucked into a system that is both despicable and incomprehensible to us in this country. I want the court to understand fully what Sir David did to rescue, at some risk to his own life, and rehabilitate the woman who was to repay him by removing his child from their home and herself leaving him for another man.'

David could see Mr. Justice Cole becoming restive, but Maxwell knew when to stop, and now he said: 'Sir David, please tell the court as much as you can recall of the first time you saw the woman who was later to become Lady Kade.'

As he began to speak, images and scenes came back to him. He began to recreate for the court that first night in the *etape* when he had seen her. Here in this hushed and gloomy room he was able to listen to his own voice and it seemed to him that the events he was recounting might have been experienced on a different planet. How could he make them see the wasted bodies, the spongy gums, the thin faces and burning eyes? How could he expect them to know what it was like to be covered by lice, to lie in mud, to breathe the fumes of excrement and urine to the exclusion of all else? How could he expect them to understand what it was like to shuffle twenty miles in leg-irons with icy mud coming through the rotten foot-coverings with every step?

As he talked, a kind of dread entered him. He had thought that the depression and the illness, the nightmares and the waking dreams were things of the past. Now he felt the memory of that terrible time reach out for him. He was talking of the march and how they shuffled through the *taiga* with the carts crashing behind them and the children crying and their mothers trying to comfort them, and he reached that point of the journey when finally they had no food and the prisoners were given permission to sing the beggars' song. He could see it all like a bioscope film running through his mind. He could hear the threnody and see Alexa with the others as the song rose and fell. He felt himself choking and put out a hand to steady himself on the rail. A voice, sounding from far away, said, 'Are you all right, Sir David?'

He looked through a film to the distorted figure of the judge and realised that he must have been silent for some moments. 'Thank you, my Lord.'

'Would you like a chair?'

He asked instead for a glass of water.

When he had pulled himself together he heard the judge say, 'I think this is a good point to adjourn, Mr. Maxwell.'

The court rose, and that was the end of the first day.

He had a drink with Jewel and Michael at their flat in Kensington. They talked of Nash, but there had been no news and David was beginning to feel that something terrible might have happened to him. He was still shaken from his ordeal in court and left early.

He slept badly that night and woke in the early morning with a cry on his lips, but to whom he had been crying, or why, he did not immediately know. Then the dream came back to him. They were in the rowing-boat with the ice cracking and groaning all around them as the river froze. They were impatient to be off. Alexa sat in the stern in the furs which Munku had given her. They were arguing about whether to stay and bury Guy. And then he looked up and saw a figure at the edge of the *taiga*. It was waving its arms. He wanted them to wait, but they would not. Munku cast off and Perfiliev and Cyril pushed away the ice with the long wooden poles. And still he argued for them to wait because he knew there was something they should know. The figure began to run heavily through the snow towards them, but long before it reached them, it stopped. And then David was no longer in the boat. *He was the figure in the snow.*

When he resumed his evidence Maxwell questioned him about the meeting between Alexa and Guy on the march. He described how they had met at the noon halts. He realised that Maxwell was beginning the process of destroying Alexa. But by making him recall those meetings, he was forcing him to remember too much. He had not bargained for self-inflicted wounds.

'That was excellent, excellent,' Maxwell said as they left the court-room. 'You could have heard a pin drop. Very moving indeed.' But it was said the way one actor might admire another's performance; there was a hollow ring to it. Stratos was looking gloomy, but then he rarely looked cheerful. David put on his coat and scarf and straightened his shoulders. When Maxwell smiled and said, 'I'm afraid you go through the mill tomorrow,' he replied, 'I've been through quite a few mills in my time.'

Mr. Russell Ashton, Q.C., did not cut nearly as grand a figure as Maxwell. He was smaller and slighter and beneath the gown could be seen a conservative suit of clerical grey worsted. He reminded David of the kind of minor businessman who came every day to the City wearing a bowler and carrying a furled umbrella. Even his manner was self-effacing, almost meek. But David knew that none of these things counted. Stratos had said he was a good man; that's what counted.

Ashton rose almost diffidently to his feet and spent a long

time asking a series of establishing questions, fleshing out some of David's earlier statements, and then, as he looked down at his notes, he raised his right hand and placed it on top of his wig as though to stroke his hair. It was the first time David saw a gesture with which he was to become familiar.

'Sir David, I think you said that when you were mistakenly held at the first of these road-side prisons, these *etapes*, you gave your real identity to the officer-in-charge. Is that correct?'

'Yes.'

Alexa was seated directly in front of Ashton. She was simply dressed in a dark suit and a light grey cloche hat. David tried to look over her head as he answered, for her presence so near him was disturbing.

'In your petition you have said you protested your mistaken identity to *some* of the officers, not all. Did you continue to protest all those weeks you were in captivity?'

'No.'

'Did anyone else in the group?'

'Not as far as I know.'

'You were the leader and if any dialogue were to take place between your group and the authorities you would be the one to represent your party. Were you pressed by members of your delegation to continue arguing your mistaken identity after you had ceased to do so?'

'Yes. Commander Jerrold pressed me.'

'Could you tell us then why, under his urging, you made no further effort?'

'My Lord,' Maxwell said, rising to his feet. 'I really must protest. This has all the hallmarks of a snide character assassination by innuendo.'

'Well, Mr. Ashton?' said the judge.

'My Lord, we have spent some time listening to a narrative account of this unfortunate journey in Russia. I'm not saying it was Sir David's intention, but at the end of it he emerges as something of a hero figure. I'm trying to balance this account by showing that he is as human as we all are. More so, in fact. As your Lordship knows, we are testing two parties. . .'

'Thank you, Mr. Ashton,' the judge said dryly. 'I'm well aware of what we are testing and I think it might be as well to consider this in a different way. It is the future of the infant which is the court's main concern. However, I take your point. Please go on.'

'Could you say then, Sir David, why you stopped protesting even when urged to continue by Commander Jerrold?'

'I felt we might end up worse off than we were. I thought that Mr. Amsterdam might be forced to walk. There were many ways they could have punished us.'

'I see.' His hand went up to his wig again. 'I'd like to take you now to the tragic story of Mr. Amsterdam. You state that he became weak and ill right from the beginning of the imprisonment. At this point you and the others were relatively fit. Is it true that he could not walk?'

'Yes. He travelled in a cart.'

'And it was because of his condition that you did not try to escape?'

'Yes.'

'Would it not have been wiser to have left him in a lazarette. He could hardly have been worse off there than in a cart bumping along a road, and sleeping on mud floors. Then you could have made your escape at once.'

'You mean, left him to die while we saved our own skins?'

'No, Sir David. I did not mean that. I simply meant that with your strength at that time you would have stood more chance of getting away and bringing back help.'

David suddenly found himself on the stinking floor of the *etape* with Connie lying next to him making him promise not to leave him. *Say it. Say you promise, David.* And he had promised.

'I put it to you that by delaying until winter came you made it unlikely for an escape to take place successfully, thereby endangering Mr. Amsterdam to the point that he eventually. . .'

Maxwell was on his feet. But Mr. Justice Cole intervened on his behalf. 'You are asking Sir David to speculate. I don't think we can have that, Mr. Ashton, do you?'

'As your Lordship pleases.'

Just then the door at the back of the court opened and

234

David saw someone slip quietly onto the public bench at the rear. It was Guy Jerrold. He was wearing a uniform, which David assumed was that of the Transatlantic Line.

Ashton was speaking again. 'Now, Sir David, I would like to move on to that part of your journey when you reached this hut – this *povarnia*, I understand it is called – in the snows which you say saved your lives. And the arrival of the hunter Munku. As I understand it, Munku had been tracking you and would have handed you over to the authorities for a bounty of ten roubles each had you not struck a bargain with him over the rifles and ammunition. Is that correct?'

'Yes.'

He scratched his wig as though it was a canopy of his own hair. 'But in the midst of this there is this problem of the diamonds, which I find most confusing. According to your statement, you thought that when he showed you the diamonds he carried in his little tin, he was giving you some sort of test. What made you think that?'

'I had told him exactly who we were and how we got there. At first I don't think he believed me, but then I had the feeling that he began to have doubts. I found it difficult to judge what was taking place in his mind.'

'You had told him that you were a mining magnate. Do you not think he believed that?'

'He had never heard the name New Chance.'

'But if you were who you said you were, he realised there was a chance of making money out of you?'

'I assumed so. He worked out that I would be more valuable to him if he guided us to freedom than if he handed us to the authorities.'

'To test you, he showed you diamonds which he had collected over the years. You recognised the stones, but then you smashed one. That does not sound like a conciliatory action.'

'I needed to dominate him. He had come into the hut with his rifle and until then he had been dominating us. It was he who would decide our future. It seemed to me that I should take some initiative. He was only a simple hunter, after all.'

Ashton frowned. 'So in order to dominate him, you smashed a stone he thought was a diamond?'

235

'It *was* a diamond.'

Mr. Justice Cole leant forward. 'Are you saying that it is possible to take a piece of iron as you did and crush a diamond to dust? Surely a diamond is the hardest stone on earth.'

'My Lord, given the right circumstances, this is possible. It is not generally known outside the industry, but diamonds have sometimes fallen from the cutting and polishing tables and burst into pieces when they hit the floor. It was the one piece of knowledge I had which I thought Munku did not. I assumed that, like you, he would have believed it impossible. There is no reason why anyone outside the trade should know any different.'

'Thank you. Please continue, Mr. Ashton.'

'You say that diamonds are crushable "given the right circumstances". What are the circumstances?'

'If they are flawed, there is a point at which they can be struck which will cause them to break.'

'And this one was flawed?'

'Yes.'

'Have you ever struck a diamond before and broken it?'

'No.'

'Have you ever cut a diamond on a cutting bench?'

'No.'

'Have you ever had anything to do with that end of the business?'

'No.'

'So you would not claim to be an expert?'

'No.'

'I put it to you then, that you were taking an unforgivable chance with the lives of your party by indulging in such a trick.'

'It is not a trick.'

'You yourself called it a game at the time. Do you deny that Lady Kade remonstrated with you?'

'She was afraid of the consequences.'

'Not unnaturally, I would have thought. What would have happened if your game had gone wrong and the diamond had not smashed?'

'It was a chance I had to take.'

'I put it to you that it was rash and ill-advised; that you could have achieved your object in other ways.'

'It was my decision.'

'That is my point. Now, did you offer Munku money or guns or ammunition or whatever he wanted *before* you played your game?'

'I did not think it advisable. He did not know us.'

'So in your judgement, in spite of the fact that Mr. Amsterdam was dying and, in fact, did die that night, and that Commander Jerrold was grievously ill – in your judgement it wasn't worth offering him what he wanted right at the beginning?'

'I felt I had to prove I was someone of importance so that when I made an offer it would be taken seriously.'

'I see.' He looked down at his notes. 'Now we come to the stay at Munku's house. You have stated that Commander Jerrold was already in the grip of fever.'

'Yes.'

'In fact, he had been taken on Mr. Munku's sled?'

'That's right.'

'Lady Kade or, as we should call her, the Countess Kropotkin, was already nursing him?'

'Yes.'

'Did you know that he had typhus?'

'She called it gaol fever. It was only later I knew that it was typhus.'

'But he was in a bad way.'

'Very bad.'

'She nursed him at Mr. Munku's house, but he became worse?'

'Yes.'

'And it was at this point that you decided to leave?'

'It had nothing to do with his illness getting worse. It had to do with the river freezing.'

'I have a difficulty here. First of all we have the weakness of Mr. Amsterdam. You say in your petition that you feared for him if you left him, and you were stern with me in cross-examination when you made the point that you would not, and I quote your words, "save our own skins" at the expense of his. Do you not think there is here a similar situation?

Commander Jerrold was very ill. There was no knowing whether he would die or not. Yet you decided to leave him. I wonder if you would explain that to me. Did you like Commander Jerrold?'

David hesitated. 'He was a very capable officer.'

'That doesn't answer the question. Had you got on well with him after leaving England?'

'Well enough.'

'Had he not been urging you to escape all along?'

'I could not leave Mr. Amsterdam.'

'He was a friend of yours, wasn't he?'

'I hadn't seen him for twenty years.'

'But he had been at one time?'

'Yes.'

'You could not say that of Commander Jerrold. He was not a friend?'

'No.'

Ashton leaned back to talk to his junior, then said, 'When you first saw the Countess, were you attracted to her?'

'Yes.'

'As far as you could tell, was that attraction reciprocated?'

David swung his eyes from side to side. Alexa was looking down at her hands. He was aware of Guy's shadowy shape at the back. Finally he focused on Maxwell, who was leaning forward and talking softly to Stratos. David had expected him to object to what clearly called for a conclusion, but he seemed not to be listening.

'I don't know,' he said.

'But she was clearly attracted to Commander Jerrold, in view of what happened later?'

'I suppose so.'

'Come, Sir David!'

'Yes. Yes, she seemed attracted to him.'

'Were you jealous?'

'I . . . uh . . . No.'

'Let me put that question to you again. You say you were attracted to Countess Kropotkin. She was attracted, on the other hand, to Commander Jerrold. Now, Sir David, were you or were you not jealous?'

'I envied him. Let me put it that way.'

'Were you or were you not jealous of an affection that quite clearly grew up between the two of them and from which you were excluded? Did they not meet in secret? Did they not have conversations in secret? Were they not going to escape together? When you were on the march through the snows did they not go and spend the night together away from the others in the camp?'

'You make it sound like some smutty play!' David snapped. 'You weren't there! We were trying to survive. We had no time for emotions like that!' He saw Stratos shaking his head. Maxwell was glowering at him.

Ashton looked at him for some moments. David felt trapped in the box. He wanted Ashton to stop. But the small, mild-looking man began again.

'I will ask you once more, Sir David. Were you or were you not jealous?'

'I may have been.'

'Thank you. Now, given those circumstances and given your feelings, I put it to you that you made a rash and subjective decision to abandon – and I use the word advisedly – to abandon Commander Jerrold in the middle of the Siberian wilderness.'

'I deny that. If we had not left then, the river would have frozen and I assumed at the time that we would have been recaptured. That would have been the end of us.'

He knew what Ashton was implying. But Alexa had said she was staying with Guy. The time he should have taken some other action was when she had joined them in the boat. Why hadn't he? *That* was the question he feared. But Ashton missed the opportunity and after another series of questions resumed his seat.

Maxwell rose to re-examine. 'Sir David, you were the leader of the British delegation. Once you were ensnared in the Russian prison system, what was your main ambition?'

'To bring us all out safely.'

'Did you think that Mr. Amsterdam was going to die?'

'I wasn't sure.'

'So you hoped to bring him out as well?'

'Yes. The longer we stayed alive, the more chance there was of something happening to make them believe us.'

'When Commander Jerrold fell ill, what arrangements did you make?'

'I arranged with the hunter, Tungus Munku, and his wife to nurse him. Once we had reached civilisation I thought I could make the Russian authorities understand what had occurred and we could have brought him out.'

'And he was also being nursed by the Countess?'

'Yes.'

'Why did you decide to leave?'

'To save the others. Mr. Hankey was already ill with tuberculosis.'

'You also saved Major Perfiliev?'

'We brought him out.'

'You owed him nothing. He was not part of your original party. You saved him out of simple humanity?'

'I suppose so.'

'Thank you, Sir David.'

When David stepped down from the box he thought his legs were giving way. He had to pass Alexa and it was impossible not to catch her eye. Her face was drawn and he wondered if she had been re-living the past as intensely as he had. They did not smile at each other. He nodded, and she inclined her head slightly in acknowledgement. He wondered if she had seen Guy. Then he was past her and taking his own seat on the far side of Stratos.

He looked inquiringly at the solicitor.

'As well as can be expected,' Stratos whispered. 'I knew he'd get that bone between his teeth.'

Cyril Hankey was next to take the stand and David did not hear the first part of his examination-in-chief. He felt physically and mentally exhausted and it took him some time to recover from Ashton's attack.

'. . . and he took charge right from the very beginning?' Maxwell was saying.

'Yes, sir.'

David studied Cyril. He was looking older. His hair, or what was left of it, was nearly white. Russia had taken its toll of him, too.

'Once things went wrong, it was Sir David who made the decisions?'

'Yes, sir.'

'Did you disagree with any of them?'

'No, sir. I thought he was right to do what he did. They were pretty rough, sir, them Russians. If he'd gone on pestering them . . . well, anything could have happened. Mr. Amsterdam riding in one of them carts – that was an arrangement, sir, it wasn't legal, like. You had to be inspected by a doctor and he had to give a letter which said you couldn't walk. That was the legal way. There wasn't no doctor around when they captured us.'

David had rarely heard him speak so freely.

'In your opinion then, if Sir David had made a nuisance of himself, things may have gone the worse for Mr. Amsterdam?'

'Yes, sir.'

'You've heard it suggested that Sir David should have organised an escape much earlier, what do you say to that?'

'Well, he couldn't, sir, because of Mr. Amsterdam. We wouldn't have got ten yards with him.'

'What would have happened if you had left him?'

'They did talk about it, sir. Commander Jerrold wanted to leave him.'

'But not Sir David?'

'Wouldn't budge, sir.'

'But if you had escaped early on and left Mr. Amsterdam, you might have been able to bring help, might you not?'

'Couldn't do it, sir. Mr. Amsterdam made Sir David promise.'

'Indeed?'

'I heard them, sir. One night in one of them *etapes*. Mr. Amsterdam was lying next to Sir David and he must have got the feeling that he was going to leave him. He may have heard Commander Jerrold talking about it. So he made Sir David give his word. I heard him say, "Promise me you won't leave me." Those were his words, sir, and he made Sir David say the promise out loud, like a swear.'

'Now we come to the question of the escape. You have heard Sir David tell us about that, but I would like to hear one thing from you. Were you ill at the time?'

'Lungs, sir.' Cyril tapped his chest.

'Bad?'

'I was spitting blood, sir, if you'll pardon me.'

'Did Sir David know how sick you were?'

'I think so, sir. He kept his eye on all of us.'

'What do you think would have happened to you if he had not decided to go down the river when he did?'

'I would have died, sir.'

Ashton was on his feet. 'My Lord, that is pure hypothesis.'

'Mr. Maxwell?'

'My Lord, Mr. Hankey spent two years in a sanatorium, recovering. It seems doubtful, to say the least, that he would have survived a winter in Siberia.'

Maxwell took Cyril briefly through the escape down the river, the sea voyage, the period in America. His gratitude to David was touching, but embarrassing. Even Mr. Justice Cole shifted uneasily in his chair.

'Now Mr. Hankey,' Ashton said, rising slowly. 'I'm sure we have all been most moved by your statement and I have only one or two questions which emerge from that. I understood you to say that you heard Mr. Amsterdam make Sir David promise that he would not leave him. Did you hear Commander Jerrold make a similar request?'

'No, sir.'

'When you were sick in America and were sent to the sanatorium in the Rocky Mountains, who paid the bills?'

'Sir David.'

'And since your retirement, is it true to say that you were given a cottage in Sussex, plus a pension by Sir David?'

'Yes, sir.'

'Thank you, Mr. Hankey.'

It was clear to David that Ashton would work this vein of gratitude, thereby reducing the value of evidence in his favour.

Perfiliev was next. David would hardly have recognised the Cossack officer in the crumpled uniform he had first met on the train. He was dressed in a black and white hounds' tooth check with a red waistcoat and large tie with stick-pin. David had received reports of him every now and then from New York: he had started off as a driver, but was now in charge of the car pool. He had married an American girl and was the father of a baby boy.

He looked eager and confident, as though pleased that he was at the centre of the court's attention.

'I'd like to touch on one area of your original statement,' Maxwell began. 'This relates to the time when you had escaped from the prison barge. As I understand it, you found yourself alone in the forest until you came upon Sir David and his little party?'

'That is correct.'

'What occurred next?'

'I say, I wish to join with you. But she say no.'

'Who is she?'

'She is she.' He pointed to Alexa. 'Then was Countess. She say leave Perfiliev to die. She no give damn.'

His tortured English was now overlaid with a New York accent and slang.

'Why did you wish to go with Sir David's party?'

'He is my pal. English are my pals. I say we must go together, but she say she don't want me. She say to kill me.'

There was a stir, a rustling in the court-room, and Maxwell allowed a moment's pause before he said, 'I would like to be clear on this. You wished to make your escape through the forest with Sir David Kade and his group, but the Countess Kropotkin, later Lady Kade, wished to have you killed rather than allow you to go with them. Is that what you are saying?'

' "Kill him," she say.'

'And what happened then?'

'Sir David said. . .' Perfiliev shook an admonitory finger at Mr. Justice Cole. '. . . he say Maxim Perfiliev is my friend. He must come with us.'

'I see. And what, in your opinion, would have happened to you all if Sir David had not decided to go down the river before it froze?'

'We are dying.'

'My Lord. . .' Ashton began.

But Maxwell interrupted. 'My Lord, I think it would be true to say that Major Perfiliev's opinion is expert. He himself served in a Cossack regiment in eastern Siberia for five years. His opinion on what would have occurred had they been stranded in the Siberian winter therefore has importance.'

Mr. Justice Cole turned his long, ascetic face to Perfiliev

and said, 'Major Perfiliev, why do you believe you would have died in those circumstances?'

'He would killed us.'

'Who would have killed you?'

'The hunter, Munku. We are eating his food. He cannot feed us for whole winter. We are too many. So he kill us. He get ten roubles for each, dead or alive.' It was said with complete confidence.

Maxwell touched on what had happened in America, anticipating that Ashton would also mention it. Again David sensed the conflict: Maxwell was showing him as a generous, caring person; Ashton's object was to show that his grateful companions would therefore be biased in his favour.

Ashton rose and began his cross-examination. 'You say that when you wished to go with them after the barge had sunk, Countess Kropotkin said, "Kill him," or words to that effect. Do you think now that she meant them or were they said in the heat of the moment?'

'She say them, she mean them.'

'Can you think of any reason why a woman like Countess Kropotkin would wish to see you dead?'

Perfiliev scowled. 'She no like me.'

'And the others?'

'They like me. They are pals.'

'Why would she not like you? Did she know you previously?'

'I never see her before.'

'Mr. Maxwell has said that you were in a Cossack regiment which spent part of its time in eastern Siberia. Where were you before that?'

'St. Petersburg. Other places.'

'What were your main functions in peacetime?'

'I no understand.'

Ashton picked up a heavy file and said, 'I have in this file copies of documents, extracts from newspaper articles and books, copies of sworn statements which have emerged from Russia in the past twenty years, describing how the Cossacks were used by the Tsar to attack his enemies.'

'It is so. We attack Tsar's enemies.'

'Farmers. Land-owners. Some nobility. Would you agree

that the Cossacks were sent in to burn out private individuals, to kill them and their wives and children?'

'They enemies of Tsar,' Perfiliev said. 'We must obey.'

'Is it true that Cossacks were used for this all over Russia?'

'Because we are best.' He nodded and smiled.

'You are proud you were a Cossack?'

'Very proud.'

'But you weren't always proud, were you?'

'What do you mean?'

'I mean that when you were taken prisoner with Sir David's party, did you not beg him and the other members not to mention that you were a Cossack?'

Perfiliev hesitated. 'I no remember.'

'Were you not afraid of being found out? Afraid of what the other prisoners might do to you?'

'I no remember.'

'So if the Countess knew that you were a Cossack, it might be understandable for her to say what you allege she said – in the heat of the moment? Would you agree with that?'

Perfiliev seemed to gnaw at this, and suddenly he blurted out: 'They say Cossacks always want blood. They say Cossacks murder women. Children. I not kill children.'

'And women?' Ashton said quickly.

'Not women. Not child. Sir, I am Cossack. I am told, you go there, you do that, you do this. I must do it.'

Ashton paused, then said, 'I'd like to ask you about these snow hurricanes. The *purgas*.' A look of relief crossed Perfiliev's face. 'Had you ever experienced one before?'

'Not in *taiga*.'

'Were you physically weak at that time?'

'All weak.'

'Starving?'

'Yes.'

'Did the Countess talk to you at all during your march?'

'Only once. She come to me to ask for knife.'

'Did you know what she wanted it for?'

'No.'

'Was she carrying anything in her arms at the time?'

'Small dog.'

'Did she appear to have affection for that dog?'

'She love dog. In *etapes* she carry always dog in her arms and ask food for it. On march she carry dog. Everywhere she carry dog. She talk to dog. She petting dog. She loving dog.'

'And what did she do when you gave her the knife?'

'She killing dog.'

'Did you eat soup made from the dog?'

'Yes.'

'Do you think you would have lived through the storm without that food?'

'Maybe. Maybe not.'

'Did the Countess stop you from eating the soup?'

'No,' he said reluctantly. 'She give it to me.'

'Then you don't think she wished you dead at that point?'

He hesitated, then said, 'Maybe not. But I no kill dog. I no kill children. I no kill women.'

'Thank you, Mr. Perfiliev.'

David had turned to look at Alexa when the dog was mentioned. Her face was cold, and he remembered a moment in the Cape, after they had come back from Kimberley. He had suggested that he buy her a dog as a companion. 'Are you mad?' she had said. 'I never want another dog!'

Annie Bester was the last witness to be called that day. Her plump brown face was tense with fright, her dark eyes outlined by white. She had been uneasy ever since she had arrived in London. The city had overawed her, and now she showed all the signs of a lengthy period of worry. She was dressed in a dark frock, dark summer coat and navy blue straw hat. She gave the impression of being a Methodist from an exotic clime.

Maxwell established her as Sophie's nanny at the Cape of Good Hope. At first she was so afraid of the judge and the court that her answers were hesitant and barely audible. Mr. Justice Cole asked her to speak a little louder.

'I'm sorry, Master,' she said, falling automatically into the vernacular of the Cape.

'That's quite all right, Mrs. Bester,' he said. 'I understand perfectly how you must be feeling. There is no need to be afraid. No one is going to bully you or make a fool of you in my court. Just answer to the best of your ability.'

Maxwell took her through the ritual of her day at the Cape

with Sophie, the bathing and the feeding and the entertaining, and as she spoke her voice gradually grew more confident and there was a warmth in it that had been absent before. It was apparent to David that her love for the child shone out in that gloomy court-room. He had already decided he would ask Annie to stay on in London when he had custody of Sophie.

'Now, Mrs. Bester, you have given us a typical day in looking after Sophie. What part did Lady Kade play in all this?'

'Master?'

'You say you bathed and fed the child, changed her, took her on picnics. What, we would like to know, was her mother doing? Did she not help?'

'No, Master.'

'Would you tell us how much of the day she spent with her child?'

'She come in after breakfast for a while.'

'Is that all?'

'Yes.'

'Did she feed Sophie herself?'

'No, Master.'

'Did she bath her?'

'No, Master.'

'Did she take her for walks?'

Annie thought for a moment, then said, 'I think once, Master.'

'In how long?'

'Two, three months.'

'So you were left in charge of Sophie?'

'I and Miss Jewel.'

'Miss Jewel being Sir David's daughter-in-law?'

'That's so, master.'

With growing confidence, Annie looked around the court as Maxwell took his seat. She caught David's eye and smiled.

'Now, Mrs. Bester,' Ashton said, in a voice that almost matched her own low-key tones. 'You say that Lady Kade only visited Sophie after breakfast. Are you sure that was the only time?'

247

Annie thought for a moment and said, 'Sometimes she come at supper-time.'

'And she *never* fed Sophie? She never took the spoon from your hand and fed Sophie herself?'

'I think. . .'

'Yes?'

'I think she do that sometimes.'

'Those walks that you took with Sophie, did Lady Kade never follow you out into the garden, perhaps take the pram for a little while?'

'No, Master.'

'I understand there are vineyards around the house. Did she never walk with you through the vineyards and take the pram?'

Again she paused to think. 'Maybe a couple of times.'

'So in fact, Lady Kade did see her child, she did take part in the feeding and entertainment and the general caring for her? You forgot those things, didn't you, Mrs. Bester?'

Suddenly Annie's whole demeanour changed. She spoke to Ashton, but it was plain she was addressing Alexa. 'Madam never took Miss Sophie out in the motor-car. She never came with us when we took her for picnics. Miss Jewel was the one who looked after Sophie more than Madam. Miss Jewel was there all the time. Miss Jewel took her on picnics. Madam never loved Miss Sophie!'

The last sentence was delivered on a rising nasal inflection and the court was suddenly silent.

Maxwell half rose. There was a satisfied expression around his mouth. 'No further questions, my lord.'

As Annie stepped down David's mind was caught by the vision of Alexa holding Sophie by the window. He forced himself not to think of it.

[7]

'Ashton had no right to cross-examine you in that way,' Jewel said.

'That's his job,' David said. 'I don't say I liked it, but he was only doing what he thought best for his client. Maxwell will do the same to Alexa.'

They were in his Bayswater house. Michael had gone down to Sussex and Jewel had dropped by, as she often did, for their London apartment was only five minutes away, in Hyde Park Gardens, and the summer evening was fine. He supposed she had come to give him moral support, and wished she hadn't. He was so tired that he felt an iron ring was clamped round his forehead.

'He tried to make you look like a coward, or at least someone without a sense of responsibility,' she said. 'It's so unfair after all you did for them. If it hadn't been for you they would probably all have died.'

'I don't think so. Anyway, Maxwell and Stratos think we've had a good day.'

He had gone straight from the Courts of Justice to have a late tea with Maxwell in his chambers in New Square.

'He's trying too hard,' Maxwell had said of Ashton. 'He hasn't anything solid, so he's trying to turn things on their heads. It's a good ploy for a jury because it confuses them, but not with Cole.'

Jewel was not to be satisfied. 'It was horrible the way he kept sniping at you.'

'But we knew it was going to be horrible. That's inevitable in a case like this.'

She wasn't listening. 'It's ridiculous. The person everyone should be most concerned with is Sophie, and yet she's

249

completely lost, hardly mentioned. And if it wasn't for her, none of this would be happening.'

'Sometimes I wish it wasn't. I hadn't realised it was going to be this destructive.'

'Don't forget what she did! She took Sophie!'

'I've been thinking about the Cape a lot lately,' he said. 'Annie underlined it today. Maxwell's cock-a-hoop about her. He thinks Ashton lost sympathy with the judge by trying to make her into a liar. It's just that looking at it from Alexa's viewpoint. . .'

'Stop trying to see it through her eyes,' Jewel said. 'You know what she did to you! And Guy was sitting there in court as if butter wouldn't melt!'

David held up his hand. 'What I was going to say was that we must have made a pretty formidable pair, you and I, at the Cape. And with Annie on our side as well, that made us three to one. We did monopolise Sophie, you know.'

'You mean I did,' Jewel said.

'Not at all.'

'Yes, you do. Michael's been at me, too. He thinks . . . well, it's obvious what you both think. But I *wasn't* trying to take Sophie over. I promise you I wasn't.'

'Of course you weren't. I'm just saying it was hard for Alexa coming into a strange society without friends or even acquaintances. We outweighed her. We were always taking Sophie out on picnics or to the beach or somewhere else.'

'But we always invited her.'

He smiled grimly. 'That was nice of us, wasn't it?'

She rose. 'I must go.'

He didn't try to stop her. 'I'll walk back with you.'

He said good-night to her on her doorstep and thought about a brisk walk in the park to restore his physical balance, but after he had crossed the Bayswater Road he found the park was filled with young people who all seemed wrapped in each other, and he felt a sudden bitter pang of envy, as though he was standing on the far side of a window, looking in at a world he could not join.

As he reached home, the telephone was ringing.

A voice said: 'Is that Sir David Kade?'

'Yes.'

'This is Cable and Wireless, sir. We have a cable from Moscow for you. We would normally deliver it in the morning, but it's marked urgent and full-rate. Would you like me to read it?'

'Yes. Read it slowly. I'll take it down.'

'The text reads: "Am bringing back vital evidence. Leaving Moscow immediately by rail. Arriving Liverpool Street Thursday, imperative you get postponement." The signature is Nash.'

'But what *is* the evidence, Mr. Maxwell?' Mr. Justice Cole asked. 'You say it is vital, but what is it?'

'At this stage I am unable to say, my Lord. We only received the telegram last evening.'

'I really don't see how I can help you. This case is consuming rather more time than I had foreseen and as you know, the long vacation is not far off. It would mean postponing until the autumn.' He looked down at his diary and shook his head. 'No, we shall just have to soldier on, Mr. Maxwell.'

'Very well, my Lord.' Maxwell resumed his seat.

'I would have given odds on that,' Stratos said to David. 'Never an earthly.'

Alexa took the stand.

When Ashton had established her, he turned to the Bench and said, 'My Lord, there are certain aspects of this case that make it unique in my experience. According to the evidence so far given, my learned friend is well on the way to showing that my client is an unnatural mother. The only way we can counter this is if we can go back and show who and what she is. She has not wanted to talk about herself, but sees now that unless she is able to explain her motives, the court will be out of sympathy after what it has already heard.'

David was staring at Alexa. Her face was drawn and pale and her black suit, black beret and white blouse only served to heighten her pallor. As she had never spoken of her past, even to him, he realised how desperate she must feel to be prepared to expose it in court.

The judge looked across and said, 'Mr. Maxwell?'

'We have no objection, my Lord. The more we know about Lady Kade, the better.'

David registered the irony of the situation. Nothing would please Maxwell more, for if her stay at Kara was introduced by Ashton, he would be able to cross-examine, and Nash's discoveries would be vital. David found himself holding his breath as the trap opened before her.

There is a curious phenomenon that sometimes occurs in the Royal Courts of Justice when a case takes an unexpected or interesting turn. The first reaction is seen in the courtroom itself. People stop whispering, the judge leans forward a little more, silks who have been sprawled on the benches, seemingly oblivious to what is going on, untangle their legs and sit up straighter. Like ripples on a pond, the word spreads through the great neo-Gothic building and soon barristers between cases or waiting for juries, enter the court and stand in small clumps near the doors, listening.

This is what occurred soon after Alexa began to give evidence. A feeling arose that the case had reached a critical point, that things were being said that had not been expected. No one was more aware of this than David. He stared up at Alexa's pale face, listening to every word, straining to catch some of the sentences, which were said so softly that the judge had difficulty hearing them.

At first she answered Ashton's questions haltingly, but then, the more deeply she delved into her past, the stronger her voice became. It was as though she was coming to terms with thoughts and memories she had tried to bury long ago.

Ashton struck a low-key approach to match her own, prompting softly, drawing her on.

She told the court first about her childhood as the daughter of a first secretary in the Imperial Russian Embassy, first in London, then in Washington; how she had been educated at a girls' boarding-school in Sussex and later in America and Switzerland; how as a young woman she had married Count Kropotkin. All of which David knew.

And then, suddenly, he was in a different world: the world of Tsarist informers, of sudden disappearances, of night arrests, of censorship, of imprisonment without trial, of 'accidents' which occurred to liberal thinkers, of the outlawing of societies, of terror and panic and exile.

Count Kropotkin, she said, had been born into one of the oldest families in St. Petersburg. The first time he came into contact with the secret police was when he was a student at the University. He was arrested for having a copy of Emerson's *Self-Reliance* and refusing to say where he had got it from. In fact, it had been lent him by his professor and Kropotkin might have saved himself a spell in the cells if he had said so at the beginning. But he was not that sort of man. He combined, according to Alexa, impetuousness with a sense of honour and an outspokenness that made him enemies. When his professor discovered what had happened, he soon secured his release. But from that moment, there was a police file bearing his name.

At the end of his University career he joined the Government service and soon held an important post in the Post-Office. It was at this time he married Alexa.

His career was checked when he came into headlong conflict with the Minister of the Interior, who ordered him to spy on several individuals in St. Petersburg by taking notes of all telegrams which they received or sent. He refused. From that moment, he and Alexa were watched constantly by the secret police.

After the birth of his son, he decided to give up his job and retire to his estate about fifty miles from the city.

'Can you tell us why he made this decision?' Ashton asked.

'We were being followed everywhere,' Alexa said. 'Even when I took my child to the city or walked with him by the river, they would follow us. They knew that neither I nor my husband had anything to do with politics. It was their way of harassing us. If we had not had a child, I think my husband would have stayed to fight them. But we went into the country because he thought it would be better for us.'

'And what happened there?'

'It was the only tranquil time in our marriage. . .'

The estate had been remote and the peasants still unaffected by the new feeling of independence and impending change which was beginning to spread across Russia. Time seemed to have stood still, life moved at a slow pace. The house had been in the Kropotkin family for more than a hundred years. At one time it had been a hunting-lodge and was built mainly of wood. They lived there in isolation, but in a dreamy kind of happiness, with their small son and their dogs, while Kropotkin carried out scientific experiments in cross-breeding cattle, trying to increase their meat-to-bone ratio. He became one of the first scientific agriculturalists in his area.

But soon the idyll was to end.

Several of their friends in St. Petersburg were arrested for joining banned societies and one day a troop of Cossacks rode out to the estate and burnt the house to the ground.

'Had you done anything to provoke them?' Ashton asked.

'No. At first we thought they were passing by. My husband asked them if they wanted water. Then they stopped and we knew they had come to see us. "Paying a visit from the Tsar," as it was called.'

'Was anyone injured?'

'My husband. An officer tried to take my son from my arms. My husband struggled with him and a trooper hit him on the left side of his head with a gun-butt. Forever afterwards he had a ringing in that ear, and sometimes it would bleed. He always had to wear cotton-wool in it.'

Maxwell rose. 'My Lord, is this all really necessary?'

The judge looked irritated. 'Sir David was given great latitude, Mr. Maxwell. I think it would be courteous to extend the same facilities to Lady Kade.'

Alexa went on: 'We took my husband to his mother's house in St. Petersburg and I nursed him until he was better. Then they arrested him and sent him into exile.'

'Will you tell the court what the charge was,' Ashton said.

'My Lord, there was a charge in Russia at that time which said that you could be arrested for being a person who intended at some time in the future to overthrow the existing form of Government.'

'And your husband was tried on this charge?' Ashton said.

'There was no trial. He was "processed". You did not need to be tried for a political offence.'

'Did you accompany him into exile?'

'No. The baby was too small.'

'How long was he to be exiled?'

'Three years.'

'He wrote you letters during that time?'

'Yes.'

'Would you tell us what happened to him.'

Kropotkin had been sent to a small town about two hundred miles from the Mongolian border. It comprised fifty or sixty houses and, as places of exile went, it was not too bad. There were half-a-dozen other political exiles and they were allowed to meet in each other's houses.

The system, as Alexa described it, was that a political exile could rent rooms, or a house if it were available, take a certain number of books and personal possessions, and live out his exile in comparative comfort.

At first Kropotkin found his life not too onerous, except for the central fact that he missed his wife and baby. He took with him a telescope and other pieces of scientific apparatus.

For nearly a year he lived in comparative peace, but then his unbending character brought him into conflict with the authorities once more. He and his fellow exiles had been reporting to the police once a month, as laid down in regulations. The authorities in the town were relaxed, and exiles were able to travel in the district, even to spend nights away on expeditions, provided they did not leave the area.

After several escapes from neighbouring towns, a directive arrived from St. Petersburg ordering all exiles to report once a week. Kropotkin refused. He was willing, he said, to report once a month, but not once a week. His fellow exiles begged him to reconsider but, as he wrote to Alexa, he found that he could not bring himself to comply with an unfair directive. Travelling about the huge district on his own, camping out, studying the local flora, were the only things that made his exile bearable. He was arrested, held in the small gaol, until orders came through changing his place of exile to a different area, hundreds of miles away in north-east Siberia, near a place called Verkhoyansk. The village was so small it was not marked on many maps.

'I applied to the authorities in St. Petersburg to be allowed to join him,' Alexa said.

'And did they grant you permission?' Ashton asked.

'Yes.'

'Will you tell the court how you got there.'

'I had to travel with a batch of prisoners from St. Petersburg. It was the only way. First by train, then by steamer down the Lena, then by sled.'

'How long did it take?'

'Four months.'

The court was hushed. David stared at her and inwardly cringed at the thought of what she had endured.

'Did you take your child?'

'No. He was old enough to leave with my mother-in-law.'

She had reached the village in the autumn, having travelled the last section by sled over a vast, wintry landscape, and had found her husband living in one of fewer than a dozen houses crouched on the bank of a small river. It was more of a burrow than a house. Half of it was underground. It comprised a single room about fourteen feet square with four windows facing the east and south, which gave it sun. In the mornings it glittered through the ice panes which covered the glass both inside and out. It was heated by a small stove and the furniture consisted of two tables, several chairs, a bed and a cupboard. The wood stove was too small to warm the house and in all the months Alexa lived there she could not bring the temperature higher than fifty degrees Fahrenheit even in summer. They had to wear thick clothing indoors all the year round. At night when the stove went out, everything froze, even the ink in Kropotkin's ink-well. Their diet comprised a little meat – dried reindeer, which made them long for fat – but mainly fish. They bought cereals in Verkhoyansk and vegetables when there were any.

Kropotkin had a dog-team and sled which was vital for his trips to Verkhoyansk. When Alexa arrived she found he had already fallen foul of the police chief there. His reputation as a haughty aristocrat who had refused to report to the police in his last place of exile, had preceded him. Here, although the village was twenty miles from the town, he was forced to report once a week. In summer this was arduous enough, but in winter it became a nightmare.

'We have heard a great deal of the cold in Siberia,' Ashton said, 'but I think Verkhoyansk is something special, is it not?'

'It is the Pole of Cold. The coldest place on earth.'

The town, she said, lay in a basin surrounded by mountains which produced a strange, still, windless climate. In winter the freezing air could not be moved away on wind so instead, being heavy, it settled in the basin. Temperatures had been registered as low as minus ninety-four degrees Fahrenheit. It was a place where, in winter, a glass of water flung into the air landed as ice crystals; where spittle froze before reaching the ground; where partridges were seen to fall like stones in flight, freezing to death in the air; where live wood became petrified and sparks flew if one attempted to chop it.

Summer was as bad in its own way and the inhabitants feared it even more than winter. Then the place was infested by mosquitoes and people moving in the *taiga* were enveloped by clouds of the insects. Domestic animals were frequently bitten to death. During the humid months of summer, smoky fires were kept going in all the houses as a protection against them and huge areas of the forest were set alight for the same reason. It became difficult to breathe.

Verkhoyansk was considered the worst of all places in which to be exiled, and a number of prisoners had committed suicide there; others had died from the unendurable conditions.

Alexa told the court she thought she and her husband might have survived had it not been for the regularity with which he had to report to the police. He had begged to be allowed to change his place of exile and live in the town itself, but this was refused. It meant that in winter he had to struggle through snowstorms to reach Verkhoyansk. He might be only half way back to his house before he had to turn round again so as not to be late for the next report. In summer he was almost choked to death by the smoke or eaten alive by mosquitoes. She sometimes went with him, but mostly she would have to stay in the house to keep it clear of snow which blew in during the frequent storms.

Conditions became so intolerable after a time that Kropotkin began to suffer from what was called 'Arctic hysteria'. It stemmed directly from the climate and took the form of a mimicry mania, the victim mechanically repeating whatever he heard, words he did not understand, even animal sounds. When Kropotkin showed signs of this hysteria she knew he would die there unless they could get away.

They began to talk of escape and concocted a plan in which she would return to St. Petersburg while he would travel north during the short summer, making for the Arctic Sea, where several nations, including America and Japan, came to hunt the whales. Exiles had escaped this way before. He was to try to reach America, where she would join him.

'I went back to my mother-in-law's house, but it was almost half a year before we heard what had happened to my husband,' she said. 'He had managed to get down the Lena to the sea and found a Japanese whalerman who was willing to take him to Yokohama, but the ship was searched before it left and he was found. He was brought back to St. Petersburg and sentenced to five years at the mines of Kara.'

'Were you allowed to see him before he was removed?' Ashton asked.

'Once. They kept him in one of the casemates of the fortress of St. Peter and St. Paul. It was a dark place, a dungeon. He had lost weight and he wore a thin beard. He looked old, not the man I had married. I knew that if he went to Kara by himself he would soon die, so I joined him. I had to take my son, because his grandmother had died. I could not leave him.'

'Did you travel with the prisoners this time?'

'No. We followed in the train.'

'We have heard these mines mentioned before, Lady Kade. Would you describe them to us?'

'They are not really mines. The Kara is a small river in eastern Siberia where they have built prisons, so that the people can work. They are what you would call "placer mines".'

'Where the river gravels were washed for gold?'

'Yes.'

'And this is what your husband had to do?'

'No. He was a "political". They did not have to work.'

'Where did you and your son live?'

She was silent for some moments and Ashton said, 'Would you like me to repeat the question?'

She shook her head. 'I find it difficult to describe it. They

258

call it the Free Command. It is where relatives stay, or prisoners who have served the first half of their sentence. But you can hardly imagine such places. They are like . . . I don't know . . . kennels for dogs. The prisoners and their families build them. The authorities do nothing. They are made of sticks and planks and tar paper and pieces of corrugated iron. You would call them shanties.'

'You lived in one of these with your son?'

'Yes.'

'How old was he then?'

'Seven.'

'Were you not worried about him?'

'All the time. Before we left St. Petersburg we had been told that there was a village with proper houses to rent, but there was not.'

'What did you do there?'

'Tried to live as normally as possible. I gave my son lessons every day. We waited for my husband to be released to the Free Command.'

'But he was never released, was he?'

'No. There was an escape. Six men made a plan to break out, using dummies on the sleeping platforms. They were not missed for three days. But then one was caught and brought back. He told how my husband had helped to make the dummies.' For the first time, David heard a weakness in her voice. 'They took him and put him in one of the secret cells. They are small rooms without windows or furniture. Just a bucket. They gave him bread and water and meat once a week.'

'And what were you doing at this time?'

'Nursing my son. He had caught typhus.'

Mr. Justice Cole said, 'If you would like to stop now, Lady Kade, please tell me and I will adjourn while you rest and collect yourself.'

'Thank you, my Lord, but I would like to get this over. I knew that my son was very ill and I went to the Governor to ask for permission for my husband to come to him. I thought it might help. But he refused. My son died. I didn't want the news to reach my husband, but in a place like that you can keep nothing to yourself. When he heard, he killed himself. I

think the solitary confinement had harmed his mind. He had
always kept a piece of glass wrapped in paper in his shoe. He
showed it to me once. He said he would only use it as a last
resort. When he heard about our son, he cut his wrists and
bled to death.'

David had listened to her with a mounting sense of horror.
Nothing in his life with her had prepared him for what he
had heard. Even the march they had endured together had
been trivial compared with what she had already gone
through.

She went on: 'I buried them in the cemetery on the hillside.
Others in the Free Command helped me to dig the graves.
Then I went to the Governor for travel documents that would
allow me to return to St. Petersburg. I carried a kitchen knife
under my coat. After a clerk had given me the documents I
begged permission to pay my farewell respects to the
Governor. I was told I could go in for half a minute, but that
was all I needed. I stabbed him. He died a few days later.
They kept me in a secret cell and then took me back to St.
Petersburg for trial. I was held in the same fortress as my
husband had been.'

'And what was your sentence?'

'To spend the remainder of my life at the Kara mines.'

'Never to be released?'

'Never.'

'It was on the journey there that you met your present
husband?'

'Yes.'

The evening meeting in New Square between David, Stratos
and Maxwell was grim. Maxwell sat at the round rosewood
table and ate a plate of buttered muffins, gulping them down
with long draughts of tea. He dabbed at his lips and said,
'We're going to lose if we're not careful.'

At that moment David disliked him intensely. He reminded
him of a petulant baby and it was clear he was looking for
someone to blame for imminent failure.

'It's only her word,' Stratos said.

'Every single point we had has already been explained,
already admitted – though in the context it's hardly an

admission of anything. Her story is like one of those unread-able Russian novels, and if I press her too hard, the judge will protect her. You heard him today. It's quite clear he is sympathetic towards her.' He rose and paced restlessly about the room. 'I thought those letters from Nash would do it, but she's anticipated what's in them, explained and expanded on them.'

'There are areas still to be explained,' Stratos said, but Maxwell took no notice of him.

'Try and see it from the court's point of view,' he said. 'The child's future is its main preoccupation, but it cannot, indeed, must not, divorce itself from the other parties. Here is a case of two warring parents, one of whom has committed misconduct. But you'll remember that I told you at the begin-ning misconduct is no reason alone to remove a child from the mother's custody. Sir David, your daughter is a baby, an infant, and who is the ideal person to look after an infant if not the mother? And now we hear the mother's life-story, one of loyalty and courage. . .' He paused, then said in a firmer voice. 'We have to find something to attack her story with. There *must* be something. No one is as brave and selfless as that; no one can endure so much. But how?'

'There's Nash,' Stratos said. 'He's due tomorrow.'

Maxwell scratched his head. 'Well, let's hope there's no hitch. We're going to need this "vital" information, whatever it is.'

[8]

The noon boat train from Harwich, which connected with the steamer from the Hook of Holland, was nearly an hour late because of fog in the North Sea. David waited impatiently at the barrier on a close summer's day. The station was full of the smell of hot oily steam as the L.N.E.R. locomotives came and went to a cacophony of shrilling whistles and slam-ming doors. When his train arrived the passengers and porters passed him in waves. He craned to see over their heads, but finally had to accept the fact that Nash was not on it. He telephoned Jewel and asked her to meet the following train, then took a cab back to the court.

Maxwell was already well into his cross-examination of Alexa. He glowered when David shook his head in silent reply to the unspoken question.

The court-room was fuller than it had been on the previous days: word had gone round that the case of the millionaire and the Countess was reaching its climax. As Stratos had said, if the press had been reporting the evidence, there would have been queues out to the pavement.

Alexa was once again dressed in dark colours which contrasted with her white face. She seemed less composed than earlier. Her hands gripped the rail in front of her. David soon discovered why. It was clear that Maxwell had weighed his tactics against the possibility of alienating the Bench and had decided that he would have to break her down in some way, for his tone was truculent and overbearing.

'This person Zagarin,' he was saying. 'You tell us he was your "protector". What precisely do you mean by that?'

'He protected me from the others.'

'Can you be more clear on that.'

'It was dangerous for a woman in the *etapes*. Things could happen. . .'

'What kind of things?'

'Some of the men were wild. They had committed crimes of violence. And there were the guards as well. They wanted favours. I knew from experience what could happen.'

'Are you saying you were afraid they would interfere with you?'

'Many of the women were raped. Not once, but many times.'

'This man Zagarin was to protect you from such . . . ah . . . interference? Did he do this out of pure altruism?'

She looked confused.

'What are you trying to suggest, Mr. Maxwell?' the judge said coldly.

'My Lord, we have heard a good deal about courage and

262

fidelity and I am simply exploring those avenues to find out what else may lie down them.'

'It was better to be the woman of one man only,' Alexa said bitterly. 'And he was the leader of the *artel*. In Kara he would have had power. The rest of my life was to be spent in Kara.'

'So you were using him for your own benefit?'

'Yes.'

'What was your attitude to Commander Jerrold. Was he also a "protector"?'

The word hung in the air in its quotations marks and David felt a sour taste in his mouth. Maxwell was able to turn ordinary words into something different and he recalled how he had been warned of this at the start.

'No.'

'What was he?'

'He seemed like someone from another world.'

'And you decided to become friendly with him?'

'Yes.'

'Would you say that Commander Jerrold was a good-looking man?'

'Yes.'

'So it was natural you would seek him out?'

'No. It wasn't because of his looks.'

'Why then?'

She hesitated. 'Because he wished to escape.'

'And you wished him to take you with him?'

'Yes.'

'So in fact, you were also using Commander Jerrold, is that it?'

'In the beginning, yes.'

'Did none of the others in the *etapes* talk of escape?'

'Yes, but they were weak from sickness and starvation.'

'And Commander Jerrold was strong?'

'He hadn't suffered like the others. I thought he would have a chance.'

'If you had escaped, what then?'

'I hoped he would take me out of Russia.'

'Are you saying that you had no affection at all for Commander Jerrold?'

263

'Not at the beginning.'

'But later you did?'

'Yes.'

'And did you become "his woman", too?'

Ashton leapt to his feet. 'My Lord, I must object most strongly. . .'

'I've warned you before, Mr. Maxwell,' the judge said, with distaste. 'I will not have you bullying the witness.'

'I withdraw the question, my Lord.'

Unperturbed, Maxwell moved the papers in front of him into a neat pile, then looked up at Alexa again. 'Let me get this straight, Lady Kade. All Commander Jerrold meant to you in the beginning was a possible way out of your circumstances?'

'Yes.'

'Then you approached him quite coldly. If it hadn't been for Commander Jerrold, you would have directed your attention to Sir David Kade, as indeed you did later?'

'I suppose so.'

'You suppose?'

'I mean, yes.'

'And if neither had been there, to Mr. Hankey or, if he had been well enough, to Mr. Amsterdam?'

'Yes.'

'I cannot hear you.'

'Yes.'

'In fact, it wouldn't really have mattered so long as the person offered some chance of escape?'

'Yes.'

'Your whole affair, if I may term it such, with Commander Jerrold, was based on falsehood and self-advantage? Is that what you're saying?'

'Only in the beginning.'

'When did your feelings change?'

'He looked after me, especially on the barge. No one had done this for a long time. I had forgotten that there could be such a relationship.'

'Did you love him?'

'In a way.'

'What sort of way?'

264

'If you mean, did I give myself to him? Not then. Not in Russia.'

'You have stated that you and he slept apart from the others once you had escaped from the barge. Are you saying that nothing occurred between you?'

'Yes.'

Maxwell raised his eyes to the ceiling in an eloquent indication of disbelief.

'He was already becoming ill,' she said.

'I see. This is the illness from which you believed he had died?'

'Yes.' She spoke so softly that David could hardly hear.

'I'd like to come to that now. He had typhus?'

'Yes.'

'You were certain of that?'

'Yes.'

'You had already begun to nurse him in the travellers' hut, and continued to do so in the dwelling of the hunter Tungus Munku and his wife, Bou-Ta?'

'Yes.'

'In your opinion, was he too ill to move?'

'Yes.'

'Did you know that Mr. Hankey was also ill?'

'He had an infection of the chest.'

'An infection which turned out to be tuberculosis, for which he had to spend a long time in a sanatorium?'

'Yes.'

'Do you think, therefore, it was correct for Sir David to take him away from the hut?'

'I'm not a doctor.'

'Do you think Mr. Hankey would possibly have recovered if he had spent the winter there?'

'He would probably have got worse.'

'Were you given the opportunity of leaving?'

'Yes.'

'Did Sir David, in fact, wait for you until the very last moment?'

'Yes.'

'So you, of your own free will, elected to remain to nurse Commander Jerrold?'

'Yes.'

'But you did not stay. In the time between the other men leaving the dwelling and getting into the boat, you thought that Commander Jerrold had died. Is that correct?'

'Yes.'

'Tragic for Commander Jerrold – had it been true – but fortunate for you, Lady Kade.'

'I thought he was dead! You don't know how it was!' Her voice had risen. 'The hunter's wife was there! She knew. She could tell you!'

'But she cannot tell us. And that is the point. So much of your testimony cannot be supported that I. . .' He paused as Jewel came into the court-room. She was flushed and had been hurrying.

She leant over towards David and whispered: 'Crossley is here. You must come.'

Maxwell excused himself and listened to her for a moment, then said: 'My Lord, something has occurred which bears on the case. With the court's permission, I would request a short adjournment.'

Mr. Justice Cole looked at the clock. 'It's almost time to adjourn anyway.' The court rose.

Gown flapping, Maxwell led the way from the court-room. As David followed them into the corridor, he felt someone touch his sleeve. He turned, to see Guy Jerrold, smart in his First Officer's uniform, his wedge-shaped face tanned. But his eyes were angry.

'You must stop this!' he said.

'Stop what?'

'What you're doing to Alexa!'

David tried to shake him off, but his fingers were powerful. People were staring at them. 'It's none of your business. Take your hand off my arm.'

Guy released him. 'You say you love her. Is this how you show it?'

'Keep your voice down!'

'Don't you see what you're doing to her?'

'It has nothing to do with you.'

'You're destroying her!'

'Get out of my way!'

'My God, Kade, you're a twenty-four carat shit! First you abandon me, then you. . .' He paused. His eyes moved away from David's face and looked over his shoulder. His face paled. David turned. He saw a splash of colour, red and blue against the walls. It was Bou-Ta, Tungus Munku's wife. She was standing on the edge of a little group made up of Crossley Nash, Maxwell, Stratos, Jewel. But she seemed curiously disassociated from them. Her Buryat gown blazed in the dim light. She looked more like a doll than a human-being.

David heard Guy swear under his breath. Then Bou-Ta saw him. She gave a cry and ran towards him. For a moment, Guy seemed too confused to move. He turned towards a side corridor, but before he could leave she had reached his side and grasped his arm. She spoke rapidly in Russian, too rapidly for David to understand, but she kept repeating Guy's name. He struggled to throw her off, but she held on, tears pouring down her cheeks.

Then he shouted in English: 'For God's sake, leave me alone!'

He flung her off. She staggered across the corridor and slipped to her knees against the far wall. Guy, his eyes wide with shock, paused for a second and took a step forward as though to help her. As he did so, he caught sight of Alexa. She was standing in the doorway of the court-room and she had seen it all. Her face was like chalk and she was holding the side of the door for support. David saw Guy open his mouth, but no words came. Then he was gone, running down the side corridor, his eyes on the ground.

David and Alexa were left and it was as though, momentarily, they were in a vacuum, the only two people in the building. They looked at each other in silence.

Then David heard a whimper and turned to help Bou-Ta. When she was on her feet Nash, Maxwell and Stratos joined them. By the time he looked again, Alexa had vanished.

In his chambers, Maxwell ordered tea, then ushered them all into his conference room, where they settled around a long table.

Maxwell pulled a yellow legal pad towards him, and turned to Nash. 'I want to hear it again exactly as you said it before.'

He seemed to communicate a suppressed energy to everyone except David, who watched the proceedings as though at one remove, not part of them.

'The main thing is that Bou-Ta says Alexa knew before she left,' Nash said.

'The Countess knew Jerrold was still alive?'

'That's what she says.'

'The men had left the dwelling and gone down to the boat. Is that correct?'

'Yes.'

'What then?'

'She says that Alexa was sitting on one of the bunks with Jerrold, wiping his face. He was drenched in sweat, and shaking. The two women were discussing what would happen if he died, and Bou-Ta said her brother would come to help them bury him.'

'Let's get this straight. There were only the two women in the *yurta*, the Countess and Bou-Ta?'

'Yes.'

'Then the Countess. . .' He paused. 'What happened next?'

'She says Alexa suddenly ran out of the *yurta*. Bou-Ta thought she had gone to say good-bye to the men and was coming back. After a while she went across to Commander Jerrold. He seemed calmer, as though the fever had broken. She went outside to tell Alexa, but didn't see her. She ran down to the tree-line. Alexa was in the boat. She called and called, but the boat went on down the river.'

'Excellent!' Maxwell said. 'Excellent, excellent! She *knew* that Jerrold was still alive. She left him. Abandoned him to save her own skin. That's what it amounts to. She cut and ran. The man she loved is lying there in a bath of sweat, in extremis, and she sees her last chance of escape begin to disappear, so she abandons him.' He threw down his pen.

Stratos said: 'And you see what this does to the rest of her evidence? All her courage and self-sacrifice. It's all suspect now. The whole kaboodle.'

'She shouldn't really be in here with us now,' Maxwell said, looking at Bou-Ta. 'Still I suppose it's all right if she can't understand a word.'

The centre of their attention was sitting quite still, as

remote from the discussion as David himself. Her round Mongolian face was covered with white powder through which the tears had made runnels. Her lips were reddened, her eyes swollen with weeping. Her expression was dead.

The two lawyers were looking at each other. It was as though there was no one else present. It was *their* case and they were scenting *their* victory.

It seemed incredible to David that they were talking of Alexa as though she were a stranger whom they wished to punish; her feelings meant nothing to them. Then he realised that in fact her feelings did *not* mean anything to them, and she *was* a stranger, a quarry to be trapped, caught, destroyed.

And it was he who had put her in this position. Stratos had warned him that in a case such as this they would seek to destroy each other. Maxwell had warned him that it would be nasty. Yet he had gone ahead. Fight. Destroy. Attack. Those had been the words. And now they had her.

There could be no doubt that this evidence would make a difference. If she was proved to have deserted the man she loved, then could the rest of her testimony, unsupported, be trusted? And would someone who had abandoned her lover be the best person to look after an infant, even though it was her own?

Suddenly, it seemed to David that he had always known what had occurred on the banks of that freezing river. Bou-Ta's story was neither a surprise nor a shock. And deep down, he understood Alexa; understood that in all that strength, there had to be one flaw; to be otherwise was to be inhuman.

He heard a brisk exchange of views around him, but the picture in his mind was of the river. He had dreamt the scene so often that now he found it difficult to winnow out the reality. He saw again Alexa coming down to the boat and taking her seat next to him in the stern, her face white and set, half hidden by the heavy furs. She had told them Guy was dead.

How long had it been since they left the *yurta*, half an hour? Time enough for a fever to break. He remembered his own half-hearted move to go back. But that decision had been easily overcome by Perfiliev and Cyril. So they had said a prayer for Guy instead. If he had really felt strongly, he would have returned. Perhaps Alexa *had* thought him dead, perhaps for a moment or two he had seemed dead. The fact was that he, David, was as much to blame as she. Had his motive for setting off down the river really been only to save Cyril or Perfiliev? What about himself?

He remembered the difficulty with which they had pushed through the ice-channels, but could he say with his hand on his heart that the channels would have frozen within the next day or two? Would it not have been better to have wrapped Guy up in furs and taken him with them?

He saw again the snowscape that ended at the black treeline half a mile from the river. He saw Bou-Ta run to the edge of the trees as they were shoving off. He saw her waving. No! He knew now that she had not been waving. That was the mistake he had made. She had been beckoning, calling them back to tell them that Guy was alive, and was going to continue to live; to tell them that it would have been possible then to have taken him. But he had simply waved back and the boat had shot out into the channel and soon he was fending off the ice-floes and he had no time to look back at Bou-Ta.

He became aware of a silence, heads turned towards him.

'David?' Jewel said.

He did not know what they had been saying, nor what required an answer. 'I can understand her,' he said.

Stratos said clearly, as though repeating himself: 'But if we can show that she knew, it puts in question. . .'

'He was my responsibility, too.'

'. . . everything else she said.'

'And if you're saying that because she left him she is less worthy of looking after Sophie, then it goes for me as well.'

'You'll have to leave those decisions to the judge,' Maxwell said impatiently.

'You mean I do nothing? Opt out?'

'That's why we're in court.'

David said: 'What do you think, Crossley? You were at Kara. You're the only one of us who knows it, except Alexa. Do you think its horrors could be exaggerated?'

Nash was thinner and looked tired. As usual, he only spoke

when spoken to. He was a different personality when he wrote, David thought.

'No,' he said. 'You couldn't exaggerate it.'

David turned to the rest of them. 'Do you really believe that all we heard of her life with her first husband and the death of her child, do you really think that was all lies?' He wished he could answer his own question, but he couldn't. He wanted to be definite, but that would presuppose he knew her well enough. And he didn't. He could not be certain. He knew now that he had never really known her, had never been certain of anything.

'She lied about Commander Jerrold,' Stratos said.

'She watched her own son die of typhus. Perhaps she couldn't bear to see someone else she loved die in the same way.' He turned to Crossley. 'Did you ask Bou-Ta what she thought of Jerrold's chances?'

'She said he was on the point of death.'

'On the point of death. As far as Alexa was concerned, he was dead. She just. . .'

'If you'll forgive me for saying so, Sir David, that's sentimental,' Maxwell said. 'The point was, and she acknowledged it, you were her last chance of escape.'

'Even if that's so, what's so wrong with it? What would have happened to her, do you think, if she had been arrested again?'

Stratos interrupted. 'I'm not sure whether you're playing devil's advocate or if you really mean what you're saying.'

David shrugged off the question. 'Can you conceive of what would have happened if she'd been caught? Can you conceive of what it might be like to face living out your life in a place like Kara? What do you think, Crossley?'

'I thought about it while I was there. Even being a visitor, I'd have done anything to free myself. Anything.'

'You'd have let someone die?' Jewel said sharply.

'I'd have killed someone if need be.'

'Fortunately, we do not have to conceive of living out our lives in a Russian prison,' Maxwell said.

'I can imagine it,' David said. 'Just. I know what the *etapes* were like and I know what our lives were like and I can *just* imagine what something worse might be like. Don't you think she's suffered enough?'

'What about you?' Jewel broke in. 'Haven't you suffered? Didn't she take Sophie from you?'

'All this is airy-fairy conjecture,' Maxwell said. 'You're confused and you're confusing the issue, Sir David. The point is this: do you want your daughter?'

David paused. 'Of course I do. But if we put Bou-Ta on the stand, we'll destroy Alexa. And after what she's already suffered, she might never recover.'

'You're still in love with her!' Jewel said. 'After all she's done to you!'

'You're probably right.'

Maxwell leant back in his chair. 'It's up to you. If we are not going to put this lady on the stand, you have very little hope. And I must tell you I don't relish the idea of fighting with both hands tied behind my back.'

There was a silence as they watched David. Only Bou-Ta was not looking towards him, but into a private world of her own misery.

[9]

David walked slowly along the Strand, a lonely, isolated figure among the homeward-hurrying crowds.

Tired and depressed, he reached Bayswater and let himself into the house. A cold supper had been left on a tray in his study. He wasn't hungry. He poured himself a large whisky and soda and sat down. Throughout the long walk his thoughts had been moving steadily in one direction as he tried to put himself in Alexa's position.

It must have been shattering for her to see Bou-Ta and Guy, for clearly she had not suspected what had gone on between them in the *yurta*. It must have been even more shattering when she realised that Bou-Ta had been brought to London to destroy her. There was that word again. When had it all started, this process of destruction? As far back as

272

Cape Town, he thought, remembering the way he had talked to her when he had found out about Guy. His whole attitude had been both self-righteous and patronising. And yet she hadn't behaved like a woman who had been pleased to see her lover; she had been more like someone who had seen a ghost. Now he knew why: she had believed she owed Guy a life.

Holding the glass in his hand, he paced through the ground floor rooms of the house, through the dining-room and the drawing-room, up and down the passage, like some animal caged in alien territory.

He could not destroy her. After what he had heard, he knew he could not do it. There had to be some other way of coming to an agreement about their daughter. He was sick to death of listening to lawyers and to his family. If he had ignored Jewel's advice and gone to Alexa the moment Guy had left her, all this might have been avoided. Then Stratos had instructed him not to go near her, and he had obeyed. But now the time had come for the principals in the case to decide their own futures, to find a solution with which they could both live, without any further destruction. What he had gone through was bad enough in terms of self-inflicted wounds, but what Alexa had endured, and the expectation of what she would endure if Bou-Ta took the stand, hardly bore thinking about. It had to be stopped. *Now.*

He put on his hat, left the house and walked quickly in the direction of the Bayswater Road. He flagged down a cab and told the driver to take him to Pimlico.

It was a warm, close evening with a hint of thunder, and traffic was moving slowly. The streets were filled with people taking the air. Finally they reached Alexa's apartment and he paid off the cab. As he reached her front door he became aware of running feet and a man raced round the corner towards him. Intent on the door, he took little notice, until the man, panting as though in the last stages of exhaustion, halted beside him. He turned and looked into the eyes of Jimmy Cairns.

Both stood, immobilised with shock for a second. Cairn's face was the colour of suet patterned by purple capillaries. Sweat was pouring down his cheeks, his hair was awry and his eyes were wild. In that instant, David knew that something was dreadfully wrong.

'What is it, Jimmy? What's happened?'

Cairns's mouth opened and closed like a boated fish.

'Take it gently, man,' David said. 'Just tell me what's happened.'

Cairns pointed towards the river. 'Alexa! Alexa and Sophie . . . the bridge!'

David ran.

He reached the Embankment; Chelsea Bridge was ahead. There was not much traffic now, but people were strolling across to a summer carnival at Battersea Park on the south side of the river. He ran up onto the bridge and saw ahead a crowd fifty or sixty strong. They were peering into the water, mildly inquisitive, enjoying a bonus to their evening out. But no one seemed to know why they were there and David's questions were shrugged off.

He fought his way to the railings where a policeman stood, with an open note-book. The centre of attention was an elderly, gnomish figure dressed in the scarlet walking-out coat of the Royal Hospital, Chelsea, his high-crowned Peninsular cap a strange silhouette against the fading light.

'I seen her! She fell from there!' he was saying. His upper jaw was toothless and had fallen inwards like a tortoise, but his eyes were sharp and bright and he seemed delighted to be the centre of attention. He pointed to one of the stanchions. 'Climbed up and jumped.' The arm made a falling semi-circle. 'And down and down. . .'

'Who?' David shouted.

'Just a minute, sir,' the constable said.

'For God's sake! I think he's talking about my wife!'

'And who would you be?'

'My wife was seen coming here with her baby.' He turned to the old soldier. 'Was she carrying a child?'

'I don't know about no baby. But she was about so high.' He put up his hand. 'And she jumped. Splash!'

David drew the constable aside, identified himself and said desperately. 'I must get down there!'

'There's a launch been sent for, sir,' the policeman said.

They looked down at the river. The tide was on the turn.

Swallows were dipping. In the dusk, Chelsea Reach looked magical.

'That's her now, sir.' The constable pointed to the opposite side of the bridge and David saw a small launch with a powerful light on the cabin roof sweeping towards them from the direction of Westminster.

'What will they do?' he said.

'Use grappling hooks, sir. We know where she fell. There's no tide running. They've got a good chance to hook her.'

He turned away, feeling bile rise into his throat. At that moment a middle-aged women with a dog tapped his arm. 'Did I hear you ask if she'd been holding a baby?'

He nodded, unable to speak.

'She was holding something. It could have been a baby. I think it's disgusting, taking a young life like that. She should be punished.'

Several more policemen had arrived. The constable led David across the bridge and pointed to a path that came onto the river wall near a small concrete jetty. 'If they find her, they'll bring her to the jetty, sir. You'll see some steps.'

He went towards the path. A voice called his name and he looked around and saw Cairns. The light was going rapidly and his white face seemed almost phosphorescent.

'Have they –?'

David shook his head. 'Tell me about it,' he said.

'I was there, with the Princess, when she came in from the court. She was badly upset.' In his mind, David saw Alexa supporting herself against the court-room door, and guilt overwhelmed him.

Cairns took a deep breath. 'We had an argument. . .'

'What about?'

'Another article for the *Examiner*. It was to appear after the case was over.'

'So it was you. . . ?'

'Yes. Look, I didn't want. . . What can I say?'

'Nothing. Just tell me about Alexa.'

'She never wanted anything in the press. She didn't even know beforehand. It was the Princess and I –'

'Never mind the bloody articles! Tell me about *her*!'

'She was crying. Then, while we were still arguing, she

275

picked up Sophie and wrapped her in a blanket and left the house. Oh, God, I should have stopped her! I talked with the Princess for a few more minutes, then I thought, hell, I'd better go and have a look for her. Only I couldn't find her. And then I heard someone say there'd been an accident on the bridge and I knew, I just knew, it was Alexa. I was on my way back to telephone the police when I saw you.'

They reached the wall and saw the steps and the small jetty below. It was almost dark now and the launch was using powerful searchlights to search the surface of the river. David could hear shouted orders, the splash of the grapple as it hit the water, the pom . . . pom . . . pom . . . of the launch's engines. Behind him rose the shrill, throaty music of a calliope and shouts and screams of excitement as the big dipper swung and plunged along its wooden tracks.

Cairns was still talking, apologising, justifying, but he was no longer interested, he knew why Jimmy had provided information for the article. His mind was concentrated on the launch.

Just then he heard a shout and a sudden clanking of the launch's winch. He could see crowds on the bridge, craning forward, and then there was a burst of laughter.

Someone shouted: 'A bloody bedstead!'

He saw an old iron-framed bed, flung over the bridge at some time in the past by owners who no longer needed it.

The minutes ticked by. He realised that he had been there for an hour. They could not be alive; perhaps they had not even been alive when he had reached the bridge. Perhaps they had been dead or dying while he was still in the taxi.

The launch moved closer to the bridge, working slowly towards the south bank. It was full dark now and everything was stark. Great shadows were thrown up by the lights, white blobs of faces hung from the bridge. In spite of the warmth of the evening, he began to shiver, and put up his coat collar. He realised that Cairns was still beside him. Suddenly, he wanted to say something savage and brutal, but could think of nothing that was adequate.

He heard another shout but this time there was no following laughter. Something white came to the surface of the water, as though a huge fish or ray had been captured. Two policemen leaned over the launch's gunwale and raised something. He saw a leg and a foot without a shoe, and he knew they had found her.

Slowly, the launch swung out of the stream and came towards them. The constable from the bridge was at his side and said, 'You come with me, sir.'

They reached the jetty and David stepped aboard the boat. There were four policemen, each wearing a life-jacket. Two were soaking wet. There was something lying in the cockpit, under a dark blanket.

One man canted a small searchlight downwards, another flicked back the top of the blanket. He looked down at her. Her eyes were wide open and staring and mud had oozed from her nose and formed two lines down her lips and over her teeth and onto her chin. She was wearing a white dress. A dark woollen jumper was entangled in her hands. She looked so young, so vulnerable.

'Well, sir?'

Unable to control himself, he turned away and said thickly: 'I've never seen her in my life.'

He stumbled back the way he had come. As he did so, he passed a young man with a distraught face running towards the boat and heard him shout, 'Alice! Alice! Oh, my God!' There was more misery in the tone than he had ever heard before, and yet he himself was crying with happiness.

He walked back to Alexa's apartment with Cairns. The Princess was in the shop, cowed and tearful.

He looked at her coldly. 'Have you any idea where she might have gone?'

She shook her head.

There was a telephone on the wall of the shop.

'When she comes in, please tell her to telephone me, no matter how late. Do you understand?'

'I'll see to it,' Cairns said.

All the way home in the taxi he kept thinking of the young girl with the mud on her face and thanking God it was not Alexa.

He let himself into the house, and saw that he had left the study light on in his haste. He had already decided to spend the night downstairs near the telephone, and he needed a drink. As he went down to the kitchen to fetch a new soda siphon he considered what he should do. Alexa could not have gone far without luggage. If he had not heard from her by morning, he would put Currie onto the job; he had found her once before and could probably do it again. He went into the study.

She was lying on the sofa. In the armchair nearby Sophie was propped up by pillows. Her head had dropped to one side. Both were asleep. He stood in the doorway for a moment, looking at them, unwilling to make a sound that would break the spell, as relief surged through him. Alexa's face was calm and just as vulnerable as that of the woman in the river.

She opened her eyes and smiled.

'Don't move,' he said softly. 'You must be exhausted. We'll both have a drink.'

She nodded and pulled herself along so that she was curled up in a corner of the sofa. He handed her a glass and said, 'I've been looking for you. I saw Jimmy Cairns and the Princess.' He decided not to tell her just then about the river.

She sipped her drink, then said, 'I'm sorry to have barged in, but the servants had left the door unlocked and I wanted to speak to you.'

'I can't begin to tell you how glad I am. . .'

'I haven't come back,' she said quickly, as though to forestall what he might be thinking.

He shook his head. 'It isn't that.'

'I had to get away. I couldn't think of anywhere else to go.'

'While you were coming here, I was crossing London to see you.'

She looked surprised. 'And you met Jimmy? So you know about the newspaper articles. Hadn't you guessed it was him?'

'In a way, I can't blame him.'

'I hated it. He found me through one of the South African newspaper offices. Then he and the Princess got to work. She wanted money. He's got it in his mind that Molly died, in fact, that everything went wrong because of you.' She paused. 'Why were you coming to see me?'

'I've made some bloody awful mistakes. First, I listened to

Jewel when she told me not to see you just after Guy had gone.'

'I remember. You told me that.'

'And then Stratos made me swear I wouldn't talk to you in case I jeopardised our case. If we'd talked, none of this might have happened.'

'Do you really believe that? Don't you remember the last time we met? We said we'd fight each other.'

'Fight! Attack! Destroy! I seem to have been hearing nothing else.'

'I know. Ashton talks like that, too. He looks so mild, yet you'd have thought we were going to war.'

'That's what it's been, a kind of war. Well, it was over for me today.' She glanced up sharply. 'I mean it. I've had enough.'

She frowned. 'I don't understand. You want Sophie. You've won. I've come to see if we can't get some agreement.'

'And I was coming to you to tell you that I wasn't fighting any longer, that I didn't want Sophie on those terms.'

'What terms?'

'They would have destroyed you. When I saw Bou-Ta, I realised that.'

She looked away. 'You know what happened, of course.'

'I think I've always suspected.'

'At one time I managed to tell myself he really had been dead, but I knew I was lying to myself. If it had come out in court . . . well, I would have lost Sophie anyway, but lost her in ways even more final when she was older. Someone would have told her. Someone always does. What would she have thought of me then? Perhaps you can't understand that.'

'I think I can.'

'It was never easy to be myself with her. You must have thought I was cold, that I didn't care for her.'

'I understand that now, too, after hearing what happened at Kara.'

She nodded. 'So I thought I would see if we could work something out between us. I'll do anything you say.'

He poured them each another drink. 'Tell me what you did when you left Gloucester Street this evening.'

Surprised at the abrupt change of subject, she said, 'I went out to look for a taxi. I couldn't find one, but there was a carnival over in Battersea Park so I crossed the bridge and picked one up there.'

He told her what had happened on the bridge that evening. As Sophie slept on, regardless of their conversation, he said, 'It may be a terrible thing to say about my own child, but when I looked down at that young woman in the bottom of the launch my first thoughts were not for Sophie. I was thanking God that the dead woman wasn't you. All the way back in the taxi that thought remained in my mind and I realised that while I love her very much indeed, I love her as part of you. I can see that in the future this will change. I remember how it did with my other children. They become human-beings with their own personalities, not part of anyone else. But it was you I wanted back. It seems the final irony that, wanting you, I should be fighting you. But there's something I'd like you to tell me: had you made up your mind to leave me from the moment Guy arrived in Cape Town?'

'No. Just the opposite. I'd decided not to go with him, but telling him was so difficult. After what I'd done to him. If you'd gone to Kimberley for Molly's funeral, I think I could have worked things out. It was the fact that you didn't seem to trust me that made me . . . oh, I don't know how I felt –'

'I wasn't coming back because I didn't trust you. I was coming back to tell you how much I wanted you: how bloody awful I felt about adopting that self-righteous attitude. If the telephone lines hadn't been down, I would have told you on the phone.'

They were silent for a while, not uncomfortably so, then she said: 'Don't you think we should talk about what we're going to do? Or, I should say, what *you're* going to do?'

He crossed to the sofa and sat down beside her, taking her hand. At first she seemed about to withdraw it, but finally the stiffness went out of her muscles and it lay in his fingers like a talisman.

'You haven't been listening,' he said.

'Yes, I have. David, things aren't as easy as that.'

'I'm not saying that for one moment. What I am saying is that nothing is impossible. Will you grant that?'

'You sound like Maxwell.'

'I hope that's a joke. If I thought it would do any good I would beg you, but –'

'Don't ever beg! Don't ever use that word!'

'I wasn't going to beg. There's been too much in both our lives. Think of the future rather like a journey. If you thought of the whole thing you'd never start. But if you take a step at a time. . .'

'What's the first step?'

'To put Sophie to bed and get some sleep myself.'

'And the second?'

'Let tomorrow come. Think about the second then.'

'David, there's so much to –'

'Just the first step. That's all.'

She nodded. She picked Sophie up. At the door, she turned to him. She smiled uncertainly, but there was more warmth in it than he could possibly have hoped for.

He heard them upstairs: sounds he had not known for a long time, domestic, ordinary. It filled him with intense pleasure and he sat in the armchair. It was warm from Sophie and he could smell her powder.

He knew their journey might be a long one, but at least they had taken the first step.

AUTHOR'S NOTE

In 1917, at the request of the Russian Government, Britain sent the diamond magnate, Mr. Solly Joel, to negotiate for the sale of the Russian Crown Jewels. Payment was to be made in coal. The negotiations broke down and the jewels remained in Russia.